THE
CHAMPDOCE MYSTERY

"Speak to me, Mademoiselle, I entreat you"
From a drawing by John Sloan

THE CHAMPDOCE MYSTERY

A Sequel to "Caught in the Net"

Translated from the French of

EMILE GABORIAU

WILDSIDE PRESS: MMIII

Published by:

Wildside Press
P.O. Box 301
Holicong, PA 18928-0301
www.wildsidepress.com

CONTENTS

CONTENTS

THE CHAMPDOCE MYSTERY

CHAPTER I.

A DUCAL MONOMANIAC.

THE traveller who wishes to go from Poitiers to London by the shortest route will find that the simplest way is to take a seat in the stage-coach which runs to Saumur; and when you book your place, the polite clerk tells you that you must take your seat punctually at six o'clock. The next morning, therefore, the traveller has to rise from his bed at a very early hour, and make a hurried and incomplete toilet, and on arriving, flushed and panting, at the office, discover that there was no occasion for such extreme haste.

In the hotel from whence the coach starts every one seems to be asleep, and a waiter, whose eyes are scarcely open, wanders languidly about. There is not the slightest good in losing your temper, or in pouring out a string of violent remonstrances. In a small restaurant opposite a cup of hot coffee can be procured, and it is there that the disappointed travellers congregate, to await the hour when the coach really makes a start.

At length, however, all is ready, the conductor utters a tremendous execration, the coachman cracks his whip, the horses spring forward, the wheels rattle, and

the coach is off at last. Whilst the conductor smokes
his pipe tranquilly, the passengers gaze out of the
windows and admire the beautiful aspect of the sur-
rounding country. On each side stretch the woods
and fields of Bevron. The covers are full of game,
which has increased enormously, as the owner of the
property has never allowed a shot to be fired since
he had the misfortune, some twenty years ago, to
kill one of his dependents whilst out shooting. On
the right hand side some distance off rise the
tower and battlements of the Château de Mussidan.
It is two years ago since the Dowager Countess of
Chevanche died, leaving all her fortune to her niece,
Mademoiselle Sabine de Mussidan. She was a kind-
hearted woman, rough and ready in her manner, but
very popular amongst the peasantry. Farther off, on
the top of some rising ground, appears an imposing
structure, of an ancient style of architecture; this is
the ancient residence of the Dukes of Champdoce.
The left wing is a picturesque mass of ruins; the roof
has fallen in, and the mullions of the windows are
dotted with a thick growth of clustering ivy. Rain,
storm, and sunshine have all done their work, and
painted the mouldering walls with a hundred varied
tints. In 1840 the inheritor of one of the noblest names
of France resided here with his only son. The name of
the present proprietor was Cæsar Guillaume Duepair
de Champdoce. He was looked upon both by the gentry and peasantry of the country side as a most eccentric individual. He could be seen any day wandering
about, dressed in the most shabby manner, and wearing a coat that was frequently in urgent need of re-
pair, a leathern cap on his head, wooden shoes, and
a stout oaken cudgel in his hand. In winter he

supplemented to these an ancient sheepskin coat. He was sixty years of age, very powerfully built, and possessing enormous strength. The expression upon his face showed that his will was as strong as his thews and sinews. Beneath his shaggy eyebrows twinkled a pair of light-gray eyes, which darkened when a fit of passion overtook him, and this was no unusual occurrence.

During his military career in the army of the Condé, he had received a sabre cut across his cheek, and the cicatrice imparted a strange and unpleasant expression to his face. He was not a bad-hearted man, but headstrong, violent, and tyrannical to a degree. The peasants saluted him with a mixture of respect and dread as he walked to the chapel, to which he was a regular attendant on Sundays, with his son. During the Mass he made the responses in an audible voice, and at its conclusion invariably put a five-franc piece into the plate. This, his subscription to the newspaper, and the sum he paid for being shaved twice each week, constituted the whole of his outlay upon himself. He kept an excellent table, however; plump fowls, vegetables of all kinds, and the most delicious fruit were never absent from it. Everything, however, that appeared upon his well-plenished board was the produce of his fields, gardens, or woods. The nobility and gentry of the neighborhood frequently invited him to their hospitable tables, for they looked upon him as the head and chief of the nobility of the county; but he always refused their invitations, saying plainly, " No man who has the slightest respect for himself will accept hospitalities which he is not in a position to return." It was not the grinding clutch of poverty that drove the Duke to this exercise

of severe economy, for his income from his estates
brought him in fifty thousand francs per annum; and it
was reported that his investments brought him in as
much more. As a matter of course, therefore, he was
looked upon as a miser, and a victim to the sordid
vice of avarice.

His past life might, in some degree, offer an explanation of this conduct. Born in 1780, the Duke
de Champdoce had joined the band of emigrants
which swelled the ranks of Condé's army. An im-
placable opposer of the Revolution, he resided, during the glorious days of the Empire, in London, where
dire poverty compelled him to gain a livelihood as a
fencing master at the Restoration. He came back
with the Bourbons to his native land, and, by an almost
miraculous chance, was put again in possession of
his ancestral domains. But in his opinion he was
living in a state of utter destitution as compared to
the enormous revenues enjoyed by the dead-and-gone
members of the Champdoce family; and what pained
him more was to see rise up by the side of the old
aristocracy a new race which had attached itself to
commerce and entered into business transactions. As
he gazed upon the new order of things, the man
whose pride of birth and position almost amounted to
insanity, conceived the project to which he determined to devote the remainder of his life. He imagined that he had discovered a means by which he
could restore the ancient house of Champdoce to all
its former splendor and position. "I can," said he,
"by living like a peasant and resorting to no unnecessary expense, treble my capital in twenty years; and
if my son and my grandson will only follow my

example, the race of Champdoce will again recover
the proud position that it formerly held. Faithful
to this idea, he wedded, in 1820, although his heart
was entirely untouched, a young girl of noble birth
but utterly devoid of beauty, though possessed of a
magnificent dowry. Their union was an extremely
unhappy one, and many persons did not hesitate to
accuse the Duke of treating with harshness and severity
a young girl, who, having brought her husband five
hundred thousand francs, could not understand why
she should be refused a new dress when she urgently
needed it. After twelve months of inconceivable unhappiness, she gave birth to a son who was baptized
Louis Norbert, and six months afterwards she sank
into an untimely grave.

The Duke did not seem to regret his loss very deeply.
The boy appeared to be of a strong and robust constitution, and his mother's dowry would go to swell
the revenues of the Champdoce family. He made
his recent loss, too, the pretext for further retrench-
ments and economies.

Norbert was brought up exactly as a farmer's son
would have been. Every morning he started off
to work, carrying his day's provisions in a basket
slung upon his back. As he grew older, he was taught
to sow and reap, to estimate the value of a standing
crop at a glance, and, last but not least, to drive a hard
bargain. For a long time the Duke debated the ex-
pediency of permitting his son to be taught to read
or write; and if he did so at last, it was owing to
some severe remarks by the parish priest upon the
day on which Norbert took the sacrament for the
first time.

All went on well and smoothly until the day when Norbert, on his sixteenth birthday, accompanied his father to Poitiers for the first time.

At sixteen years of age, Louis Norbert de Champdoce looked fully twenty, and was as handsome a youth as could be seen for miles round. The sun had given a bronzed tint to his features which was exceedingly becoming. He had black hair, with a slight curl running through it, and large melancholy blue eyes, which he inherited from his mother. Poor girl! it was the sole beauty that she had possessed. He was utterly uncultured, and had been ruled with such a rod of iron by his father that he had never been a league from the Château. His ideas were barred by the little town of Bevron, with its sixty houses, its town hall, its small chapel, and principal river; and to him it seemed a spot full of noise and confusion. In the whole course of his life he had never spoken to three persons who did not belong to the district. Bred up in this secluded manner, it was almost impossible for him to understand that any one could lead a different existence to that of his own. His only pleasure was in procuring an abundant harvest, and his sole idea of excitement was High Mass on Sunday.

For more than a year the village girls had cast sly glances at him, but he was far too simple and innocent to notice this. When Mass was over, he generally walked over the farm with his father to inspect the work of the past week, or to set snares for the birds. His father at last determined to give him a wider experience, and one day said that he was to accompany him to Poitiers.

At a very early hour in the morning they started in one of the low country carts of the district, and under the seat were small sacks, containing over forty thousand francs in silver money. Norbert had long wished to visit Poitiers, but had never done so, though it was but fifteen miles off. Poitiers is a quaint old town, with dilapidated pavements and tall, gloomy houses, the architecture of which dates from the tenth century; but Norbert thought that it must be one of the most magnificent cities in the world. It was market day when they drove in, and he was absolutely stupefied with surprise and excitement. He had never believed there could be so many people in one place, and hardly noticed that the cart had pulled up opposite a lawyer's office. His father shook him roughly by the shoulder.

" Come, Norbert, lad, we are there," said he.

The young man jumped to the ground, and assisted mechanically to remove the sacks. The servile manner of the lawyer did not strike him, nor did he listen to the conversation between him and his father. Finally, the business being concluded, they took their departure, and, driving to the Market Place, put up the horse and cart at an old-fashioned, dingy inn, where they took their breakfast in the public room at a table where the wagoners were having a violent quarrel over their meal. The Duke, however, had other business to transact than the investment of his money, for he wanted to find the whereabouts of a miller who was somewhat in his debt. Norbert waited for him in front of the inn, and could not help feeling rather uncomfortable at finding himself alone. All at once some one came up and touched him lightly on the shoulder. He turned round sharply, and found himself face to face with a young man, who, seeing his look of surprise, said,—

" What! have you entirely forgotten your old friend Montlouis?"

Montlouis was the son of one of the Duke's farmers, and he and Norbert had often played together in past years. They had driven their cows to the meadows together, and had spent long days together fishing or searching for birds' nests. The dress now worn by Montlouis had at first prevented Norbert from recognizing him, for he was attired in the uniform of the college at which his father had placed him, being desirous of making something more than a mere farmer of his son.

" What are you doing here?" asked Norbert.

" I am waiting for my father."

" So am I.   Let us have a cup of coffee together."

Montlouis led his playmate into a small wine shop near at hand.   He seemed a little disposed to presume upon the superior knowledge of the world which he had recently acquired.

" If there was a billiard-table here," said he, " we could pass away the time with a game, though, to be sure, it runs into money."

Norbert never had had more than a few pence in his pocket at one time, and at this remark the color rose to his face, and he felt much humiliated.

" My father," added the young collegian, " gives me all I ask for.   I am certain of getting one, if not two prizes at the next examination; and when I have taken my degree, the Count de Mussidan has promised to make me his steward.   What do you think that you will do?"

" I—I don't know," stammered Norbert.

" You will, I suppose, dig and toil in the fields, as your father has done before you.   You are the son of the noblest and the richest man for miles round, and yet you are not so happy as I am."

Upon the return of the Duke de Champdoce some little time after this conversation, he did not detect any change in his son's manner; but the words spoken by Montlouis had fallen into Norbert's brain like a subtle poison, and a few careless sentences uttered by an inconsiderate lad had annihilated the education of sixteen years, and a complete change had taken place in Norbert's mind, a change which was utterly unsuspected by those around him, for his manner of bringing up had taught him to keep his own counsel.

The fixed smile on his features entirely masked the angry feelings that were working in his breast. He went through his daily tasks, which had once been a pleasure to him, with utter disgust and loathing. His eyes had been suddenly opened, and he now understood a host of things which he had never before even endeavored to comprehend. He saw now that his proper position was among the nobles, whom he never saw except when they attended Mass at the little chapel in Bevron. The Count de Mussidan, so haughty and imposing, with his snow-white hair; the aristocratic-looking Marquis de Laurebourg, of whom the peasants stood in the greatest awe, were always courteous and even cordial in their salutations, while the noble dames smiled graciously upon him. Proud and haughty as they were, they evidently looked upon his father and himself as their equals, in spite of the coarse garments that they wore. The realization of these facts effected a great change in Norbert. He was the equal of all these people, and yet how great a gulf separated him from them. While he and his father tramped to Mass in heavy shoes, the others drove up in their carriages with powdered footmen to open the doors. Why was this extraordinary difference? He knew enough of the value of crops and land to know that his father was as wealthy as any of these gentlemen. The laborers on the farm said that his father was a miser, and the villagers asserted that he got up at night and gazed with rapture upon the treasure that was hidden away from men's eyes.

"Norbert is an unhappy lad," they would say. "He who ought to be able to command all the pleasures of life is worse off than our own children."

He also recollected that one day, as his father was talking to the Marquis de Laurebourg, an old lady, who was doubtless the Marchioness, had said, "Poor boy! he was so early deprived of a mother's care!" What did that mean unless it was a reflection upon the arbitrary behavior of his father? Norbert saw that these people always had their children with them, and the sight of this filled him with jealousy, and brought tears of anguish to his eyes. Sometimes, as he trudged wearily behind his yoke of oxen, goad in hand, he would see some of these young scions of the aristocracy canter by on horseback, and the friendly wave of the hand, with which they greeted him almost appeared to his jaundiced mind a premeditated insult. What could they find to do in Paris, to which they all took wing at the first breath of winter? This was a question which he found himself utterly unable to solve. To drink to intoxication offered no charms to him, and yet this was the only pleasure which the villagers seemed to enjoy. Those young men must have some higher class of entertainment, but in what could it consist? Norbert could hardly read a line without spelling every word; but these new thoughts running through his mind caused him to study, so as to improve his education. His father had often told him that he did not like lads who were always poring over books; and so Norbert did not discontinue his studies, but simply avoided bringing them under his father's notice. He knew that there was a large collection of books in one of the upstairs rooms of the Château. He managed to force the lock of the door, and he found some thousands of volumes, of which at least two hundred were novels, which had been the solace of his mother's unhappy life. With all the eagerness of a man who is at the point of starvation and finds an unexpected store of provisions, Norbert seized upon them. At first he had great difficulty in dividing fact from fiction.

He arrived at two conclusions from perusing this heterogeneous mass of literature—one was, that he was most unhappy; and the other was, that he hated his father with a cold and determined loathing. Had he dared, he would have shown this feeling openly, but the Duke de Champdoce inspired him with an unconquerable feeling of terror. This state of affairs continued for some months, and at the end of that time the Duke felt that he ought to make his son acquainted with his projects. One Sunday, after supper, he commenced this task. Norbert had never seen his father so animated as he was at this moment, when all his ancestral pride blazed in his eyes. He explained at length the acts and deeds of those heroes who had been the ornament of their house, and enumerated the influential marriages which had been made by them in the days when their very name was a power in the land. And what remained of all their power and rank, save their Parisian domicile, their old Châ-

teau, and some two hundred thousand francs of income?

Norbert could hardly credit what he heard; he had
never believed that his father possessed such enormous wealth. " Why, it is inconceivable! " he muttered. And yet, as he looked round, he saw that the
surroundings were those of a peasant's cottage. How
could he endure so many discomforts and wounds to
his pride? In his anger he absolutely started to his
feet with the intention of reproaching his father, but
his courage failed him, and he fell back into a chair,
quivering with emotion.

The Duke de Champdoce was pacing up and down
the room.

" Do you think it so little? " asked he angrily.

Norbert knew that not one of the neighboring nobility who had the reputation of being wealthy possessed half this annual income, and it was with a feeling of bitter anger in his heart that he listened to the
broken words which fell from his father's lips. All
at once the Duke halted in front of his son's chair.

" What fortune I have now," said he in a hoarse
voice, " is little or nothing in times like these, when
the tradesman contrives to make an almost unlimited
income, and, setting up as a gentleman, imitates, not
our virtues, but our vices; while the nobles, not understanding the present hour, are in poverty and want.
Without money, nothing can be done. To hold his
own against these mushroom fortunes, a Champdoce
should possess millions. Neither you nor I, my son,
will see our coffers overflowing with millions, but our
descendants will reap the benefit of our toil. Our ancestors gained their name and glory by their determi-

nation; let us show that we are their worthy offspring."

As he approached the subject which had occupied
his mind entirely for years, the old noble's voice
quivered and shook.

" I have done my duty," said he, calming himself by
a mighty effort, "and it is now your turn to do yours.
You shall marry some wealthy heiress, and you shall
bring up your son as I have reared and nurtured you.
You will be able to leave him fifteen millions; and if
he will only follow in our footsteps, he will be able to
bequeath to his heir a fortune that a monarch might
envy. And this shall and will come to pass, because it
is my fixed determination."

This strange outburst of confidence petrified Norbert.

" The task is heavy and painful," continued the
Duke, "but it is one that several scores of illustrious
houses have accomplished. He who wishes to revive
the fallen fortunes of some mighty house must live
only in the future, and have no thought but for the
prosperity of his descendants. More than once I have
faltered and hesitated, but I have conquered my weakness, and now only live to make the line of Champdoce the most wealthy in France. You have seen me
haggle for an hour over a wretched louis, but it was
for the reason that at a future day one of our descendants might fling it to a beggar from the window of his
magnificent equipage. Next year I will take you to
Paris and show you our house there. You will see
in it the most wonderful tapestry, pictures by the best
masters, for I have ornamented and embellished it as
a lover adorns a house for a beloved mistress, and that

house, Norbert, is the home that your grandchildren will dwell in."

The Duke uttered these words in a tone of jubilant triumph.

"I have spoken to you thus," resumed he, after a short pause, "because you are now of an age to listen to the truth, and because I wished you to understand the rules by which you are to regulate your life. You have now arrived at years of discretion, and must do of your own free will what you have up to this time done at my bidding. This is all that I have to say. To-morrow you will take twenty-five sacks of wheat to the miller at Bevron."

Like all tyrannical despots, the Duke never contemplated for a moment the possibility of any one disobeying his commands; yet at this very moment Norbert was registering a solemn mental oath that he would never carry out his father's wishes. His anger, which his fears had so long restrained, now burst all bounds, and it was in the broad chestnut tree avenue, behind the Château, far from any listening ear, that he gave way to his despair. So long as he had only looked upon his father as a mere miser, he had permitted himself to indulge in hope; but now he understood him better, and saw that life-long plans, such as the Duke had framed, were not to be easily overruled.

"My father is mad," said he; "yes; decidedly mad."

He had made up his mind that for the present he would yield to his despotism, but afterwards, in the future, what was he to do?

It is an easy thing to find persons to give you bad

advice, and the very next day Norbert found one at Bevron in the shape of a certain man called Daumon, a bitter enemy of the Duke.

CHAPTER II.

A DANGEROUS ACQUAINTANCE.

DAUMON was not a native of this part of the country, and no one knew from whence he came. He said that he had been an attorney's clerk, and had certainly resided for a long time in Paris. He was a little man of fifty years of age, clean shaved, and with a sharp and cunning expression of countenance. His long nose, sharp, restless eyes, and thin lips, attracted attention at first sight. His whole aspect aroused a feeling of distrust. He had come to Bevron, some fifteen years before, with all his provisions in a cotton handkerchief slung over his shoulder. He was willing to make money in any way, and he prospered and rose. He owned fields, vineyards, and a cottage, which is at the juncture of the highway to Poitiers and the cross road that leads to Bevron. His aim and object were to be seen everywhere, to know everybody, and to have a finger in every pie in the neighborhood around. If any of the farmers or the laborers wanted small advances, they went to him, and he granted them loans at exorbitant rates of interest. He gave most disputants counsel, and had every point of law at his fingers' ends. He could teach people how to sail as close to the wind as possible, and yet to be beyond the reach of the law. He affected to be only too anxious to ameliorate the lot of the peasant class, and yet he was drawing heavy sums from them by way of interest. He endeavored by every means in his power to rouse their feelings of animosity against both the priest-hood and the gentry. His artful way of talking, and the long black coat which he wore, had given him the nickname of the " Counsellor " in the district. The reason why he disliked the Duke was because the lat-ter had more than once shown himself hostile to him, and had taken him before the court of justice, from which Daumon only escaped by means of bribery of suborned witnesses. He vowed that he would be re-venged for this, and for five years had been watching his opportunity, and this was the man whom Norbert met when he went to deliver his corn to the miller. As he was coming back with his empty wagon, Dau-mon asked for a lift back as far as the cross road that led to his cottage.

" I trust, sir," said he with the most servile courtesy, "that you will excuse the liberty I take, but I am so utterly crippled with rheumatism that I can hardly walk, Marquis."

Daumon had read somewhere that the eldest son of a Duke was entitled to be styled *Marquis,* and it was the first time that Norbert had been thus addressed. Before this he would have laughed at the appellation, but now his wounded vanity, and his exasperation at the unhappy condition in which he found himself, tempted him to accept the title without remonstrance.

" All right, I can give you a lift," said he, and the Counsellor clambered into the cart.

All the time that he was showering thanks upon Norbert for his courtesy he was watching the young man's face carefully.

"Evidently," thought the Counsellor to himself, "something unusual has taken place at the Château de Champdoce. Was not the opportunity for revenge here?"

Long since he had decided that through the son he could strike the father. But he must be cautious.

"You must have been up very early, Marquis," said he.

The young man made no reply.

"The Duke," resumed Daumon, "is most fortunate in having such a son as you. I know more than one father who says to his children, 'See what an excellent example the young Marquis de Champdoce sets to you all. He is not afraid of hard work, though he is noble by birth, and should not soil his hands by labor.'"

A sudden lurch brought the Counsellor's eloquence to a sudden close, but he speedily resumed again.

"I was watching you as you hefted the sacks. Heavens! what muscles! what a pair of shoulders!"

At any other moment Norbert would have gloried in such laudation, but now he felt displeased and annoyed, and vented his anger by a sharp cut at his team.

"When people say that you are as innocent as a girl," continued Daumon, "I always say that you are a sensible young fellow after all, and that if you choose to lead a regular life, it is far better than wasting your future fortune in wine, billiards, cards, or women."

"I don't know that I might not do something of the kind," returned Norbert.

"What did you say?" answered his wily companion.

" I said that if I were my own master, I would live as other young men."

The lad paused abruptly, and Daumon's eyes gleamed with joy.

" Aha," murmured he to himself; " I have the game in my own hands. I will teach his Grace to interfere with me."

Then, in a voice which could reach Norbert's ears, he continued,—

" Of course some parents are far too strict."

An impatient gesture from Norbert showed him that he had wounded him deeply.

" Yes, yes," put in the wily Counsellor, " as the head grows bald, and the blood begins to stagnate, they forget,—they forget the days when all was so different. They forget the time when they were young, and when they sowed their wild oats with so lavish a hand. When your father was twenty-five, he was precious wild. Ask your father, if you do not believe me."

At this moment the wagon passed the cross road, and Norbert pulled up.

" I cannot thank you enough, Marquis," said the Counsellor as he alighted with difficulty; " but if you would condescend to come and taste my brandy, I should esteem it a great honor."

Norbert hesitated for an instant: his reasoning powers urged him to decline the offer, but he refused to listen to them, and, fastening his horses to a tree, he followed Daumon down the by-road. The cottage was an excellent one, and extremely well furnished. A woman, who acted as Daumon's housekeeper, served the refreshments. The office—for he called his room an office, just as if he was a professional man—was

a strange-looking place. On one side was a desk
covered with account books, and against the wall were
sacks of seed. A number of books on legal matters
crowded the shelves, and from the ceiling hung a
quantity of dried herbs. The Counsellor welcomed
the heir to the dukedom of Champdoce with the
greatest deference, seated him in his own capacious
leathern arm-chair, and pressed the brandy which he
had refused upon him.

"Come, sir, another drop," said he, and, without
waiting for Norbert's assent, he replenished the glass
which stood before him.

"I got this brandy from a man down Arcachon way
in return for a kindness that I did him; for, without
boasting, I may say that I have done kindnesses for
many people in my time." He raised his glass to his
lips as he spoke. "It is good, is it not?" said he.
"You can't get stuff with an, aroma like that here-
abouts."

The extreme deference of the man, coupled with the
excellence of the spirit, opened Norbert's heart in a
very short space of time. Up to the present the conduct of poor Norbert had been blameless, but now,
without knowing anything of the Counsellor's character
or reputation, he poured out all the secret sorrows of
his heart, while Daumon chuckled secretly, preserving
all the time the imperturbable face of a physician
called in to visit a patient.

"Dear me! dear me!" said he; "this is really too
bad. Poor fellow! I really pity you. Were it not
for the deep respect that I have for the Duke, your
father, I should feel inclined to say that he was not
quite in his right senses."

"Yes," continued Norbert, the tears starting to his

eyes, "this is just how I am situated. My destiny has been marked out for me, and I am helpless to alter it. I had better a thousand times be lying under the cold greensward, than vegetate thus above ground."

The peculiar smile on Daumon's lips caused him to pause in his complaint.

"Perhaps," he went on, "you think that I am childish in talking thus?"

"Not at all, Marquis, you have suffered too deeply; but forgive me if I say that you are foolish to despond so much over the future that lies before you."

"Future!" repeated Norbert angrily, "what is the use of speaking to me of the future, when I may be kept in this horrible servitude for the next thirty years? My father is still hale and hearty."

"What of that? You will be of age soon, and then you will have full right to claim your mother's fortune."

The extreme surprise displayed by Norbert at this intelligence convinced the Counsellor that he was much more unsophisticated than he had supposed him to be.

"A man," continued he, "can, when he attains his majority, dispose of his inheritance as he thinks fit, and your mother's fortune will render you independent of your father."

"But I should never dare to claim it; how could I venture to do so?"

"You need not make the application personally; your solicitor would manage all that for you; but, of course, you must wait until you are of age."

"But I cannot wait until then," said Norbert; "I must at once free myself from this tyranny."

" Luckily there are ways."

" Do you really think so, Daumon? "

" Yes, and I will show you what is done every day. Nothing is more common in noble families. Would you like to be a soldier? "

" No, I do not care for that, and yet——"

" That is your last resource, Marquis. First, then, we could lay a plaint before the court."

" A plaint? "

" Certainly. Do you suppose that our laws do not provide for such a case as a father exceeding the proper bounds of parental authority? Tell me, has the Duke, your father, ever struck you? "

" Never once."

" Well, that is almost a pity. We will say that your father's property is worth two millions, and yet you derive so slight a benefit from this that you are known everywhere as the ' Young Savage of Champdoce '! "

Norbert started to his feet.

" Who dares speak of me like that? " said he furiously. " Tell me his name."

This outburst of passion did not in the smallest degree discompose Daumon.

" Your father has many enemies, Marquis," he resumed, " for his manners are overbearing and exacting; but you have many friends, and among them all you will find none more devoted than myself, humble though my position may be. Many ladies of high rank take a great interest in you. Only a day or two ago some persons were speaking of you in the presence of Mademoiselle de Laurebourg, and she blushed crimson at your name. Do you know Mademoiselle Diana? "

Norbert colored.

"Ah, I understand," replied Daumon. "And when you have broken the fetters that now bind you, we shall see something one of these days. And now——"

But at this moment Norbert's eyes caught a glimpse of the old-fashioned cuckoo clock that hung on the wall in one corner of the room. He started to his feet.

"Why, it is dinner-time!" said he. "What upon earth will my father say?"

"What, does he keep you in such order as that?"

But, never heeding the sarcastic question of the Counsellor, Norbert had regained his cart, and was driving off at full speed.

CHAPTER III.

A BOLD ADVENTURE.

DAUMON had in no way exaggerated when he said that Norbert was spoken of as the "Young Savage of Champdoce," though no one used this appellation in an insulting form. Public opinion had changed considerably regarding the Duke of Champdoce. The first time that he had made his appearance, wearing wooden shoes and a leathern jacket, every one had laughed, but this did not affect him at all, and in the end people began to term his dogged obstinacy indomitable perseverance. The gleam that shone from his hoarded millions imparted a brilliant lustre to his shabby garments. Why should they waste their pity upon a man who would eventually come into a gigantic fortune, and have the means of gratifying all his desires?

Mothers, with daughters especially, took a great interest in the young man, for to get a girl married to the "Young Savage of Champdoce" would be a feat to be proud of; but unluckily his father watched him with all the vigilance of a Spanish duenna. But there was a young girl who had long since secretly formed a design of her own, and this bold-hearted beauty was Diana de Laurebourg. It was with perfect justice that she had received the name of the "Belle of Poitiers." She was tall and very fair, with a dazzling complexion and masses of lustrous hair; but her eyes gleamed with a suppressed fire, which plainly showed the constitution of her nature. She had been brought up in a convent, and her parents, who had wished her to take the veil, had only been induced to remove her owing to her obstinate refusal to pronounce the vows, coupled with the earnest entreaties of the lady superior, who was kept in a constant state of ferment owing to the mutinous conduct of her pupil. Her father was wealthy, but all the property went over to her brother, ten years older than herself; and so Diana was portionless, with the exception of a paltry sum of forty thousand francs.

"My child," said her father to her the first day of her return, "you have come back to us once more, and now all you have to do is to fascinate some gentleman who is your equal in position and who has plenty of money. If you fail in that, back you go to the convent."

"Time enough to talk about that some years hence," answered the girl with a smile; "at present I am quite contented with being at home with you."

M. de Laurebourg had commented with some severity upon the conduct of the Duke de Champdoce towards his son, but he was perfectly willing to sacrifice his daughter's heart for a suitable marriage.

"I shall gain my end," murmured the girl, "I am sure of it."

She had heard a friend of her father's speaking of Norbert and his colossal expectations.

"Why should I not marry him?" she asked of her own heart; and, with the utmost skill, she applied herself to the execution of her design; for the idea of being a duchess, with an income of two hundred thousand francs, was a most fascinating one. But how was she to meet Norbert? and how bring over the money-raking Duke to her side? Before, however, she could decide on any plan, she felt that she must see Norbert. He was pointed out to her one day at Mass, and she was struck by his beauty and by an ease of manner which even his shabby dress could not conceal. By the quick perception which many women possess, she dived into Norbert's inmost soul; she felt that he suffered, and her sympathy for him brought with it the dawn of love, and by the time she had left the chapel she had registered a solemn vow that she would one day be Norbert's wife. But she did not acquaint her parents with this determination on her part, preferring to carry out her plans without any aid or advice. Mademoiselle Diana was shrewd and practical, and not likely to err from want of judgment. The frank and open expression of her features concealed a mind of superior calibre, and one which well knew how to weigh the advantages of social rank and position. She affected a sudden sympathy with the poor, and visited them constantly, and might be frequently met in the lanes carrying soup and other comforts to them. Her father declared, with a laugh, that she ought to have been a Sister of Charity, and did not notice the fact that all Diana's pensioners resided in the vicinity of Champdoce. But it was in vain that she wandered about, continually changing the hour of her visits. The "Savage of Champdoce" was not to be seen, nor was he even a regular attendant at Mass. At last a mere trifle changed the whole current of the young man's existence; for, a week after the conversation in which the Duke had laid bare his scheme to his son, he again referred to it, after their dinner, which they had partaken of at the same table with forty laborers, who had been hired to get in the harvest.

"You need not, my son," began the old gentleman, "go back with the laborers to-day."

"But, sir——"

"Allow me to continue, if you please. My confidential conversation with you the other night was merely a preliminary to my telling you that for the future I did not expect you to toil as hard as you had hitherto done, for I wish you to perform a duty less laborious, but more responsible; you will for the future act as farm-bailiff."

Norbert looked up suddenly into his father's face.

"For I wish you to become accustomed to independent action, so that at my death your sudden liberty may not intoxicate you."

The Duke then rose from his seat, and took a highly finished gun from a cupboard.

"I have been very much pleased with you for some time past," said he, "and this is a sign of my satisfaction. The gamekeeper has brought in a thor-

oughly trained dog, which will also be yours. Shoot
as much as you like, and, as you cannot go about without money in your pocket, take this, but be careful
of it; for remember that extravagance on your part
will procrastinate the day upon which our descendants
will resume their próper station in the world."

The Duke spoke for some time longer, but his son
paid no heed to his words, and was too much astonished to accept the six five-franc pieces which his
father tendered to him.

"I suppose," said the Duke at last in angry accents,
"that you will have the grace to thank me."

"You will find that I am not ungrateful," stammered Norbert, aroused by this reproach.

The Duke turned away impatiently.

"What has the boy got into his head now?" muttered he.

It was owing to the advice of the priest of Bevron
that the Duke had acted as he had done; but this in-
dulgence came too late, for Norbert's detestation of
his tyrant was too deeply buried in his heart to be
easily eradicated.

A gun was not such a wonderful present after all—
a matter of a few francs, perhaps. Had the Duke
offered him the means of a better education, it would
be a different matter; but as it was, he would still
remain the "Young Savage of Champdoce."

However, Norbert took advantage of the permission accorded to him, and rambled daily over the
estate with his gun and his dog Bruno, to which he
had become very much attached. His thoughts often
wandered to Daumon; but he had made inquiries, and
had heard that the Counsellor was a most dangerous
man, who would stick at nothing; but for all that, he

had made up his mind to go back to him again for further advice, though his better nature warned him of the precipice on the brink of which he was standing.

CHAPTER IV.

A FINANCIAL TRANSACTION.

DAUMON was expecting a visit from the young man, and had been waiting for him with the cool complacency of a bird-catcher, who, having arranged all his lines and snares, stands with folded arms until his feathered victims fall into his net. The line that he had displayed before the young man's eyes was the sight of liberty. Daumon had emissaries everywhere, and knew perfectly well what was going on at the Château de Champdoce, and could have repeated the exact words made use of by the Duke in his last conversation with his son, and was aware of the leave of liberty that had been granted to Norbert, and was as certain as possible that this small concession would only hasten the rebellion of the young Marquis.

He often took his evening stroll in the direction of Champdoce, and, pipe in mouth, would meditate over his schemes. Pausing on the brow of a hill that overlooked the Château, he would shake his fist, and mutter,—

"He will come; ah, yes, he must come to me!"

And he was in the right, for, after a week spent in indecision, Norbert knocked at the door of his father's bitterest enemy. Daumon, concealed behind the window curtain, had watched his approach, and it was

with the same air of deference that he welcomed the
Marquis, as he took care to call him; but he affected
to be so overcome by the honor of this visit that he
could only falter out,—

"Marquis, I am your most humble servant."

And Norbert, who had expected a very warm greet-
ing, was much disconcerted. For a moment he
thought of going away again, but his pride would
not permit him to do so, for he had said to himself
that it would be the act of a fool to go away this
time without having accomplished anything.

"I want to have a bit of advice from you, Counsellor," said he; "for, as I have but little experience in
a certain matter, I should like to avail myself of your
knowledge."

"You do me too much honor, Marquis," murmured
the Counsellor with a low bow.

"But surely," said the young man, "you must feel
that you are bound to assist me after all you told me
a day or two back. You mentioned two means by
which I could regain my freedom, and hinted that
there was a third one. I have come to you to-day to
ask you what it was."

Never did any man more successfully assume an
air of astonishment than did Daumon at this moment.

"What," said he, "do you absolutely remember
those idle words I made use of then?"

"I do most decidedly."

The villain's heart of Daumon was filled with delight, but he replied,—

"Oh, Marquis! you must remember that we say
many things that really have no special meaning, for
between act and intention there is a tremendous dif-

ference. I often speak too freely, and that has more than once got me into trouble."

Norbert was no fool, in spite of his want of education, and the hot blood of his ancestors coursed freely through his veins. He now struck the butt-end of his gun heavily upon the floor.

"You treated me like a simpleton, then, it appears?" remarked he angrily.

"My dear Marquis——"

"And imagined that you could trifle with me. You managed to learn my real feelings for your own amusement; but, take care; this may cost you more than you think."

"Ah, Marquis, can you believe that I would act so basely?"

"What else can I think?"

Daumon paused for a moment, and then said,—

"You will be angry when you hear what I have to say, but I cannot help speaking the truth."

"I shall not be angry, and you can speak freely."

"I am but a very poor and humble man. What have I to gain by securing any note, and by encouraging you to brave your father's anger? Just think what must happen if I opposed the all-powerful Duke de Champdoce; why, I might find myself in prison in next to no time."

"And for what reason, if you please?" asked Norbert.

"Have you never studied law in the slightest degree, Marquis? Dear me, how neglectful some parents are! You are not of age, and there is a certain article, 354 in the code, that could be so worked that a poor humble creature like me could be locked up for perhaps five years. The law deals very hardly when any one has dealings with a minor, the more especially when the father is a man of untold wealth. If the Duke should ever discover——"

"But how could he ever do so?"

Daumon made no reply, and his silence so plainly showed Norbert that the Counsellor did not trust him, that he repeated the question in an angry voice.

"Your blind subservience to your father is too well known."

"You believe that I should confess everything to him?"

"You yourself told me that when his eyes were fixed on yours you could not avoid yielding to his will."

Norbert's anger gradually died away, as he replied in accents of intense bitterness,—

"I may be a savage, but I am not likely to become a traitor. If I once promised to keep a secret, no measures or tortures would tear it from me. I may fear my father, but I am a Champdoce, and fear no other mortal man. Do you understand me?"

"But, Marquis——"

"No other mortal man," interrupted Norbert sternly, "will ever know from me that we have ever exchanged words together."

An expression passed over the features of the Counsellor which cast a ray of hope upon the young man's heart.

"Upon my word," said he, "any one would judge from my hesitation that I had some wrong motive in acting as I am doing, but I never give bad advice, and any one will tell you the same about me, and this is the breviary by which I regulate all my actions."

As he spoke, he took a book from his desk, and waved it aloft.

Norbert looked puzzled and angry.

"What do you mean?" asked he.

"Nothing, Marquis, nothing; have patience; your majority is not far off, and you have only a few years to wait. Remember that your father is an old man; let him carry out his plan for a few years longer, and——"

Norbert struck his fist savagely upon the table, crying out furiously. "It was not worth my coming here if this was all that you had to say;" and, whistling to Bruno, the young man prepared to quit the room.

"Ah, Marquis! you are far too hasty," said the Counsellor humbly.

Norbert paused. "Speak then," answered he roughly.

In a low, impressive voice, Daumon went on.

"Remember, Marquis, that though I should like to see you have a better understanding with your father, yet, at the same time, I should like to work for the happiness of you both. I am like a judge in court, who endeavors to bring about a compromise between the litigants. Can you not, while affecting perfect submission, live in a manner more suited to you? There are many young men of your age in a precisely similar position."

Norbert took a step forward and began to listen earnestly.

"You have more liberty now," continued Daumon. "Pray, does your father know how you employ your time?"

"He knows that I can do nothing but shoot."

"Well, I know what I would do if I were your age."

" And what would that be? "

" First of all, I would stay at home sufficiently often
not to arouse papa's suspicions, and the rest of my leisure I would spend in Poitiers, which is a very pleasant
town. I could take nice rooms in which I could be
my own master. At Champdoce I could keep to my
peasant's clothes, but in Poitiers I would be dressed by
the best tailor. I should pick up a few boon companions amongst the jolly students, and have plenty of
friends, ladies as well as gentlemen. I would dance,
sing, and drink, and would dip into every kind of life,
so that——"

He paused for a second and then said, " There ought
to be a fast horse or so in your father's stables, eh?
Well then, if there are, why not take one for your own
riding? Then at night, when you are supposed to be
snug between the sheets, creep down to the stable, clap
a bridle on the horse, and, hey, presto! you are in Poitiers. Put on the clothes suitable to the handsome
young noble you are, and have a joyous carouse with
your many companions; and if you do, next day, not
choose to go back until the morning, the servants will
only tell your father that you are out shooting."

Norbert was a thoroughly strong, honest youth, and
the idea of meanness and duplicity were most repugnant to his feelings in general; and yet he listened
eagerly to this proposition, for oppression had utterly
changed his nature. The career of dissipation and
pleasure proposed so adroitly by Daumon dazzled his
imagination and his eyes began to sparkle.

" Well," asked the Counsellor invidiously, " and,
pray, what is there to prevent you doing all this? "

" Want of funds," returned Norbert, with a deep
sigh; " I should want a great deal, and I have hardly

any; if I were to ask my father for any, he would refuse me, and wonder——"

"Have you no friends who would find you such a sum as you would require until you came of age?"

"None at all;" and, overwhelmed with the sense of his utter helplessness, Norbert sank back upon a chair.

After a brief period of reflection, Daumon spoke with apparent reluctance,—

"No, Marquis, I cannot see you so miserably unhappy without doing my best to help you. A man is a fool who puts out his hand to interfere between father and son, but I will find money to lend you what you want."

"Will you do so, Counsellor?"

"Unluckily I cannot, I am only a poor fellow, but some of the neighboring farmers intrust me with their savings for investment. Why should I not use them to make you comfortable and happy?"

Norbert was almost choked with emotion. "Can this be done?" asked he eagerly.

"Yes, Marquis; but you understand that you will have to pay very heavy interest on account of the risk incurred in lending money to a minor. For the law does not recognize such transactions, and I myself do not like them. If I were in your place, I would not borrow money on these terms, but wait until some friend could help me."

"I have no friends," again answered the young man.

Daumon shrugged his shoulders with the air of a man who says: "Well, I suppose I must give in, but at any rate I have done my duty." Then he began aloud, "I am perfectly aware, Marquis, that, considering the wealth that must one day be yours, this transaction is a most paltry one."

He then went on to enumerate the conditions of the loan, and at each clause he would stop and say, " Do you understand this? "

Norbert understood him so well that at the end of the conversation, in exchange for the thousand francs, he handed to the Counsellor the promissory notes for four thousand francs each, which were made payable to two farmers, who were entirely in Daumon's clutches. The young man, in addition, pledged his solemn word of honor that he would never disclose that the Counsellor had anything to do with the transaction.

" Remember, Marquis, prudence must be strictly observed. Come here to me only after the night has set in."

This was the last piece of advice that Daumon gave his client; and when he was again left alone, he perured with feelings of intense gratification, the two notes that Norbert had signed. They were entirely correct and binding, and drawn up in proper legal form. He had made up his mind to let the young man have all his savings, amounting to some forty thousand francs, and not to press for payment until the young man came into his fortune.

All this, however, hinged upon Norbert's silence and discretion, for, at the first inkling of the matter, the Duke would scatter all the edifice to the winds; but of this happening Daumon had no fear.

As Norbert walked along, followed by his dog, he could not resist putting his hands into his pockets and fingering the tempting, crisp banknotes which lurked there, and making sure that it was a reality and not a dream. That night seemed interminable; and the next morning, with his gun on his shoulder and his dog at his heels, he walked briskly along the road to Poitiers.

He had determined to follow Daumon's advice,—to have suitable rooms, and to make the acquaintance of some of the students. On his arrival at Poitiers, which he had only once before visited, Norbert felt like a half-fledged bird who knows not how to use its wings. He wandered about the streets, not knowing how to commence what he wanted. Finally, after a sojourn in the town of a very brief duration, he went to the inn where he had breakfasted with his father on his former visit, and, after an unsatisfactory meal, returned to Champdoce, as wretched as he had been joyful and hopeful at his early start in the morning. But later on he went to Daumon, who put him in communication with a friend who, for a commission, took the unsophisticated lad about, hired some furnished rooms, and finally introduced him to the best ladies in the town, while Norbert ordered clothes to the tune of five hundred francs. He now thought himself on the high road to the full gratification of his desires; but, alas! the reality, compared with what his imagination had pictured, appeared rank and chilling. His timidity and shyness arrested all his progress; he required an intimate friend, and where could he hit upon one?

One evening he entered the Café Castille. He found a large number of students collected there, and was a little disgusted at their turbulent gayety, and, hastily withdrawing, he spent the rest of the weary evening in his own rooms with Bruno, who, for his part, would have much preferred the open country. He had really only enjoyed the four evenings on which he had visited the Martre; but these limited hours of happiness did not make up for the web of falsehood in which he had enmeshed himself, or the daily dread of detection in which he lived.

The Duke had noticed his son's absence, but his suspicions were very wide of the truth. One morning he laughed at Norbert on the continued non-success of his shooting.

"Do your best to-day, my boy," said he, "and try and bring home some game, for we shall have a guest to dinner."

"To dinner, here?"

"Yes," answered the Duke suppressing a smile. "Yes, actually here; M. Puymandour is coming, and the dining-room must be opened and put into proper order."

"I will try and kill some game," answered Norbert to himself as he started on his errand.

This, however, was more easily resolved on than executed. At last he caught sight of an impudent rabbit near a hedge; he raised his gun and fired. A shriek of anguish followed the report, and Bruno dashed into the hedge, barking furiously.

CHAPTER V.

A BAD START.

DIANA DE LAUREBOURG was a strange compound; under an appearance of the most artless simplicity she concealed an iron will, and had hidden from every one of her family, and even from her most intimate friends, her firm resolve to become the Duchess of Champdoce. All her rambles in the neighborhood had turned out of no avail; and as the weather was now very uncertain, it seemed as if her long strolls in the country roads and fields would soon come to an end. "The day must eventually come," murmured she, "when this invisible prince must make his appearance." And at last the long-expected day arrived.

It was in the middle of the month of November, and the weather was exceedingly soft and balmy for the time of year. The sky was blue, the few remaining leaves rustled on the trees, and an occasional bird whistled in the hedgerows. Diana de Laurebourg was walking slowly along the path leading to Mussidan, when all at once she heard a rustling of branches. She turned round sharply, and all the blood in her body seemed to rush suddenly to her heart, for through an opening in the hedge she caught sight of the man who for the past two months had occupied all her waking thoughts. Norbert was waiting for something with all the eagerness of a sportsman, his finger on the trigger of his gun.

Here was the opportunity for which she had waited so long, and with such ill-concealed impatience; and yet she could derive no advantage from it, for what would happen? Simply this: Norbert would bow to her, and she would reply by a slight inclination of her head, and perhaps two months might pass away before she met him again. Just as she was about to take some bold and decisive step she saw Norbert raise his gun and point it in her direction. She endeavored to call out to him, but her voice failed her, and in another moment the report rang out, and she felt a sharp pang, like the touch of a red-hot iron upon her ankle. With a wild shriek she threw up her arms and fell upon the pathway. She did not lose her senses, for she heard a cry in response to her own, and the crashing of something forcing its way through the hedge. Then she felt a hot breath upon her face, and then something cold and wet touched her cheek. She opened her eyes languidly, and saw Bruno licking her face and hands.

At the same moment Norbert dashed through the hedge and stood before her. At once she realized the advantage of her position and closed her eyes once more. Norbert, as he hung over the seemingly unconscious form of this fair young creature, felt that his senses were deserting him, for he greatly feared that he had killed Mademoiselle de Laurebourg. His first impulse was to fly precipitately, and his second to give what aid he could to his victim. He knelt down by her, and, to his infinite relief, found that life was not extinct. He raised her beautiful head.

"Speak to me, mademoiselle, I entreat you," cried he.

All this time Diana was returning thanks to kind Providence for the fulfilment of her wishes. After a time she made a slight move, and Norbert uttered an exclamation of joy. Then, opening her beautiful eyes, she gazed upon the young man with the air of a person just awaking from a dream.

"It is I," faltered the distracted young man, "Norbert de Champdoce. But forgive me, and tell me if you are in pain?"

Pity came over the wounded girl. She gently drew herself away from the arm that encircled her, and said softly,—

"It is I who ought to apologize for my foolish weakness; for I am really more frightened than hurt."

Norbert felt that heaven had opened before his very eyes. "Let me go for help," exclaimed he.

"No, no; it was a mere scratch." And, raising her

skirt, she displayed a foot that might have turned a
steadier head than Norbert's. "See," said she, "it is
there that I am in pain."

And she pointed to a spot of blood upon the delicate
white stocking. At the sight of this the young man's
terror increased, and he started to his feet.

"Let me run to the Château," said he, "and in less
than an hour——"

"Do nothing of the kind," interrupted the girl; "it
is a mere nothing. Look, I can move my foot with
ease."

"But let me entreat you——"

"Hush! we shall soon see what it is that has happened." And she inspected what she laughingly termed
his terrible wound.

It was, as she had supposed, a mere nothing. One
pellet had grazed the skin, another had lodged in the
flesh, but it was quite on the surface.

"A surgeon must see to this," said Norbert.

"No, no." And with the point of a penknife she
pulled out the little leaden shot. The young man remained still, holding his breath, as a child does when he
is putting the topmost story in a house of cards. He
had never heard so soft a voice, never gazed on so perfectly lovely a face. In the meantime Diana had torn
up her handkerchief and bandaged the wound. "Now
that is over," exclaimed she, with a light laugh, as she
extended her slender fingers to Norbert, so that he
might assist her to rise.

As soon as she was on her feet, she took a few steps
with the prettiest limp imaginable.

"Are you in pain?" said he anxiously.

"No, I am not indeed; and by this evening I shall

have forgotten all about it. But confess, Marquis,"
she added, with a coquettish laugh, "that this is a
droll way of making an acquaintance."

Norbert started at the word Marquis, for no one
but Daumon had ever addressed him thus.

"She does not despise me," thought he.

"This little incident will be a lesson to me," continued she. "Mamma always has told me to keep to
the highroad; but I preferred the by-paths because of
the lovely scenery."

Norbert, for the first time in his life, realized that
the view was a beautiful one.

"I am this way nearly every day," pursued Diana,
"though I am very wicked to disobey my mother. I
go to see poor La Berven. She is dying of consump-
tion, poor thing, and I take her a little soup and wine
every now and then."

She spoke like a real Sister of Mercy, and, in Norbert's opinion, wings only were lacking to transform
her into a perfect angel.

"The poor woman has three children, and their
father does nothing for them, for he drinks what he
earns," the young girl went on.

Berven was one of the identical men to whom Norbert had given his promissory note for four thousand
francs, for he was one of the two men who had intrusted Daumon with their savings for investment; but
the young man was not in a condition to notice this.
Diana had meantime slung her basket on her arm.

"Before I leave you to-day," said she, "I should so
much like to ask a favor of you."

"A favor of me, mademoiselle?"

"Yes; oblige me by saying nothing of what has occurred to-day to any one; for should it come to my

parents' ears, they would undoubtedly deprive me of the little liberty that they now grant me."

"Mademoiselle," answered Norbert, "be sure that I will never mention the terrible accident that my awkwardness has caused."

"Thank you, Marquis," answered the girl, with a half-mocking courtesy. "Another time let me advise you, before you shoot, to look that no one is behind a hedge."

With these words she tripped away, without her tiny feet showing any signs of lameness. She had read Norbert's heart like the pages of a book, and felt that there was every chance of her winning the game. "I am sure of it now," said she; "I shall be the Duchess of Champdoce." How grateful she felt for that untimely shot! and she felt sure that Norbert had understood what she meant when she had said that she went along that path. She felt certain that the young man had not lost one word. She believed that the only opposition would come from his father. As she looked round for a moment, she saw Norbert standing fixed and motionless as the trees around him.

After Diana had departed, the unhappy lad felt as if she had taken half his life with her. Was it all a dream? He knelt down, and, after a slight search, discovered the little pellet, the cause of all the mischief; and, taking it up carefully, returned home. To his extreme surprise, he found the main gateway wide open, and from a window he heard his father's voice calling out in kindly accents,—

"Come up quickly, my boy, for our guest has arrived."

CHAPTER VI.

THE COUNT DE PUYMANDOUR.

SINCE the death of the Duchess of Champdoce the greater portion of the Château had been closed, but the reception rooms were always ready to be used at a very short notice.

The dining-room was a really magnificent apartment. There were massive buffets of carved oak, black with age, ornamented with brass mountings. The shelves groaned beneath their load of goblets and salvers of the brightest silver, engraved with the haughty armorial bearings of the house of Champdoce.

Standing near one of the windows, Norbert saw a man, stout, robust, bald and red-faced, wearing a mustache and slight beard. His clothes were evidently made by a first-rate tailor, but his appearance was utterly commonplace.

" This is my son," said the Duke, " the Marquis de Champdoce. Marquis, let me introduce you to the Count de Puymandour."

This was the first time that his father had ever addressed Norbert by his title, and he was greatly surprised. The great clock in the outer hall, which had not been going for fifteen years, now struck, and instantly a butler appeared, bearing a massive silver soup tureen, which he placed on the table, announcing solemnly that his Grace was served, and the little party at once seated themselves. A dinner in such a vast chamber would have been rather dull had it not been enlivened by the amusing tales and witty anecdotes of the Count de Puymandour, which he narrated in a jovial

but rather vulgar manner, seasoned with bursts of
laughter. He ate with an excellent appetite, and
praised the quality of the wine, which the Duke himself
had chosen from the cellar, which he had filled with
an immense stock for the benefit of his descendants.
The Duke, who was generally so silent and morose,
smiled buoyantly, and appeared to enjoy the plea-
santries of his guest. Was this only the duty of the
host, or did his geniality conceal some hidden scheme?
Norbert was utterly unable to settle this question, for
though not gifted with much penetration, he had
studied his father's every look as a slave studies his
master, and knew exactly what annoyed and what
pleased him.

The Count de Puymandour lived in a magnificent
house, with his daughter Marie, about three miles
from Champdoce, and he was exceedingly fond of en-
tertaining; but the gentry, who did not for a moment
decline to accept his grand dinners, did not hesitate to
say that Puymandour was a thief and a rogue. Had he
been convicted of larceny, he could not have been
spoken of with more disdainful contempt. But he was
very wealthy, and possessed at least five millions of
francs. Of course this was an excellent reason for
hating him, but the fact was, that Puymandour was a
very worthy man, and had made his money by specula-
tion in wool on the Spanish frontier. For a long period
he had lived happy and respected in his native town of
Orthez, when all at once he was tempted by the thought
of titular rank, and from that time his life was one
long misery. He took the name of one of his estates,
he bought his title in Italy, and ordered his coat-of-
arms from a heraldic agent in Paris, and now his ambition was to be treated as a real nobleman. The mere

fact of dining with the eccentric Duke de Champdoce, who never invited any one to his table, was to him, as it were, a real patent of nobility.

At ten o'clock he rose and declared he must leave, and the Duke escorted him the length of the avenue to the great gates opening on the main road, and Norbert, who walked a few paces in the rear, caught now and then a few words of their conversation.

" Yes," remarked Puymandour, " I will give a million down."

Then came a few words from the Duke, of which Norbert could only catch the words, " thousands and millions."

He paid, however, but little attention, for his mind was many miles away. Since the unlooked-for meeting with that fair young face, he had thought of nothing else, and he mechanically shook hands with, and bade his guest " Good-night " when his father did.

When the Duke was sure that M. de Puymandour could not hear his voice, he took his son by the arm, and the bitterness of feeling which he had so long repressed burst forth in words.

" This," said he, " is a specimen of the mushroom aristocracy that has sprung up, and not a bad sample either; for though he is puffed up by ridiculous vanity, the man is shrewd and intelligent enough, and his descendants, who will have the advantages of a better education than their progenitors, will form a new class, with more wealth and as much influence as the old one."

For more than an hour the Duke de Champdoce enlarged on his favorite topic; but he might as well have been alone, for his son paid no attention to what he said, for his mind was still dwelling upon his ad-

ventures of the morning. Again that sweet, soft laugh,
and that modulated voice rang in his ears. How foolish he must have seemed to her! and what a ridiculous
figure he must have cut in her eyes! He had by no
means omitted to engrave on the tablet of his memory
the fact that Diana passed daily down the little path on
her errand of bounty, and that there he had the chance
of again seeing her. He fancied that he had so much
to say to her; but as he found that his bashfulness
would deprive him of the power of utterance, he determined to commit his sentiments to paper. That
night he composed and destroyed some fifty letters.
He did not dare to say openly, " I love you," and yet
that was exactly what he wanted to express, and he
strove, but in vain, to find words which would veil its
abruptness and yet disclose the whole strength of his
feelings. At last, however, one of his efforts satisfied
him. Rising early, he snatched up his gun, and whistling to Bruno, made his way to the spot where he had
the day before seen Diana stretched upon the ground.
But he waited in vain, and hour after hour passed
away, as he paced up and down in an agony of suspense. Diana did not come. The young lady had considered her plans thoroughly and kept away. The
next day he might have been again disappointed but
for a lucky circumstance. Norbert was seated on the
turf, awaiting with fond expectation the young girl's
approach and as Diana passed the opening to the pathway Bruno scented her, and rushed forward with a
joyous bark. She had then no option but to walk up
to the spot where Norbert was seated. Both the young
people were for the moment equally embarrassed, and
Norbert stood silent, holding in his hand the letter
which had caused him so much labor to indite.

"I have ventured to wait for you here, mademoiselle," said he in a voice which trembled with suppressed emotion, "because I was full of anxiety to know how you have been. How did you contrive to return home with your wounded foot?"

He paused, awaiting a word of encouragement, but the girl made no reply, and he continued,—

"I was tempted to call and make inquiries at your father's house, but you had forbidden me to speak of the accident, and I did not dare to disobey you."

"I thank you sincerely," faltered Diana.

"Yesterday," the young man went on, "I passed the whole day here. Are you angry with me for my stupidity? I had thought that perhaps you had noticed my anxiety, and might have deigned to——"

He stopped short, terrified at his own audacity.

"Yesterday," returned Diana with the most ingenuous air in the world, and not appearing to perceive the young man's embarrassment, "I was detained at home by my mother."

"Yes," replied he, "for the past two days your form, lying senseless and bleeding on the ground, has ever been before my eyes, for I felt as if I were a murderer. I shall always see your pale, white face, and how, when I raised up your head it rested on my arm for a moment, and all the rapture——"

"You must not talk like that, Marquis," interrupted Diana, but she spoke in such a low tone that Norbert did not hear her and went on,—

"When I saw you yesterday my feelings so overpowered me that I could not put them into words; but as soon as you had left me, it appeared as if all grew dark around me, and throwing myself on my knees, I searched for the tiny leaden pellet that might have

caused your death. I at last found it, and no treasure
upon earth will ever be more prized by me."

To avoid showing the gleam of joy that flashed from
her eyes, Diana was compelled to turn her head on one
side.

" Forgive me, mademoiselle," said Norbert, in despair, as he noticed this movement; " forgive me if I
have offended you. Could you but know how dreary
my past life has been, you would pardon me. It seemed
to me, the very moment that I saw you, I had found a
woman who would feel some slight interest in me, and
that for her sweet compassion I would devote my whole
life to her. But now I see how mad and foolish I have
been, and I am plunged into the depths ' of despair.' "

" At your age, Marquis, you must not make use of
a word like despair."

She accompanied these words with a glance sufficiently tender to restore all Norbert's courage.

" Ah, mademoiselle," said he; " do not trifle with me,
for that would be too cruel."

She let her head droop on her bosom, and, falling
upon his knees, he poured a stream of impassioned
kisses upon her hands. Diana felt herself swept away
by this stream of passion; she gasped, and her fingers
trembled, as she found that she was trapped in the
same snare that she had set for another. Her reason
warned her that she must bring this dangerous interview to a conclusion.

" I am forgetting all about my poor pensioners," said
she.

" ·Ah, if I might but accompany you! "

" And so you may, but you must walk fast."

It is quite true that great events spring from very
trivial sources; and had Diana gone to visit La Besson,

Norbert might have heard something concerning Daumon that would have put him on his guard; but, unfortunately, to-day Diana was bound on a visit to an old woman in another part of the parish.

Norbert looked on whilst this fair young creature busied herself in her work of charity, and then he silently placed two louis from the money he had borrowed, on the table, and left the cottage. Diana followed him, and, laying her finger upon her lips with the significant word "to-morrow," turned down the path that led to her father's house. Norbert could hardly believe his senses when he found himself again alone. Yes, this lovely girl had almost confessed her affection for him, and he was ready to pour out his life blood for her. He tore up the letter which had cost him so much trouble to compose, for he felt that he could make no use of it. He had now no anxieties regarding the future, and he thanked Providence for having caused him to meet Diana de Laurebourg. It never entered his brain that this apparently frank and open-hearted girl had materially furthered the acts of Providence. At supper that night he was so gay, and in such excellent spirits, that even his father's attention was at last attracted.

"I would lay a wager, my boy," remarked the Duke, "that you have had a good day's sport."

"You would win your wager," answered the young man boldly.

His father did not pursue the subject further; but as Norbert felt that he must give some color to his assertion, he stopped the next day, and purchased some quails and a hare. He waited fully half an hour for Diana; and when she did appear, her pale face and the

dark marks under her eyes showed that anxiety had
caused her to pass a sleepless night.

No sooner had she parted from Norbert than she
saw the risk that she was running by her imprudent
conduct. She was endangering her whole future and
her reputation,—all indeed that is most precious to a
young girl. For an instant the thought of confiding
all to her parents entered her brain; but she rejected
the idea almost as soon as she had conceived it, for
she felt that her father would believe that the parsimonious Duke de Champdoce would never consent to
such a marriage, and that her entire liberty would be
taken from her, and that she might even be sent back
to the convent.

"I cannot stop now," she murmured, "and must be
content to run all risks to effect an object in which I
am now doubly interested."

Diana and Norbert had a long conversation together
on this day in a spot which had become so dear to
them both, and it was only the approach of a peasant
that recalled the girl to the sense of her rash imprudence, and she insisted on going on her ostensible errand of charity. Norbert, as before, escorted her, and
even went so far as to offer his arm, upon which she
pressed when the road was steep or uneven.

These meetings took place daily, and after a few
short minutes spent in conversation, the young lovers
would set off on a ramble. More than once they were
met by the villagers, and a little scandal began to arise.
This was very imprudent on Diana's side; but it had
been a part of her plan to permit her actions to be
talked of by the tongue of scandal. Unfortunately the
end of November was approaching, and the weather

growing extremely cold. One morning, as Norbert arose from his couch, he found that a sharp icy blast was swaying the bare branches of the trees, and that the rain was descending in torrents. On such a day as this he knew that it was vain to expect Diana, and, with his heart full of sadness, he took up a book and sat himself down by the huge fire that blazed in the great hall.

Mademoiselle de Laurebourg had, however, gone out, but it was in a carriage, and she had driven to a cottage to see a poor woman who had broken her leg, and who had nothing but the scanty earnings of her daughter Françoise upon which to exist. As soon as Diana entered the cottage she saw that something had gone wrong.

" What is the matter? " asked she.

The poor creature, with garrulous volubility, exhibited a summons which she had just received, and said that she owed three hundred francs, and that as she could no longer pay the interest, she had been summoned, and that her little property would be seized, and so a finishing stroke would be put to her troubles.

" It is the Counsellor," said she, " that rogue Daumon, who has done all this."

The poor woman went on to say that when she went to her creditor to implore a little delay, he had scoffingly told her to send her pretty daughter to him to plead her cause.

Mademoiselle de Laurebourg was disgusted at this narrative, and her eyes gleamed with anger.

" I will see this wicked man," said she, " and will come back to you at once."

She drove straight to the Counsellor's house. Daumon was engaged in writing when the housekeeper ushered Diana into the office. He rose to his feet, and, taking off his velvet skull cap, made a profound bow, advancing at the same time a chair for his visitor's accommodation.

Though Diana knew nothing of this man, she was not so unsophisticated as Norbert, and was not imposed upon by the air of servile obsequiousness that he assumed. With a gesture of contempt, she declined the proffered seat, and this act made Daumon her bitter enemy.

"I have come," said she in the cold, disdainful words in which young girls of high birth address their inferiors,—"I have come to you from Widow Rouleau."

"Ah! you know the poor creature then?"

"Yes, and I take a great interest in her."

"You are a very kind young lady," answered the Counsellor with a sinister smile.

"The poor woman is in the most terrible distress both of mind and body. She is confined to her bed with a fractured limb, and without any means of support."

"Yes, I heard of her accident."

"And yet you sent her a summons, and are ready to seize all she possesses in the world."

Daumon put on an air of sympathy.

"Poor thing!" said he. "How true it is that misfortunes never come singly!"

Diana was disgusted at the man's cool effrontery.

"It seems to me," answered she, "that her last trouble is of your making."

"Is it possible?"

"Why, who is it but you who are the persecutor of this poor lone creature?"

"I!" answered he in extreme astonishment; "do

you really think that it is I? Ah! mademoiselle, why
do you listen to the cruel tongues of scandal-mongers?
To make a long story short, this poor woman bought
barley, corn, potatoes, and three sheep from a man in
the neighborhood, who gave her credit to the extent of
I daresay three hundred francs. Well, in time, the
man asked—most naturally—for his money, and fail-
ing to get it, came to me. I urged him to wait, but he
would not listen to me, and vowed that if I did not do
as he wished he would go to some one else. What was
I to do? He had the law on his side too. Ah!" continued he, as though speaking to himself, "if I could
only see a way of getting this poor creature out of her
trouble! but that cannot be done without money."

He opened a drawer and pulled out about fifty
francs.

"This is all my worldly wealth," said he sadly.
"But how foolish I am! for, of course, when poor
Widow Rouleau has a wealthy young lady to take an
interest in her, she must have no further fear."

"I will speak to my father on the matter," answered
Diana in a voice which showed that she had but little
hope of interesting him in the widow's misfortunes.

Daumon's face fell.

"You will go to the Marquis de Laurebourg?"
asked he. "Now, if you would take my advice, I
should say, go to some intimate friend,—to the Marquis de Champdoce, for instance. I know," he went
on, "that the Duke does not make his son a very
handsome allowance; but the young gentleman will
find no difficulty in raising whatever he may desire—
as it will not be long before he is of age—without
counting his marriage, which will put an enormous
sum at his disposal even before that."

Diana fell in an instant into the trap the wily Daumon had laid for her.

"A marriage!" exclaimed she.

"I know very little about it; only I know that if the young man wishes to marry without his father's consent, he will have to wait at least five years."

"Five years?"

"Yes; the law requires that a young man who marries against his father's desire should be twenty-five years of age."

This last stroke was so totally unexpected, that the girl lost her head.

"Impossible!" cried she. "Are you not making a mistake?"

The Counsellor gave a quiet smile of triumph.

"I am not mistaken," said he, and calmly pointed out in the code the provision to which he had alluded. As Diana read the passage to which his finger pointed, he watched her as a cat watches a mouse.

"After all, what does it matter to me?" remarked Diana, making an effort to recover herself. "I will speak about this poor woman's case to my father;" and, with her limbs bending under her, she left the room.

As Daumon returned from accompanying her to the door, the Counsellor rubbed his hands.

"Things are getting decidedly warm," muttered he.

He felt that he must gain some further information, and this he could not get from Norbert. It would be also as well, he thought, to tell the sheriff to stay proceedings relative to the Widow Rouleau. By this means he might secure another interview with Mademoiselle de Laurebourg, and perhaps win the poor girl's confidence.

As Diana rode home, she abandoned herself to the grief which the intelligence that she had just heard had caused her, for the foresight of the framers of the law had rendered all her deeply laid plans of no avail.

"The Duke de Champdoce," murmured she to herself, "will never consent to his son's marriage with so scantily a dowered woman as I am; but as soon as Norbert is of age he can marry me, in spite of all his father's opposition; but, oh! 'tis a dreary time to wait."

For a moment she dared to think of the possible death of the old man; but she shuddered as she remembered how strong and healthy he was, and felt that the frail edifice of her hope had been crushed into ten thousand atoms. For all this, however, she did not lose courage. She was not one of those women who, at the first check, beat a retreat. She had not yet decided upon a fresh point of departure, but she had fully made up her mind that she would gain the victory. The first thing was to see Norbert with as little delay as possible. Just then the carriage pulled up at the widow's cottage, which she entered hastily.

"I have seen Daumon," said she. "Do not be alarmed; all matters will be arranged shortly."

Then, without listening to the thanks and blessings which the poor woman showered upon her, she said,—

"Give me a piece of paper to write on," and, standing near the casement, she wrote in pencil on a soiled scrap of paper the following words:—

"Diana would, perhaps, have been at the usual meeting place to-day, in spite of the weather, had she not been compelled to visit a poor woman in a contrary direction. Upon the same business, she will have to call to-morrow at the house of a man named Daumon."

She folded the note and said,—

" This letter must be taken at once to M. Norbert de Champdoce. Who will carry it ? "

Françoise had made a smock frock for one of the farm servants at Champdoce, and the delivery of it formed a good excuse for going up to the Château, and she willingly undertook the errand.

The next day, in the midst of a heavy shower of rain, Norbert made his appearance at Daumon's office, saying, as a pretext for his visit, that he had exhausted his stock of money, and required a fresh supply. He too was feeling very unhappy, for he feared that his father might entertain matrimonial designs for him which would be utterly opposed to his passion for Mademoiselle de Laurebourg.

Had not the inexorable old man once said, " You will marry a woman of wealth "? But in the event of this matter being brought up, Norbert swore that he would no longer be obedient, but would resist to the last; and he calculated on receiving assistance from Daumon. He was on the point of referring to this matter, when a carriage drew up at the door of the cottage, and Mademoiselle de Laurebourg descended from it.   Daumon at once saw how matters stood, and wasted no time in addressing Diana.

" The sheriff will stop proceedings," said he.   " I can show you his letter to that effect."

He turned away, and searched as diligently for the letter as if it had existed anywhere except in his own imagination.

" Dear me," said he at length.   " I cannot find it. I must have left it in the other room. I have so much to do, that really there are times when I forget everything. I must find it, however. Excuse me, I will be back immediately."

His sudden departure from the room had been a mere matter of calculation; for, guessing that an assignation had been planned, he thought that he might know what took place at it by a little eavesdropping. He therefore applied first his ear and then his eye to the keyhole, and by these means acquired all the information he desired.

A moment of privacy with the object of his affections seemed to Norbert an inestimable boon. When Diana had first entered, he was horrified at the terrible alteration that had taken place in the expression of her face. He seized her hand, which she made no effort to withdraw, and gazed fixedly into her eyes.

"Tell me," murmured he in accents of love and tenderness, "what it is that has gone wrong."

Diana sighed, then a tear coursed slowly down her cheek. Norbert was in the deepest despair at these signs of grief.

"Great heavens!" cried he. "Will you not trust me? Am not I your truest and most devoted friend?"

At first she refused to answer him, but at length she yielded to his entreaties, and confessed that the evening before her father had informed her that a young man had sought her hand in marriage, and one who was a perfectly eligible suitor.

Norbert listened to this avowal, trembling from head to foot, with a sudden access of jealousy.

"And did you make no objections?" asked he.

"How could I?" retorted she. "What can a girl do in opposition to the will of all her family, when she has to choose between the alternative that she loathes, or a life-long seclusion in a convent?"

Daumon shook with laughter, as he kept his ear closely to the keyhole.

"Good business," muttered he. "Not so bad. Here's a little girl from a convent. She has a clever brain and a glib tongue, and under my tuition would be a perfect wonder. If this country booby does not make an open declaration at once, I wonder what her next move will be?"

"And you hesitated," said Norbert reproachfully. "Remember you may escape from the walls of the convent, but not from the bonds of an ill-assorted marriage."

Diana, who looked more beautiful than ever in her despair, wrung her hands.

"What reason can I give to my father for declining this offer?" said she. "Every one knows that I am almost portionless, and that I am sacrificed to my brother, immolated upon the altar erected before the cruel idol of family pride; and how dare I refuse a suitable offer when one is made for my hand?"

"Have you forgotten me?" cried Norbert. "Have you no love for me?"

"Ah, my poor friend, you are no more free than I am."

"Then you look on me as a mere weak boy?" asked he, biting his lips.

"Your father is very powerful," answered she in tones of the deepest resignation; "his determination is inflexible, and his will inexorable. You are completely in his power."

"What do I care for my father?" cried the young man fiercely. "Am not I a Champdoce too? Woe be to any one, father or stranger, who comes between me and the woman I love devotedly; for I do love you, Diana, and no mortal man shall take you from me."

He clasped Diana to his breast, and pressed a loving kiss upon her lips.

"Aha," muttered Daumon, who had lost nothing from his post of espial, "this is worth fifty thousand francs at least to me."

For a moment Diana remained clasped in her lover's embrace, and then, with a faint cry, released herself from him. She then felt that she loved him, and his kiss and caresses sent a thrill like liquid fire through her veins. She was half pleased and half terrified. She feared him, but she feared herself more.

"What, Diana! would you refuse me?" asked he, after a moment's pause. "Do you refuse me, when I implore you to be my wife, and to share my name with me? Will you not be the Duchess of Champdoce?"

Diana only replied with a glance; but if her eyes spoke plainly, that look said "Yes."

"Why, then," returned Norbert, "should we alarm ourselves with empty phantoms? Do you not trust me? My father may certainly oppose my plans, but before long I shall escape from his tyrannical sway, for I shall be of age."

"Ah, Norbert," returned she sadly, "you are feeding upon vain hopes. You must be twenty-five years of age before you can marry and give the shelter of your name to the woman whom you have chosen for your wife."

This was exactly the explanation for which Daumon had been waiting.

"Good again, my young lady," cried he. "And so this is why she came here. There is some credit in giving a lesson to so apt a pupil."

"It is impossible," cried Norbert, violently agitated; "such an iniquitous thing cannot be."

"You are mistaken," answered Diana calmly. "Unfortunately I am telling you exactly how matters stand. The law clearly fixes the age at twenty-five. During all this time will you remember that a broken-hearted girl——"

"Why talk to me of law? When I am of age, I shall have plenty of money," broke in Norbert; "and do you think that I will tamely submit to my father's oppression? No, I will wrest his consent from him."

During this conversation the Counsellor was carefully removing the dust from the knees of his trousers.

"I will pop in suddenly," thought he, "and catch a word or two which will do away with the necessity of all lengthy explanations."

He suited the action to the word, and appeared suddenly before the lovers. He was not at all disconcerted at the effect his entrance produced upon them, and remarked placidly, "I could not find the sheriff's letter, but I assure you that Widow Rouleau's matter shall be speedily and satisfactorily arranged."

Diana and Norbert exchanged glances of annoyance at finding their secret at the mercy of such a man. This evident distrust appeared to wound Daumon deeply.

"You have a perfect right," remarked he dejectedly, "to say, 'Mind your own business;' but the fact is, that I hate all kinds of injustice so much that I always take the side of the weakest, and so, when I come in and find you deploring your troubles, I say to myself, 'Doubtless here are two young people made for each other.'"

"You forget yourself," broke in Diana haughtily.

"I beg your pardon," stammered Daumon. "I am

but a poor peasant, and sometimes I speak out too
plainly. I meant no harm, and I only hope that you
will forgive me."

Daumon looked at Diana; and as she made no reply, he went on: "Well," says I to myself, "here are
two young folks that have fallen in love, and have
every right to do so, and yet they are kept apart by
unreasonable and cruel-minded parents. They are
young and know nothing of the law, and without help
they would most certainly get into a muddle. Now,
suppose I take their matter in hand, knowing the law
thoroughly as I do, and being up to its weak as well
as its strong points."

He spoke on in this strain for some minutes, and
did not notice that they had withdrawn a little apart,
and were whispering to each other.

"Why should we not trust him?" asked Norbert.
"He has plenty of experience."

"He would betray us; he would do anything for
money."

"That is all the better for us then; for if we promise him a handsome sum, he will not say a word of
what has passed to-day."

"Do as you think best, Norbert."

Having thus gained Diana's assent, the young man
turned to Daumon. "I put every faith in you, and
so does Mademoiselle de Laurebourg. You know our
exact situation. What do you advise?"

"Wait and hope," answered the Counsellor. "The
slightest step taken before you are of age will be fatal
to your prospects, but the day you are twenty-one I
will undertake to show you several methods of bringing the Duke on his knees."

Nothing could make this speech more explicit; but

he was so cheerful and confident, that when Diana left the office, she felt a fountain of fresh hope well up in her heart.

This was nearly their last interview that year, for the winter came on rapidly and with increased severity, so that it was impossible for the lovers to meet out of doors, and the fear of spying eyes prevented them from taking advantage of Daumon's hospitality. Each day, however, the widow's daughter, Françoise, carried a letter to Laurebourg, and brought back a reply to Champdoce. The inhabitants of the various country houses had fled to more genial climates, and only the Marquis de Laurebourg, who was an inveterate sportsman, still lingered; but at the first heavy fall of snow he too determined to take refuge in the magnificent house that he owned in the town of Poitiers. Norbert had foreseen this, and had taken his measures accordingly. Two or three times in the week he mounted his horse and rode to the town. After changing his dress, he made haste to a certain garden wall in which there was a small door. At an agreed hour this door would gently open, and as Norbert slipped through he would find Diana ready to welcome him, looking more bewitching than ever. This great passion, which now enthralled his whole life, and the certainty that his love was returned, had done away with a great deal of his bashfulness and timidity. He had resumed his acquaintanceship with Montlouis, and had often been with him to the Café Castille. Montlouis was only for a short time at Poitiers, for as soon as spring began he was to join the young Count de Mussidan, who had promised to find some employment for him. The approaching departure was not at all to Montlouis' taste, as he was madly in love with a young girl who resided in the town. He told all to Norbert; and as confidence begets confidence, he more than once accompanied the young Marquis to the door in the garden wall of the Count de Laurebourg's town house.

April came at last. The gentry returned to their country houses, and in time the happy day arrived when Diana de Laurebourg was to return to her father's country mansion. The lovers had now every opportunity to meet, and would exhort each other to have patience, and a week after Diana's return they spent a long day together in the woods. After this delicious day, Norbert, happy and light-hearted, returned to his father's house.

" Marquis," said the Duke, plunging at once into the topic nearest his heart, " I have found a wife for you, and in two months you will marry her."

CHAPTER VII.

AN UNLUCKY BLOW.

THE falling of a thunderbolt at his feet would have startled Norbert less than these words did. The Duke took, or affected to take, no notice of his son's extreme agitation, and in a careless manner he continued,—

" I suppose, my son, that it is hardly necessary for me to tell you the young lady's name. Mademoiselle Marie de Puymandour cannot fail to please you. She is excessively pretty, tall, dark, and with a fine figure. You saw her at Mass one day. What do you think of her ? "

"Think!" stammered Norbert. "Really I——"

"Pshaw," replied the old gentleman; "I thought that you had begun to use your eyes. And look here, Marquis, you must adopt a different style of dress. You can go over with me to Poitiers to-morrow, and one of the tailors there will make you some clothes suitable to your rank, for I don't suppose that you wish to alarm your future wife by the uncouthness of your appearance."

"But, father——"

"Wait a moment, if you please. I shall have a suite of apartments reserved for you and your bride, and you can pass your honeymoon here. Take care you do not prolong it for too lengthened a period; and when it is all over, we can break the young woman into all our ways."

"But," interrupted Norbert hastily, "suppose I do not fancy this young lady?"

"Well, what then?"

"Suppose I should beg you to save me from a marriage which will render me most unhappy?"

The Duke shrugged his shoulders. "Why this is mere childishness," said he. "The marriage is a most suitable one, and it is my desire that it should take place."

"But, father," again commenced Norbert.

"What! Are you opposing my will?" asked his father angrily. "Pray, do you hesitate?"

"No," answered his son coldly, "I do not hesitate."

"Very good, then. A man of no position can consult the dictates of his heart when he takes a wife, but with a nobleman of rank and station it is certainly a different matter, for with the latter, marriage should be looked upon as a mere business transaction. I have made excellent arrangements. Let me repeat to you the conditions. The Count will give two-thirds of his fortune, which is estimated at five millions—just think of that!—and when we get that, we shall be able to screw and save with better heart. Think of the restoration of our house, and the colossal fortune that our descendants will one day inherit, and realize all the beauties of a life of self-denial."

While the Duke was uttering this string of incoherent sentences, he was pacing up and down the room, and now he halted immediately in front of his son. "You understand," said he; "to-morrow you will go to Poitiers, and on Sunday we will dine at the house of your future father-in-law."

In this fearful crisis Norbert did not know what to say or how to act.

"Father," he once more commenced, "I have no wish to go to Poitiers to-morrow."

"What are you saying? What in heaven's name do you mean?"

"I mean that as I shall never love Mademoiselle de Puymandour, she will never be my wife."

The Duke had never foreseen the chance of rebellion on the part of his son, and he could not bring his mind to receive such an unlooked-for event.

"You are mad," said he at last, "and do not know what you are saying."

"I know very well."

"Think of what you are doing."

"I have reflected."

The Duke was making a violent effort to compose his ordinarily violent temper.

"Do you imagine," answered he disdainfully, "that I shall be satisfied with an answer of this kind? I hope that you will submit to my wishes, for I think that, as the head of the family, I have conceived a splendid plan for its future aggrandizement; and do you think that, for the mere whim of a boy, I will be turned aside from my fixed determination?"

"No, father," answered Norbert, "it is no boyish whim that makes me oppose your wishes. Tell me, have I not ever been a dutiful son to you? Have I ever refused to do what I was ordered? No; I have obeyed you implicitly. I am the son of the wealthiest man in Poitiers, and I have lived like a laborer's child. Whatever your mandates were, I have never complained or murmured at them."

"Well, and now I order you to marry Mademoiselle de Puymandour."

"Anything but that; I do not love her, and I shall never do so. Do you wish my whole life to be blighted? I entreat you to spare me this sacrifice!"

"My orders are given, and you must comply with them."

"No," answered Norbert quietly, "I will not comply with them."

A purple flush passed across the Duke's face, then it faded away, leaving every feature of a livid whiteness.

"Great heavens!" said he in a voice before which Norbert, at one time, would have quailed. "Whence comes the audacity that makes you venture to dispute my orders?"

"From the feeling that I am acting rightly."

"How long is it that it has been right for children to disobey their parents' commands?"

"Ever since parents began to issue unjust commands."

This speech put the finishing stroke to the Duke's rage. He made a step across the room, towards his son, raising the stick that he usually carried high in the air. For a moment he stood thus, and then, casting it aside, he exclaimed,—

"No, I cannot strike a Champdoce."

Perhaps it was Norbert's intrepid attitude that restrained the Duke's frenzy, for he had not moved a muscle, but stood still, with his arms folded, and his head thrown haughtily back.

"No, this is an act of disobedience that I will not put up with," exclaimed the old man in a voice of thunder, and, springing upon his son, he grasped him by the collar and dragged him up to a room on the second floor, and thrust him violently through the doorway.

"You have twenty-four hours in which to reflect whether you will be willing to accept the wife that I have chosen for you," said he.

"I have already decided on that point," answered Norbert quietly.

The Duke made no reply, but slammed the door, which was of massive oak, and secured by a lock of enormous proportions.

Norbert gazed round; the only other exit from the room was by means of a window some forty feet from the ground. The young man, however, imagined that some one would surely come to make up his bed for the night; that would give him two sheets; these he could knot together and thus secure a means of escape. He might not be able to see Diana at once, but he could easily send her a message by Daumon, warning her of what had taken place. Having arranged his plans, he threw himself into an arm-chair with a more easy mind than he had experienced for many months past. The decisive step had been taken, and the relations between his father and himself clearly defined, and thus he naturally considered great progress had been made, and the task before him seemed as nothing to what he had already performed.

"My father," thought he, "must be half mad with passion."

And Norbert was not wrong in his opinion. When the Duke, as usual, took his place at the table, at which the farm laborers ate their meals, not one of them had the courage to make a single observation. Every one knew that a serious altercation had taken place between father and son, and each one was devoured by the pangs of ungratified curiosity.

As soon as the meal was concluded, the Duke called an old and trustworthy servant, who had been in his employment for over thirty years.

"Jean," said he, "your young master is locked up in the yellow room. Here is the key. Take him something to eat."

"Very good, your Grace."

"Wait a little. You will spend the night in his room and keep a strict watch upon him. He may design to make his escape. If he attempts it, restrain him, if necessary, by physical force. Should he prove too strong for you, call to me; I shall be near, and will come to your aid."

This unexpected precaution upon the Duke's part upset all Norbert's plans of escape. He endeavored to persuade Jean to allow him to go out for a couple of hours, giving his word of honor that he would return at the expiration of that time. Prayers and menaces, however, had no effect. Had the young man gazed from the window, he would have seen his father striding moodily up and down the courtyard, with the thought gnawing at his heart that perhaps after all these many years of waiting his plans might yet be frustrated.

"There is a woman at the bottom of all this," said he to himself. "It is only woman's wiles that in this brief space of time would effect so complete a change in a young man's disposition. Besides, he would not have so obstinately declined to listen to the proposal I made him had not his affections been engaged elsewhere. Who can she be? and by what means shall I find her out?"

It would be absurd to question Norbert, and the Duke was excessively unwilling to institute any regular inquiry into the matter. He passed the whole night in gloomy indecision, but towards morning an inspiration came to him which he looked upon as a special interposition of Providence.

"Bruno," he exclaimed with a mighty oath. "The dog will show me the place that his master frequents and perhaps lead me to the very woman who has bewitched him."

This brilliant idea soothed him a great deal, and at one o'clock he took his seat as usual at the head of the table, and ordered food to be taken up to Norbert, but that none of the measures for his safe custody were to be relaxed.

When he thought the moment was a favorable one, he whistled to Bruno, and, though the dog rarely followed him, yet in the absence of his master, he condescended to accompany the Duke down the avenue to the front gates. Three roads branched off from here, but the dog did not hesitate for a moment, and took the one to the left, like an animal who knew his destination perfectly well. Bruno went ahead for nearly half an hour, until he reached the exact spot where Diana had met with her accident. He made a cast round, but finding nothing, sat down, clearly saying,—

" Let us wait."

" This, then," muttered the Duke, " is the place where the lovers have been in the habit of meeting each other."

The place was a very lonely one, and, standing on rising ground, commanded a view of the country for a long way round.

The Duke noticed this, and took up a position where the trunk of a giant oak almost concealed him from observation. He was delighted at his sagacity, and was almost in a good humor; for now that he had reflected, the danger did not seem by any means so great, for to whom could Norbert have lost his heart? To some little peasant girl, perhaps, who, thinking that the lad was an easy dupe, had tried to induce him to marry her. As these thoughts passed through the Duke's brain, Bruno gave a joyous bark.

" Here she is," muttered he, as he emerged from his hiding place, and at that moment Diana de Laurebourg made her appearance; but as soon as she saw the Duke she uttered a faint cry of alarm. She was inclined to turn and fly, but her strength failed her, and, extending her hands, she grasped the boughs of a slender birch tree that grew close by, to prevent herself from falling. The Duke was quite as much astonished as the young lady. He had expected to see a peasant girl, and here was the daughter of the Marquis de Laurebourg. But anger soon succeeded to surprise; for though he might have had nothing to fear from the peasant, the daughter of the Marquis de Laurebourg was an utterly different antagonist. He could not rely upon aid from her family, as, for all he knew, they might be aiding and abetting her.

"Well, my child," began he, "you do not seem very glad to see me."

"Your Grace."

"Yes, when you come out to meet the son, it is annoying to meet the father; but do not blame poor Norbert, for I assure you he is not in fault."

Though Mademoiselle de Laurebourg had been startled at first, she was possessed of too strong a will to give in, and soon recovered her self-possession.

She never thought to screen herself by a denial of her reasons for being on the spot, for such a course she would have looked on as an act of treacherous cowardice.

"You are quite right," answered she. "I came here to meet your son, and therefore you will pardon me if I take my leave of you."

With a deep courtesy she was about to move away, when the Duke laid a restraining grip upon her arm.

"Permit me, my child," said he, endeavoring to put on a kind and paternal tone,—"let me say a few words to you. Do you know why Norbert did not come to meet you?"

"He has doubtless some very good reason."

"My son is locked up in a room, and my servants have my orders to prevent his making his escape by force, if necessary."

"Poor fellow! He deserves the deepest commiseration."

The Duke was much surprised at this piece of impertinence, as he considered it.

"I will tell you," returned he in tones of rising anger, "how it comes that I treat my son, the heir to my rank and fortune, in this manner."

He looked savagely angry as he spoke, but Diana answered negligently, "Pray go on; you quite interest me."

"Well then, listen to me. I have chosen a wife for Norbert; she is as young as you are—beautiful, clever, and wealthy."

"And of noble birth, of course."

The sarcasm conveyed in this reply roused the Duke to fury.

"Fifteen hundred thousand francs as a marriage portion will outweigh a coat of arms, even though it should be a tower argent on a field azure." The Duke paused as he made this allusion to the Laurebourg arms, and then continued, "In addition to this, she has great expectations; and yet my son is mad enough to refuse the hand of this wealthy heiress."

"If you think that this marriage will cause your son's happiness, you are quite right in acting as you have done."

"Happiness! What has that to do with the matter, as long as it adds to the aggrandizement of our house and name? I have made up my mind that Norbert shall marry this girl; I have sworn it, and I never break my oath. I told him this myself."

Diana suffered acutely, but her pride supported her, whilst her confidence in Norbert was so great that she had the boldness to inquire, "And what did he say to that?"

"Norbert will become a dutiful son once more when he is removed from the malignant influence which has been so injurious to him," returned the Duke fiercely.

"Indeed."

"He will obey me, when I show him that though he may not value his name and position, there are others who do so; and that many a woman would fight a brave battle for the honor of being the Duchess of Champdoce. Young lady, my son is a mere boy; but I have known the world, and when I prove to the poor foul that it was only grasping ambition which assumed the garb of love, he will renounce his folly and resume his allegiance to me. I will tell him what I think of the poverty-stricken adventuresses of high birth, whose only weapons are their youth and beauty, and with which they think that they can win a wealthy husband in the battle of life."

"Continue, sir," broke in Diana haughtily. "Insult a defenceless girl with her poverty! It is a noble act, and one worthy of a high-born gentleman like yourself!"

"I believed," said the Duke, "that I was addressing the woman whose advice had led my son to break into open rebellion against my authority. Am I right or wrong? You can prove me to be mistaken by urging upon Norbert the necessity for submission."

She made no reply, but bent her head upon her bosom.

"You see," continued the Duke, "that I am correct, and that if you continue to act as you have done, I shall be justified in retaliating in any manner that I may deem fit. You have now been warned. Carry on this intrigue at your peril."

He placed such an insulting emphasis upon the word " intrigue " that Diana's anger rose to boiling point. At that instant, for the sake of vengeance, she would have risked her honor, her ambition, her very life itself.

Forgetting all prudence, she cast aside her mask of affected indifference, and, with her eyes flashing angry gleams of fire, and her cheeks burning, she said,—

"Listen to me. I, too, have sworn an oath, and it is that Norbert shall be my husband; and I tell you that he shall be so! Shut him up in prison, subject him to every indignity at the hands of your menials, but you will never break his spirit, or make him go back from his plighted word. If I bid him, he will resist your will even unto the bitter end. He and I will never yield. Believe me when I tell you, that before you attack a young girl's honor, you had better pause; for one day she will be a member of your family. Farewell."

Before the Duke could recover his senses, Diana was far down the path on her way homewards; and then he burst into a wild storm of menaces, oaths, and insults. He fancied that he was alone, but he was mistaken; for the whole of that strange scene had a hidden witness, and that witness was Daumon. He had heard of the treatment of the young Marquis from one of the servants at the Château, and his first thought had been to acquaint Diana with it. Unfortunately he saw no means of doing this. He dared not go to Laurebourg, and he would have died sooner than put pen to paper. He was in a position of the deepest embarrassment when the idea struck him of going to the lovers' trysting place. The little cry that Diana had uttered upon perceiving the Duke had put him upon his guard. Bruno had found him out; but, as he knew him, merely fawned upon him. He was delighted at the fury of the Duke, whom he hated with cold and steady malignity; but the courage of Diana filled him with admiration. Her sublime audacity won his warmest praises, and he longed for her as an ally to aid him in his scheme of revenge. He knew that the girl would find herself in a terribly embarrassing position, and thus she would be sure to call upon him for advice before returning home.

"Now," thought he, "if I wish to profit by her anger, I ought to strike while the iron is hot; and to do so, I should be at home to meet her."

Without a moment's delay, he dashed through the woods, striving to get home without the young girl's perceiving him. His movements in the underwood caught the Duke's eye.

"Who is there?" exclaimed he, moving towards the spot from whence the rustling came. There was no reply. Surely he had not been mistaken. Calling to Bruno, he strove to put him on the scent, but the dog showed no signs of eagerness. He sniffed about for a time, and seemed to linger near one special spot. The Duke moved towards it, and distinctly saw the impression of two knees upon the grass.

"Some one has been eavesdropping," muttered he, much enraged at his discovery. "Who can it be? Has Norbert escaped from his prison?"

As he returned through the courtyard, he called one of the grooms to him.

"Where is my son?" asked he.

"Upstairs, your Grace," was the answer.

The Duke breathed more freely. Norbert was still in security, and therefore it could not have been the person who had been listening.

"But," added the lad, "the young master is half frantic."

"What do you mean?"

"Well, he declared that he would not remain in his room an instant longer; so old Jean called for help. He is awfully strong, and it took six of us to hold him. He said that if we would let him go, he would return in two hours, and that his honor and life were involved."

The Duke listened with a sarcastic smile. He cared nothing about the frantic struggles of his son, for his heart had grown cold and hard from the presence of the fixed idea which had actuated his conduct for so many years, and it was with the solemn face of a man who was fulfilling a sacred duty that he ascended to the room in which his son was imprisoned. Jean threw open the door, and the Duke paused for a moment on the threshold. The furniture had been overturned, some of it broken, and there were evident signs of a furious struggle having taken place.

A powerful laborer stood near the window, and Norbert was lying on the bed, with his face turned to the wall.

"Leave us," said the Duke, and the man withdrew at once.

"Get up, Norbert," he added; "I wish to speak to you."

His son obeyed him. Any one but the Duke would have been alarmed by the expression of the young man's face.

"What is the meaning of all this?" asked the old

nobleman in his most severe voice. "Are not my orders sufficient to insure obedience? I hear that absolute force has had to be used towards you during my absence. Tell me, my son, what plans you have devised during these hours of solitude, and what hopes you still venture to cherish."

"I intend to be free, and I will be so."

The Duke affected not to hear the reply, uttered as it was in a tone of decision.

"It was very easy for me to discover, from your obstinacy, that some woman had endeavored to entrap you, and by her insidious counsels inducing you to disobey your best friend."

He paused, but there was no reply.

"This woman—this dangerous woman—I have been in search of, and as you can conceive, I easily found her. I went to the Forest of Bevron, and there I need not tell you I found Mademoiselle de Laurebourg."

"Did you speak to her?"

"I did so, certainly. I told her my opinion of those manœuvring women who fascinate the dupes they intend to take advantage of——"

"Father!"

"Can it be possible that you, simple boy even as you are, could have been deceived by the pretended love of this wily young woman? It is not you, Marquis, that she loves, but our name and fortune; but *I* know if *she* does not that the law will imprison women who contrive to entrap young men who are under age."

Norbert turned deadly pale.

"Did you really say that to her?" asked he, in a low, hoarse voice, utterly unlike his own. "You dare to insult the woman I love, when you knew that I was

far away and unable to protect her! Take care, or
I shall forget that you are my father."

"He actually threatens me," said the Duke, "my
son threatens me;" and, raising the heavy stick he
held in his hand, he struck Norbert a violent blow.
By a fortunate movement the unhappy boy drew back,
and so avoided the full force of the stroke, but the
end of the stick struck him across the temple, inflicting
a long though not a serious wound. In his blind rage
Norbert was about to throw himself upon his father,
when his eyes caught sight of the open door. Liberty
and safety lay before him, and, with a bound, he was
on the stairs, and before the Duke could shout for aid
from the window, his son was tearing across the park
with all the appearance and gesture of a madman.

CHAPTER VIII.

THE LITTLE GLASS BOTTLE.

IN order to avoid being seen by Mademoiselle de
Laurebourg, Daumon had to take a much longer route
to regain his home than the one that Diana had followed. This, however, he could not help. As soon as
he arrived at his home he ran hastily upstairs and took
from a cleverly concealed hiding-place in the wains-
coting of his bedroom a small bottle of dark green
glass, which he hastily slipped into his pocket. When
he had once more descended to his office, he again took
it out and examined it carefully to see that it had in
no way been tampered with; then, with a hard, cruel
smile, he placed it upon his desk among his ledgers

and account books. Diana de Laurebourg might pay
him a visit as soon as she liked, for he was quite prepared for her, for he had slipped on his dressing-gown
and placed his velvet skull cap upon his head, as if
he had not quitted the house that day.

"Why on earth does she not come?" muttered he.

He began to be uneasy. He went to the window
and glanced eagerly down the road; then he drew out
his watch and examined the face of it, when all at
once his ears detected a gentle tapping at the door of
the office.

"Come in," said he.

The door opened, and Diana entered slowly, without
uttering a word, and took no notice of the servile obsequiousness of the Counsellor; indeed, she hardly
seemed to notice his presence, and with a deep sigh
she threw herself into a chair.

In his inmost heart Daumon was filled with the utmost delight; he now understood why Diana had
taken so long in reaching his house; it was because her
interview with the Duke had almost overcome her.

She soon, however, recovered her energy, and shook
off the languor that seemed to cling to her limbs, and,
turning towards her host, said abruptly,—

"Counsellor, I have come to you for advice, which
I sorely need. About an hour ago——"

With a gesture of sympathy Daumon interrupted
her,—

"Alas!" said he; "spare me the recital, I know all."

"You know——"

"Yes, I know that M. Norbert is a prisoner at the
Château. Yes, mademoiselle, I know this, and I know,
too, that you have just met the Duke de Champdoce in
the Forest of Bevron. I know, moreover, all that you

said to the old nobleman, for I have heard every word from a person who has just left."

In spite of her strong nerves, Diana was unable to restrain a movement of dismay and terror.

" But who told you of this?" murmured she.

" A man who was out cutting wood. Ah! my dear young lady, the forest is not a safe place to tell secrets in, for you never know whether watchful eyes and listening ears are not concealed behind every tree. This man, and I am afraid some of his companions, heard every word that was spoken, and as soon as you left the Duke the man scampered off to tell the story. I made him promise not to say a word, but he is a married man and is sure to tell it to his wife. Then there are his companions; dear me! it is most annoying."

" Then all is lost, and I am ruined," murmured she.

But her despair did not last long, for she was by no means the woman to throw down her arms and sue for mercy. She grasped the arm of the Counsellor.

" The end has not come yet, surely? Speak! what is to be done? You must have some plan. I am ready for anything, now that I have nothing to lose. No one shall ever say that that cowardly villain, the Duke de Champdoce, insulted me with impunity. Tell me, will you help me?"

" In the name of heaven!" cried he, " do not speak so loud. You do not know the adversary that you have to contend with."

" Are you afraid of him?"

" Yes, I do fear him; and what is more, I fear him very much. He is a determined man, and will gain his object at any cost or risk. Do you know that he did his best to crush me because I summoned him to court on behalf of one of my clients? So that now, when any one comes to me and wishes to proceed against the Duke, I am glad to decline to take up the matter."

"And so," returned the young girl in a tone of cold contempt, "after leading us to this compromising position, you are ready to abandon us at the most critical moment?"

"Can you think such a thing, mademoiselle?"

"You can act as you please, Counsellor; Norbert is still left to me; he will protect me."

Daumon shook his head with an air of deep sorrow.

"How can we be sure that at this very moment the Marquis has not given in to all his father's wishes?"

"No," exclaimed the girl; "such a supposition is an insult to Norbert. He would sooner die than give in. He may be timid, but he is not a coward; the thoughts of me will give him the power to resist his father's tyranny."

Daumon allowed himself to fall into his great arm-chair as though overcome by the excitement of this interview.

"We can talk coolly enough here and with no one to threaten us; but the Marquis, on the other hand, is exposed to all his father's violence and ill treatment, moral as well as physical, without any defence or aid from a soul in the world, and in such times as these the strongest will may give way."

"Yes, I see it all; Norbert may give in, he may marry another woman, and I shall be left alone, with my reputation gone, and the scorn and scoff of all the neighborhood."

" But, mademoiselle, you still have——"

" All I have left is life, and that life I would gladly give for vengeance."

There was something so terribly determined in the young girl's voice that again Daumon started, and this time his start was sincere and not simulated.

" Yes, you are right," said he, " and there are many besides myself who have vowed to have revenge on the Duke, and their time will come, have no fear. A quiet shot in the woods in the dusk of the evening would settle many a long account. It has been tried, but the old man seems to have the luck of the evil one; and if the gun did not miss fire, the bullets flew wide of the mark. A judge might take a very serious view of such a matter, and term a crime what was merely an act of justice. Who can say whether the death of the Duke de Champdoce might not save him from the commission of many acts of tyranny and oppression and render many deserving persons happy? "

The face of Diana de Laurebourg turned deadly pale as she listened to these specious arguments.

" As things go," continued Daumon, " the Duke may go on living to a hundred; he is wealthy and influential, and to a certain degree looked up to. He will die peacefully in his bed, there will be a magnificent funeral, and masses will be sung for the repose of his soul."

While he spoke the Counsellor had taken the little bottle from beside his account books and was turning it over and over between his fingers.

" Yes," murmured he, thoughtfully; " the Duke is quite likely to outlive us all, unless, indeed——"

He took the cork from the bottle, and poured a little of the contents into the palm of his hand. A few grains of fine white powder, glittering like crystal, appeared on the brown skin of the Counsellor.

"And yet," he went on, in cold, sinister accents, "let him but take a small pinch of this, and no one need fear his tyranny again in this world. No one is much afraid of a man who lies some six feet under ground, shut up in a strong oak coffin, with a finely carved gravestone over his head."

He stopped short, and fixed his keen eyes upon the agitated girl, who stood in front of him. For at least two minutes the man and the girl stood face to face, motionless, and without exchanging a word. Through the dead, weird silence, the pulsations of their hearts were plainly audible. It seemed as if before speaking again each wished to fathom the depths of guilt that lay in the other's heart. It was a compact entered into by look and not by speech; and Daumon so well understood this, that at length, when he did speak, his voice sank to a hoarse whisper, as though he himself feared to listen to the utterance of his own thoughts.

"A man taking this feels no pain. It is like a heavy, stunning blow on the forehead—in ten seconds all is over, no gasp, no cry, but the heart ceases to beat forever; and, best of all, it leaves no trace behind it. A little of this, such a little, in wine or coffee, would be enough. It is tasteless, colorless, and scentless, its presence is impossible to be detected."

"But in the event of a *post-mortem* examination?"

"By skilful analysts in Paris or the larger towns, there would be a chance; but in a place like this, never! Never, in fact, anywhere, unless there had been previous grounds for suspicion. Otherwise only apoplectic symptoms would be observed; and even if it was traced, there comes the question, By whom was it administered?"

He stopped short, for a word rose to his lips which he did not dare utter; he raised his hands to his mouth, coughed slightly, and went on,—

"This substance is not sold by chemists; it is very rarely met with, difficult to prepare, and terribly expensive. The smallest quantity might be met with in the first-class laboratories for scientific purposes, but it is most unlikely for any one in these parts to possess any of this drug, or even to know of its existence."

"And yet you——"

"That is quite another matter. Years ago, when I was far away from here, it was in my power to render a great service to a distinguished chemist, and he made me a present of this combination of his skill. It would be impossible to trace this bottle; I have had it ten years, and the man who gave it to me is dead. Ten years? no, I am wrong, it is now twelve."

"And in all these years has not this substance lost any of its destructive powers?"

"I tried it only a month ago. I threw a pinch of it into a basin of milk and gave it to a powerful mastiff. He drank the milk and in ten seconds fell stark and dead."

"Horrible!" exclaimed Diana, covering her face with her hand, and recoiling from the tempter.

A sinister smile quivered upon the thin lips of the Counsellor.

"Why do you say horrible?" asked he; "the dog had shown symptoms of *rabies*, and had he bitten me, I might have expired in frightful torture. Was it not fair self-defence? Sometimes, however, a man is more dangerous than a dog. A man blights the whole of my life; I strike him down openly, and the law convicts me and puts me to death; but I do not contemplate doing so, for I would suppress such a man secretly."

Diana placed her hands on the man's mouth and stopped a further exposition of his ideas.

"Listen to me," said she. But at this moment a heavy step was heard outside. "It is Norbert," gasped she.

"Impossible! it is more likely his father."

"It is Norbert," cried Mademoiselle de Laurebourg, and snatching the little bottle from the Counsellor's hands, she thrust it into her bosom. The door flew open, and Norbert appeared on the threshold. Diana and the Counsellor both uttered a shriek of terror. His livid countenance seemed to indicate that he had passed through some terrible scene; his gait was unsteady, his clothes torn and disordered, and his face stained with blood, which had flowed from a cut over his temple. Daumon imagined that some outrage had taken place.

"You have been wounded, Marquis?" said he.

"Yes, my father struck me."

"Can it be possible?"

"Yes, he struck me."

Mademoiselle Diana had feared this, and she trembled with the terror of her vague conjectures as she made a step towards her lover.

"Permit me to examine your wound," said she.

She placed both her hands at the side of his head and stood on tip-toe, the better to inspect the cut. As she did so, she shuddered; an inch lower, and the consequences might have been fatal.

"Quick," she said, "give me some rags and water."

Norbert gently disengaged himself. "It is a mere nothing," said he, "and can be looked after later on. Fortunately I did not receive the whole weight of the blow, which would otherwise have brought me senseless to the ground, and perhaps I should have been slain by my father's hand."

"By the Duke? and for what reason did he strike you?"

"Diana, he had grossly insulted you, and he dared to tell me of it. Had he forgotten that the blood of the race of Champdoce ran in my veins as well as in his?"

Mademoiselle de Laurebourg burst into a passion of tears.

"I," sobbed she, "I have brought all this upon you."

"You? Why, it is to you that he owes his life. He dared to strike me as if I had been a lackey, but the thoughts of you stayed my hand. I turned and fled, and never again will I enter that accursed house. I renounce the Duke de Champdoce, he is no longer my father, and I will never look upon his face again. Would that I could forget that such a man existed; but, no, I would rather that I remembered him for the sake of revenge."

Again the heart of Daumon overflowed with joy. All his deeply malignant spirit thrilled pleasantly as he heard these words.

"Marquis," said he, "perhaps you will now believe with me that in all misfortunes there is an element of luck, for your father has committed an act of imprudence which will yet cost him dear. It is very strange that so astute a man as the Duke de Champdoce should have allowed his passion to carry him away."

" What do you mean? "

" Simply that you can be freed from the tyranny of your father whenever you like now. We now have all that is necessary for lodging a formal plaint in court. We have sequestration of the person, threats and bodily violence by the aid of third parties, and words and blows which have endangered life; our case is entirely complete. A surgeon will examine your wound, and give a written deposition. We can produce plenty of evidence, and the wound on the head will tell its own story. As a commencement we will petition that we may not be ordered back to our father's custody, and it will further be set forth that our reason for this is that a father has assaulted a son with undue and unnecessary violence. We shall be sure to gain the day, and——"

" Enough," broke in Norbert; " will the decision give me the right to marry whom I please without my father's consent? "

Daumon hesitated. Under the circumstances, it seemed to him very likely that the court would grant Norbert the liberty he desired; he, however, thought it advisable not to say so, and answered boldly, " No, Marquis, it will not do so."

" Well, then, the Champdoce family have never exposed their differences to the public, nor will I begin to do so," said Norbert decisively.

The Counsellor seemed surprised at this determination.

" If, Marquis," he began, " I might venture to advise you——"

" No advice is necessary, my mind is entirely made up, but I need some help, and in twenty-four hours I require a large sum of money—twenty thousand francs."

"You can have them, Marquis, but I warn you that you will have to pay heavily for the accommodation."

"That I care nothing for."

Mademoiselle de Laurebourg was about to speak, but with a gesture of his hand Norbert arrested her.

"Do you not comprehend me, Diana?" said he; "we must fly, and that at once. We can find some safe retreat where we can live happily, where no one will harm us."

"But this is mere madness!" cried Diana.

"You will be pursued," remarked the Counsellor; "and most likely overtaken."

"Can you not trust your life to me?" asked Norbert reproachfully. "I swear that I will devote everything to you, life, thought and will. On my knees I entreat you to fly with me."

"I cannot," murmured she; "it is impossible."

"Then you do not love me," said he in desponding accents. "I have been a thrice-besotted fool to believe that your heart was mine, for you can never have loved me."

"Hear him, merciful powers! he says that I, who am all his, do not love him."

"Then why cast aside our only chance of safety?"

"Norbert, dearest Norbert!"

"I understand you too well; you are alarmed at the idea of the world's censure, and——"

He paused, checked by the gleam of reproach that shone in Diana's eyes.

"Must it be so?" said she; "must I condescend to justify myself? You talk to me of the world's cen-

sure? Have I not already defied it, and has it not
sat in judgment upon me? And what have I done,
after all? Every act and word that has passed between
us I can repeat to my mother without a blush rising
to my cheek; but would any one credit my words? No,
not a living soul. Most likely the world has come to
a decision. My reputation is gone, is utterly lost, and
yet I am spotless as the driven snow."

Norbert was half-mad with anger.

"Who will dare to treat you with anything save
with the most profound respect?" said he.

"Alas! my dear Norbert," replied she, "to-morrow
the scandal will be even greater. While your father
was talking to me with such brutal violence and
contempt, he was overheard by a woodcutter and perhaps by some of his companions."

"It cannot be."

"No, it is quite true," returned Daumon. "I had
it from the man myself."

Mademoiselle de Laurebourg shot one glance at
the Counsellor; it was only a glance, but he compre-
hended at once that she wished to be left alone with
her lover.

"Pardon me," said he, "but I think I have a visitor, and I must hinder any one from coming in
here."

He left the room as he spoke, closing the door
noisily behind him.

"And so," resumed Norbert when alone, "it
seems that the Duke de Champdoce did not even take
the ordinary precaution of assuring himself that you
were in privacy before he spoke as he did, and was
so carried away by his fury that he never thought that
in casting dishonor upon you, he was heaping infamy

on me. Does he think by these means to compel me
to marry the heiress whom he has chosen for me,
the Mademoiselle de Puymandour?"

For the first time Diana learned the name of her
rival.

"Ah!" moaned she between her sobs, "so it is
Mademoiselle de Puymandour that he wants you to
marry?"

"Yes, the same, or rather her enormous wealth;
but may my hand wither before it clasps hers. Do
you hear me, Diana?"

She gave a sad smile and murmured, "Poor Norbert!"

The heart of the young man sank; so melancholy
was the tone of her voice.

"You are very cruel," said he. "What have I done
to deserve this want of confidence?"

Diana made no reply, and Norbert, believing that
he understood the reason why she refused to fly with
him, said, "Is it because you have no faith in me,
that you will not accompany me in my flight?"

"No; I have perfect faith in you."

"What is it, then? Do I not offer you fortune and
happiness? Tell me what it is then."

She drew herself up, and said proudly, "Up to
this time, my conscience has enabled me to hold my
own against all the scandalous gossip that has been
flying about, but now it says, 'Halt, Diana de Laurebourg! you have gone far enough.' My burden is
heavy, my heart is breaking, but I must draw back
now. No, Norbert; I cannot fly with you."

She paused for a moment, as though unable to
proceed, and then went on with more firmness, "Were
I alone and solitary in the world, I might act dif-

ferently; but I have a family, whose honor I must guard as I would my own."

"A family indeed, which sacrifices you to your elder brother."

"It may be so, and therefore my task is all the greater. Who ever heard of virtue as something easy to practise?"

Norbert never remembered what an example of rebellion she had set.

"My heart and my conscience dictate the same course to me. The result must ever be fatal, when a young girl sets at defiance the rules and laws of society; and you would never care to look with respect on one upon whom others gazed with the eye of contempt."

"What sort of an opinion have you of me, then?"

"I believe you to be a man, Norbert. Let us suppose that I fly with you, and that the next day I should hear that my father had been killed in a duel fought on my account; what then? Believe me that when I tell you to fly by yourself, I give you the best advice in my power. You will forget me, I know; but what else can I hope for?"

"Forget you!" said Norbert angrily. "Can *you* forget me?"

His face was so close to hers that she felt the hot breath upon her cheek.

"Yes," stammered she, with a violent effort, "I can."

Norbert drew a pace back, that he might read her meaning more fully in her eyes.

"And if I go away," asked he, "what will become of you?"

A sob burst from the young girl's breast, and her strength seemed to desert her limbs.

"I," answered she, in the calm, resigned voice of a Christian virgin about to be cast to the lions that roared in the arena, " I have my destiny. To-day is the last time that we shall ever meet. I shall return to my home, where everything will shortly be known. I shall find my father angry and menacing. He will place me in a carriage, and the next day I shall find myself within the walls of the hated convent."

" But that life would be one long, slow agony to you. You have told me this before."

" Yes," answered she, " it would be an agony, but it would also be an expiation; and when the burden grows too heavy, I have this."

And as she spoke, she drew the little bottle from its hiding-place in her bosom, and Norbert too well understood her meaning. The young man endeavored to take it from her, but she resisted. This contest seemed to exhaust her little strength, her beautiful eyes closed, and she sank senseless into Norbert's arms. In an agony of despair, the young man asked himself if she was dying; and yet there was sufficient life in her to enable her to whisper, soft and low, these words, "My only friend—let me have it back, dear Norbert." And then, with perfect clearness, she repeated all the deadly properties of the drug, and the directions for its use that the Counsellor had given to her.

On hearing the woman whom he loved with such intense passion confess that she would sooner die than live apart from him, Norbert's brain reeled.

"Diana, my own Diana!" repeated he, as he hung over her.

But she went on, as though speaking through the promptings of delirium.

"The very day after such a fair prospect! Ah, Duke de Champdoce! you are a hard and pitiless man. You have robbed me of all I held dear in the world, blackened my reputation, and tarnished my honor, and now you want my life."

Norbert uttered such a cry of anger, that even Daumon in the passage was startled by it. He placed Diana tenderly in the Counsellor's arm-chair, saying,—

"No, you shall not kill yourself, nor shall you leave me."

She smiled faintly, and held out her arms to him. Her magic spells were deftly woven.

"No," cried he; "the poison which you had intended to use on yourself shall become my weapon of vengeance, and the instrument of punishment of the one who has wronged you."

And with the gait of a man walking in his sleep, he left the Counsellor's office.

Hardly had the young man's footsteps died away, than Daumon entered the room. He had not lost a word or action in the foregoing scene, and he was terribly agitated; and he could scarcely believe his eyes when he saw Diana, whom he had supposed to be lying half-insensible in the arm-chair, standing at the window, gazing after Norbert, as he walked along the road leading from the Counsellor's cottage.

"Ah! what a woman!" muttered he. "Gracious powers, what a wonderful woman!"

When Diana had lost sight of her lover, she turned round to Daumon. Her face was pale, and her eyelids swollen, but her eyes flashed with the conviction of success.

"To-morrow, Counsellor," said she, "to-morrow I shall be the Duchess de Champdoce."

Daumon was so overwhelmed that, accustomed as he was to startling events and underhand trickery, he could find no words to express his feelings.

"That is to say," added Diana thoughtfully, "if all goes as it should to-night."

Daumon felt a cold shiver creep over him, but summoning up all his self-possession, he said, "I do not understand you. What is this that you hope will be accomplished to-night?"

She turned so contemptuous and sarcastic a look on him, that the words died away in his mouth, and he at once saw his mistake in thinking that he could sport with the girl's feelings as a cat plays with a mouse; for it was she who was playing with him, and she, a simple girl, had made this wily man of the world her dupe.

"Success is, of course, a certainty," answered she coldly; "but Norbert is impetuous, and impetuous people are often awkward. But I must return home at once. Ah, me!" she added, as her self-control gave way for a moment, "will this cruel night never pass away, and give way to the gentle light of dawn? Farewell, Counsellor. When we meet again, all matters will be settled, one way or other."

The Parthian dart which Mademoiselle de Laurebourg had cast behind her went true to the mark; the allusion to Norbert's impetuosity and awkwardness rendered the Counsellor very unhappy. He sat down in his arm-chair, and, resting his head on his hands, and his elbows on his desk, he strove to review the position thoroughly. Perhaps by now all might be over. Where was Norbert, and what was he doing? he asked himself.

At the time that Daumon was reflecting, Norbert was on the road leading to Champdoce. He had entirely lost his head, but he found that his reason was clear and distinct. Those who have been accustomed to the treatment of maniacs know with what startling rapidity they form a chain of action, and the cloud that veiled Norbert's brain appeared to throw out into stronger relief the murderous determination he had formed. He had already decided how the deed was to be done. The common wine of the country was always served to the laborers at the table, but the Duke kept a better quality for his own drinking, and the bottle containing this was after meals placed on a shelf in a cupboard in the dining-room. It was thus within every one's reach, but not a soul in the household would have ventured to lay a finger upon it. Norbert's thoughts fell upon this bottle, and in his mind's eye he could see it standing in its accustomed place. He crossed the courtyard, and the laborers, engaged in their tasks, gazed at him curiously. He passed them, and entered the dining-room, which was untenanted. With a caution that was not to be expected from the agitation of his mind, he opened each door successively, in order to be certain that no eyes were gazing upon him. Then, with the greatest rapidity, he took down the bottle, drew the cork with his teeth, and dropped into the wine, not one, but two or three pinches of the contents of the little vial. He shook the bottle gently, to facilitate the dissolution of the powder. A few particles of the poison clung to the lip of the bottle; he wiped off these, not with a napkin, a pile of which lay on the shelf beside him, but

with his own handkerchief. He replaced the bottle
in its accustomed place, and seating himself by the
fire, awaited the course of events.

At this moment the Duke de Champdoce was coming
up the avenue at a rapid pace. For the first time,
perhaps, in his life, this man perceived that one of
his last acts had been insensate and foolish in the
extreme. All the possibilities of the law to which
Daumon had alluded struck the Duke with overwhelming force, and he at once saw that his violent
conduct had given ample grounds upon which to base
a plaint, with results which he greatly feared. If the
court entertained the matter, his son would most likely
be removed from his control. He knew that such an
idea would never cross Norbert's brain, but there were
plenty of persons to suggest it to him. The danger of
his position occurred to him, and at the same time he
felt that he must frame his future conduct with extreme
prudence. He had not given up his views regarding
his son's marriage with Mademoiselle de Puymandour. No; he would sooner have resigned life itself,
but he felt that he must renounce violence, and gain
his ends by diplomacy. The first thing to be done
was to get Norbert to return home, and the father
greatly doubted whether the son would do so. While
thinking over these things, with a settled gloom upon
his face, one of the servants came running up to him
with the news of Norbert's return.

"I hold him at last," muttered he, and hastened
on to the Château.

When the Duke entered the dining-room, Norbert
did not rise from his seat, and the Duke was dis-
agreeably impressed by this breach of the rules of
domestic etiquette.

"On my word," thought he, "it would appear that the young booby thinks that he owes me no kind of duty whatever."

He did not, however, allow his anger to be manifest in his features; besides, the sight of the blood, with which his son's face was still smeared, caused him to feel excessively uncomfortable.

"Norbert, my son," said he, "are you suffering? Why have you not had that cut attended to?"

The young man made no reply, and the Duke continued,—

"Why have you not washed the blood away? Is it left there as a reproach to me? There is no need for that, I assure you; for deeply do I deplore my violence."

Norbert still made no answer, and the Duke became more and more embarrassed. To give himself time for reflection, more than because he was thirsty, he took a glass, and filled it from his own special bottle.

Norbert trembled from head to foot as he saw this act.

"Come, my son," continued the Duke, "just try if you cannot find some palliation for what your old father has done. I am ready to ask your forgiveness, and to apologize, for a man of honor is never ashamed to acknowledge when he has been in the wrong."

He raised his glass, and raised it up to the light half mechanically. Norbert held his breath; the whole world seemed turning round.

"It is hard, very hard," continued the Duke, "for a father thus to humiliate himself in vain before his son."

It was useless for Norbert to turn away his head; he saw the Duke place the glass to his lips. He was about to drink, but the young man could endure it no longer, and with a bound he sprang forward, snatched the glass from his father's hand, and hurled it from the window, shouting in a voice utterly unlike his own,—

"Do not drink."

The Duke read the whole hideous truth in the face and manner of his son. His features quivered, his face grew purple, and his eyes filled with blood. He strove to speak, but only an inarticulate rattle could be heard; he then clasped his hands convulsively, swayed backwards and forwards, and then fell help-lessly backwards, striking his head against an oaken sideboard that stood near. Norbert tore open the door.

"Quick, help!" cried he. "I have killed my father."

CHAPTER IX.

THE HONOR OF THE NAME.

THE account that the Duke de Champdoce had given of M. de Puymandour's mad longing for rank and title was true, and afforded a melancholy instance of that peculiar kind of foolish vanity. He was a much happier man in his younger days, when he was known simply as Palouzet, which was his father's name, whose only wish for distinction was to be looked upon as an honest man. In those days he was much looked up to and respected, as a man who had pos-sessed brains enough to amass a very large fortune by strictly honest means. All this vanished, however, when the unhappy idea occurred to him to affix the title of Count to the name of an estate that he had recently purchased.

From that moment, all his tribulations in life may have been said to have commenced. The nobility laughed at his assumption of hereditary rank, while the middle classes frowned at his pretensions to be superior to them, so that he passed the existence of a shuttlecock, continually suspended in the air, and struck at and dismissed from either side.

It may, therefore, be easily imagined how excessively anxious he was to bring about the marriage between his daughter Marie and the son of that mighty nobleman, the Duke de Champdoce. He had offered to sacrifice one-third of his fortune for the honor of forming this connection, and would have given up the whole of it, could he but have seen a child in whose veins ran the united blood of Palouzet and the Champdoce seated upon his knee. A marriage of this kind would have given him a real position; for to have a Champdoce for a son-in-law would compel all scoffers to bridle their tongues.

The day after he had received a favorable reply from the Duke, M. de Puymandour thought that it was time to inform his daughter of his intentions. He never thought that she would make any opposition, and, of course, supposed that she would be as delighted as he was at the honor that awaited her. He was seated in a magnificently furnished room which he called his library when he arrived at this conclusion, and ringing the bell, ordered the servant to inquire of mademoiselle's maid if her mistress could grant him an interview. He gave this curious message, which did not appear to surprise the servant in the least, with an air of the utmost importance. The communication between the father and daughter was always carried on upon this basis; and scoffers wickedly asserted that M. de Puymandour had modelled it upon a book of etiquette, for the guidance of her household, written by a venerable archduchess.

Shortly after the man had departed on his errand, a little tap came to the door.

"Come in," exclaimed M. de Puymandour.

And Mademoiselle Marie ran in and gave her father a kiss upon each cheek. He frowned slightly, and extricated himself from her embrace.

"I thought it better to come to you, my dear father," said she, "than to give you the trouble of coming all the way to me."

"You always forget that there are certain forms and ceremonies necessary for a young lady of your position."

Marie gave a little gentle smile, for she was no stranger to her father's absurd whims; but she never thwarted them, for she was very fond of him. She was a very charming young lady, and in the description that the Duke had given of her to his son, he had not flattered her at all. Though she differed greatly in appearance from Mademoiselle de Laurebourg, Marie's beauty was perfect in a style of its own. She was tall and well proportioned, and had all that easy grace of movement, characteristic of women of Southern parentage. Her large soft dark eyes offered a vivid contrast to her creamy complexion; her hair, in utter disregard of the fashionable mode of dressing, was loosely knotted at the back of her head. Her nature was soft and affectionate, capable of the deepest devotion, while she had the most equable temper that can be imagined.

"Come, my dear papa," said she; "do not scold me any more. You know that the Marchioness of Arlanges has promised to teach me how to behave myself according to all the rules of fashionable society next winter, and I declare to you that I will so practise them up in secret, that you will be astonished when you behold them."

"How woman-like!" muttered her father. "She only scoffs at matters of the most vital importance."

He rose from his seat, and, placing his back to the fireplace, took up an imposing position, one hand buried in his waistcoat, and the other ready to gesticulate as occasion required.

"Oblige me with your deepest attention," commenced he. "You were eighteen years of age last month, and I have an important piece of intelligence to convey to you. I have had an offer of marriage for you."

Marie looked down, and endeavored to hide her confusion at these tidings.

"Before coming to a conclusion upon a matter of such importance," continued he, "it was, of course, necessary for me to go into the question most thoroughly. I spared no means of obtaining information, and I am quite certain that the proposed connection would be conducive to your future happiness. The suitor for your hand is but little older than yourself; he is very handsome, very wealthy, and is a Marquis by hereditary right."

"Has he spoken to you then?" inquired Marie in tones of extreme agitation.

"He! Whom do you mean by he?" asked M. de

Puymandour; and as his daughter did not reply, he repeated his question.

"Who? Why, George de Croisenois."

"Pray, what have you to do with Croisenois? Who is he, pray? Not that dandy with a mustache, that I have seen hanging about you this winter?"

"Yes," faltered Marie; "that is he."

"And why should you presume that he had asked me for your hand? Did he tell you that he was going to do so?"

"Father, I declare——"

"What, the daughter of a Puymandour has listened to a declaration of love unknown to her father? Ten thousand furies! Has he written to you? Where are those letters?"

"My dear father——"

"Silence; have you those letters? Let me see them. Come, no delay; I will have those bits of paper, if I turn the whole house upside down."

With a sigh Marie gave the much prized missives to her father; there were four only, fastened together with a morsel of blue ribbon.

He took one out at random, and read it aloud, with a running fire of oaths and invectives as a commentary upon its contents.

" MADEMOISELLE,—

"Though there is nothing upon earth that I dread so much as your anger, I dare, in spite of your commands to the contrary, to write to you once again. I have learned that you are about to quit Paris for several months. I am twenty-four years of age. I have neither father nor mother, and am entirely my own master. I belong to an ancient and honorable family. My fortune is a large one, and my love for you is of

the most honorable and devoted kind. My uncle, M.
de Saumeuse, knows your father well; and will convey
my proposals to him upon his return from Italy, in
about two or three weeks' time.   Once more intreat-
ing you to forgive me,
    " I remain,
        " Yours respectfully,
            " GEORGE DE CROISENOIS."

"Very pretty indeed," said M. de Puymandour,
as he replaced the letter in its envelope. "This is
sufficient, and I need not read the others; but pray,
what answer did you give?"

"That I must refer him to you, my dear father."

"Indeed, on my word, you do me too much honor;
and did you really think that I would listen to such
proposals? Perhaps you love him?"

She turned her lovely face towards her father,
with the great tears rolling down her cheeks for her
sole reply.

This mute confession, for as such he regarded it,
put the finishing touch to M. de Puymandour's exasperation.

"You absolutely love him, and have the impudence
to tell me so?"

Marie glanced at her father, and answered,—

"The Marquis de Croisenois is of good family."

"Pooh! you know nothing about it. Why, the
first Croisenois was one of Richelieu's minions, and
Louis XIII. conferred the title for some shady piece
of business which he carried out for him. Has this
fine Marquis any means of livelihood?"

"Certainly; about sixty thousand francs a year."

"Humbug! What did he mean by addressing you
secretly? Only to compromise your name, and so

to secure your fortune, and perhaps to break off your marriage with another."

" But why suppose this ? "

" I suppose nothing; I am merely going upon facts. What does a man of honor do when he falls in love ? "

" My dear father——"

" He goes to his solicitor, acquaints him with his intentions, and explains what his means are; the solicitor goes to the family solicitor of the young lady, and when these men of the law have found out that all is satisfactory, then love is permitted to make his appearance upon the scene. And now you may as well attend to me. Forget De Croisenois as soon as you can, for I have chosen a husband for you, and, having pledged my word of honor, I will abide by it. On Sunday the eligible suitor will be introduced to you, and on Monday we will visit the Bishop, asking him to be good enough to perform the ceremony. On Tuesday you will show yourself in public with him, in order to announce the betrothal. Wednesday the marriage contract will be read. Thursday a grand dinner-party. Friday an exhibition of the marriage presents; Saturday a day of rest; Sunday the publication of the banns, and at the end of the following week the marriage will take place."

Mademoiselle Marie listened to her father's determination with intense horror.

" For pity's sake, my dear father, be serious," cried she.

M. de Puymandour paid no attention to her entreaty, but added, as an afterthought:

" Perhaps you would wish to know the name of the gentleman I have selected as a husband for you. He is the Marquis Norbert, the son and heir of the Duke de Champdoce."

Marie turned deadly pale.

"But I do not know him; I have never seen him," faltered she.

"*I* know him, and that is quite sufficient. I have often told you that you should be a duchess, and I mean to keep my word."

Marie's affection for George de Croisenois was much deeper than she had told her father, much deeper even than she had dared to confess to herself, and she resented this disposal of her with more obstinacy than any one knowing her gentle nature would have supposed her capable of; but M. de Puymandour was not the man to give up for an instant the object which he had sworn to attain. He never gave his daughter an instant's peace, he argued, insisted, and bullied until, after three days' contest, Marie gave her assent with a flood of tears. The word had scarcely passed her lips, before her father, without even thanking her for her terrible sacrifice, exclaimed in a voice of triumph:

"I must take these tidings to Champdoce without a moment's delay."

He started at once, and as he passed through the doorway said:

"Good-by, my little duchess, good-by."

He was most desirous of seeing the Duke, for, on taking leave of him, the old nobleman had said, "You shall hear from me to-morrow"; but no letter had as yet reached him from Champdoce. This delay, however, had suited M. de Puymandour's plans, for it had enabled him to wring the consent from his daughter; but now that this had been done, he began to feel very anxious, and to fear that there might be some unforeseen hitch in the affair.

When he reached Bevron, he saw Daumon talking earnestly with Françoise, the daughter of the Widow Rouleau. M. de Puymandour bowed graciously, and stopped to talk with the man, for he was just now seeking for popularity, as he was a candidate, and the elections would shortly take place; and, besides, he never failed to talk to persons who exercised any degree of influence, and he knew that Daumon was a most useful man in electioneering.

"Good morning, Counsellor," said he gayly. "What is the news to-day?"

Daumon bowed profoundly.

"Bad news, Count," answered he. "I hear that the Duke de Champdoce is seriously indisposed."

"The Duke ill—impossible!"

"This girl has just given me the information. Tell us all about it, Françoise."

"I heard to-day at the Château that the doctors had quite given him over."

"But what is the matter with him?"

"I did not hear."

M. de Puymandour stood perfectly aghast.

"It is always the way in this world," Daumon philosophically said. "In the midst of life we are in death!"

"Good morning, Counsellor," said De Puymandour; "I must try and find out something more about this."

Breathless, and with his mind filled with anxiety, he hurried on.

All the servants and laborers on the Champdoce estate were gathered together in a group, talking eagerly to each other, and as soon as M. de Puymandour

appeared, one of the servants, disengaging himself
from his fellows, came towards him. This was the
Duke's old, trustworthy servant.

"Well?" exclaimed M. de Puymandour.

"Oh, sir," cried the old man, "this is too horrible;
my poor master will certainly die."

"But I do not know what is the matter with him;
no one has told me anything, in fact."

"It was terribly sudden," answered the man. "It
was about this time the day before yesterday that the
Duke was alone with M. Norbert in the dining-room.
All at once we heard a great outcry. We ran in and
saw my poor master lying senseless on the ground, his
face purple and distorted."

"He must have had a fit of apoplexy."

"Not exactly; the doctor called it a rush of blood
to the brain; at least, I think that is what he said, and
he added that the reason he did not die on the spot
was because in falling he had cut open his head against
the oaken sideboard, and the wound bled profusely.
We carried him up to his bed; he showed no signs of
life, and now——"

"Well, how is he now?"

"No one dare give an opinion; my poor master is
quite unconscious, and should he recover—and I do
not think for a moment that he will—the doctor says
his mind will have entirely gone."

"Horrible! too horrible! and a man of such intel-
lectual power, too. I shall not ask you to let me
look at him, for I could do no good, and the sight
would upset me. But can I not see M. Norbert?"

"Pray, do not attempt to do so, sir."

"I was his father's intimate friend, and if the condolences of such a one could assuage the affliction under which——"

" Impossible ! " answered the man in a quick, eager manner. " M. Norbert was with his father at the time of his seizure, and has given strict orders that he is not to be disturbed on any account; but I must go to him at once, for we are expecting the physicians who are coming from Poitiers."

" Very well, then I will go now, but to-night I will send up one of my people for news."

With these words, M. de Puymandour walked slowly away, absorbed in thought. The manner and expression of the servant had struck him as extremely strange. He noted the fact that Norbert was alone with his father at the time of the seizure, and, recalling to mind the opposition he had met with from his daughter, he began to imagine that the Duke had found his son rebellious, and that the apoplectic fit had been brought on by a sudden access of passion. Interest and ambition working together brought him singularly near the truth.

" If the Duke dies, or becomes a maniac," thought he to himself, " the end as regards us will be the same, for Norbert will break off the match to a certainty."

He felt that such a proceeding would cause him to be more jeered at and ridiculed than ever, and that the only path of escape left open to him was to marry his daughter to the Marquis de Croisenois, which was a most desirable alliance, in spite of all he had said against it. A voice close to his ear aroused him from his reflections: it was that of Daumon, who had come up unperceived.

"Was the girl's information correct, Count?" asked he. "How are the Duke and M. Norbert, for of course you have seen them both?"

"M. Norbert is too much agitated by the sad event to see any one."

"Of course that was to be looked for," returned the wily Counsellor; "for the seizure was terribly sudden."

M. de Puymandour was too much occupied with his own thoughts to spare much pity for Norbert. He would have given a great deal to have known what the young man was doing, and especially what he was thinking of at the present moment.

The poor lad was standing by the bedside of his dying father, watching eagerly for some indication, however slight, of returning life or reason. The hours of horror and self-reproach had entirely changed his feelings and ideas; for it was only at the instant when he saw his father raise the poisoned wine to his lips that he saw his crime in all its hideous enormity. His soul rose up in rebellion against his crime, and the words, "Parricide! murderer!" seemed to ring in his ears like a trumpet call. When his father fell to the ground, his instinct made him shout for aid; but an instant afterwards terror took possession of him, and, rushing from the house, he sought the open country, as though striving to escape from himself.

Jean, the old servant, who had noticed Norbert's strange look, was seized with a terrible fear. Trusted as he was by both the Duke and his son, he had many means of knowing all that was going on in the household, and was no stranger to the differences that had arisen recently between father and son. He knew how violent the tempers of both were, and he also knew that some woman was urging on Norbert to a course of open rebellion. He had seen the cruel blow dealt by the Duke, and had wondered greatly when he saw Norbert return to the Château. Why had he done so? He had been in the courtyard when Norbert threw the glass from the window. Putting all these circumstances together, as soon as the inanimate body of the Duke had been laid upon a bed, Jean went into the dining-room, feeling sure that he should make some discovery which would confirm his suspicions. The bottle from which the Duke had filled his glass stood half emptied upon the table. With the greatest care, he poured a few drops of its contents into the hollow of his hand, and tasted it with the utmost caution. The wine still retained its customary taste and scent. Not trusting, however, to this, Jean, after making sure that he was not observed, carried the bottle to his own room, and concealed it. After taking this precaution, he ordered one of the other servants to remain by the side of the Duke until the arrival of the doctor, and then went in search of Norbert.

For two hours his efforts were fruitless. Giving up his search in despair, he turned once more to regain the Château, and, taking the path through the wood, suddenly perceived a human form stretched on the turf beneath a tree. He moved cautiously towards the figure, and at once recognized Norbert. The faithful servant bent over his young master, and shook him by the arm to arouse him from his state of stupor. At the first touch, Norbert started to his feet with a shriek of terror. With mingled fear and pity, Jean noticed the look that shone in the young man's eyes, more like that of some hunted animal than a human being.

"Do not be alarmed, M. Norbert; it is only I," said he.

"And what do you want?"

"I came out to look for you, and to entreat you to come back with me to Champdoce."

"Back to Champdoce?" repeated Norbert hoarsely; "no, never!"

"You must, Master Norbert; for your absence now would cause a terrible scandal. Your place at this critical time is by the bedside of your father."

"Never! never!" repeated the poor boy; but he yielded passively when Jean passed his arm through his, and led him away towards the Château. Supported thus by the old man's arm, he crossed the courtyard, and ascended the staircase; but at his father's door he withdrew his hand, and struggled to get away.

"I will not; no, no, I cannot," gasped he.

"You must and you shall," returned the old man firmly. "Whatever your feelings may be, no stain shall rest on the family honor."

These words roused Norbert; he stepped across the room, and dropped on his knees by the bed, placing his forehead upon his father's icy hand. He burst into a passion of tears and sobs, and the simple peasants, who surrounded the couch of the insensible nobleman, breathed a sigh; for, from his pallid face and burning eyes, they believed he must be mad. They were not far out in this surmise; but the tears relieved his over-wrought brain, and with this relief came the sense of intense suffering. When the physician arrived, he was able to appear before him merely as a deeply anxious son.

"There is no hope for the Duke, I regret to say," said the medical man, who felt that it was useless to keep Norbert in suspense. "There is a feeble chance of saving his life; but even should we succeed in doing so, his intellect will be irretrievably gone. This is a sad truth, but I feel it my duty to inform you of it. I will come again to-morrow."

As the doctor left the room, Norbert threw himself into a chair, and clasped his hands round his head, which throbbed until it seemed as if it would burst. For more than half an hour he sat motionless, and then started to his feet with a stifled cry; for he remembered the bottle into which he had poured the poison, and which had been left on the table. Had any one drunk from it? What had become of it? The agony of his mind gave him the necessary strength to descend to the dining-room; but the bottle was not on the table, nor was it in its customary place in the cupboard. The unhappy boy was looking for it everywhere, when the door silently opened, and Jean appeared on the threshold. The expression upon his young master's face so startled the faithful old man that he nearly dropped the lighted candle that he carried in his hand.

"Why are you here, Master Norbert?" asked he in a voice that trembled with emotion.

"I was looking for—— I wanted to find——," faltered Norbert.

Jean's suspicions at once became certainties; he walked up to his young master, and whispered in his ear,—

"You are looking for the Duke's bottle of wine, are you not? It is quite safe; for I have taken it to my room. To-morrow the contents shall be emptied away, and there will be no proof existing."

Jean spoke in such a low voice that Norbert guessed rather than heard his words, and yet it seemed that the accusing whisper resounded like thunder through the Château, filling the old house from cellar to roof-tree.

"Be quiet," said he, laying his hand on the old man's lips, and gazing around him with wild and affrighted glances.

A more complete confession could hardly have been made.

"Fear nothing, Master Norbert," answered Jean; "we are quite alone. I know that there are words which should never be even breathed; and if I have ventured to speak, it was because it was my duty to warn you, and to inculcate on you the necessity of caution."

Norbert was filled with horror when he saw that the old man believed him to be really guilty.

"Jean," cried he, "you are wrong in your suspicions. I tell you that my father never tasted that wine. I snatched the glass from him before his lips had touched it. I flung it out into the courtyard, and, if you search, you will find its scattered fragments there still."

"I am not sitting in judgment upon you; what you tell me to believe I am ready to accept."

"Ah;" cried Norbert passionately, "he does not believe me; he thinks that I am guilty. I swear to you by all that I hold most sacred in this world, that I am innocent of this deed."

The attached servant shook his head with a melancholy air.

"Of course, of course," said he; "but it is for us two to save the honor of the house of Champdoce. Should it happen that any suspicions should be aroused, put all the guilt upon my shoulders. I will defend myself in a manner which will only fix the crime more firmly upon me. I will not throw away the bottle, but will retain it in my room, so that it may be found there, and its contents will be a damnatory evidence against me. What matters it how a poor man like me is sent out of the world? but with you it is different. You——"

Norbert wrung his hands in abject despair; the sublime devotion of the old servant showed how firmly Jean believed in his criminality. He was about to assert his innocence further, when the loud sound of a closing door was heard above stairs.

"Hush!" said the old man; "some one approaches; we must not be seen whispering together like two plotters, for their suspicions would be certainly awakened; and I fear that my face or your eyes will reveal the secret. Quick, go upstairs, and endeavor, as soon as possible, to resume your calmness. I beg you not to compromise the honor of your name, which is in deadly peril."

Without another word Norbert obeyed. His father was alone, and only the man to whom Jean had delegated the task of watcher remained by his bedside. At the sight of his young master he rose.

"The prescription which the doctor ordered to be made up has arrived," said he. "I have administered a dose to the Duke, and it seems to me that the result has been favorable."

Norbert drew up a heavy arm-chair to the foot of the bed, and took his seat upon it. From this position he could see his father's face. His brain was dazed, and it was with the utmost difficulty that he could recall the chain of events which had drawn him towards the abyss into which he had so nearly been precipitated.

The veil had been taken from his eyes, and he now saw with perfect clearness and seemed again to hear his father's voice as it roughly warned him that the woman he loved was a mere plotter, who cared not for him, but was scheming for his fortune and his name. Then he had been furiously indignant and looked upon the words as almost blasphemous, but now he saw that his father was right. How was it that he had not before seen that Diana was flinging herself in his way, and that all her affected openness and simplicity were merely the perfections of art, and that step by step she had led him to the brink of the terrible precipice which yawned before him? The whole hideous part as played by Daumon was no longer a sealed book to him. She whom he had looked on as a pure and innocent girl was merely the accomplice of a scheming villain like the Counsellor, and after exciting his hatred and anger almost to madness, had placed the poison which was to take his father's life in his hands. A cold shiver ran through him as he realized this, and all his ardent love for Diana de Laurebourg was changed into a feeling of loathing and disgust.

At last the first pale rays of dawn broke through the casement, but before that Norbert, worn out with conflicting emotions, had fallen into a restless and uneasy sleep, and when he awoke the doctor was standing by the bedside of the sick man. At the first sound made by Norbert as he stirred in the chair, the doctor came towards him, saying, "We shall preserve his life."

This prognostication was complete, for that very evening the Duke de Champdoce was able to move in his bed, the next day he uttered some incoherent words, and later on asked for food; but the will of iron had passed away, the features had lost their expression of determination, and the eye the glitter of pride and power. Never again would the Duke be able to exert that keen, stern intellect which had enabled him to influence all those around him; and in this terrible state of imbecility the haughty nobleman would ever remain, fed and looked after like a child, with no thought beyond his desires and his warm fire, and without a care for anything that was going on in the world around him.

After the enormity of his crime had been brought before him, the greatness of the punishment that he must endure now came across Norbert's mind. It was only now that Jean had ventured to tell him of M. de Puymandour's visit; and such a change had taken place in Norbert that he looked upon this visit as a special arrangement made by Providence.

"My father's will shall be carried out in every respect," said he to himself, and without an hour's delay he wrote to M. du Puymandour, begging him to call, and hoping that the grief which had fallen upon him had in no way altered the plan which had already been arranged.

CHAPTER X.

A THUNDERBOLT.

As the miner, who sets fire to the fuse and seeks shelter from the coming explosion, so did Diana de Laurebourg return to her father's house after her visit to Daumon. During dinner it was impossible for her to utter a word, and it was with the greatest difficulty that she succeeded in swallowing a mouthful. Fortunately neither her father nor mother took any notice of her. They had that day received a letter announcing the news that their son, for whose future prosperity they had sacrificed Diana, was lying dangerously ill in Paris, where he was living in great style. They were in terrible affliction, and spoke of starting at once, so as to be with him. They therefore expressed no surprise when, on leaving the table, Diana pleaded a severe headache as an excuse for retiring to her own room. When once she was alone, having dismissed her maid, she heaved a deep sigh of relief. She never thought of retiring to bed, but throwing open her window, leaned out with her elbow on the window-sill.

It seemed to her that Norbert would certainly make some effort to see her, or at any rate by some means to let her know whether he had succeeded or failed.

"But I must be patient," murmured she, "for I can't hear anything until the afternoon of to-morrow."

In spite, however, of her resolutions, patience fled from her mind, and as soon as the servants had begun moving about, she went out into the garden and took up a position which commanded a view of the highroad, but no one appeared. The bell rang for breakfast. Again she had to seat herself at table with her parents, and the terrible penance of the past evening had to be repeated. At three o'clock she could endure the suspense no longer, and making her escape from the Château, she went over to Daumon, who, she felt, must have obtained some intelligence. Even if she found that he knew nothing, it would be a relief to speak to him and to ask him when he thought that this terrible delay would come to an end. But she got no comfort at Daumon's, for he had passed as miserable a night as herself, and was nearly dead with affright. He had remained in his office all the morning, starting at the slightest sound, and though he was as anxious as Diana for information, he had only gone out a little before her arrival. He met Mademoiselle Laurebourg on his return at the door of his cottage, and taking her inside, he informed her that at a late hour the night before the doctor had been sent for to Champdoce to attend on the Duke, who was supposed to be dying. Then he reproved her bitterly for her imprudence in visiting him.

"Do you wish," said he, "to show all Bevron that you and I are Norbert's accomplices?"

"What do you mean?" asked she.

"I mean that if the Duke does not die, we are lost. When I say we, I mean myself, for you, as the daughter of a noble family, will be sure to escape scot free, and I shall be left to pay for all."

"You said that the effect was immediate."

"I did say so, and I thought so too. Ah, if I had but reflected a little! You will however see that I do not intend to give in without a fight. I will defend myself by accusing you. I am an honest man, and have been your dupe. You have thought to make me a mere tool; your fine Norbert is a fool, but he will pay for his doings with his head all the same."

At these gross insults Mademoiselle de Laurebourg rose to her feet and attempted to speak, but he cut her short.

"I can't stop to pick and choose my words, for I feel at the present moment as if the axe of the guillotine were suspended over my head. Now just oblige me by getting out of this, and never show your face here again."

"As you like. I will communicate with Champdoce."

"You shall not," exclaimed Daumon with a gesture of menace. "You might as well go and ask how the Duke enjoyed the taste of the poison."

His words, however, did not deter Diana, for any risk seemed preferable to her than the present state of suspense.

With a glance of contempt at the Counsellor she left the cottage, determined to act as she thought fit.

After Diana's departure, Daumon felt too that he must learn how matters were going on, and going over to the Widow Rouleau's, he despatched her daughter Françoise to the Château de Champdoce, under the pretext that he wanted some money which he had lent to one of the Duke's servants. He had instructed the girl so cunningly that she had no suspicion of the real end and object of her mission, and set out on it with the most implicit confidence. He had not long to wait for her return, for in about half an hour his messenger returned.

"Well," said he anxiously, "has the scamp sent my money?"

"No, sir, I am sorry to say that I could not even get to speak to him."

"How was that? Was he not at Champdoce?"

"I cannot even tell you that. Ever since the Duke has been ill, the great gates of the Château have been bolted, for it seems that the poor old gentleman is at his last gasp."

"Did you not hear what was the matter with him?"

"No, sir, the little I have told you I got from a stable boy, who spoke to me through a grating in the gate, but before he could say ten words Jean came up and sent him off."

"Do you mean Jean, the Duke's confidential man?"

"Just so," returned the girl, "and very angry he was. He abused the lad and told him to be off to the stables, and then asked, 'Well, my girl, and pray what do you want?' I told him that I had come with a message to the man Mechenit; but before I could say any more he broke in with, 'Well, he isn't here, you can call again in a month.'"

"You silly little fool, was that all you said?"

"Not quite, for I said that I must see Mechenit. Then, looking at me very suspiciously, he said, 'And who sent you here, you little spy?'"

The Counsellor started.

"Indeed! and what did you say in return?" asked he.

"Why, of course I said that you had sent me."

"Yes, yes, that was right."

"And then Jean rubbed his hand over his chin, and looking at me very curiously, said sternly,—

"'So you have come from the Counsellor, have you? Ah, I see it all, and so shall he one of these days.'"

At these words Daumon felt his knees give way under him; but all further questioning was stopped by the appearance of M. de Puymandour on his way to Champdoce. He therefore dismissed Françoise, and awaited the return of this gentleman, from whom he hoped to gain the fullest information regarding the Duke's malady. The intelligence which he re-received calmed him a little, and repenting of his treatment of Diana, he went and hung about the gates of the Château de Laurebourg, until he was lucky enough to catch sight of the girl in the garden, for her anxiety would not permit her to remain in the house. He beckoned to her, and then said,—

"M. Norbert did not make the dose strong enough. The Duke is as strong as a horse; but it is all right, for should he live, he will be an idiot, and so our end is as much gained as if he had died."

"But why does not Norbert write to me?" asked Diana seriously.

"Why, because he has some faint glimmerings of common sense. How do you know that he may not have half a dozen spies about him? You must wait."

Diana and the Counsellor waited for a week, but Norbert made no sign. Diana suffered agonies, and the days seemed to pass with leaden feet. Sunday came at last. The Marchioness de Laurebourg had attended early Mass, and had given orders that her daughter should go to high Mass under the escort of her maid. Diana was highly pleased with this arrangement, for she hoped to have a chance of seeing Norbert, but she was disappointed. The Mass had commenced when she entered, but the spot occupied by the Duke and his son was vacant. She followed the service in a purely mechanical manner, and at last noticed that the priest had taken his place in the pulpit.

This was generally an exciting moment for the inhabitants of Bevron, for it was immediately before the sermon that the banns of marriage were published. The priest gazed blandly down upon the expectant crowd, coughed slightly, used his handkerchief, and finally took from his breviary a sheet of paper.

" I have," said he, " to publish the banns of marriage between——" here he made a little pause, and all the congregation were on the tenterhooks of expectation; " between," he continued, " Monsieur Louis Norbert, Marquis de Champdoce, a minor, and only legitimate son of Guillaume Cæsar, Duke de Champdoce, and of his wife, Isabella de Barnaville, now deceased, but who both formerly resided in this parish, and Desirée Anne Marie Palouzet, minor, and legitimate daughter of René Augustus Palouzet, Count de Puymandour, and of Zoe Staplet, his wife, but now deceased, also residents of this parish."

This was the thunderbolt launched from the pulpit, which seemed to crush Diana into the earth, and her heart almost ceased to beat.

" Let any one," continued the priest, " who knows of any impediment to this marriage, take warning that he or she must acquaint us with it, under the penalty of excommunication. And at the same time let him be warned under the same penalty to bring forward nothing in malice or without some foundation."

An impediment! What irony lay veiled beneath that word. Mademoiselle de Laurebourg knew of more than one. A wild desire filled her heart to start from her seat and cry out,—

"It is impossible for this marriage to take place, for that Norbert was her affianced husband in the sight of Heaven, and that he was bound to her by the strongest of all links, that of crime."

But by a gigantic effort she controlled herself, and remained motionless, pallid as a spectre, but with a forced smile on her lips, and with unparalleled audacity made a little sign to one of her female friends, which plainly meant, "This is, indeed, something unexpected." All her mind was concentrated to preserve a calm and unmoved aspect. The singing of the choir seemed to die away, the strong odor of the incense almost overpowered her, and she felt that unless the service soon came to an end, she must fall insensible from her chair. At last the priest turned again to the congregation and droned out the *Ita missa est,* and all was over. Diana grasped the arm of her maid and forced her away, without saying a word. As she reached home, a servant ran up to her with a face upon which agitation was strongly painted.

"Ah, mademoiselle," gasped he, "such a frightful calamity. Your father and mother are expecting you; it is really too terrible."

Diana hastened to obey the summons. Her father and mother were seated near each other, evidently in deep distress. She went towards them, and the Marquis, drawing her to him, pressed her against his heart.

"Poor child! my dear daughter!" murmured he, "you are all that is left to us now."

Their son had died, and the sad news had been brought to the Château while Diana was at Mass. By her brother's death she had succeeded to a princely fortune, and would now be one of the richest heiresses for many a mile round. Had this event happened but a week before, her marriage to Norbert would have met with no opposition from his father, and she would never have plunged into this abyss of crime. It was more than the irony of fate; it was the manifest punishment of an angry Divinity. She shed no tear for her brother's death. Her thoughts were all firmly fixed on Norbert, and that fearful announcement made in the house of God rang still in her ears. What could be the meaning of this sudden arrangement, and why had the marriage been so suddenly decided on?

She felt that some mystery lay beneath it all, and vowed that she would fathom it to its nethermost depths. What was it that had taken place at Champdoce? Had the Duke, contrary to Daumon's prognostications, recovered? Had he discovered his son's insidious attack upon his life, and only pardoned it upon a blind compliance being given to his will? She passed away the whole day in these vain suppositions, and tried to think of every plan to stay the celebration of this union, for she had not given up her hopes, nor did she yet despair of ultimate success. Her new and unlooked-for fortune placed a fresh weapon at her disposal, and she felt that the victory would yet be hers if she could but see Norbert again, were it but for a single instant. Was she not certain of the absolute power that she exercised over him, for had she not by a few words induced him to enter upon the terrible path of crime? She must see him, and that without a moment's delay, for the danger was imminent. A day now would be worth a year hereafter. She determined that, upon that very night, she would visit Champdoce. A little after midnight, when all the inhabitants of the Château were wrapped in slumber, she crept on tiptoe down the grand staircase, and made her exit by a side door. She had arranged her plan as to how she would find Norbert, for he had often described the interior arrangements of the Château to her. She knew that his room was on the ground floor, with two windows looking on to the courtyard. When, however, she reached the old Château, she hesitated. Suppose that she should go to the wrong window. But she had gone too far to recede, and determined that if any one else than Norbert should open the window, she would turn and fly. She tapped at the window softly, and then more loudly. She had made no mistake. Norbert threw open the window, with the words,—

"Who is there?"

"It is I, Norbert; I, Diana."

"What do you want?" asked Norbert in an agitated tone of voice. "What do you want to do here?"

She looked at him anxiously and hardly recognized his face, so great was the change that had come over it. It absolutely terrified her.

"Are you going to marry Mademoiselle de Puymandour?" asked she.

"Yes I am."

"And yet you pretended to love me?"

"Yes, I loved you ardently, devotedly, with a love that drove me to crime; but you had no love; you cared but for rank and fortune."

Diana raised her hands to heaven in an agony of despair.

"Should I be here at this hour if what you say is true?" asked she wildly. "My brother is dead, and I am as wealthy as you are, Norbert, and yet I am here. You accuse me of being mercenary, and for what reason? Was it because I refused to fly with you from my father's house? Oh, Norbert, it was but the happiness of our future life that I strove to protect. It was——"

Her speech failed her, and her eyes dilated with horror, for the door behind Norbert opened, and the Duke de Champdoce entered the room, uttering a string of meaningless words, and laughing with that mirthless laugh which is so sure a sign of idiotcy.

"Can you understand now," exclaimed Norbert, pointing to his father, "why the remembrance of my love for you has become a hateful reminiscence? Do you dare to talk of happiness to me, when this spectre of a meditated crime will ever rise between us?" and with a meaning gesture he pointed to the open gate of the courtyard.

She turned; but before passing away, she cast a glance upon him full of the deepest fury and jealousy. She could not forgive Norbert for his share in the crime that she had herself prompted,—for the crime which had blighted all her hopes of happiness. Her farewell was a menace.

"Norbert," she said, as she glided through the gate like a spectre of the night, "I will have revenge, and that right soon."

CHAPTER XI.

MARRIAGE BELLS; FUNERAL KNELLS.

THREE days of hard work had completed all the arrangements necessary for the marriage of Norbert and Mademoiselle de Puymandour. He had been presented to the lady, and neither had received a favorable impression of the other. At the very first glance each one felt that inevitable repugnance which the lapse of years can never efface. While dreading the anger of her obdurate father, Marie had at one time thought of confiding the secret of her attachment to George de Croisenois to Norbert, for she had the idea that if she told him that her heart was another's, he might withdraw his pretensions to her hand; but several times, when the opportunity occurred, fear restrained her tongue, and she let the propitious moment pass away. Had she done so, Norbert would at once have eagerly grasped at a pretext for absolving himself from a promise which he had made mentally of obeying in all things a father who now, alas! had no means of enforcing his commands.

Each day he paid his visit to Puymandour as an accepted suitor, bearing a large bouquet with him, which he regularly presented to his betrothed upon his entrance into the drawing-room, which she accepted with a painful flush rising to her cheek. The pair conversed upon indifferent topics, while an aged female connection sat in the room to play propriety. For many hours they would remain thus, the girl bending over her fancy work, and he vainly striving to find topics of conversation, and, consequently, saying hardly anything, in spite of Marie's feeble efforts to assist in the conversation. It was a slight relief when M. de Puymandour proposed a walk; but this was a rare occurrence, for that gentleman usually declared that he never had a moment's leisure. Never had he seemed so gay and busy since the approaching marriage of his daughter had been the theme of every tongue. He took all the preparations for the ceremony into his own hands, for he had determined that everything should be conducted on a scale of unparalleled magnificence. The Château was refurnished, and all the carriages repainted and varnished, while the Champdoce and the Puymandour arms were quartered together on their panels. This coat of arms was to be seen everywhere—over the doors, on the walls, and engraved on the silver, and it was believed that M. de Puymandour would have made no objection to their being branded on his breast.

In the midst of all this turmoil and bustle Norbert and Marie grew sadder and sadder as each day passed on. One day M. de Puymandour heard so astounding a piece of intelligence that he hurried into the drawing-room, where he knew that he should find the lovers (as he styled them) together.

" Well, my children," exclaimed he, " you have set such an excellent example, that everybody seems disposed to copy you, and the mayor and the priest will be kept to their work rather tightly this year."

His daughter tried to put on an appearance of interest at this speech.

" Yes," continued M. de Puymandour, " I have

just heard of a marriage that will come off almost directly after yours has been celebrated, and will make a stir, I can assure you."

"And whose is that, pray?"

"You are acquainted, I presume," returned her father, addressing himself to Norbert, "with the son of the Count de Mussidan?"

"What, the Viscount Octave?"

"The same."

"He lives in Paris, does he not?"

"Yes, generally; but he has been staying at Mussidan, and in the short space of a week has managed to lose his heart here; and to whom do you think? Come, give a guess."

"We cannot think who it can be, my dear father," said Marie, "and we are devoured with curiosity."

"It is reported that the Viscount de Mussidan has proposed for the hand of Mademoiselle de Laurebourg."

"Why," remarked Marie, "it is only three weeks since her brother died!"

Norbert flushed scarlet, and then turned a livid white; so great was his agitation at hearing this news, that he nearly dropped the album which he held in his hand.

"I like the Viscount," continued M. de Puymandour, "while Mademoiselle Diana is a charming girl. She is very handsome, and, I believe, has many talents; and she is a good model for you to copy, Marie, as you are so soon to become a duchess."

When he got upon his favorite hobby, it was very difficult to check M. de Puymandour. His daughter, therefore, waited until he had concluded, and then left the room, under the pretext of giving an order to the servants. The Count hardly noticed her absence, as he had still Norbert at his mercy.

"Reverting again to Mademoiselle Diana," said he: "she looks charming in black, for women should look upon a death in the family as a most fortunate occurrence; but I ought not to be praising her to you, who are so well acquainted with her."

"I?" exclaimed Norbert.

"Yes, you. I do not suppose that you intend to deny that you have had a little flirtation with her?"

"I do not understand you."

"Well, *I* do then, my boy; I heard all about your making love to her. Why, you are really blushing! What is up now?"

"I can assure you——"

De Puymandour burst into a loud laugh.

"I have heard a good deal of your little country walks, and all the pretty things that you used to say to each other."

In vain did Norbert deny the whole thing, for his intended father-in-law would not believe him; and at last he got so annoyed that he refused to remain and dine with the Count, alleging anxiety for his father as an excuse. He returned home as soon as he possibly could, much agitated by what he had heard; and as he was walking rapidly on, he heard his name called by some one who was running after him: Norbert turned round, and found himself face to face with Montlouis.

"I have been here a week," said the young man. "I am here with my patron, for I have one now. I am now with the Viscount de Mussidan, as his private secretary. M. Octave is not the most agreeable man in the world to get on with, as he gets into

the most violent passions on very trivial occasions;
but he has a good heart, after all, and I am very
pleased with the position I have gained."

"I am very glad to hear it, Montlouis, very much
pleased indeed."

"And you, Marquis, I hear, are to marry Mademoiselle de Puymandour; I could scarcely credit the
news."

"And why, pray?"

"Because I remembered when we used to wait outside a certain garden wall, until we saw a certain
door open discreetly."

"But you must efface all this from your memory,
Montlouis."

"Do not be alarmed; save to you, my lips would
never utter a word of this. No one else would ever
make me speak."

"Stop!" said Norbert, with an angry gesture.
"Do you venture to say——"

"To say what?"

"I wish you to understand that Mademoiselle
Diana is as free from blame to-day as she was when
first I met her. She has been indiscreet, but nothing
more, I swear it before heaven!"

"I believe you perfectly."

In reality Montlouis did not believe one word of
Norbert's assertion, and the young Marquis could
read this in his companion's face.

"The more so," continued the secretary, "as the
young lady is about to be married to my friend and
patron."

"But where," asked Norbert, "did the Viscount
meet with Mademoiselle de Laurebourg?"

"In Paris; the Viscount and her brother were very

intimate, and nursed him during his last illness, and as soon as the scheming parents heard of the Viscount being in the neighborhood they asked him to call on them. Of course he did so, and saw Mademoiselle Diana, and returned home in a perfect frenzy of love."

Norbert seemed so incensed at this that Montlouis broke off his recital, feeling confident that the Marquis still loved Diana, and was consumed with the flame of jealousy.

" But, of course," he added carelessly, " nothing is yet settled."

Norbert, however, was too agitated to listen to the idle gossip of Montlouis any longer, so he pressed his hand and left him rather abruptly, walking away at the top of his speed, leaving his friend silent with astonishment. It seemed to Norbert as if he was imprisoned in one of those iron dungeons he had read of, which slowly contracted day by day, and at last crushed their victims to atoms. He saw Diana married to the Viscount de Mussidan, and compelled to meet daily the man who knew all about her illicit meetings with her former lover, and who had more than once, when Norbert was unable to leave Champdoce, been intrusted with a letter or a message for her. And how would Montlouis behave under the circumstances? Would he possess the necessary tact and coolness to carry him through so difficult a position? What would be the end of this cruel concatenation of circumstances? Would Diana be able to endure the compromising witness of her youthful error? She would eagerly seek out some pretext for his dismissal; he could easily detect this, and in his anger at the loss of a position which he had long desired, would turn on her and repeat the whole story. Should Montlouis let loose his tongue, the Viscount, indignant at the imposition that had been practised upon him, would separate from his wife. What would be Diana's conduct when she found herself left thus alone, and despised by the society of which she had hoped to be a queen? Would she not, in her turn, seek to revenge herself on Norbert? He had just asked himself whether at this juncture death would not be a blessing to him, when he caught sight of Françoise, the daughter of the Widow Rouleau, close by him. For two hours she had been awaiting his coming, concealed behind a hedge.

"I have something to give you, my lord Marquis," said she.

He took the letter that she held out to him, and, opening it, he read,—

"You said that I did not love you—perhaps this was but a test to prove my love. I am ready to fly with you to-night. I shall lose all, but it will be for your sake. Reflect, Norbert; there is yet time, but to-morrow it will be too late."

These were the words that Mademoiselle de Laurebourg had had the courage to pen, which to the former lover were full of the most thrilling eloquence. The usually bold, firm writing of Diana was, in the letter before him, confused and almost illegible, showing the writer's frame of mind. There were blurs and blisters upon the paper as though tears had fallen upon it, perhaps because the writing had been made purposely irregular and drops of water are an excellent substitute for tears.

"Does she really love me?" murmured he.

He hesitated; yes, he absolutely hesitated, impressed by the idea that for him she was ready to sacrifice position and honor, that he had but to raise his finger and she was his, and that in the space of a couple of hours she might be the companion of his flight to some far-distant land. His pulse throbbed madly, and he could scarcely draw his breath, when some fifty paces down the road he caught sight of the figure of a man; it was his father. This was the second time that the Duke by his mere presence had spread the web of Diana's temptations and allurements.

"Never!" exclaimed Norbert, with such fire and energy that the girl fell back a pace. "Never! no, never!" and crushing up the letter, he dashed it upon the ground, from whence Françoise picked it up as he ran forward to meet his father. The Duke had recovered from his attack as far as the mere fact of his life not having been sacrificed; he could walk, sleep, eat and drink as he had formerly done. He could look at the laborers in the fields or the horses in the stables, but five minutes afterwards he had no recollection of what he heard or saw. The sudden loss of his father's aid would have caused Norbert much embarrassment had it not been for the shrewdness and sagacity of M. de Puymandour, who had assisted him greatly. But all these arrangements which had to be made had necessarily delayed the wedding. But it came at last; M. de Puymandour took absolute possession of him, and after the unhappy young man had passed a sleepless night, he was allowed no time for reflection. At eleven o'clock he entered the carriage, and was driven fast to the Mayor's office, and from thence to the chapel, and by twelve o'clock all was finished and he fettered for life. A little before dinner the Viscount de Mussidan came to offer his congratulations, and gained them at the same time for himself by announcing his speedy union with Mademoiselle Diana de Laurebourg.

Five days later the newly married pair took possession of their mansion at Champdoce. Hampered with a wife whom he had never affected to love, and whose tearful face was a constant reproach to him, and with a father who was an utter imbecile, the thoughts of suicide more than once crossed Norbert's brain. One day a servant informed Norbert that his father refused to get up. A doctor was sent for, and he declared that the Duke was in a highly critical condition. A violent reaction had taken place, and all day the invalid was in a state of intense excitement. The power of speech, which he had almost entirely lost, seemed to have returned to him in a miraculous manner; at length, however, he became delirious, and Norbert dismissed the servants who had been watching by his father's bed, lest in the incoherent ravings of the invalid, the words "Parricide" or "Poison" should break forth. At eleven o'clock he grew calmer, and slept a little, when all at once he started up in bed, exclaiming: "Come here, Norbert," and Jean, who had remained by his old master's side, ran up to the bed and was much startled at the sight. The Duke had entirely recovered his former appearance. His eyes flashed, and his lips trembled, as they always did when he was greatly excited.

"Pardon, father; pardon," cried Norbert, falling upon his knees.

The Duke softly stretched out his hand. "I was mad with family pride," said he; "and God punished me. My son, I forgive you."

Norbert's sobs broke the stillness of the chamber. "My son, I renounce my ideas," continued the Duke. "I do not desire you to wed Mademoiselle de Puymandour if you feel that you cannot love her."

"Father," answered Norbert, "I have obeyed your wishes, and she is now my wife."

A gleam of terrible anguish passed over the Duke's countenance; he raised his hands as though to shield his eyes from some grizzly spectre, and in tones of heartrending agony exclaimed: "Too late! too late!"

He fell back in terrible convulsions, and in a moment was dead. If, as has been often asserted, the veil of the hereafter is torn asunder, then the Duke de Champdoce had a glimpse into a terrible future.

CHAPTER XII.

"RASH WORD, RASH DEED."

AFTER her repulse by Norbert, Diana, with the cold chill of death in her heart, made her way back to the Château of the De Laurebourgs, over the same road which but a short time before she had traveled full of expectation and hope. The sudden appearance of the Duke de Champdoce had filled her with alarm, but her imagination was not of that kind upon which unpleasant impressions remain for any long period; for after she had regained her room, and thrown aside her out-door attire, and removed all signs of mud-stains, she once more became herself, and even laughed a little rippling laugh at all her own past alarms. Overwhelmed with the shame of her repulse, she had threatened Norbert; but as she reasoned calmly, she felt that it was not he for whom she felt the most violent animosity. All her hatred was reserved for that woman who had come between her and her lover—for Marie de Puymandour. Some hidden feeling warned her that she must look into Marie's past life for some reason for the rupture of her engagement with Norbert, though the banns had been already published. This was the frame of mind in which Diana was when the Viscount de Mussidan was introduced to her, the friend of the brother whose untimely death had left her such a wealthy heiress. He was tall and well made, with handsomely chiseled features; and, endowed with physical strength and health, Octave de Mussidan had the additional advantages of noble descent and princely fortune. Two women, both renowned for their wit and beauty, his aunt and his mother, had been intrusted with the education which would but enable him to shine in society.

Dispatched to Paris, with an ample allowance, at the age of twenty, he found himself, thanks to his birth and connections, in the very center of the world of fashion. At the sight of Mademoiselle de Laurebourg his heart was touched for the first time. Diana had never been more charmingly fascinating than she was at this period. Octave de Mussidan did not suit her fancy; there was too great a difference between him and Norbert, and nothing would ever efface from her memory the recollection of the young Marquis as he had appeared before her on the first day of their meeting in the Forest of Bevron, clad in his rustic garb, with the game he had shot dangling from his hand. She delighted to feast her recollection, and thought fondly of his shyness and diffidence when he hardly ventured to raise his eyes to hers. Octave, however, fell a victim at the first glance he caught of Diana, and permitted himself to be swept away by the tide of his private emotions, which upon every visit that he paid to Laurebourg became more powerful and resistless. Like a true knight, who wishes that he himself should gain the love of his lady fair, Octave addressed himself directly to Diana, and after many attempts succeeded in finding himself alone with her, and then he asked her if she could permit him to crave of her father, the Marquis de Laurebourg, the honor of her hand. This appeal surprised her, for she had been so much absorbed in her own troubles that she had not even suspected his love for her. She was even frightened at his declaration, as is the patient when the surgeon informs him that he must use the knife. She glanced at De Mussidan strangely as he put this question to her, and after a moment's hesitation, replied that she would give him a reply the next day. After thinking the matter over, she wrote and dispatched the letter which Françoise had carried to Norbert. The prisoner in the dock, as he anxiously awaits the sentence of his judge, can alone appreciate Diana's state of agonized suspense as she stood at the end of the park at Laurebourg awaiting the return of the girl. Her anxiety of mind lasted nearly three hours, when Françoise hurried up breathless.

"What did the Marquis say?" asked Diana.

"He said nothing; that is, he cried out very angrily, 'Never! no, never!'"

In order to prevent any suspicions arising in the girl's mind, Mademoiselle de Laurebourg contrived to force a laugh, exclaiming: " Ah! indeed, that is just what I expected."

Françoise seemed as if she had something to say on the tip of her tongue, but Diana hurriedly dismissed her, pressing a coin into her hand. All anxiety was now at an end; for her there was no longer any suspense or anguish; all her struggles were now futile, and she felt grateful to Octave for having given her his love. " Once married," thought she, " I shall be free, and shall be able to follow the Duke and Duchess to Paris."

Upon her return to the Château, she found Octave awaiting her. His eyes put the question that his lips did not dare to utter; and, placing her hand in his with a gentle inclination of her head, she assented to his prayer.

This act on her part would, she believed, free her from the past; but she was in error. Upon hearing that his dastardly attempt at murder had failed, the Counsellor was for the time utterly overwhelmed with terror, but the news that he had gained from M. de Puymandour calmed his mind in a great measure. He was not, however, completely reassured until he heard for certain that the Duke had become a helpless maniac, and that the doctor, having given up all hopes of his patient's recovery, had discontinued his visits to the Château. As soon as he had heard that Norbert's marriage had been so soon followed by his father's death, he imagined that every cloud had disappeared from the sky. All danger now seemed at an end, and he recalled with glee that he had in his strong box the promissory notes, signed by Norbert, to the amount of twenty thousand francs, which he could demand at any moment, now that Norbert was the reigning lord of Champdoce. The first step he took was to hang about the neighborhood of Laurebourg, for he thought that some lucky chance would surely favor him with an opportunity for a little conversation with Mademoiselle Diana. For several days in succession he was unsuccessful, but at last he was delighted at seeing her alone, walking in the direction of Bevron. Without her suspecting it, he followed her until the road passed through a small plantation, when he came up and addressed her.

"What do you want with me?" asked she angrily.

He made no direct reply; but after apologizing for his boldness, he began to offer his congratulations upon her approaching marriage, which was now the talk of the whole neighborhood, and which pleased him much, as M. de Mussidan was in every way superior to——

"Is that all you have to say to me?" asked Diana, interrupting his string of words.

As she turned from him, he had the audacity to lay his hand upon the edge of her jacket.

"I have more to say," said he, "if you will honor me with your attention. Something about—you can guess what."

"About whom or what?" asked she, making no effort to hide her supreme contempt.

He smiled, glanced around to see that no one was within hearing, and then said in a low voice,—

"It is about the bottle of poison."

She recoiled, as though some venomous reptile had started up in front of her.

"What do you mean?" cried she. "How dare you speak to me thus?"

All his servile manner had now returned to him, and he uttered a string of complaints in a whining tone of voice. She had played him a most unfair trick, and had stolen a certain little glass bottle from his office; and if anything had leaked out, his head would have paid the penalty of a crime in which he had no hand. He was quite ill, owing to the suspense and anxiety he had endured; sleep would not come to his bed, and the pangs of remorse tortured him continually.

"Enough," cried Diana, stamping her foot angrily on the ground. "Enough, I say."

"Well, mademoiselle, I can no longer remain here. I am far too nervous, and I wish to go to some foreign country."

"Come, let me hear the real meaning of this long preface."

Thus adjured, Daumon spoke. He only wished for some little memento to cheer his days and nights of exile, some little recognition of his services; in fact, such a sum as would bring him in an income of three thousand francs.

"I understand you," replied Diana. "You wish to be paid for what you call your kindness."

"Ah, mademoiselle!"

"And you put a value of sixty thousand francs upon it; that is rather a high price, is it not?"

"Alas! it is not half what this unhappy business has cost me."

"Nonsense; your demand is preposterous."

"Demand!" returned he; "I make no demand. I come to you respectfully and with a little charity. If I were to demand, I should come to you in quite a different manner. I should say, 'Pay me such and such a sum, or I tell everything.' What have I to lose if the whole story comes to light? A mere nothing. I am a poor man, and am growing old. You and M. Norbert are the ones that have something to fear. You are noble, rich, and young, and a happy future lies before you."

Diana paused and thought for an instant.

"You are speaking," answered she at last, "in a most foolish manner. When charges are made against people, proofs must be forthcoming."

"Quite right, mademoiselle; but can you say that these proofs are not in my hands? Should you, however, desire to buy them, you are at liberty to do so. I give you the first option, and yet you grumble."

As he spoke, he drew a battered leather pocket-book from his breast, and took from it a paper, which, after having been crumpled, had been carefully smoothed out again. Diana glanced at it, and then uttered a stifled cry of rage and fear, for she at once recognized her last letter to Norbert.

"That wretch, Françoise, has betrayed me," exclaimed she, "and I saved her mother from a death by hunger and cold."

The Counsellor held out the letter to her. She thought that he had no suspicion of her, and made an attempt to snatch it from him; but he was on his guard, and drew back with a sarcastic smile on his face.

"No, mademoiselle," said he; "this is not the little bottle of poison; however, I will give it to you, together with another one, when I have obtained what I ask. Nothing for nothing, however; and if I must go to the scaffold, I will do so in good company."

Mademoiselle de Laurebourg was in utter despair.

"But I have no money," said she. "Where is a girl to find such a sum?"

" M. Norbert can find it."

" Go to him, then."

Daumon made a negative sign with his head.

" I am not quite such a fool," answered he; " I know M. Norbert too well. He is the very image of his father. But you can manage him, mademoiselle; besides, you have much interest in having the matter settled."

" Counsellor !"

" There is no use in beating about the bush. I come to you humbly enough, and you treat me like so much dirt. I will not submit to this, as you will find to your cost. *I* never poisoned any one; but enough of this kind of thing. To-day is Tuesday; if on Friday, by six o'clock, I do not have what I have asked for, your father and the Count Octave will have a letter from me, and perhaps your fine marriage may come to nothing after all."

This insolence absolutely struck Diana dumb, and Daumon had disappeared round a turning of the road before she could find words to crush him for his vile attempt at extortion. She felt that he was capable of keeping his word, even if by so doing he seriously injured himself without gaining any advantage.

A nature like Diana's always looks danger boldly in the face. She had, however, but little choice how she would act—for to apply to Norbert was the only resource left to her—for she knew that he would do all in his power to ward off the danger which threatened both of them so nearly. The idea, however, of applying to him for aid was repugnant to her pride. To what depths of meanness and infamy had she descended! and to what avail had been all her aspirations of ambition and grandeur?

She was at the mercy of a wretch—of Daumon, in fact. She was forced to go as a suppliant to a man whom she had loved so well that she now hated him with a deadly hatred. But she did not hesitate for a moment. She went straight to the cottage of Widow Rouleau, and despatched Françoise in quest of Norbert.

She ordered the girl to tell him that he must without fail be at the wicket gate in the park wall at Laurebourg on the coming night, where she would meet him, and that the matter was one of life and death.

As Diana gave these orders to Françoise, the woman's nervous air and flushed features plainly showed that she was a mere creature of Daumon's; but Mademoiselle de Laurebourg felt it would be unwise to take any notice of her discovery, but to abstain from employing her in confidential communications for the future.

As the hour of the meeting drew near a host of doubts assailed her. Would Norbert come to the meeting? Had Françoise contrived to see him? Might he not be absent from home? It was now growing dark, and the servants brought candles into the dining-room, and Diana, contriving to slip away, gained the appointed spot. Norbert was waiting, and when he caught sight of her, rushed forward, but stopped as though restrained by a sudden thought, and remained still, as if rooted to the ground.

" You sent for me, mademoiselle ? " said he.

" I did."

After a pause, in which she succeeded in mastering her emotion, Diana began with the utmost volubility to explain the extortion that Dawson was endeavoring to practise upon her, magnifying, though there was

but little need to do so, all the threats and menaces that
he had made use of. She had imagined that this last
piece of roguery on the part of Daumon would drive
Norbert into a furious passion, but to her surprise
it had no such effect. He had suffered so much and
so deeply, that his heart was almost dead against any
further emotion.

"Do not let this trouble you," answered he apathet-
ically; "I will see Daumon and settle with him."

"Can you leave me thus, at our last meeting, without even a word?" asked she.

"What have I to say? My father forgave me on his
death-bed, and I pardon you."

"Farewell, Norbert; we shall see no more of each
other. I am going to marry, as you have doubtless
been informed. Can I oppose my parent's will? Besides, what does it signify? Farewell; remember no
one wishes more sincerely for your future happiness
than I do."

"Happy!" exclaimed Norbert. "How can I ever
be happy again? If you know the secret, for pity's
sake break it to me. Tell me how to forget and how
to annihilate thought. Do you not know that I had
planned a life of perfect happiness with you by my
side? I had visions; and now plans and visions are
alike hateful to me. And as they ever and anon recur
to my memory, they will fill me with terror and
despair."

As Diana heard these words of agony, a wild gleam
of triumph shot from her eyes, but it faded away
quickly, and left her cold and emotionless as a marble
statue; and when she reappeared in the drawing-room,
after taking leave of Norbert, her face wore so satis-

fied an expression, that the Viscount complimented her upon her apparent happiness.

She made some jesting retort, but there was a shade of earnestness mixed with her playfulness, for to her future husband she only wished to show the amiable side of her character; but all the time she was thinking. Will Norbert see Daumon in time?

The Duke kept his word, and the next day the faithful Jean discreetly handed her a packet. She opened it, and found that besides the two letters of which the Counsellor had spoken, it contained all her correspondence with Norbert—more than a hundred letters in all, some of great length, and all of them compromising to a certain extent. Her first thought was to destroy them, but on reflection she decided not to do so, and hid the packet in the same place as she had concealed the letters written by Norbert to her.

Norbert had given Daumon sixty thousand francs, and in addition owed him twenty thousand on his promissory notes. This sum, in addition to what he had already saved, would form such a snug little fortune that it would enable the Counsellor to quit Bevron, and take up his abode in Paris, where his peculiar talents would have more scope for development. And eight days later the village was thrown into a state of intense excitement by the fact becoming known that Daumon had shut up his house and departed for Paris, taking Françoise, the Widow Rouleau's daughter, with him. The Widow Rouleau was furious, and openly accused Mademoiselle de Laurebourg of having aided in the committal of the act which had deprived her of her daughter's services in her declining years; and the old woman who had acted as housekeeper, who on Daumon's departure had thrown open the place, did not hesitate to assert that all her late master's legal lore had been acquired in prison, where he had undergone a sentence of ten years' penal servitude.

In spite of all this, however, Mademoiselle de Laurebourg was secretly delighted at the departure of Daumon and Françoise; for she experienced an intense feeling of relief at knowing that she no longer was in any risk of meeting her accomplice in her daily walks. Norbert, too, was going to Paris with his wife; and M. de Puymandour was going about saying that his daughter, the Duchess of Champdoce, would not return to this part of the country for some time to come.

Diana drew a long breath of relief, for it seemed to her as if all the threatening clouds, which had darkened the horizon, were fast breaking up and drifting away. Her future seemed clear, and she could continue the preparations for her marriage, which was to be celebrated in a fortnight's time; and the friend of Octave who had been asked to act as his best man had answered in the affirmative.

Diana had taken accurate measurement of the love that Octave lavished upon her, and did her utmost to increase it. She had another cruel idea, and that was, that the bewitching manner which she had assumed towards her betrothed was excellent practice, and by it she might judge of her future success in society when she resided in Paris. Octave was utterly conquered, as any other man would have been under similar circumstances.

Upon the day of her wedding she was dazzling in her beauty, and her face was radiant with happiness; but it was a mere mask, which she had put on to con-

ceal her real feelings. She knew that many curious
eyes were fixed upon her as she left the chapel; and
the crowd formed a lane for her to pass through. She
saw many a glance of dislike cast upon her; but a
more severe blow awaited her, for on her arrival at
the Château de Mussidan, to which she was driven
directly after the ceremony, the first person she met
was Montlouis, who came forward to welcome her.
Bold and self-possessed as she was, the sight of this
man startled her, and a bright flush passed across her
face. Fortunately Montlouis had had time to prepare
himself for this meeting, and his face showed no token
of recognition. But though his salutation was of the
most respectful description, Madame de Mussidan
thought she saw in his eyes that ironical expression of
contempt which she had more than once seen in Daumon's face.

" That man must not, shall not, stay here," she
murmured to herself.

It was easy enough for her to ask her husband to
dismiss Montlouis from his employ, but it was a
dangerous step to take; and her easiest course was to
defer the dismissal of the secretary until some really
good pretext offered itself. Nor was this pretext long
in presenting itself; for Octave was by no means satisfied with the young man's conduct. Montlouis,
who had been full of zeal while in Paris, had renewed
his *liaison,* on his return to Mussidan, with the girl
with whom he had been formerly entangled at Poitiers.
This, of course, could not be permitted to go on, and
an explosion was clearly to be expected; but what Diana dreaded most was the accidental development of
some unseen chance.

After she had been married some two weeks, when

Octave proposed in the afternoon that they should go for a walk, she agreed. Her preparations were soon completed, and they started off, blithe and lively as children on a holiday ramble. As they loitered in a wooded path, they heard a dog barking in the cover. It was Bruno, who rushed out, and, standing on his hind legs, endeavored to lick Diana's face.

" Help, help, Octave! " she exclaimed, and her husband, springing to her side, drove away the animal.

" Were you very much alarmed, dearest? " asked he.

" Yes," answered she faintly; " I was almost frightened to death."

" I do not think that he would do you any harm," remarked Octave.

" No matter; make him go away"; and as she spoke she struck at him with her parasol. But the dog never for a moment supposed that Diana was in earnest, and, supposing that she intended to play with him, as she had often done before, began to gambol round her, barking joyously the whole time.

" But this dog evidently knows you, Diana," observed the Viscount.

" Know me? Impossible! " and as she spoke Bruno ran up and licked her hand. " If he does, his memory is better than mine; at any rate, I am half afraid of him. Come, Octave, let us go."

They turned away, and Octave would have forgotten all about the occurrence had not Bruno, delighted at having found an old acquaintance, persisted in following them.

" This is strange," exclaimed the Viscount, " very strange indeed. Look here, my man," said he, addressing a peasant, who was engaged in clipping a hedge by the roadside, " do you know whose dog this is? "

"Yes, my lord, it belongs to the young Duke of Champdoce."

"Of course," answered Diana, "I have often seen the dog at the Widow Rouleau's, and have occasionally given it a piece of bread. He was always with Françoise, who ran off with that man Daumon. Oh, yes, I know him now; here, Bruno, here!"

The dog rushed to her, and, stooping down, she caressed him, thus hoping to conceal her tell-tale face.

Octave drew his wife's arm within his without another word. A strange feeling of doubt had arisen in his mind. Diana, too, was much disturbed, and abused herself mentally for having been so weak and cowardly. Why had she not at once confessed that she knew the dog? Had she said at once, "Why, that is Bruno, the Duke of Champdoce's dog," her husband would have thought no more about the matter; but her own folly had made much of a merely trivial incident.

Ever since that fatal walk the Viscount's manner appeared to have changed, and more than once Diana fancied that she caught a look of suspicion in his eyes. How could she best manage to make him forget this unlucky event? She saw that for the rest of her life she must affect a terror of dogs; and, for the future, whenever she saw one, she uttered a little cry of alarm, and insisted upon all Octave's being chained up. But for all this she lived in a perfect atmosphere of suspicion and anxiety, while the very ground upon which she walked seemed to have been mined beneath her feet. Her sole wish now was to fly from Mussidan, and leave Bevron and its environs, she cared not for what spot. It had been first arranged that immediately after the marriage they should make a short tour;

but, in spite of this, they still lingered at Mussidan; and all that Diana could do was to keep this previous determination before her husband, without making any direct attack.

The blow came at last, and was more unexpected and terrible than she had anticipated. On the afternoon of the 26th of October, as Diana was gazing from her window, an excited crowd rushed into the courtyard of the Château, followed by four men bearing a litter covered with a sheet, under which could be distinguished the rigid limbs of a dead body, while a cruel crimson stain upon one side of the white covering too plainly showed that some one had met with a violent death.

The hideous sight froze Diana with terror, and it was impossible for her to leave the window or quit the object on the litter, which seemed to have a terrible fascination for her. That very morning her husband, accompanied by his friend the Baron de Clinchain, Montlouis, and a servant named Ludovic, had gone out for a day's shooting. It was evident that something had happened to one of the party; which of them could it be? The doubt was not of very long duration; for at that moment her husband entered the courtyard, supported by M. de Clinchain and Ludovic. His face was deadly pale, and he seemed scarcely able to drag one leg after the other. The dead man therefore must be Montlouis. She need no longer plot and scheme for the dismissal of the secretary, for his tongue had been silenced for ever.

A ray of comfort dawned in Diana's heart at this idea, and gave her the strength to descend the staircase. Halfway down she met M. de Clinchain, who was ascending. He seized her by the arm, and said hoarsely,—

"Go back, madame, go back!"

"But tell me what has happened."

"A terrible calamity. Go back to your room, I beg of you. Your husband will be here presently"; and, as Octave appeared, he absolutely pushed her into her own room.

Octave followed, and, extending his arms, pressed his wife closely to his breast, bursting as he did so into a passion of sobs.

"Ah!" cried M. de Clinchain joyously, "he is saved. See, he weeps; I had feared for his reason."

After many questions and incoherent answers, Madame de Mussidan at last arrived at the fact that her husband had shot Montlouis by accident. Diana believed this story, but it was far from the truth. Montlouis had met his death at her hands quite as much as the Duke de Champdoce had done. He had died because he was the possessor of a fatal secret.

This was what had really occurred. After lunch, Octave, who had drunk rather freely, began to rally Montlouis regarding his mysterious movements, and to assert that some woman must be at the bottom of them. At first Montlouis joined in the laugh; but at length M. de Mussidan became too personal in remarks regarding the woman his secretary loved, and Montlouis responded angrily. This influenced his master's temper, and he went on to say that he could no longer permit such doings, and he reproached his secretary for risking his present and future for a woman who was worthy neither of love nor respect, and who was notoriously unfaithful to him. Montlouis heard this last taunt with compressed lips and a deep cloud upon his brow.

"Do not utter a word more, Count," said he; "I forbid you to do so."

He spoke so disrespectfully that Octave was about to strike him, but Montlouis drew back and avoided the blow; but he was so intoxicated with fury that this last insult roused him beyond all bounds.

"By what right do you speak thus," said he, "who have married another man's mistress? It well becomes you to talk of woman's virtue, when your wife is a——"

He had no time to finish his sentence, for Octave, levelling his gun, shot him through the heart.

M. de Mussidan kept these facts from his wife because he really loved her, and true love is capable of any extreme; and he felt that, however strong the cause might be, he should never have the courage to separate from Diana; that whatever she might do in the future, or had already done in the past, he could not choose but forgive her.

Acquitted of all blame, thanks to Clinchain's and Ludovic's evidence—for they had mutually agreed that the tragical occurrence should be represented to have been the result of an accident—the conscience of M. de Mussidan left him but little peace. The girl whom Montlouis had loved had been driven from her home in disgrace, owing to having given birth to a son. Octave sought her out, and, without giving any reason for his generosity, told her that her son, whom she had named Paul, after his father, Montlouis, should never come to want.

Shortly after this sad occurrence, M. de Mussidan and his wife quitted Poitiers, for Diana had more than

once determined that she would make Paris her residence for the future. She had taken into her service
a woman who had been in the service of Marie de
Puymandour, and through her had discovered that,
previous to her marriage with Norbert, Marie had
loved George de Croisenois; and she intended to use
this knowledge at some future date as a weapon with
which to deal the Duke de Champdoce a deadly blow.

CHAPTER XIII.

A SCHEME OF VENGEANCE.

THE marriage between Norbert and Mademoiselle
de Puymandour was entirely deficient in that brief,
ephemeral light that shines over the honeymoon. The
icy wall that stood between them became each day
stronger and taller. There was no one to smooth away
inequalities, no one to exercise a kindly influence over
two characters, both haughty and determined. After
his father's death, when Norbert announced his intention of residing in Paris, M. de Puymandour highly
approved of this resolution, for he fancied that if he
were to remain alone in the country, he could to a
certain extent take the place and position of the late
Duke, and, with the permission of his son-in-law, at
once take up his residence at Champdoce.

Almost as soon as the young Duchess arrived in
Paris she realized the fact that she was the most unfortunate woman in the world. As Champdoce was
almost like her own home, her eyes lighted on familiar
scenes; and if she went out, she was sure of being

greeted by kindly words and friendly features; but in Paris she only found solitude, for everything there was strange and hostile. The late Duke, pinching and parsimonious as he had been towards himself and his son, launched out into the wildest extravagances when he imagined he was working for his coming race, and the home which he had prepared for his great-grand-children was the incarnation of splendor and luxury.

Upon the arrival of Norbert and his wife, they could almost fancy that they had only quitted their town house a few days before, so perfect were all the arrangements. Had Norbert been left to act for himself, he might have felt a little embarrassed, but his trusty servant Jean aided him with his advice, and the establishment was kept on a footing to do honor to the traditions of the house of Champdoce. Everything can be procured in Paris for money, and Jean had filled the ante-rooms with lackeys, the kitchens and offices with cooks and scullions, and the stables with grooms, coachmen, and horses, while every description of carriage stood in the place appointed for their reception.

But all this bustle and excitement did not seem in the eyes of the young Duchess to impart life to the house. It appeared to her dead and empty as a sepulchre. It seemed as if she were living beneath the weight of some vague and indefinable terror, some hideous and hidden spectre which might at any moment start from its hiding place and drive her mad with the alarm it excited. She had not a soul in whom she could confide. She had been forbidden by Norbert to renew her acquaintance with her old Parisian friends, for Norbert did not consider them of sufficiently good family, and in addition he had used the

pretext of the deep mourning they were in to put off
receiving visitors for a twelvemonth at least. She felt
herself alone and solitary, and, in this frame of mind,
how was it possible for her not to let her thoughts
wander once again to George de Croisenois. Had
her father been willing, she might have been his wife
now, and have been wandering hand in hand in some
sequestered spot beneath the clear blue sky of Italy.
He had loved her, while Norbert——.

Norbert was leading one of those mad, headstrong
lives which have but two conclusions—ruin or suicide. His name had been put up for election at a
fashionable club by his uncle, the Chevalier de Sep-
traor, as soon as he arrived in Paris. He had been
elected at once, being looked on as a decided acquisi-
tion to the list of members. He bore one of the oldest
names to be found among the French nobility, while
his fortune—gigantic as it was—had been magnified
threefold by the tongue of common report. He was
received with open arms everywhere, and lived in a
perfect atmosphere of flattery. Not being able to shine
by means of cultivation or polish, he sought to gain
a position in his club by a certain roughness of de-
meanor and a cynical mode of speech. He flung away
his money in every direction, kept racers, and was
uniformly fortunate in his betting transactions. He
frequented the world of gallantry, and was constantly
to be seen in the company of women whose reputations
were exceedingly equivocal. His days were spent on
horseback, or in the fencing room, and his nights in
drinking, gambling, and all kinds of debauchery. His
wife scarcely ever saw him, for when he returned home
it was usually with the first beams of day, either half
intoxicated or savage from having lost large sums at

the gambling table. Jean, the old and trusty retainer
of the house of Champdoce, was deeply grieved, not
so much at seeing his master so rapidly pursuing the
path to ruin as at the fact that he was ever surrounded
by dissolute and disreputable acquaintances.

"Think of your name," he would urge; "of the
honor of your name."

"And what does that matter," sneered Norbert,
"provided that I live a jolly life, and shuffle out of the
world rapidly?"

There was one fixed star in all the dark clouds that
surrounded him, which now seemed to blaze brightly,
and this star was Diana de Mussidan. Do what he
would, it was impossible to efface her image from his
memory. Even amidst the fumes of wine and the de-
bauched revelry of the supper table he could see the
form that he had once so passionately loved standing
out like a pillar of light, clear and distinct against the
darkness. He had led this demoralizing existence for
fully six months, when one day, as he was riding down
the Avenue des Champs Elysées, he saw a lady give
him a friendly bow. She was seated in a magnificent
open carriage, wrapped in the richest and most costly
furs. Thinking that she might be one of the many
actresses with whom he was acquainted, Norbert
turned his horse's head towards the carriage; but as
he got nearer he saw, to his extreme amazement and
almost terror, that it was Diana de Mussidan who was
seated in it. He did not turn back, however; and as
the carriage had just drawn up, he reined in his horse
alongside of it. Diana was as much agitated as he
was, and for a moment neither of them spoke, but
their eyes were firmly fixed upon each other, and they
sat pale and breathless, as if each had some sad pre-

sentiment which fate was preparing for them both.
At last Norbert felt that he must break the silence, for
the servants were beginning to gaze upon them with
eyes full of curiosity.

"What, madame, you here, in Paris?" said he with
an effort.

She had drawn out a slender hand from the mass of
furs in which she was enveloped, and extended it to
him, as she replied in a tone which had a ring of tenderness beneath its commonplace tone,—

"Yes, we are established here, and I hope that we
shall be as good friends as we were once before. Fare--
well, until we meet again."

As if her words had been a signal, the coachman
struck his horses lightly with his whip, and the magnificent equipage rolled swiftly away. Norbert had
not accepted Diana's proffered hand, but presently he
realized the whole scene, and plunging his spurs into
his horse dashed furiously up the Avenue in the direction of the Arc de Triomphe.

"Ah," said he, as a bitter pang of despair shot
through his heart, "I still love her, and can never care
for any one else; but I will see her again. She has not
forgotten me. I could read it in her eyes, and detect
it in the tones of her voice." Here a momentary
gleam of reason crossed his brain. "But will a woman
like Diana ever forgive an offence like mine? and when
she seems most friendly the danger is the more
near."

Unfortunately he thrust aside this idea, and refused
to listen to the voice of reason. That evening he
went down to his club with the intention of asking a
few questions regarding the Mussidans. He heard
enough to satisfy himself, and the next day he met

Madame de Mussidan in the Champs Elysées, and for many days afterwards in rapid succession. Each day they exchanged a few words, and at last Diana, with much simulated hesitation, promised to alight from her carriage when next they met in the Bois, and talk to Norbert unhampered by the presence of the domestics.

Madame de Mussidan had made the appointment for three o'clock, but before two Norbert was on the spot, in a fever of expectation and doubt.

"Is it I," asked he of himself, "waiting once more for Diana, as I have so often waited for her at Bevron?"

Ah, how many changes had taken place since then! He was now no longer waiting for Diana de Laurebourg, but for the Countess de Mussidan, another man's wife, while he also was a married man. It was no longer the whim of a monomaniac that kept them apart, but the dictates of law, honor, and the world.

"Why," said he, in a mad burst of passion, "why should we not set at defiance all the cold social rules framed by an artificial state of society; why should not the woman leave her husband and the man his wife?" Norbert had consulted his watch times without number before the appointed hour came. "Ah," sighed he, "suppose that she should not come after all."

As he said these words a cab stopped, and the Countess de Mussidan alighted from it. She came rapidly along towards him, crossing an open space without heeding the irregularities of the ground, as that diminished the distance which separated her from Norbert. He advanced to meet her, and taking his arm, they plunged into the recesses of the Bois. There had been heavy rain on the day previous, and the pathway was wet and muddy, but Madame de Mussidan did not seem to notice this.

"Let us go on," said she, "until we are certain of not being seen from the road. I have taken every precaution. My carriage and servants are waiting for me in front of St. Philippe du Roule; but for all that I may have been watched."

"You were not so timid in bygone days."

"Then I was my own mistress; and if I lost my reputation, the loss affected me only; but on my wedding day I had a sacred trust confided to me—the honor of the man who has given me his name, and that I must guard with jealous care."

"Then you love me no longer."

She stopped suddenly, and overwhelming Norbert with one of those glacial glances which she knew so well how to assume, answered in measured accents,—

"Your memory fails you; all that has remained to me of the past is the rejection of a proposal conveyed in a certain letter that I wrote."

Norbert interrupted her by a piteous gesture of entreaty.

"Mercy!" said he. "You would pardon me if you knew all the horrors of the punishment that I am enduring. I was mad, blind, besotted, nor did I love you as I do at this moment."

A smile played round Diana's beautiful mouth, for Norbert had told her nothing that she did not know before, but she wished to hear it from his own lips.

"Alas!" murmured she; "I can only frame my reply with the fatal words, 'Too late!'"

"Diana!"

He endeavored to seize her hand, but she drew it away with a rapid movement.

"Do not use that name," said she; "you have no right to do so. Is it not sufficient to have blighted the young girl's life? and yet you seek to compromise the honor of the wife. You must forget me; do you understand? It is to tell you this that I am here. The other day, when I saw you again, I lost my self-command. My heart leapt up at the sight of you, and, fool that I was, I permitted you to see this; but base no hopes on my weakness. I said to you, Let us be friends. It was a mere act of madness. We can never be friends, and had better, therefore, treat each other as strangers. Do you forget that lying tongues at Bevron accused me of being your mistress? Do you think that this falsehood has not reached my husband's ears? One day, when your name was mentioned in his presence, I saw a gleam of hatred and jealousy in his eye. Great heavens! should he, on my return, suspect that my hand had rested in yours, he would expel me from his house like some guilty wretch! The door of our house must remain for ever closed to you. I am miserable indeed. Be a man; and if your heart still holds one atom of the love you once bore for me, prove it by never seeking me again."

As she concluded she hurried away, leaving in Norbert's heart a more deadly poison than the one she had endeavored to persuade the son to administer to his father, the Duke de Champdoce. She knew each chord that vibrated in his heart, and could play on it at will. She felt sure that in a month he would again be her slave, and that she could exercise over him a sway more despotic than she had yet done, and, in addition to this, that he would assist her in executing a cruel scheme of revenge, which she had long been plotting.

After having followed Diana about like her very
shadow for several days, Norbert at last again ventured to approach her in the Champs Elysées. She was
angry, but not to such an extent that he feared to
repeat his offence. Then she wept, but her tears could
not force him to avoid her. At first her system of
defence was very strong, then it gradually grew
weaker. She granted him another interview, and then
two others followed. But what were those meetings
worth to him? They took place in a church or a public gallery, in places where they could scarcely exchange a grasp of the hand. At length she told him
that she had thought of a place which would render
their interviews less perilous, but that she hardly
dared tell him where it was. He pressed her to tell
him, and, by degrees, she permitted herself to be persuaded. Her idea was to become the friend of the
Duchess of Champdoce.

Norbert now felt that she was more an angel than a
woman, and it was agreed that on the next day he
himself would introduce her to his wife.

* * *

CHAPTER XIV.

FALSE FRIEND, OLD LOVER.

It was on a Wednesday morning that the Duke de
Champdoce, instead of, as usual, going to his own or
one of his friends' clubs to breakfast, took his seat at
the table where his wife was partaking of her morning meal. He was in excellent spirits, gay, and full
of pleasant talk, a mood in which his wife had never
seen him since their ill-fated marriage. The Duchess

could not understand this sudden change in her husband; it terrified and alarmed her, for she felt that it was the forerunner of some serious event, which would change the current of her life entirely.

Norbert waited until the domestics had completed their duty and retired, and as soon as he was alone with his wife he took her hand and kissed it with an air of gallantry.

"It has been a long time, my dear Marie, since I had resolved to open my heart to you entirely, and now a full and open explanation has become absolutely necessary."

"An explanation!" faltered Marie.

"Yes, certainly; but do not let the word alarm you. I fear that I must have appeared in your eyes the most morose and disagreeable of husbands. Permit me to explain. Since we came here, I have gone about my own affairs, I have gone out early and returned extremely late, and sometimes three days have elapsed without our even setting eyes on each other."

The young Duchess listened to him like a woman who could not believe her ears. Could this be her husband who was heaping reproaches upon himself in this manner?

"I have made no complaint," stammered she.

"I know that, Marie; you have a noble and forgiving nature; but, however, it is impossible, as a woman, that you should not have condemned me."

"Indeed, but I have not done so."

"So much the better for me. On this I shall not have to find either defence or excuse for my conduct; you must know, however, that you are ever foremost in my thoughts, even when I am away from you."

He was evidently doing his best to put on an air

of tenderness and affection, but he failed; for though his words were kind, the tone of his voice was neither tender nor sympathetic.

"I hope I know my duty," said the Duchess.

"Pray, Marie," broke in he, "do not let the word duty be uttered between us. You know that you have been much alone, because it was impossible for the friends of Mademoiselle de Puymandour to be those of the Duchess de Champdoce!"

"Have I made any opposition to your orders?"

"Then, too, our mourning prevents us going out into the world for five months longer at least."

"Have I asked to go out?"

"All the more reason that I should endeavor to make your home less dull for you. I should like you to have with you some person in whose society you could find pleasure and distraction. Not one of those foolish girls who have no thought save for balls and dress, but a sensible woman of the world, and, above all, one of your own age and rank,—a woman, in short, of whom you could make a friend. But where can such a one be found? It is a perilous quest to venture on, and upon such a friend often depends the happiness and misery of a home.

"But," continued he, after a brief pause, "I think that I have discovered the very one that will suit you. I met her at the house of Madame d'Ailange, who spoke eloquently of her charms of mind and body, and I hope to have the pleasure of presenting her to you to-day."

"Here, at our house?"

"Certainly; there is nothing odd in this. Besides, the lady is no stranger to us; she comes from our own part of the country, and you know her."

A flush came over his face, and he busied himself with the fire to conceal it as he added,—

" You recollect Mademoiselle de Laurebourg ? "

" Do you mean Diana de Laurebourg ? "

" Exactly so."

" I saw very little of her, for my father and hers did not get on very well together. The Marquis de Laurebourg looked on us as too insignificant to——"

" Ah, well," interrupted he, " I trust that the daughter will make up for the father's shortcomings. She married just after our wedding had been celebrated, and her husband is the Count de Mussidan. She will call on you to-day, and I have told your servants to say that you are at home."

The silence that followed this speech lasted for nearly a couple of minutes, and became exceedingly embarrassing, when suddenly the sound of wheels was heard on the gravel of the courtyard, and in a moment afterwards a servant came and announced that the Countess de Mussidan was in the drawing-room. Norbert rose, and, taking his wife's arm, led her away.

" Come, Marie, come," said he ; " she has arrived."

Diana had reflected deeply before she had taken this extraordinarily bold step. In paying a visit so contrary to all the usual rules of etiquette, she exposed herself to the chance of receiving a severe rebuff. The few seconds that elapsed while she was still alone in the drawing-room seemed like so many centuries ; but the door was opened, and Norbert and his wife appeared. Then, with a charming smile, Madame de Mussidan rose and bowed gracefully to the Duchess de Champdoce, making a series of half-jesting apologies for her intrusion. She had been utterly unable, she said, to resist the pleasure she should experience in seeing an old county neighbor, the more so as they were now separated by so short a distance. She had, therefore, disregarded all the rules of etiquette so that they might have a cosy chat about Poitiers, Bevron, Champdoce, and all the county where she had been born, and which she so dearly loved.

The Duchess listened in silence to this torrent of words, and the expression of her face showed how surprised she was at this unexpected visit. A less perfectly self-possessed woman than Diana de Mussidan might have felt abashed, but the slight annoyance was not to be compared to the prospective advantages that she hoped to gain, and she brought all the mettle of her talent and diplomacy into play.

Norbert was moving about the room, half ashamed of the ignoble part that he was playing. As soon as he thought that the welcome between the two ladies had been partially got over, and imagined that they were conversing more amicably together, he slipped out of the room, not knowing whether to be pleased or angry at the success of the trick.

The trick was rather a more difficult one than Diana had, from Norbert's account, anticipated, as she had thought that she would have been received by the Duchess like some ministering angel sent down to earth to console an unhappy captive. She had expected to find a simple, guileless woman, who, upon her first visit, would throw her arms round her visitor's neck and yield herself entirely to her influence. Far, however, from being dismayed, Diana was rather pleased at this unexpected difficulty, and so fully exerted all her powers of fascination, that when she took her leave, she believed that she had made a little progress.

On that very evening the Duchess remarked to her husband,—

"I think that I shall like Madame de Mussidan; she seems an excellent kind of woman."

"Excellent is just the proper word," returned Norbert. "All Bevron was in tears when she was married and had to leave, for she was a real angel among the poor."

Norbert was intensely gratified by Diana's success; for was it not for him that she had displayed all her skill, and was not this a proof that she still cherished a passion for him?

He was not, however, quite so much pleased when he met Madame de Mussidan the next day in the Champs Elysées. She looked sad and thoughtful.

"What has gone wrong?" asked he.

"I am very angry with myself for having listened to the voice of my own heart and to your entreaties," answered she, "and I think that both of us have committed a grave error."

"Indeed, and what have we done?"

"Norbert, your wife suspects something."

"Impossible! why, she was praising you after you had left."

"If that is the case, then she is indeed a much more clever woman than I had imagined, for she knows how to conceal her suspicions until she is in a position to prove them."

Diana spoke with such a serious air of conviction, that Norbert became quite alarmed.

"What shall we do?" asked he.

"The best thing would be to give up meeting each other, I think."

"Never; I tell you, never!"

"Let me reflect; in the meantime be prudent; for both our sakes, be prudent."

To further his ends, Norbert entirely changed his mode of life. 'He gave up going to his clubs, refused invitations to fast suppers, and no longer spent his nights in gambling and drinking. He drove out with his wife, and frequently spent his evenings with her, and at the club began to be looked on as quite a model husband. This great change, however, was not effected without many a severe inward struggle. He felt deeply humiliated at the life of deception that he was forced to lead, but Diana's hand, apparently so slight and frail, held him with a grip of steel.

"We must live in this way," said she, in answer to his expostulations, "first, because it must be so; and, secondly, because it is my will. On our present mode of conduct depends all our future safety, and I wish the Duchess to believe that with me happiness and content must have come to her fireside."

Norbert could not gainsay this very reasonable proposition on the part of Madame de Mussidan, for he was more in love than ever, and the terrible fear that if he went in any way contrary to her wishes that she would refuse to see him any more, stayed the words of objection that rose to his lips.

After hesitating for a little longer, the Duchess made up her mind to accept the offer of friendship which Diana had so ingenuously offered to her, and finished by giving herself up to the bitterest enemy that she had in the world. By degrees she had no secrets from her new friend, and one day, after a long and confidential conversation, she acknowledged to Diana the whole secret of the early love of her girlish days, the memory of which had never faded from the inmost recesses of her heart, and was rash enough to mention George de Croisenois by name. Madame de Mussidan was overjoyed at what she considered so signal a victory.

"Now I have her," thought she, "and vengeance is within my grasp."

Marie and Diana were now like two sisters, and were almost constantly together; but this intimacy had not given to Norbert the facile means of meeting Diana which he had so ardently hoped for. Though Madame de Mussidan visited his house nearly every day, he absolutely saw less of her than he had done before, and sometimes weeks elapsed without his catching a glimpse of her face. She played her game with such consummate skill, that Marie was always placed as a barrier between Norbert and herself, as in the farce, when the lover wishes to embrace his mistress, he finds the wrinkled visage of the duenna offered to his lips. Sometimes he grew angry, but Diana always had some excellent reason with which to close his mouth. Sometimes she held up his pretensions to ridicule, and at others assumed a haughty air, which always quelled incipient rebellion upon his part.

"What did you expect of me?" she would say, "and of what base act did you do me the honor to consider me capable?"

He was treated exactly like a child, or more cruel still, like a person deficient in intellect, and this he was thoroughly aware of. He could not meet Madame de Mussidan as he had formerly done, for now in the Bois, at Longchamps, or at any place of public amusement she was invariably surrounded by a band of fashionable admirers, among whom George de Croisenois was always to be found. Norbert disliked all these

men, but he had a special antipathy to George de
Croisenois, whom he regarded as a supercilious fool;
but in this opinion he was entirely wrong, for the Marquis de Croisenois was looked upon as one of the most
talented and witty men in Parisian society, and in this
case the opinion of the world was a well-founded one.
Many men envied him, but he had no enemies, and his
honest and straightforward conduct was beyond all
doubt. He had all the noble instincts of a knight of the
days of chivalry.

" Pray," asked Norbert, " what is it that you can
see in this sneering dandy who is always hanging about
you ? "

But Diana, with a meaning smile, always made the
same reply,—

" You ask too much; but some time you will learn
all."

Every day she contrived, when with the Duchess, to
turn the conversation skilfully upon George de Croisenois, and she had in a manner accustomed Marie to
look certain possibilities straight in the face, from the
very idea of which she would a few months back have
recoiled with horror. This point once gained, Madame
de Mussidan believed that the moment had arrived to
bring the former lovers together again, and fancied
that one sudden and unexpected encounter would advance matters much more quickly than all her half-
veiled insinuations. One day, therefore, when the
Duchess had called on her friend, on entering the
drawing-room, she found it only tenanted by George
de Croisenois. An exclamation of astonishment fell
from the lips of both as their eyes met; the cheek of
each grew pale. The Duchess, overcome by her feelings, sank half-fainting into a chair near the door.

"Ah," murmured he, scarcely knowing the meaning of the words he uttered, "I had every confidence in you, and you have forgotten me."

"You do not believe the words you have just spoken," returned the Duchess haughtily; "but," she added in softer accents, "what could I do? I may have been weak in obeying my father, but for all that I have never forgotten the past."

Madame de Mussidan, who had stationed herself behind the closed door, caught every word, and a gleam of diabolical triumph flashed from her eyes. She felt sure that an interview which began in this manner would be certain to be repeated, and she was not in error. She soon saw that by some tacit understanding the Duchess and George contrived to meet constantly at her house, but this she carefully abstained from noticing. Things were working exactly as she desired, and she waited, for she could well afford to do so, knowing that the impending crash could not long be delayed.

CHAPTER XV.

A STAB IN THE DARK.

SEPTEMBER had now arrived; and though the weather was very bad, the Duke de Champdoce, accompanied by his faithful old servant, Jean, left Paris on a visit to his training stables. Having had a serious difference with Diana, he had made up his mind to try whether a long absence on his part would not have the effect of reducing her to submission, and at the same time remembering the proverb, that "absence makes the heart grow fonder."

He had already been away two whole days, and was growing extremely anxious at not having heard from Madame de Mussidan, when one evening, as he was returning from a late inspection of his stud, he was informed that there was a man waiting to see him. The man was a poor old fellow belonging to the place, who eked out a wretched subsistence by begging, and executing occasional commissions.

"Do you want me?" asked the Duke.

With a sly look, the man drew from his pocket a letter.

"This is for you," muttered he.

"All right; give it to me, then."

"I was told to give it to you only in private."

"Never mind that; hand it over."

"Well, if I must, I must."

Norbert's sole thought was that this letter must have come from Diana, and throwing the man a coin, hurried to a spot where it was light enough to read the missive. He did not, however, recognize Diana's firm, bold hand on the envelope.

"Who the devil can this be from?" thought Norbert, as he tore open the outer covering. The paper within was soiled and greasy, and the handwriting was of the vilest description, it was full of bad spelling, and ran thus:—

" SIR,—
"I hardly dare tell you the truth, and yet my conscience will give me no relief until I do so. I can no longer bear to see a gentleman such as you are deceived by a woman who has no heart or honorable feeling. Your wife is unfaithful to you, and will soon make you

a laughing stock to all. You may trust to this being
true, for I am a respectable woman, and you can easily
find out if I am lying to you. Hide yourself this evening, so that you may command a view of the side-door
in the wall of your garden, and between half-past ten
and eleven you will see your wife's lover enter. It is
a long time since he has been furnished with a key.
The hour for the meeting has been judiciously fixed,
for all the servants will be out; but I implore you not to
be violent, for I would not do your wife any harm, but
I feel that you ought to be warned.

"From one

"WHO KNOWS."

Norbert ran through the contents of this infamous
anonymous letter in an instant. The blood surged
madly through his brain, and he uttered a howl of fury.
His servants ran in to see what was the matter.

" Where is the fellow who brought this letter? " said
he. " Run after him and bring him back to me."

In a few minutes the sturdy grooms made their appearance, pushing in the messenger, who seemed overpowered with tears.

" I am not a thief," exclaimed he. " It was given to
me, but I will give it back."

He was alluding to the louis given to him by Norbert, for the largeness of the sum made him think that
the donor had made a mistake.

" Keep the money," said the Duke; " I meant it for
you; but tell me who gave this letter to you."

" I can't tell you," answered the man. " If I ever
saw him before, may my next glass of wine choke me.
He got out of a cab just as I was passing near the
bridge, and calling to me, said, ' Look at this letter;
at half-past seven take it to the Duke de Champdoce,
who lives by his stables in the road to the Forest. Do

you know the place?' 'Yes,' I says, and then he slips the letter and a five-franc piece into my hand, got back into the cab, and off he went."

"What was the man like?" asked he.

"Well, I can hardly say. He wasn't young or old, or short or tall. I recollect he had a gold watch-chain on, but that was about all I noticed."

"Very well; you can be off."

At this moment Norbert's anger was turned against the writer of the letter only, for he did not place the smallest credence in the accusations against his wife. If he did not love her, he at any rate respected her. "My wife," said he to himself, "is an honorable and virtuous woman, and it is some discharged menial who has taken this cowardly mode of revenge." A closer inspection of the letter seemed to show him that the faults in caligraphy were intentional. The concluding portion of the letter excited his attention, and, calling Jean, he asked him if it was true that all his servants would be absent from the house to-day.

"There will be none there this evening; not until late at night," answered the old man.

"And why, pray?"

"Have you forgotten, your Grace, that the first coachman is going to be married, and the Duchess was good enough to say that all might go to the wedding dinner and ball, as long as some one remained at the porter's lodge?"

After the first outburst, Norbert affected an air of calmness, and laughed at the idea of having permitted himself to be disturbed for so trivial a cause. But this was mere pretence, for doubt and suspicion had entered his soul, and no power on earth could expel them. "Why should not my wife be unfaithful to me?"

thought Norbert. "I give her credit for being honorable and right-minded, but then all deceived husbands
have the same idea. Why should I not take advantage
of this information, and judge for myself? But no.
I will not stoop to such an act of baseness. I should
be as infamous as the writer of this letter if I was to
play the spy, as she recommends me to do." He
glanced round, and perceived that his servants were
looking at him with undisguised curiosity.

"Go to your work," said he. "Extinguish the
lights, and see that all the doors and windows are carefully closed."

He had made up his mind now, and taking out his
watch, saw that it was just eight o'clock. "I have time
to reach Paris," muttered he, "by the appointed time."
Then he called Jean to him again. There was no need
to conceal anything from this trusty adherent of the
house of Champdoce. "I must start for Paris," said
the Duke, "without an instant's delay."

"On account of that letter?" asked the old man
with an expression of the deepest sorrow upon his
features.

"Yes, for that reason only."

"Some one has been making false charges against
the Duchess."

"How do you know that?"

"It was easy enough to guess."

"Have the carriage got ready, and tell the coachman to wait for me in front of the club. I myself
will go on foot."

"You must not do that," answered Jean gravely.
"The servants may have conceived the same suspicions
as I have. You ought to creep away without any one
being a bit the wiser. The other domestics need not

even suppose that you have left the house. I can get you a horse out of the little stables without any one being the wiser. I will wait for you on the other side of the bridge."

"Good; but remember that I have not a moment to lose."

Jean left the room, and as he reached the passage Norbert heard him say to one of the servants, "Put some cold supper on the table; the Duke says that he is starving."

Norbert went into his bedroom, put on a great coat and a pair of high boots, and slipped into his pocket a revolver, the charges of which he had examined with the greatest care. The night was exceedingly dark, a fine, icy rain was falling, and the roads were very heavy. Norbert found Jean with the horse at the appointed spot, and as he leaped into the saddle the Duke exclaimed, "Not a soul saw me leave the house."

"Nor I either," returned the attached domestic. "I shall go back and act as if you were at supper. At three in the morning I will be in the wine-shop on the left-hand side of the road. When you return, give a gentle tap on the window-pane with the handle of your whip." Norbert sprang into the saddle, and sped away through the darkness like a phantom of the night. Jean had made an excellent choice in the horse he had brought for his master's use, and the animal made its way rapidly through the mud and rain; but Norbert by this time was half mad with excitement, and spurred him madly on. As he neared home a new idea crossed his brain. Suppose it was a practical joke on the part of some of the members of the club? In that case, they would doubtless be watching for his arrival, and, after talking to him on indifferent subjects, would, when he betrayed any symptoms of impatience, overwhelm him with ridicule. The fear of this made him cautious. What should he do with the horse he was riding? The wine-shops were open, and perhaps he might pick up some man there who would take charge of it for him. As he was debating this point, his eye fell upon a soldier, probably on his way to barracks.

"My man," asked the Duke, "would you like to earn twenty francs?"

"I should think so, if it is nothing contrary to the rules and regulations of the army."

"It is only to take my horse and walk him up and down while I pay a visit close by."

"I can stay out of barracks a couple of hours longer, but no more," returned the soldier.

Norbert told the soldier where he was to wait for him, and then went on rapidly to his own house, and reached the side street along which ran the garden belonging to his magnificent residence. On the opposite side of the street the houses all had porticoes, and Norbert took up his position in one of these, and peered out carefully. He had studied the whole street, which was not a long one, from beginning to end, and was convinced that he was the only person in it. He made up his mind that he would wait until midnight; and if by that time no one appeared, he would feel confident that the Duchess was innocent, and return without any one but Jean having known of his expedition. From his position he could see that three windows on the second floor of his house were lighted up, and those windows were in his wife's sleeping apartment. "She is the last woman in the world to permit a lover to visit her," thought he. "No, no; the whole thing is a hoax." He began to think of the way in which he had treated his wife. Had he nothing to reproach himself with? Ten days after their marriage he had deserted her entirely; and if during the last few weeks he had paid her any attention, it was because he was acting in obedience to the whims of another woman. Suppose a lover was with her now, what right had he to interfere? The law gave him leave, but what did his conscience say? He leaned against the chill stone until he almost became as cold as it was. It seemed to him at that moment that life and hope were rapidly drifting away from him. He had lost all count of how long he had been on guard. He pulled out his watch, but it was too dark to distinguish the hands or the figures on the dial-plate. A neighboring clock struck the half-hour, but this gave him no clue as to the time. He had almost made up his mind to leave, when he heard the sound of a quick step coming down the street. It was the light, quick step of a sportsman,— of a man more accustomed to the woods and fields than the pavement and asphalt of Paris. Then a shadow fell upon the opposite wall, and almost immediately disappeared. Then Norbert knew that the door had opened and closed, and that the man had entered the garden. There could be no doubt upon this point, and yet the Duke would have given worlds to be able to disbelieve the evidence of his senses. It might be a burglar, but burglars seldom work alone; or it might be a visitor to one of the servants, but all the servants were absent. He again raised his eyes to the windows of his wife's room. All of a sudden the light grew brighter; either the lamp had been turned up, or fresh candles lighted. Yes, it was a candle, for he saw it borne across the room in the direction of the great staircase, and now he saw that the anonymous letter had spoken the truth, and that he was on the brink of a discovery. A lover had entered the garden, and the lighted candle was a signal to him. Norbert shuddered; the blood seemed to course through his veins like streams of molten fire, and the misty atmosphere that surrounded him appeared to stifle him. He ran across the street, forced the lock, and rushed wildly into the garden.

CHAPTER XVI.

HUSBAND AND LOVER.

THE writer of the anonymous communication had only known the secret too well, for the Duchess de Champdoce was awaiting a visit that evening from George de Croisenois; this was, however, the first time. Step by step she had yielded, and at length had fallen into the snare laid for her by the treacherous woman whom she believed to be her truest friend. The evening before this eventful night she had been alone in Madame de Mussidan's drawing-room with George de Croisenois. She had been impressed by his ardent passion, and had listened with pleasure to his loving entreaties.

"I yield," said she. "Come to-morrow night, at half-past ten, to the little door in the garden wall; it will only be kept closed by a stone being placed against it inside; push it, and it will open; and when you have entered the garden, acquaint me with your presence by clapping your hands gently once or twice."

Diana had, from a secure hiding-place, overheard these words, and feeling certain that the Duchess would repent her rash promise, she kept close to her side until George's departure, to give her no chance of retracting her promise. The next day she was constantly with her victim, and made an excuse for dining with her, so as not to quit her until the hour for the meeting had almost arrived.

It was not until she was left alone that the Duchess saw the full extent of her folly and rashness. She was terrified at the promise that she had given in a weak moment, and would have given worlds had she been able to retract.

There was yet, however, one means of safety left her—she could hurry downstairs and secure the garden gate. She started to her feet, determined to execute her project; but she was too late, for the appointed signal was heard through the chill gloom of the night. Unhappy woman! The light sound of George de Croisenois' palms striking one upon the other resounded in her ears like the dismal tolling of the funereal bell. She stooped to light a candle at the fire, but her hand trembled so that she could scarcely effect her object. She felt sure that George was still in the garden, though she had made no answer to his signal. She had never thought that he would have had the audacity to open a door that led into the house from the garden, but this is what he had done. In the most innocent manner imaginable, and so that her listener in no way suspected the special reason that she had for making this communication, Diana de Mussidan had informed George de Croisenois that upon this night all the domestics of the Champdoce household would be attending the coachman's wedding, and that consequently the mansion would be deserted. George knew also that the Duke was away at his training establishment, and he therefore opened the door, and walked boldly up the main staircase, so that when the Duchess, with the lighted candle in her hand, came to the top steps she found herself face to face with George de Croisenois, pallid with emotion and quivering with excitement.

At the sight of the man she loved she started backwards with a low cry of anguish and despair.

" Fly! " she said " fly, or we are lost! "

He did not, however, seem to hear her, and the Duchess recoiled slowly, step by step, through the open door of her chamber, across the carpeted floor, until she reached the opposite wall of her room, and could go no farther.

George followed her, and pushed to the door of the room as he entered it. This brief delay, however, had sufficed to restore Marie to the full possession of her senses. " If I permit him to speak," thought she,—" if he once suspects that my love for him is still as strong as ever, I am lost."

Then she said aloud,—

" You must leave this house, and that instantly. I was mad when I said what I did yesterday. You are too noble and too generous not to listen to me when I tell you that the moment of infatuation is over, and that all my reason has returned to me, and my openness will convince you of the truth of what I say—George de Croisenois, I love you."

The young man uttered an exclamation of delight upon hearing this news.

" Yes," continued Marie, " I would give half the years of my remaining life to be your wife. Yes, George, I love you ; but the voice of duty speaks louder than the whispers of the heart. I may die of grief, but there will be no stain upon my marriage robe, no remorse eating out my heart. Farewell! "

But the Marquis would not consent to this immediate dismissal, and appeared to be about to speak.

"Go!" said the Duchess, with an air of command.
"Leave me at once!" Then, as he made no effort to
obey her, she went on, "If you really love me, let my
honor be as dear to you as your own, and never try to
see me again. The peril we are now in shows how necessary this last determination of mine is. I am the
Duchess de Champdoce, and I will keep the name that
has been intrusted to me pure and unsullied, nor will I
stoop to treachery or deception."

"Why do you use the word deception?" asked he.
"I do, it is true, despise the woman who smiles upon
the husband she is betraying, but I respect and honor
the woman who risks all to follow the fortunes of the
man she loves. Lay aside, Marie, name, title, fortune,
and fly with me."

"I love you too much, George," answered she
gently, "to ruin your future, for the day would surely
come when you would regret all your self-denial, for a
woman weighed down with a sense of her dishonor is
a heavy burden for a man to bear."

George de Croisenois did not understand her thoroughly.

"You do not trust me," said he. "You would
be dishonored. Shall I not share a portion of the
world's censure? And, if you wish me, I will be a
dishonored man also. To-night I will cheat at play at
the club, be detected, and leave the room an outcast
from the society of all honorable men for the future.
Fly with me to some distant land, and we will live happily under whatever name you may choose."

"I must not listen to you," cried she wildly. "It is
impossible now."

" Impossible!—and why? Tell me, I entreat you."

" Ah, George," sobbed she, " if you only knew——"

He placed his arm around her waist, and was about to press his lips on that fair brow, when all at once he felt Marie shiver in his clasp, and, raising one of her arms, point towards the door, which had opened silently during their conversation, and upon the threshold of which stood Norbert de Champdoce, gloomy and threatening.

The Marquis saw in an instant the terrible position in which his insensate folly had placed the woman he loved.

" Do not come any nearer," said he, addressing Norbert; " remain where you are."

A bitter laugh from the Duke made him realize the folly of his command. He supported the Duchess to a couch, and seated her upon it. She recovered consciousness almost immediately, and, as she opened her eyes, George read in them the most perfect forgiveness for the man who had ruined her life and hopes.

This look, and the fond assurance conveyed in it, restored all George's coolness and self-possession, and he turned towards Norbert.

" However compromising appearances may seem, I am the only one deserving punishment; the Duchess has nothing to reproach herself with in any way; it was without her knowledge, and without any encouragement from her, that I dared to enter this house, knowing as I did that the servants were all absent."

Norbert, however, still maintained the same gloomy silence. He too had need to collect his thoughts. As he ascended the stairs he knew that he should find the Duchess with a lover, but he had not calculated upon that lover being George de Croisenois, a man whom he loathed and detested more than any one that he was in the habit of meeting in society. When he recognized George, it was with the utmost difficulty that he restrained himself from springing upon him and endeavoring to strangle him. He had suspected this man of having gained Diana's affections, and now he found him in the character of the lover of his wife, and he was silent simply because he had not yet made up his mind what he would say. If his face was outwardly calm and rigid as marble, while the flames of hell were raging in his heart, it was because his limbs for the moment refused to obey his will; but, in spite of this, Norbert was, for the time, literally insane.

Croisenois folded his arms, and continued,—

"I had only just come here at the moment of your arrival. Why were you not here to listen to all that passed between us? Would to heaven that you had been! then you would have understood all the grandeur and nobility of your wife's soul. I admit the magnitude of my fault, but I am at your service, and am prepared to give you the satisfaction that you will doubtless demand."

"From your words," answered Norbert slowly, "I presume that you allude to a duel; that is to say, that having effected my dishonor to-night, you purpose to kill me to-morrow morning. In the game that you have been playing a man stakes his life, and you, I think, have lost."

Croisenois bowed. "I am a dead man," thought he as he glanced towards the Duchess, "and not for your sake, but on account of quite another woman."

The sound of his own voice excited Norbert, and he went on more rapidly: "What need have I to risk my life in a duel? I come to my own home, I find you with my wife, I blow out your brains, and the law will exonerate me." As he said these last words, he drew a revolver from his pocket and levelled it at George. The moment was an intensely exciting one, but Croisenois did not show any sign of emotion, Norbert did not press the trigger, and the suspense became more than could be borne.

"Fire!" cried George, "fire!"

"No," returned Norbert coldly; "on reflection I have come to the conclusion that your dead body would be a source of extreme inconvenience to me."

"You try my forbearance too far. What are your intentions?"

"I mean to kill you," answered Norbert in such a voice of concentrated ferocity that George shuddered in spite of all his courage, "but it shall not be with a pistol shot. It is said that blood will wash out any stain, but it is false; for even if all yours is shed, it will not remove the stain from my escutcheon. One of us must vanish from the face of the earth in such a manner that no trace of him may remain."

"I agree. Show me how this is to be done."

"I know a method," answered Norbert. "If I was certain that no human being was aware of your presence here to-night——"

"No one can possibly know it."

"Then," answered the Duke, "instead of taking advantage of the rights that the law gives me and shooting you down on the spot, I will consent to risk my life against yours."

George de Croisenois breathed a sigh of relief. "I am ready," replied he, "as I before told you."

"I heard you; but remember that this will be no

ordinary duel, in the light of day, with seconds to regulate the manner of our conduct."

" We will fight exactly as you wish."

" In that case, I name swords as the weapons, the garden as the spot, and this instant as the hour."

The Marquis cast a glance at the window.

" You think," observed Norbert, comprehending his look, " that the night is so dark that we cannot see the blades of our swords?"

" Quite so."

" You need not fear; there will be light enough for the death struggle of the one who remains in the garden, for you understand that one *will* remain."

" I understand you; shall we go down at once?"

Norbert shook his head in the negative.

" You are in too great a hurry," said he, " and have not given me the time to fix my conditions."

" I am listening."

" At the end of the garden there is a small plot of ground, so damp that nothing will grow there, and consequently is almost unfrequented; but for all that it is thither that you must follow me. We will each take spade and pick-axe, and in a very brief period we can hollow out a receptacle for the body of the one who falls. When this work is completed, we will take to our swords and fight to the death, and the one who can keep his feet shall finish his fallen adversary, drag his body to the hole, and shovel the earth over his remains."

" Never!" exclaimed Croisenois. " Never will I agree to such barbarous terms."

" Have a care then," returned Norbert; " for I shall use my rights. That clock points to five minutes to eleven. If, when it strikes, you have not decided to accept my terms, I shall fire."

The barrel of the revolver was but a few inches from George de Croisenois' heart, and the finger of his most inveterate enemy was curved round the trigger; but his feelings had been so highly wrought up that he thought not of this danger. He only remembered that he had four minutes in which to make up his mind. The events of the last thirty minutes had pressed upon each other's heels with such surprising alacrity that he could hardly believe that they had really occurred, and it seemed to him as if it might not, after all, be only a hideous vision of the night.

"You have only two minutes more," remarked the Duke.

Croisenois started; his soul was far away from the terrible present. He glanced at the clock, then at his enemy, and lastly at Marie, who lay upon the couch, and from her ashen complexion might have been regarded as dead, save for the hysterical sobs which convulsed her frame. He felt that it was impossible to leave her in such a condition without aid of any kind, but he saw well that any show of pity on his part would only aggravate his offence. "Heaven have mercy on us!" muttered he. "We are at the mercy of a maniac," and with a feeling of deadly fear he asked himself what would be the fate of this woman, whom he loved so devotedly, were he to die. "For her sake," he thought, "I must slay this man, or her life will be one endless existence of torture—and slay him I will."

"I accept your terms," said he aloud.

He spoke just in time, for as the words were uttered came the whirr of the machinery and then the first clear stroke of the bell.

"I thank you," answered Norbert coldly as he lowered the muzzle of his revolver.

The icy frigidity of manner in a period of extreme danger, which is the marked characteristic of a certain type of education, had now vanished from the Marquis's tone and behavior.

"But that is not all," he continued; "I, too, have certain conditions to propose."

"But we agreed——"

"Let me explain: we are going to fight in the dark in your garden without seconds. We are to dig a grave and the survivor is to bury his dead antagonist. Tell me, am I right?"

Norbert bowed.

"But," went on the Marquis, "how can you be certain that all will end here, and that the earth will be content to retain our secret? You do not know, and you do not seem to care, that if one day the secret should be disclosed and the survivor accused of being the murderer of the other, arrested, dragged before a tribunal, condemned, and sent to a life-long prison——"

"There is a chance of that, of course."

"And do you think that I will consent to run such a risk as that?"

"There is such a risk, of course," answered Norbert phlegmatically; "but that will be an incentive for you to conceal my death as I should conceal yours."

"That will not be sufficient for me," returned De Croisenois.

"Ah! take care," sneered Norbert, "or I shall begin to think that you are afraid."

"I *am* afraid; that is, afraid of being called a murderer."

"That is a danger to which I am equally liable
with yourself."

Croisenois, however, was fully determined to carry
his point. "You say," continued he, "that our chances
are equal; but if I fall, who would dream of searching
here for my remains? You are in your own house
and can take every precaution; but suppose, on the
other hand, I kill you. Shall I look to the Duchess to
assist me? Will not the finger of suspicion be pointed
at her? Shall she say to her gardener when all Paris
is hunting for you, 'Mind that you do not meddle
with the piece of land at the end of the garden.'"

The thought of the anonymous letter crossed Norbert's mind, and he remembered that the writer of it
must be acquainted with the coming of George de
Croisenois. "What do you propose then?" asked he.

"Merely that each of us, without stating the
grounds of our quarrel, write down the conditions
and sign our names as having accepted them."

"I agree; but use dispatch."

The two men, after the conditions had been sub-
scribed, wrote two letters, dated from a foreign country, and the survivor of the combat was to post his
dead adversary's letter, which would not fail to stop
any search after the vanished man. When this talk
was concluded, Norbert rose to his feet.

"One word in conclusion," said he: "a soldier is
leading the horse on which I rode here up and down in
the Place des Invalides. If you kill me, go and take
the horse from the man, giving him the twenty francs
I promised him."

"I will."

"Now let us go down."

They left the room together. Norbert was stepping aside to permit Croisenois to descend the stairs first, when he felt his coat gently pulled, and, turning round, saw that the Duchess, too weak to rise to her feet, had crawled to him on her knees. The unhappy woman had heard everything, and in an almost inaudible voice she uttered an agonized prayer:

"Mercy, Norbert! have mercy! I swear to you that I am guiltless. You never loved me; why should you fight for me? Have pity! To-morrow, by all that I hold sacred, I swear to you that I will enter a convent, and you shall never see my face again. Have pity!"

"Pray heaven, madame, that it may be your lover's sword that pierces my heart. It is your only hope, for then you will be free."

He tore his coat from her fingers with brutal violence, and the unhappy woman fell to the floor with a shriek as he closed the door upon her, and followed his antagonist downstairs.

CHAPTER XVII.

BLADE TO BLADE.

SEVERAL times in the course of this interview Norbert de Champdoce had been on the point of bursting into a furious passion, but he restrained himself from a motive of self-pride; but now that his wife was no longer present, he showed a savage intensity of purpose and a deadly earnestness that was absolutely appalling. As he followed Croisenois down the great staircase, he kept repeating the words, "Quick! quick! we have lost too much time already;" for he saw that a mere trifle might upset all his plans—such as a servant returning home before the others. When they reached the ground-floor, he led George into a by-room which looked like an armory, so filled was it with arms of all kinds and nations.

"Here," said he, with a bitter sneer, "we can find, I think, what we want"; and placing the candle he carried on the mantelpiece, he leaped upon the cushioned seat that ran round the room, and took down from the wall several pairs of duelling swords, and, throwing them upon the floor, exclaimed, "Choose your own weapon."

George was as anxious as Norbert to bring this painful scene to a close, for anything was preferable to this hideous state of suspense. The last despairing glance of the Duchess had pierced his heart like a dagger thrust, and when he saw Norbert thrust aside his trembling wife with such brutality, it was all that he could do to refrain from striking him down. He made no choice of weapons, but grasped the nearest, saying,—

"One will do as well as another."

"We cannot fight in this darkness," said Norbert, "but I have a means to remedy that. Come with me this way, so that we may avoid the observation of the porter."

They went into the stables, where he took up a large lantern, which he lighted.

"This," said he, "will afford ample light for our work."

"Ah, but the neighbors will see it, too; and at this

hour a light in the garden is sure to attract attention," observed George.

"Don't be afraid; my grounds are not overlooked."

They entered the garden, and soon reached the spot to which the Duke had alluded. Norbert hung the lantern on the bough of a tree, and it gave the same amount of light as an ordinary street lamp.

"We will dig the grave in that corner," observed he; "and when it is filled in, we can cover it with that heap of stones over there."

He threw off his great coat, and, handing a spade to Croisenois, took another himself, repeating firmly the words,—

"To work! to work!"

Croisenois would have toiled all night before he could have completed the task, but the muscles of the Duke were hardened by his former laborious life, and in forty minutes all was ready.

"That will do," said Norbert, exchanging his spade for a sword. "Take your guard."

Croisenois, however, did not immediately obey. Impressible by nature, he felt a cold shiver run through his frame; the dark night, the flickering lantern, and all these preparations, made in so cold-blooded a manner, affected his nerves. The grave, with its yawning mouth, fascinated him.

"Well," said Norbert impatiently, "are you not ready?"

"I will speak," exclaimed De Croisenois, driven to desperation. "In a few minutes one of us two will be lying dead on this spot. In the presence of death a man's words are to be relied on. Listen to me. I swear to you, on my honor and by all my hopes of fu ture salvation, that the Duchess de Champdoce is entirely free from guilt."

"You have said that before; why repeat it again?"

"Because it is my duty; because I am thinking that, if I die, it will be my insane passions that have caused the ruin of one of the best and purest women in the world. I entreat you to believe that she has nothing to repent of. See, I am not ashamed to descend to entreaty. Let my death, if you kill me, be an expiation for everything. Be gentle with your wife; and if you survive me, do not make her life one prolonged existence of agony."

"Silence, or I shall look upon you as a dastard," returned Norbert fiercely.

"Miserable fool!" said De Croisenois. "On guard, then, and may heaven decide the issue!"

There was a sharp clash as their swords crossed, and the combat began with intense vigor.

The space upon which the rays of the lantern cast a glimmering and uncertain light was but a small one; and while one of the combatants was in complete shade the other was in the light, and exposed to thrusts which he could not see. This was fatal to Croisenois, and, as he took a step forward, Norbert made a fierce lunge which pierced him to the heart.

The unfortunate man threw up his arms above his head; his sword escaping from his nerveless fingers and his knees bending under him, he fell heavily backwards without a word escaping from his lips. Thrice he endeavored to regain his feet, and thrice he failed in his attempts. He strove to speak, but he could only utter a few unintelligible words, for his life blood was suffocating him. A violent convulsion shook every limb, then arose a long, deep-drawn sigh, and then silence—George de Croisenois was dead.

Yes, he was dead, and Norbert de Champdoce stood over him with a wild look of terror in his eyes, and his hair bristling upon his head, as a shudder of horror convulsed his body. Then, for the first time, he realized the horror of seeing a man slain by his own hand; and yet what affected Norbert most was not that he had killed George de Croisenois—for he believed that justice was on his side and that he could not have acted otherwise—but the perspiration stood in thick beads upon his forehead, as he thought that he must raise up that still warm and quivering body, and place it in its unhallowed grave.

He hesitated and reasoned with himself for some time, going over all the reasons that made dispatch so absolutely necessary—the risk of detection, and the honor of his name.

He stooped and prepared to raise it, but recoiled again before his hands had touched the body. His heart failed him, and once more he assumed an erect position. At last he nerved himself, grasped the body, and, with an immense exertion of strength, hurled it into the gaping grave. It fell with a dull, heavy sound which seemed to Norbert like the roar of an earthquake. The violent emotions which he had endured had ended by acting on his brain, and, snatching up the spade which his late antagonist had used with so unpracticed a hand, shovelled the earth upon the body, flattened down the ground, and finally covered it with straw and dead leaves.

"And this is the end of a man who wronged a Champdoce; yes, his life has paid the penalty of his deed."

All at once, a few paces off, in the deep shadow of the trees, he thought that he detected the outline of a human head with a pair of glittering eyes fixed upon him. The shock was so terrible that for an instant he stopped and nearly fell, but he quickly recovered himself, and, snatching up his blood-stained sword, he dashed to the spot where he fancied he had seen this terrible witness of his deed.

At this rapid movement on the part of the Duke, a figure started up with a faint cry for mercy. It was a woman.

She fled with inconceivable swiftness towards the house, but he caught her just as she had gained the steps.

"Have mercy on me!" cried she. "Do not murder me!"

He dragged her back to where the lantern was hanging. She was a girl of about eighteen years of age, ugly, badly clothed, and dirty looking. Norbert looked earnestly at her, but could not say who she was, though he was certain that he had seen her face somewhere.

"Who are you?" asked he.

She burst into a flood of tears, but made no other reply.

"Come," resumed he, in more soothing accents; "you shall not be hurt. Tell me who you are."

"Caroline Schimmel."

"Caroline?" repeated he.

"Yes. I have been in your service as scullery maid for the last three months."

"How is it that you did not go to the wedding with the rest of them?"

"It was not my fault. I was asked, and I did so

long to go, but I was too shabby; I had no finery to
put on. I am very poor now, for I have only fifteen
francs a month, and none of the other maids would
lend me anything to wear."

"How did you come into the garden?" asked Norbert.

"I was very miserable, and was sitting in the garret crying, when I suddenly saw a light down there.
I thought it was theirs, and crept down the back
stairs."

"And what did you see?"

"I saw it all."

"All what?"

"When I got down here, you and the other were
digging. I thought you were looking for money!
but ah, dear me! I was wrong. Then the other began to say something, but I couldn't catch a word;
then you fought. Oh, it was awful! I was so frightened, I could not take my eyes off you. Then the
other fell down on his back."

"And then?"

"Then," she faltered, "you buried him, and then
——"

"Could you recognize this—this other?"

"Yes, my lord duke, I did."

"Had you ever seen him before? Do you know
who he was?"

"No."

"Listen to me, my girl. If you know how to hold
your tongue, if you can forget all you have seen to-
night, it will be the greatest piece of luck for you
in the world that you did not go to this wedding."

"I won't open my lips to a soul, my lord duke.
Hear me swear, I won't. Oh, do believe me!"

"Very well; keep your oath, and your fortune is made. To-morrow I will give you a fine, large sum of money, and you can go back to your village and marry some honest fellow to whom you have taken a fancy."

"Are you not making game of me?"

"No; go to your room and go to bed, as if nothing had happened. Jean will tell you what to do to-morrow, and you must obey him as you would me."

"Oh, my lord! oh, my lord duke!"

Unable to contain her delight, she mingled her laughter and her tears.

And Norbert knew that his name, his honor, and perhaps his life were in the hands of a wretched girl like this. All the peace and happiness of his life were gone, and he felt like some unhappy prisoner who through the bars of his dungeon sees his jailer's children sporting with lighted matches and a barrel of gunpowder. He was at her mercy, for well he knew that it would resolve into this—that the smallest wish of this girl would become an imperative command that he dared not disobey. However absurd might be her whims and caprices, she had but to express them, and he dared not resist. What means could he adopt to free himself from this odious state of servitude? He knew but of one—the dead tell no tales. There were four persons who were the sharers of Norbert's secret. First, the writer of the anonymous letter; then the Duchess; then Caroline Schimmel; and, finally, Jean, to whom he must confide all. With these thoughts ringing through his brain, Norbert carefully effaced the last traces of the duel, and then bent his steps towards his wife's chamber.

He had expected to find her still unconscious on the

spot where he had left her lying. Marie was seated in an armchair by the side of the fire; her face was terribly pale, and her eyes sparkling with the inward flame that consumed her.

"My honor has been vindicated; the Marquis de Croisenois is no more; I have slain your lover, madame."

Marie did not start; she had evidently prepared herself for this blow. Her face assumed a more proud and disdainful expression, and the light in her dark eyes grew brighter and brighter.

"You are wrong," said she, "M. de Croisenois was not my lover."

"You need no longer take the pains to lie; I ask nothing now."

Marie's utter calmness jarred inexpressibly upon Norbert's exasperated frame of mind. He would have given much to change this mood of hers, which he could not at all understand. But in vain did he say the most cutting things, and coupled them with bitter taunts, for she had reached a pitch of exaltation far above his sarcasms and abuse.

"I am not lying," answered she frigidly. "What should I gain by it? What more have I to gain in this world? You desire to learn the truth; here it is then: It was with my knowledge and permission that George was here to-night. He came because I had asked him to do so, and I left the gate in the garden wall open, so as to facilitate his entrance. He had not been more than five minutes in your room when you arrived, and he had never been there before. It would have been easy for me to have left you; but as I bear your name, I could not dishonor it. As you entered, he was entreating me to fly with him; both his

life and his honor were in my hands. Ah, why did
I pause for an instant? Had I consented, he would
still have been alive, and in some far distant country
he and I might have learned that this world has something more to offer than unhappiness and misery.
Yes, as you will have it, you shall have all. I loved
him ere I knew that you even existed. I have only
my own folly to blame, only my own unhappy weakness to deplore. Why did I not steadily refuse to become your wife? You say that you have slain
George. Not so, for in my heart his memory will
ever remain bright and ineffaceable."

"Beware!" said Norbert furiously, "beware if
——"

"Ah, would you kill me, too? Do not fear resistance; my life is a blank without him. He is dead; let
death come to me; it would be a welcome visitant.
The only kindness that you could now bestow upon
me would be my death-blow. Strike then, and end
it all! In death we should be united, George and I;
and as my limbs grew stiff and my breath passed away,
my whitening lips would murmur words of thanks."

Norbert listened to her, overwhelmed by the intensity of her passion, and marvelling that he had any
power to feel after the terrible event which had fallen
upon his devoted head.

Could this be Marie, the soft and gentle woman,
who spoke with such passionate vehemence and boldly
braved his anger? How could he have so misunder-
stood her? He forgot all his anger in his admiration. She seemed to him to have undergone a complete change. There was an unearthly style of beauty
around her—her eyes blazed and shone with the lurid
light of a far-distant planet, while her wealth of raven

hair fell in disordered masses on her shoulders. It
was passion, real passion, that he beheld to-night, not
that mere empty delusion which he had so long followed blindly. Marie was really capable of a deep-
rooted feeling of adoration for the man she loved,
while with Diana de Mussidan, the woman with the
fair hair and the steel-blue eyes, love was but the lust
of conquest, or the desire to jeer at a suitor's earnestness. Ah, what a revelation had been made to him
now! and what would he not have given to have
wiped out the past! He advanced towards her with
outstretched arms.

"Marie!" said he, "Marie!"

"I forbid you to call me Marie!" shrieked she
wildly.

He made no reply, but still advanced towards her,
when, with a terrible cry, she recoiled from him.

"Blood!" she screamed, "ah, heavens! he has blood
upon his hands!"

Norbert glanced downwards; upon the wristband
of his shirt there was a tell-tale crimson stain.

The Duchess raised her hand, and pointed towards
the door.

"Leave me," said she, with an extraordinary assumption of energy, "leave me; the secret of your
crime is safe; I will not betray you or hand you over
to justice. But remember that a murdered man
stands between us, and that I loathe and execrate
you."

Rage and jealousy tortured Norbert's soul. Though
George de Croisenois was no more, he was still his
successful rival in Marie's love.

"You forget," said he in a voice hoarse with passion, "that you are mine, and that, as your husband,

I can make your existence one long scene of agony and misery. Keep this fact in your memory. To-morrow, at six o'clock, I shall be here."

The clock was striking two as he left the house and hastened to the spot where he had left his horse.

The soldier was still pacing backwards and for-wards, leading the Duke's horse.

" My faith! " said the man, as soon as he perceived Norbert, " you pay precious long visits. I had only leave to go to the theatre, and I shall get into trouble over this."

" Pshaw! I promised you twenty francs. Here are two louis."

The soldier pocketed the money with an air of de-lighted surprise, and Norbert sprang into the saddle.

An hour later he gave the appointed signal upon the window pane, behind which the trusty Jean was waiting.

" Take care that no one sees you as you take the horse to the stable," said the Duke hastily, " and then come to me, for I want your assistance and advice."

CHAPTER XVIII.

THE HEIR OF CHAMPDOCE.

As long as she was in Norbert's presence, anger and indignation gave the Duchess de Champdoce strength; but as soon as she was left alone her energy gave way, and with an outburst of tears she sank, half fainting, upon a couch. Her despair was aug-mented from the fact that she felt that had it not been for her, George de Croisenois would never have met with his death.

"Had I not made that fatal appointment," she sobbed, "he would be alive and well now; my love has slain him as surely as if my hand had held the steel that has pierced his heart!"

She at first thought of seeking refuge with her father, but abandoned the idea almost immediately, for she felt that he would refuse to enter into her grievance, or would say, "You are a duchess; you have an enormous fortune. You must be happy; and if you are not, it must be your own fault."

In terrible anguish the night passed away; and when her maids entered the room, they found her lying on the floor, dressed as she had been the night before. No one knew what to do, and messengers were dispatched in all directions to summon medical advice.

Norbert's return was eagerly welcomed by the terrified domestics, and a general feeling of relief pervaded the establishment.

The Duke had grown very uneasy as to what might have happened during his absence. He questioned the servants as diplomatically as he could; and while he was thus engaged, the doctors who had been summoned arrived.

After seeing their patient, they did not for a moment conceal their opinion that the case was a very serious one, and that it was possible that she might not survive this mysterious seizure. They impressed upon Norbert the necessity of the Duchess being kept perfectly quiet and never left alone, and then departed, promising to call again in the afternoon.

Their injunctions were unnecessary, for Norbert had established himself by his wife's bedside, resolved not to quit her until her health was re-established or death had intervened to release her from suffering. Fever had claimed her for its own, and in her delusion she uttered many incoherent ravings, the key to which Norbert alone held, and which filled his soul with dread and terror.

This was the second time that Norbert had been compelled to watch over a sick-bed, guarding within his heart a terrible secret. At Champdoce he had sat by his father's side, who could have revealed the terrible attempt against his life; and now it was his wife that he was keeping a watch on, lest her lips should utter the horrible secret of the death of George de Croisenois.

Compelled to remain by his wife's side, the thoughts of his past life forced themselves upon him, and he shuddered to think that, at the age of twenty-five, he had only to look back upon scenes of misery and crime, which cast a cloud of gloom and horror over the rest of his days. What a terrible future to come after so hideous a past!

He had another source of anxiety, and frequently rang the bell to inquire for Jean.

"Send him to me as soon as he comes," was his order.

At last Jean made his appearance, and his master led him into a deeply-recessed window.

"Well?" asked he.

"All is settled, my lord; be easy."

"And Caroline?"

"Has left. I gave her twenty thousand francs, and saw her into the train myself. She is going to the States, where she hopes to find a cousin who will marry her; at least, that is her intention."

Norbert heaved a deep sigh of relief, for the thought of Caroline Schimmel had laid like a heavy burden upon his heart.

" And how about the other matter? " asked he.

The old man shook his head.

" What has been done? "

" I have got hold of a young fellow who believes that I wish to send him to Egypt, to purchase cotton. He will start to-morrow, and will post the two letters written by the Marquis de Croisenois, one at Marseilles, and the other at Cairo."

" Do you not think that these letters will insure my perfect security? "

" I see that any indiscretion on our agent's part, or a mere act of carelessness, may ruin us."

" And yet it must be done."

After consulting together, the doctors had given some slight hope, but the position of the patient was still very precarious. It was suggested that her intellect might be permanently affected; and during all these long and anxious hours Norbert did not even dare to close his eyes, and it was with feelings of secret terror that he permitted the maids to perform their duties around their invalid mistress.

Upon the fourth day the fever took a favorable turn, and Marie slept, giving Norbert time to review his position.

How was it that Madame de Mussidan, who was a daily visitor, had not appeared at the house since that eventful night? He was so much surprised at this that he ventured to dispatch a short note, acquainting her of the sudden illness of his wife.

In an hour he received a reply, merely containing these words:—

" Can you account for M. de Mussidan's sudden determination to spend the winter in Italy? We leave this evening. Farewell.—D."

And so she, too, had abandoned him, taking with her all the hopes he had in the world. Still, however, his infatuation held its sway over him, and he forced himself to believe that she felt this separation as keenly as he did.

Some five days afterwards, when the Duchess de Champdoce had been pronounced out of immediate danger, one of the doctors took him mysteriously aside. He said that he wanted to inform the Duke of a startling, but he hoped a welcome piece of intelligence—that the Duchess de Champdoce was in the way to present the Duke with an heir to his title and estates.

It was the knowledge of this that had decided her not to leave her husband's roof, and had steeled her heart against George's entreaties. She had hesitated, and had almost yielded to the feelings of her heart, when this thought troubled her.

Unfortunately for herself, she had not disclosed her condition to her husband, and, at the news, all Norbert's former suspicions revived, and his wrath rose once more to an extraordinary height. His lips grew pale, and his eyes blazed with fury.

" Thank you, doctor! " exclaimed he. " Of course, the news is very welcome. Good-by. I must go to the Duchess at once."

Instead of going to his wife, Norbert went and locked himself up in his own private apartment. He had need to be alone, in order to look this fresh complication more fully in the face, and the more he reflected, the more convinced was he that he had been the dupe of a guilty woman. He had begun by doubting, and he ended by being convinced that the child was not his. Was he to accept this degraded position, and rear up as his own the child of George de Croisenois? The child would grow up under his own roof-tree, bear his name, and finally inherit his title and gigantic fortune. "Never," muttered he. "No, never; for sooner than that, I will crush the life out of it with my own hands!"

The more he thought how he should have to deceive the world by feigning love and lavishing caresses upon this interloping child, the more he felt that it would be impossible to perform his task. He had, however, much to do at present. The sudden and mysterious disappearance of George de Croisenois had created much stir and excitement in Paris, and the letter which had been posted by the agent dispatched by Jean, instead of explaining matters, had only deepened the mystery and caused fresh grounds of surprise to arise in the minds of the friends of the Marquis and the police authorities. But the disappearance of the Marquis was only a nine days' wonder after all. Some other strange event excited the attention of the fickle public, and George de Croisenois' name was no longer in every one's mouth.

Norbert breathed freely once more, for he felt his secret was safe.

Diana de Mussidan had now been absent for three months and had not vouchsafed him a single line. A river of blood flowed between him and his wife. Among all his acquaintances he had not one friend on whom he could rely, and his reckless life of debauchery and dissipation began to weary him. His thoughts were always fixed upon this coming child.

How could he ever bear to bring it up as if it were his own? He had thought over many plans, but always trusted to the first one he had conceived. This was to procure an infant, it mattered not where or by what means, and substitute it for the new-born child of his wife. As time rolled on, he became more imbued with this idea, and at length he summoned Jean to him, that faithful old man, who served his master so truly out of affection to the house of Champdoce.

For the first time Jean raised an objection to his master's proposal, declaring that such an act would bring shame and misery upon all concerned in it; but when he found that Norbert was determined, and that, if he refused, his master would employ some less scrupulous agent, he, with tears in his eyes and a tremor in his voice, promised obedience.

About a month later, Jean came to his master and suggested that it would be best the *accouchement* of the Duchess should take place at a château belonging to the Champdoce family near Montroire, and that this once done, he, Jean, would arrange everything. The removal was effected almost at once, and the Duchess, who was a mere shadow of her former self, made no opposition. She and Norbert lived together as perfect strangers. Sometimes a week would elapse without their meeting; and if they had occasion to communicate, it was done by letter.

The estate to which Norbert had conducted the Duchess was admirably adapted for his purpose. The unhappy woman was entirely alone in the world, and had no one to whom she could apply for protection or advice. Her father, the Count de Puymandour, had died suddenly a month before, owing to chagrin caused by his defeat when a candidate for a seat in the Chamber. The brief note from the despairing mother, in which followed the words, " Have mercy! Give me back my child!" hardly describes the terrible events that occurred in the lonely Château to which Norbert had conducted his innocent victim.

The child of the Duchess de Champdoce had been placed by Jean in the Foundling Hospital at Vendôme, while the infant that was baptized with the grandiloquent names of Anne René, Gontran de Duepair, Marquis de Champdoce, was the bastard child of a girl living near Montroire, who was known in the neighborhood as " The Witch."

CHAPTER XIX.

MASCARIN SPEAKS.

THIS was the conclusion of the manuscript handed by Mascarin to Paul Violaine, and the young man laid down the roll of paper with the remark, " And that is all."

He had consumed six hours in reading this sad account of the follies and crimes of the owners of illustrious names.

Mascarin had listened with the complacency of an author who hears his own work read aloud to him, but all the while he was keenly watching him beneath his spectacles and the faces of his companions. The effect that was produced was immense, and exactly what he had anticipated. Paul, Hortebise, and Catenac gazed upon each other with faces in which astonishment at the strange recital, and then at the power of the man who had collected these facts together, were mingled, and Catenac was the first who spoke. The sound of his own voice seemed gradually to dispel the vague sense of apprehension that hung about the office.

"Aha!" cried he, "I always said that our old friend Mascarin would make his mark in literature. As soon as his pen touches the paper the business man vanishes; we have no longer a collection of dry facts and proofs, but the stirring pages of a sensational novel."

"Do you really consider that as a mere romance?" asked Hortebise.

"It reads like one certainly; you must allow that."

"Catenac," remarked Mascarin in his bitterly sarcastic tone, "is best able to pronounce upon the truth or falsehood of this narrative, as he is the professional adviser of this same Duke de Champdoce, the very Norbert whose life has just been read to you."

"I do not deny that there is some slight foundation to it," returned the lawyer.

"Then what is it that you do deny?"

"Nothing, nothing; I merely objected, more in jest than otherwise, to the sentimental manner in which you have set forward your case."

"Catenac," remarked Mascarin, addressing the others, "has received many confidential communications from his noble client, which he has not thought fit to communicate to us; and though he fancied that we were drifting into quicksands and among breakers, he displayed no signal of warning to save us from our danger, hoping, like a true friend, that, by this means, he might get rid of us."

Catenac began to utter protestations and denials, but Mascarin cut him short with an imperative gesture, and, after a long pause, he again commenced,—

"You must understand that my inquisitors have had but little to do in this affair, for my work has chiefly consisted in putting fragments together. It is not to me that you are indebted for the sensational (I think that that was the term used) part of my story, but rather to Madame de Mussidan and Norbert de Champdoce. I am sure that some of the phrases must have struck you considerably."

"It seems to me," objected Catenac——

"Perhaps," broke in Mascarin, "you have forgotten the correspondence which the Countess de Mussidan preserved so carefully—both his letters and her own, which Norbert returned to her."

"And have we those?"

"Of course we have, only there is a perfect romance contained in these letters. What I have read is a mere bald extract from them; and this is not all. The man who assisted me in the unravelling of this dark intrigue was the original promoter—Daumon."

"What, is the Counsellor still alive?"

"Certainly, and you know him. He is not quite in his first youth, and has aged somewhat, but his intellect is as brilliant as ever."

Catenac grew serious. "You tell me a great deal," said he.

"I can tell you even more. I can tell you that the account of the deed was written under the dictation of Caroline Schimmel," broke in Mascarin. "This unlucky woman started for Havre, intending to sail for the United States, but she got no further than that seaport town, for the good looks and the persuasive tongue of a sailor induced her to alter her plans. As long as her money lasted he remained an ardent lover, but vanished with the disappearance of her last thousand-franc note. Starving and poverty-stricken, Caroline returned to Paris and to the Duke de Champdoce, who accepted her constant demands for money as a penitent expiation of his crime. But she remained faithful to her oath; and had it not been for her terrible propensity for drink, Tantaine would never have succeeded in extracting her secret from her. If, on her recovery from her fit of drink coma, she recollects what has taken place, she will, if I read her character right, go straight to the Duke de Champdoce and tell him that his secret has passed into better hands."

At this idea being promulgated, Catenac started from his chair with a loud oath.

"Did you think," asked Mascarin, "that I should feel so much at my ease if I found that there was the slightest risk? Let us consider what it is that Caroline can say. Who is it that she can accuse of having stolen her secret from her? Why, only a poor old wretch named Tantaine. How can the Duke possibly trace any connection between this miserable writer and Catenac?"

"Yes, I think that it would be a difficult task."

"Besides," pursued Mascarin, "what have we to fear from the Duke de Champdoce? Nothing, as far as I can see. Is he not as much in our power as the woman he formerly loved—Diana de Mussidan? Do we not hold the letters of both of them, and do we not know in what corner of his garden to dig to discover a damning piece of evidence? Remember that there will be no difficulty in identifying the skeleton, for at the time of his disappearance, Croisenois had about him several Spanish doubloons, a fact which was given to the police."

"Well," said Catenac, "I will act faithfully. Tell me your plans, and I will let you know all that I hear from the Duke."

For a moment a smile hovered upon Mascarin's lips, for this time he placed firm reliance upon the good faith of the lawyer.

"Before we go further," said he, "let me conclude this narrative which Paul has just read. It is sad and simple. The united ages of the Duke and Duchess did not exceed fifty years; they had unlimited wealth, and bore one of the grandest historic names of France; they were surrounded with every appliance of luxury, and yet their lives were a perfect wreck. They simply dragged on an existence and had lost all hopes of happiness, but they made up their minds to conceal the skeleton of their house in the darkest cupboard, and the world knew nothing of their inner life. The Duchess suffered much in health, and merely went out to visit the sick and poor. The Duke worked hard to make up for the deficiencies of his early education, and made a name and reputation throughout Europe."

"And how about Madame de Mussidan?" asked Catenac.

"I am coming to that," returned Mascarin. "With that strange determination that fills the hearts of our women, she did not consider her revenge complete until Norbert learned that she was the sole instrument in heaping the crowning sorrow of his life on his head; and on her return from Italy, she sent for him and told him everything. Yes, she absolutely had the audacity to tell him that it was she who had done her best to throw his wife into De Croisenois' arms. She told him that it was she who had worked the arrangements for the meeting, and had written the anonymous letter."

"Why did he not kill her?" cried Hortebise. "Had she not all his letters, and taunted him with the production of them? Ah, my dear friends, do not let us flatter ourselves that we have the sole monopoly of blackmailing. This high-born Countess plunged her hand into the Duke's coffers just as if she had been a mere adventuress. It is only ten days ago that she borrowed—you will observe the entry of it as a loan—a large sum to settle an account of Van Klopen's. But let us now speak of the child who took the place of the boy whom the Duchess brought into the world. You know him, doctor?"

"Yes, I have often seen him. He was a good-looking young fellow."

"He was, but he was a degraded scoundrel, after all. He was educated and brought up without regard to expense, but he always displayed low tastes, and, had he lived, would have brought discredit on the name he bore. He was a thorn in the side of the Duke and Duchess, and I believe that they felt great relief when he died of brain fever, brought on by a drunken debauch. His parents, or those whom he supposed to be such, were present at his death-bed, for they had learned to consider their sorrows as the just chastisement of heaven. The boy having died, the family of Champdoce seemed likely to become extinct, and then it was that Norbert decided to do what his wife had long urged upon him, to seek for and reclaim the child which he had caused to be placed in the Foundling Hospital at Vendôme. It went against his pride to

diverge from the course he had determined on as best,
but doubts had arisen in his mind as to his wife's
guilt, and Diana's confessions had reassured him as
to the paternity of the missing boy. It was thus with
hope in his heart, and furnished with every necessary
document, that he started for Vendôme; but there a
terrible disappointment awaited him. The authorities
of the hospital, on consulting the register, found
that a child had been admitted on the day and hour
mentioned by Norbert, and that his description of the
infant's clothing tallied exactly with the entries. But
the child was no longer in the hospital, and there was
no clue to his whereabouts. He had, at the age of
twelve, been apprenticed to a tanner, but he had run
away from his master, and the most active and ener-
getic search had failed to arrest the fugitive."

Catenac listened to all these exact details with an
unpleasant feeling gnawing at his heart, for he saw
that his associates knew everything, and he had relied
upon again securing their confidence by furnishing
them with those details which were evidently already
known to them. Mascarin, however, affected not to
notice his surprise, and went on with his narrative.

" This terrible disappointment will certainly kill the
Duke de Champdoce. It seemed to him that after
having so bitterly expiated the crimes and follies of
his youth, he might hope to have his old age in peace
and quiet, with a son who might cheer the loneliness
of his desolate fireside. His countenance, as soon as
he appeared before the Duchess, who had been expecting his return in an agony of anguish and suspense, told her at once that all hope had fled. In a
few days, however, the Duke had perfectly recovered
from the shock, and had decided that to give up the

search would be an act of madness. The world is
wide, and a friendless boy, without a name, difficult
to trace; but, with ample funds, almost anything can
be done, and he was willing to sacrifice both life and
fortune to attain his object. So immense were his re-
sources, that it was easy for him to employ the most
skilful detectives; and whatever the result might be,
he had come to look upon this task as a sacred duty
to which he ought to devote all the remaining years
of his life. He swore that he would never rest or
cease from his search until he had been furnished with
the indisputable proofs of the existence or the death
of his son. He did not confide all this project to the
Duchess; for he feared—and he had by this time
learned to have some consideration for her enfeebled
frame—her health had given way so completely that
any extra degree of excitement might prove fatal to
her. He, therefore, as a preliminary, applied to that
element which in the Rue de Jérusalem acts as the
terrestrial guardians of society. But the police could
do nothing for the Duke. They heard what he had
to say gravely, took notes, told him to call again later
on, and there was an end to their proceedings. It
can easily be understood that the rank and position of
the Duke prevented him from making his name known
in his inquiries; and as he dared not divulge the whole
truth, he gave such a bald version of the case, that
it excited no deep feelings of interest. At last he was
sent to a certain M. Lecoq."

To Paul's utter astonishment, the name produced a
sudden and terrible effect upon Doctor Hortebise, who
started to his feet as if propelled from his chair by
the unexpected application of some hidden motive
power, and, fingering the locket that hung from his

chain, gazed round upon his associates with wild and excited eyes.

"Stop!" cried he. "If that fellow Lecoq is to put his nose into your case, I withdraw; I will have nothing to do with it, for it is certain to be a failure."

He appeared to be so thoroughly frightened, that Catenac condescended to smile.

"Yes, yes," said he, "I can understand your alarm; but be at ease; Lecoq has nothing to do with us."

But Hortebise was not satisfied with Catenac's assurance, and looked for confirmation from Mascarin.

"Lecoq has nothing to do with us," repeated his friend. "The fool said that his position prevented him from giving his time to any investigation of a private nature, which, by the way, is quite true. The Duke offered him a heavy sum to throw up his appointment, but he refused, saying he did not work for money, but from love for his profession."

"Which is quite true," interrupted Catenac.

"However," continued Mascarin, "to cut short my narrative, the Duke, on the refusal of Lecoq to act, applied to Catenac."

"Yes," answered the lawyer, "and the Duke has placed the conduct of the search in my hands."

"Have you formed any plan of action?"

"Not at present. The Duke said, 'Ask every living soul in the world, if you can succeed in no other way'; this is all the instruction he has given me; and," added he, with a slight shrug of his shoulders, "I am almost of Perpignan's opinion, that the search will be a fruitless one."

"Lecoq did not think so."

"He only said that he believed he should succeed if he were to take it in hand."

"Well," answered Mascarin coldly, "I have been certain of success from the very commencement."

"Have you been to Vendôme?" asked Catenac.

"Never mind, I have been somewhere, and at this very moment could place my hand upon the shoulder of the heir to the dukedom of Champdoce."

"Are you in earnest?"

"I was never more in earnest in my life. I have found him; only as it is impossible for me to appear in the matter, I shall delegate to you and Perpignan the happiness of restoring the lost son to his father's arms."

Catenac glanced from Mascarin to Hortebise, and from them to Paul, and seemed to wish to be certain that he was not being made an object of ridicule.

"And why do you not wish to appear in the matter?" asked he at last, in a suspicious tone of voice. "Do you foresee some risk, and want me to bear the brunt?"

Mascarin shrugged his shoulders.

"First," said he, "I am not a traitor, as you know well enough; and then the interests of all of us depend on your safety. Can one of us be compromised without endangering his associates? You know that this is impossible. All you have to do is to point out where the traces commence; others will follow them at their own risk, and all you will have to do will be to look calmly on."

"But——"

Mascarin lost his patience, and with a deep frown, replied,—

"That is enough. We require no more argument. I am the master, and it is for you to obey."

When Mascarin adopted this tone, resistance was

out of the question; and as he invariably made all yield to him, it was best to obey with a good grace, and Catenac relapsed into silence, completely subjugated and very much puzzled.

"Sit down at my desk," continued Mascarin, "and take careful notes of what I now say. Success is, as I have told you, inevitable, but I must be ably backed. All now depends upon your exactitude in obeying my orders; one false step may ruin us all. You have heard this, and cannot say that you are not fully warned."

CHAPTER XX.

A SUDDEN CHECK.

CATENAC seated himself at the writing-table without a word, concealing his anger and jealousy beneath a careless smile. Mascarin was no longer the plotter consulting with his confederates; he was the master issuing his orders to his subordinates. He had now taken from a box some of those square pieces of pasteboard, which he spent his time in reading over.

"Try and not miss one word of what I am saying," remarked he, bending his keen glance upon Paul; then, turning to Catenac, he continued, "Can you persuade the Duke de Champdoce and Perpignan to start for Vendôme on Saturday?"

"Perhaps I may be able to do so."

"I want a Yes or No. Can you or can you not make these people go there?"

"Well, yes, then."

"Very well. Then, on going to Vendôme, you will stop at the Hotel de Porte."

"Hotel de Porte," repeated Catenac, as he made a note of the name.

"Upon the day of your arrival at Vendôme," continued Mascarin, "you could do very little. Your time would be taken up in resting after your journey, and perhaps you may make a few preliminary inquiries. It will be on Sunday that you will go to the hospital together, and make the same inquiries which the Duke formerly made by himself. The lady superior is a woman of excellent taste and education, and she will do all that she can to be useful to you. Through her you will be able to obtain the boy's description, and the date on which he left the hospital to be apprenticed to a tanner. She will tell you that, disliking the employment, he ran away from them at the age of twelve and a half years, and that since then no trace of him has been found. You will hear from her that he was a tall, well-built lad, looking two years older than he really was, with an intelligent cast of features, and keen, bright eyes, full of health and good looks. He had on, on the day of his disappearance, blue and white striped trousers, a gray blouse, a cap with no peak, and a spotted silk cravat. Then, to assist you still further in your researches she will add that he carried in a bundle, enveloped in a red plaid cotton handkerchief, a white blouse, a pair of gray cloth trousers, and a pair of new shoes."

Catenac watched Mascarin as he was speaking with an expression of ill-concealed enmity.

"You are well informed, on my word," muttered he.

"I think I am," returned Mascarin. "After this you will go back to the hotel, and not until then—do you understand?—and you will consult as to the first steps to be taken. The plan proposed by Perpignan is an excellent one."

" What! you know it then?"

" Of course I do. He proposed to divide Vendôme and its suburbs into a certain number of circles, and to make a house-to-house visitation in each of them. Let him go to work in this manner. Of course, to do so, you will require a guide."

" Of course we should require such a person."

" Here, Catenac, I must leave a little to chance, for I am not quite omnipotent. But there are nine chances out of ten that your host will advise you to avail yourself of the services of a man called Fréjot, who acts as commissioner to the hotel. It may be, however, that he may designate some one else; but in that case you must, by some means or other, manage to employ the services of one other man."

" What am I to say to him?"

" He understands what he is to do completely. Well, these preliminaries being settled, you will commence on Monday morning to search the suburb called Areines, under the guidance of Fréjot. Leave all responsibility to Perpignan, but make sure that the Duke comes with you. Ask the denizens a series of questions which you have prepared beforehand, such as ' My friends, we are in search of a boy. A reward of ten thousand francs is offered to any one who will put us on his track. He must have left these parts in August, 1856, and some of you may have seen him.' "

Here Catenac stopped Mascarin.

" Wait a moment. Your own words are excellent; I will write them down."

" All Monday," continued Mascarin, " you will not make much progress, and for the next few days it will be the same, but on Saturday prepare yourself for a great surprise; for on that day Fréjot will take you to a large, lonely farmhouse, on the shores of a lake. This farm is held by a man named Lorgelin, who cultivates it with the assistance of his wife and his two sons. You will find these worthy people at dinner. They will offer you some refreshment, and you will accept. At the next word you utter you will find that they will glance at each other in a meaning manner, and the wife will exclaim, ' Blessed Virgin! surely the gentleman is speaking of the poor lad we have so often talked about.' "

As Mascarin went on describing his arrangements, his whole form seemed to dilate, and his face shone with the knowledge of mastery and power. His voice was so clear and his manner so full of authority and command, that it carried conviction to the minds of all those who were seated listening to him. He spoke of what would happen as if he was dealing with an absolute certainty, and went on with such wonderful lucidity and force of reasoning that they seemed to be absolutely real.

" Oh! the farmer's wife will say this, will she?" demanded Catenac, in a tone of the utmost surprise.

" Yes, this, and nothing more. Then the husband will explain that they found the poor lad half dead in a ditch by the side of the road, and that they took him home, and did what they could for him; and will add, this was in the beginning of September, 1856. You will offer to read him your description of the lad, but he will volunteer his own, which you will find exactly to tally with the one you have. Then Lorgelin

will tell you what an excellent lad he was, and how
the farm seemed quite another place as long as he remained there. All the family will join in singing his
praises—he was so good-tempered, so obliging, and at
thirteen he could write like a lawyer's clerk. And
then they will produce some of his writing in an old
copy book. But after all the old woman, with a tear
in her eye, will say that she found the lad had not
much gratitude in his composition, for at the end of
the following September he left the farm where he had
received so much kindness. Yes, he left them to go
away with some strolling performers. You will be
absolutely affected by the words of these worthy people, and before you leave they will show you the
clothes the lad left behind him."

Catenac was waiting for the conclusion, and then
exclaimed, in rather a disappointed tone,—

"But I do not see what we have gained when
Lorgelin's story has been repeated to us."

Mascarin raised his hand, as though to deprecate immediate criticism, and to ask for further patience on
the part of his audience.

"Permit me to go on," said he. "You would now
not know what to do, but Perpignan will not hesitate
for a moment. He will tell you that he holds the end
of the clue, and that all that remains to be done is to
follow it up carefully."

"I think you overrate Perpignan's talents."

"Not a bit; each man to his own line of business.
Besides, if he wanders off the course, you must get him
back to it. In this you must act diplomatically. His
first move will naturally be to take you to the office of
the mayor of the township, where a register of licenses
is kept. There you will find that in September, 1857,

there passed through the place a troop of travelling performers, consisting of nine persons, with the caravans, under the management of a man known as Vigoureux, nicknamed the Grasshopper."

Catenac rapidly jotted down these items. "Not so fast," said he; "I cannot follow you."

After a short pause, Mascarin continued.

"An attentive examination of the book will prove to you that no other troupe of itinerant performers passed through the place during that month; and it is clear that it must have been the Grasshopper with whom the lad went away. You will then peruse the man's description. Vigoureux, born at Bourgogne, Vosges. Age, forty-seven. Height, six feet two inches. Eyes, small and gray, rather near-sighted. Complexion dark. Third finger of left hand cut off at first joint. If you confound him, after reading this, with any other man of his profession, you must certainly be rather foolish."

"I shall now be able to find him," muttered Catenac.

"But that is Perpignan's business. You will see him put on an air of the greatest importance, and appear quite overjoyed at the news he has obtained at the office of the mayor. He will say that the inquiry at Vendôme is over, and that it will be best to return to Paris at once. Of course, you will make no objection. You will permit the Duke to make a handsome present to Lorgelin and Fréjot; but take care not to leave him behind you. I advise you to regain Paris without a moment's delay. The wily Perpignan, on your return, will at once take you to the head police office, where Vigoureux will have left his papers, like other men of his profession. If there is any difficulty in obtaining a sight of them, the Duke de Champdoce will act as a talisman. You will then discover that in

'1864, the man Vigoureux was sentenced to a term of imprisonment for disorderly conduct, and that he now keeps a wine-shop at the corner of the Rue Depleux."

"Stop a bit," said Catenac, "and let me take down the address."

"When you go there, you will recognize Vigoureux by the loss of his finger. He will at once admit that the lad followed him, and remained in the troupe for ten months. He was a good enough lad, but as grand as a peacock, and as lazy as a dormouse. He made great friends with an old Alsatian, called Fritz, who was the conductor of the orchestra, and by-and-by both were so fond of each other, that one day they went off in each other's company. Now you want to know what has become of Fritz? I know Vigoureux will get tired of this prolonged string of questions, and behave violently; then you will threaten him for having carried off a youth of tender years, and he will calm down, and become as mild as mother's milk, and will promise to gain information for you. In a week he will give the information that Fritz is to be found at the Hospital Magloire."

Absolutely dumb with surprise, the audience listened to these strange assertions, which dovetailed so exactly into each other, and seemed to have been the work of years of research.

"Fritz," continued Mascarin, "is a sly old dog. You will find an old, rickety, blue-eyed man at the hospital, and remember to tell the Duke de Champdoce that he must not put too much faith in him. This wily old Alsatian will tell you of all the sacrifices he made for the dear lad. He will tell you that he often went without his beer and tobacco in order to pay for the music lessons that he forced the boy to take. He will tell you that he wanted to get him into the Government School of Music, for that he possessed great vocal and instrumental talent, and he cherished the hope of one day seeing him a great composer, like Weber or Mozart. I expect that this flow of self-praise will melt the heart of your client, for he will see that his son had made an effort to rise out of the mire by his own exertions, and will, in this energy, recognize one of the characteristics of the Champdoce family; and on the strength of this testimony he will almost be ready to accept the young man as his son."

Catenac had for some time past been striving to decipher the meaning hidden behind the inscrutable countenance of Mascarin, but in vain.

"Let us get on," said the lawyer impatiently. "All that you have told me I shall hear later on in the course of the inquiry."

"If your sagacity requires no further explanation from me," rejoined Mascarin, "you will, I trust, permit me to continue them for the benefit of our young friend, Paul Violaine. You will feel compassion when the Alsatian tells you of his sufferings, at the boys' description of him, and his subsequent prosperity in the Rue d'Arras. You had better listen to the old man as long as he continues to grumble on, the more so as you will detect in the rancor and bitterness of his remarks all the vexation of a disappointed speculator. He will confess to you besides that he subsists entirely on the bounty of the lad, whom he had stigmatized as an ungrateful villain. Of course, the Duke will have to leave behind him some testimonial of his pleasure, and you will hurry off to the Rue d'Arras. The proprietor of the house will tell you that some four years ago he got rid of this musician, the only one of his class who had dared to establish himself there, and a small present and a few adroit questions will obtain for you the address of one of the young man's pupils, Madame Grandorge, a widow lady, residing in the Rue St. Louis. This lady will tell you that she does not know the address of her former master, but that he used to live at 57, Rue de la Harpe. From the Rue de la Harpe you will be sent to the Rue Jacob, and from thence to the Rue Montmartre, at the corner of the Rue Joquelet."

Mascarin paused, drew a long breath, and chuckled inwardly, as though at some excellent joke.

"Be comforted, Catenac," said he. "You have nearly reached the end of your journey. The portress at the house in the Rue Montmartre is the most obliging woman in the world. She will tell you that the musician still retains his rooms in the house, but that he resides there no longer, for he has made a lucky hit, and last month he married the daughter of a wealthy banker living close by. The young lady, Mademoiselle Rigal, saw him, and fell in love with him."

A clever man like Catenac should have foreseen what was coming, but he had not, and at this conclusion he uttered a loud exclamation of surprise.

"Yes, just so," said Mascarin, with an air of bland triumph. "The Duke de Champdoce will then drag you off to our mutual friend Martin Rigal, and there you will find our young *protégé*, the happy husband of the beautiful Flavia."

Mascarin drew himself up, and adjusted his glasses firmly on his nose.

"Now, my dear Catenac, show the liberality and amiability of your disposition by congratulating our friend Paul as Gontran, Marquis de Champdoce."

Hortebise, of course, knew what was coming; he knew the lines of the plot of the play as if he had been a joint author of it, and was as much excited as if he were assisting at a first rehearsal.

" Bravo! " he exclaimed, clapping his hands together. " Bravo, my dear Mascarin, you have excelled yourself to-day! "

Worried and perplexed as Paul had been, as Mascarin concluded he sank back in his chair, sick and giddy with emotion.

" Yes," said Mascarin in a clear and ringing voice, " I accept your praise without any affectation of false modesty. We have no reason to fear the intervention of that grain of sand which sometimes stops the working of the machine. Perpignan, poor fool though he is, will be our best friend, and will do our work quite unconsciously. Can the Duke retain any atom of suspicion after these minute investigations? Impossible. But to remove the slightest element of doubt, I have another and an additional plan. I will make him retrace the path upon which he has started. He shall take Paul to all these various places, and at all of them the statements will be even more fully confirmed. Paul, the son-in-law of Martin Rigal, the husband of Flavia, will be recognized in the Rue Montmartre, the Rue Jacob, and the Rue de la Harpe. He will be joyfully welcomed in the Rue d'Arras; Fritz will embrace his ungrateful pupil; Vigoureux will remind him of his skillful feats on the trapeze; the Lorgelin family will press the lad whom they gave shelter to, to their hearts, and this will happen, Catenac, because I will it, and because all the people from the portress in the Rue Montmartre to the Lorgelins are my slaves, and dare not disobey one single command which I may issue."

Catenac rose slowly and solemnly from his seat.

" I recognize your patience and ingenuity thoroughly, only I am going with one word to crush the fabric of hope that you have so carefully erected."

Catenac might be a coward, he might also be a traitor, but he was a clever and clear-sighted man too. Consequently Hortebise shivered as he heard these words, but Mascarin smiled disdainfully, basking in his dream of success.

" Go on then," said he.

" Well, then, let me tell you that you will not overreach and deceive the Duke."

" And why not, pray?" asked Mascarin. " But are you sure that I wish to deceive him? You have not been open with me, why should I be frank with you? Am I in the habit of confiding in those who do not repose confidence in me? Does Perpignan for a moment suspect the part that he is to play? Why may I not have judged it best to keep from you the fact that Paul is really the child you are seeking?"

Mascarin spoke so confidently that Catenac gazed upon him, hardly knowing to what conclusion to come, for his conscience was by no means clear. His intellect quickly dived into the depths of all probabilities, and yet he could not see in all these combinations any possible peril to himself.

" I only hope," said he, " that Paul is all that you represent him to be; but why all these precautions? Only, mark my words, the Duke has an infallible way of detecting, or rather of preventing, any attempt at imposition. It is ever thus, the most trivial circumstance will overset the best laid plans, and the inevitable destroy the combinations of the most astute intellect."

Mascarin interrupted his associate.

"Paul is the son of the Duke de Champdoce," said he decisively.

What was the meaning of this? Catenac felt that he was being played with, and grew angry.

"As you please; but you will, I presume, permit me to convince myself of the truth of this assertion."

Then, advancing towards Paul, the lawyer said,—

"Have the goodness to remove your coat."

Paul took it off, and threw it upon the back of a chair.

"Now," added Catenac, "roll up your right shirt sleeve to the shoulder."

Scarcely had the young man obeyed, and the lawyer cast a rapid glance at the bare flesh, than he turned to his associates and observed,—

"No, he is not the right man."

To his extreme surprise, Mascarin and Hortebise burst into a fit of unrestrained laughter.

"No," pursued the lawyer, "this is not the child who was sent to the Hospital of Vendôme, and the Duke will recognize this better than I can. You laugh, but it is because you do not know all."

"Enough," returned Mascarin, and then, turning to the doctor, he remarked, "Tell him, my friends, that we know more than he thinks."

"And so," said Hortebise, taking Paul's hand, "you are certain that this is not the lost child because he has not certain marks about him; but these will be seen upon the day on which Paul is introduced to the Duke, and legibly enough to satisfy the most unbelieving."

"What do you mean?"

"Let me explain in my own way. If in early childhood Paul had been scalded on his shoulder by boiling water, he would have a scar whose appearance would denote its origin?"

Catenac nodded. "You are quite accurate," said he.

"Well, then, listen. Paul is coming home with me. I shall take him into my consulting-room; he will lie on a couch. I shall give him chloroform, for I do not wish him to suffer any pain. Mascarin will help me. Then I shall apply, on the proper part, a piece of flannel steeped in a certain liquid which is an invention of my own. I am not a fool, as you may have discovered before this; and in a drawer at home is a piece of flannel cut so as exactly to resemble the irregular outline of a scar of the kind you describe, and a few little bits here and there will do the rest of the work artistically. When the liquid has effected its work, which will be in ten minutes, I shall remove it, and apply an ointment, another invention of my own, to the wound; then I shall restore Paul to his senses, and go to dinner."

Mascarin rubbed his hands with delight.

"But you forget that a certain space of time is required to give a scar the appearance of not having been recent," objected Catenac.

"Let me speak," broke in the doctor. "If we only needed time—six months, say, or a year—we should postpone our concluding act until then; but I, Hortebise, assure you that in two months, thanks to another discovery of my own—will show you a scar that will pass muster, not perhaps before a fellow-practitioner, but certainly before the Duke."

Catenac's sunken eyes blazed as he thought of the prospective millions.

"May the devil fly away with all scruples!" cried he. "My friends, I am yours soul and body; you may rely on your devoted Catenac."

The doctor and Mascarin exchanged a look of triumph.

"Of course we share and share alike," observed the lawyer. "It is true that I come in rather late; but the part I play is a delicate and an important one, and you can do nothing without me."

"You shall have your share," answered Mascarin evasively.

"One word more," said the lawyer. "Do you think that the Duke has kept nothing back? The infant was hardly seen by him or the Duchess; but Jean saw it, and he, though very old and infirm, would come forward at any moment to defend the name and honor of the Champdoce family."

"Well, and what then?"

"Jean, you know, was against the substitution of another child. May he not have foreseen the chance of such a case as this arising?"

Mascarin looked grave. "I have thought of that before," returned he; "but what can be done?"

"I will find out," said Catenac. "Jean has the most implicit confidence in me, and I will question him."

The cold calmness of the lawyer had vanished, and Catenac only displayed the zealous eagerness of the man who, admitted at a late hour into an enterprise which he imagines will be lucrative, burns to do as much as he can to further it.

"But," added he, as an after-thought, "how can we be certain that there is no one to recognize Paul?"

"I can answer for that; his poverty had isolated him from all but a woman named Rose, and I took care that she should be sent to the prison of St. Lazare. At one time I was a little anxious, as I heard that Paul had a patron; but he, as I have found out, was the Count de Mussidan, the murderer of Montlouis, who, as you may have guessed, was Paul's father."

"We have nothing, then, to fear from that quarter," said the doctor.

"Nothing; and while you get on with your work, I will hurry on Paul's marriage with Rigal's daughter. But this will not prevent my busying myself in another quarter; for before a month Henri de Croisenois will have floated his Company, and become the husband of Sabine de Mussidan."

"I think that it is about time for dinner," remarked Hortebise, and, turning to the *protégé* of the association, he added, "Come, Paul."

But Paul made no movement, and then for the first time it was seen that the poor boy had fainted, and they had to sprinkle cold water upon him before he regained consciousness.

"Surely," remarked the doctor, "it is not the idea of a trifling operation that you will not feel which has so frightened you?"

Paul shook his head. "It is not that," said he.

"What, then, is it?"

"Simply that the real man exists; I know him, and know where he lives."

"What do you mean?" they cried.

"I know him, I tell you—the son of the Duke de Champdoce."

"Let us hear all!" cried Mascarin, who was the first to come to his senses. "Explain yourself."

"Simply this. I know such a young man, and it was the thought of this that made me feel so ill. He is thirty-three. He was at the Foundling Hospital;

he left it at the age of twelve and a half years; and he has just such a scald on his shoulder, which he got when he was apprenticed to a tanner."

"And where," asked Mascarin quickly, "is this same young man? What is his name, and what does he do for a living?"

"He is a painter; his name is André, and he lives——"

A blasphemous oath from Mascarin interrupted him. "This is the third time," said he fiercely, "that this cursed fellow has crossed our path; but I swear that it shall be the last."

Hortebise and Catenac were livid with alarm.

"What do you intend to do?" asked they.

"I shall do nothing," answered he; "but you know that this André, in addition to being a painter, is an ornamental sculptor and house decorator, and so is often on lofty scaffolds. Have you never heard that accidents frequently happen to that class of people?"

CHAPTER XXI.

A MELANCHOLY MASHER.

WHEN Mascarin spoke of suppressing the man who stood in his way as easily as if he was alluding to extinguishing a candle, he was not aware that there was one circumstance which considerably enhanced the difficulty of his task, for André had been fore-warned, and this note of warning had been sounded on the day on which he had received that letter from

Sabine, in which she spoke in such despairing terms
of her approaching marriage, which she had been
compelled to agree to to save the honor of her family. This feeling was strengthened by a long conversation he had had with M. de Breulh-Faverlay and the
Viscountess de Bois Arden, in which it was unani-
mously decided that the Count and Countess de Mussidan were victims of some plot of which Henri de
Croisenois was certainly one of the promoters. He
had no conception on what side to look for the danger,
but he had an instinctive feeling that it was impending. He prepared, therefore, to act on the defensive.
It was not only his life that was in danger, but his love
and his future happiness. M. de Breulh-Faverlay had
also serious apprehensions for the safety of a man for
whom he entertained so great a respect and regard.

" I would lay a heavy wager," said he, " that we
have to do with some villainous blackmailers, and the
difficulty of the business is, that we must do the work
ourselves, for we dare not invite the aid of the police.
We have no proof to offer, and the police will not stir
a foot on mere suppositions, and we should not earn
the thanks of those we are desirous of assisting if
we called the attention of the law to certain acts in
their past lives; for who can say what the terrible
secret is, that some vile wretch holds over the heads
of M. and Madame de Mussidan? and it is quite on
the cards that the Count and the Countess might be
compelled to join the blackmailers and oppose us.
We must act with the greatest prudence and caution.
Remember, that if you are out at night, you must avoid
dark corners, for it would be the easiest thing in the
world to put a knife into your back."

The conclusion that was arrived at, at this interview, was that for the present André and De Breulh should cease to see each other so frequently. They felt convinced that a watch had been set on them, and that their intimacy would certainly be notified to De Croisenois; and of course they had every desire to cause him to imagine that they were not acting in any way together. The arrangement, therefore, that they entered into was that each should act from his own point of vantage against Henri de Croisenois, and that when necessary they should meet in the evening to compare notes in a small *café* in the Champs Elysées, not far from the house in which André was at work.

His courage was still as high as ever, but the first symptoms of rashness had vanished. He was a born diplomatist, and fully realized that cunning and treachery must be met by similar weapons. He must not break his engagement to M. Gandelu; but how could he superintend the workmen and keep an eye on Croisenois at the same time? Money was absolutely necessary, and yet he felt a strange disinclination to accept a loan from M. de Breulh. If he were to throw up his work, it would naturally create suspicion.

M. Gandelu had a shrewd head, and André, remembering the old man's kindness to him on all occasions, determined to confide the matter to him, and with this object he called on him the next morning as the clock was striking nine. His surprise was extreme when he saw Gaston de Gandelu in the courtyard. He was just the same looking Gaston, the lover of Madame de Chantemille, to the outward eye, but some grave calamity had evidently entirely changed the inner man. He was smoking his cigar with an air of desperation, and seemed to be utterly weary of the world and its belongings.

At the moment André entered the young man caught sight of him.

"Halloo!" said he; "here is my artistic friend. I lay ten to one that you have come to ask my father to do you a favor."

"You are quite right; is he at home?"

"The governor is in the sulks; he has shut himself up, and will not see me."

"You are joking."

"Not I; the old man is a regular despot, and I am sick of everything."

Noticing that one of the grooms was listening, Gaston had sufficient sense to draw André a little on one side.

"Do you know," asked he, "that the governor has docked my screw and vows that he will advertise himself as not responsible for the debts of yours truly; but I cannot think he will do so, for that would be a regular smash-up for me. You haven't such a trifle as ten thousand francs about you that you could lend me, have you? I'd give twenty thousand for the accommodation when I came of age."

"I must say——," began André.

"All right; never mind; I understand. If you had the ready, you wouldn't be hanging about here; but for all that, I must have the cash. Hang it all, I signed bills to that amount payable to Verminet. Do you know the fellow?"

"Not at all."

"Where were you dragged up? Why, he is the head of the Mutual Loan Society. The only nuisance is, that to make matters run a bit smooth, I wrote down the wrong name. Do you tumble, eh?"

"But, great heavens! that is forgery," said André, aghast.

"Not a bit, for I always intended to pay; besides, I wanted the money to square Van Klopen. You know *him*, I suppose?"

"No."

"Well, he is the chap to dress a girl. I had those costumes for Zora from him; but it is out and out the governor's fault. Why did he drive me to desperation? Yes, it is all the old man's doing. He wasn't satisfied with pitching into me, but he collared that poor, helpless lamb and shut her up. She never did him any harm, and I call it a right down cowardly and despicable act to hurt Zora."

"Zora," repeated André, who did not recognize the name.

"Yes, Zora; you know; you had a feed with us one day."

"Yes, yes; you mean Rose."

"That's it; but I don't like any one to call her by that ugly, common name. Well, the governor has gone mad about her, and filed a complaint against her of decoying a minor, as if I was a fellow any one could decoy. Well, the end of it was, that she is now in the prison of St. Lazare."

The tears started to the young man's eyes as he related his grievance.

"Poor Zora," he added; "I was never mashed on a woman like I was on her. And then what a splendid form she was! Why, the hairdresser said he had never seen such hair in his life; and she is at St.

Lazare. As soon as the police came for her, her first thoughts were of me, and she shrieked out, ' Poor Gaston will kill himself when he hears of this.' The cook told me this, and added that her mistress's sufferings were terrible. And she is at St. Lazare. I tried to see her, but it was no go"; and here the boy's voice broke into a sob.

" Come," said André, " keep up your spirits."

" Ah! you shall see if, as soon as I am twenty-one, I don't marry her. I don't put all the blame on the old man. He has been advised by his lawyer, a beast by the name of Catenac. Do you know *him?* "

" No."

" You don't seem to know any one. Well, I shall send him a challenge to-morrow. I have got my seconds all ready. By the way, would you like to act for me? I can easily get rid of one of the others."

" I have had no experience in such matters."

" Ah, then you would be of no use. My seconds must put him into a regular blue funk."

" In that case——"

" No; I know what you are going to say: you mean that I had best look out for a military swell; but, after all, the matter lies in a nutshell. I am the insulted party, and draw pistols at ten paces. If that frightens him, he will make the governor drop all this rubbish."

Had his mind not been so much occupied, this rhodomontade on Gaston's part would have amused André very much, but now he asked himself what would be the quickest way to escape from him.

Just at this moment a servant emerged from the house.

" Sir," said he, addressing André, " my master has seen you from his window, and begs that you will go up to him at once."

" I will be with him immediately," answered André; and, holding out his hand to Gaston, he took leave of him with a few words of encouragement.

CHAPTER XXII.

A GENTLEMAN IN DIFFICULTIES.

WHEN André had got rid of the young man, and had been ushered into M. Gandelu's presence, the change in that gentleman's appearance struck him with horror. His eyes were red and swollen as if he had been weeping, but as soon as he caught sight of André his face brightened, and he welcomed him warmly.

" Oh, it does me good to see you, and I bless the fortunate chance that has brought you here to-day."

" It is not a very fortunate chance," answered André, as he shook his head sadly.

For the first time Gandelu noticed the air of gravity which marked the young man, and the shade of sorrow upon his brow.

" What ails you, André?" asked he.

" A great misfortune is hanging over me."

" What do you mean?"

" The naked truth and this misfortune may bring death and despair to me."

" I am your friend, my dear boy," said the old man, " and would gladly be of service to you. Tell me if I can be of any use?"

" I come to you to-day to ask a favor at your hands."

"And you thought of the old man, then? I thank you for doing so. Give me your hand; I like to feel the grasp of an honest man's hand; it warms my heart."

"It is the secret of my life that I am going to confide to you," said he, with some solemnity.

M. Gandelu made no reply, but struck his clenched fist upon his breast, as though to show that any secret confided to him would be locked up in the safe security of his heart.

Then André hesitated no longer, and, with the exception of giving names, told the whole story of his love, his ambitions, and his hopes, and gave a clear account of how matters stood.

"How can I help you?" asked M. Gandelu.

"Allow me," said André, "to hand over the work with which you have intrusted me to one of my friends. I will retain the responsibility, but will merely act as one of the workmen. This, to a certain extent, will give me my liberty, while at the same time I shall be earning a little money, which is just now of vast importance to me."

"Is that what you call a favor?"

"Certainly, and a very great one, too."

Gandelu rose hastily, and, opening an iron safe which stood in one corner of the room, and taking from it a bundle of banknotes, he placed them on the table before André with an expressive look, which meant, "Take what you desire."

The unlooked-for kindness of this man, who forgot all his own sorrows in his anxiety to relieve the necessities of another, affected André deeply.

"I do not need money," began he.

With a wave of his hand Gandelu inspired silence.

"Take these twenty thousand francs," said he, "and then I can tell you why I asked you to come upstairs."

A refusal would have wounded the old man deeply, and so André took the proffered loan.

Gandelu resumed his seat, and remained in gloomy silence for some time.

"My dear boy," said he, in a voice broken by emotion, "a day or two back you saw something of the trouble that I am laboring under. I have no longer any respect or esteem for that wretched fool, my son, Pierre."

André had already guessed that he had been incensed with reference to something connected with Gaston.

"Your son has behaved very foolishly," said he; "but remember he is very young."

A sad smile passed over the old man's face.

"My son is old in vice," replied he. "I have thought the matter over only too plainly. Yesterday he declared that he would kill himself. An absurd threat. Up to this time I have been culpably weak, and it is no use now to act in an opposite direction. The unhappy boy is infatuated with a degraded woman named Rose, and I have had her locked up; but I have made up my mind to let her out again, and also to pay his debts. It is weak folly, I allow; but what am I to do? I am his father after all; and while I cannot respect her, I must love him. He has almost broken my heart, but it was his to do as he liked with."

André made no reply, and Gandelu went on.

"I have not deceived myself; my son is ruined. I can but stand by and wait for the end. If this Rose is not everything that is bad, her influence may be

of some use to him. But I want some one to undertake these negotiations, and I had hopes, André, that
you would have been able to do so."

André felt that all his efforts ought to be devoted
to the interests of Sabine, but at the same time he
could not leave the kind old man to the mercy of
others, and by a display of absolute heroism he determined to accede to the broken-hearted father's desires and briefly told him that he was at his service.
Gandelu thanked him warmly, and André, seating
himself at the table, the two men entered into a long
discussion as to the best means to be adopted. It
was finally decided that André should act with freedom and according to his own instincts, and that M.
Gandelu should, to actual appearance, remain firm in
the course he had entered upon, and should only be
induced, by André's intercession, to adopt milder measures. The result justified their anticipations, for Gaston was even more crushed and downcast than André
had imagined, and it was in an agony of suspense that
he awaited the return of the young painter. As soon
as he saw him descending the steps he sprang forward
to greet him.

" Well," said he, in a tone of eager inquiry.

" Your father," returned André, " is terribly angry
with you, but I hope to be able to induce him to do
something for you."

" Will he set Zora at liberty? "

" Perhaps he will; but first he must have something
more from you than promises—he must have stable
guarantees."

At these words Gaston's face fell. " Guarantees,"
answered he sulkily. " Is not my word of honor
enough? What sort of guarantees does he require? "

" That I cannot tell you, and you must find out for yourself; but I will do all I can for you."

Gaston gazed upon André in surprise.

" Do you mean to tell me," asked he, " that you can do pretty well what you like with the governor?"

" Not exactly; but surely you can see that I have a good deal of influence over him. If you want a proof of this, see, here is the money to take up these bills you told me of."

" What, Verminet's?"

" I suppose so. I am speaking of those to which you were mad enough to forge another man's name."

Foolish as the boy was, this act of his had caused him many a sleepless night, and he had reflected very often how he could possibly escape from the consequence of his act of rashness.

" Give me the money," cried he.

André shook his head, however. " Forgive me," said he, " but this money does not quit my hands until the bills are handed over to me. Your father's orders on this point are decided; but the sooner we settle the affair the better."

" That is too bad; the governor is as sly as a fox; but he must have his own way, I suppose, so come on. Only just wait till I slip on a coat more suitable to my position than this lounging suit."

He rushed away, and was back again in ten minutes as neat as a new pin, and full of gayety and good spirits.

" We can walk," said he, putting his arm through André's. " We have to go to the Rue St. Anne."

Verminet had his office in this street—the office of the Mutual Loan Society, of which he was the managing director. The house, in spite of its grandiloquent title, was of excessively shabby exterior. The Mutual Loan Society was frequented by those who, having lost their credit, wished to obtain a fresh amount, and who, having no money, wanted to borrow some.

Verminet's plan of financial operations was perfectly simple. A tradesman on the verge of bankruptcy would come to him. Verminet would look into his case and make him sign bills for the sum he required, handing him in exchange bills drawn by other tradesmen in quite as serious a predicament as himself, and pocketed a commission of two per cent. upon both the transactions. Verminet obtained clients from the simple fact that an embarrassed tradesman is utterly reckless, cares not what he signs, and will clutch at a straw to keep his head above water. But there were many other transactions carried on at the office of the Mutual Loan Society, for its largest means of income was drawn from even less respectable sources, and it was alleged that many of these bogus bills which are occasionally cashed by some respectable bankers were manufactured there. At any rate, Verminet managed to make money somehow.

CHAPTER XXIII.

RINGING THE CHANGES.

ANDRÉ, who was gifted with plenty of intelligence, at once judged of the kind of business done by the Mutual Loan Society by the dinginess of the brass plate on the door and the generally dilapidated aspect of the house.

"I don't like the look of it at all," said he.

"It does not go in for show," answered Gaston,

affecting an air of wisdom, "but it is deemed handy sometimes. It does all sorts of business that you would never think of. A real downy card is Verminet."

André could easily believe this, for, of course, there could be but one opinion concerning the character of a man who could have induced a mere simpleton like Gaston to affix a forged signature to the bills which he had discounted. He made no remark, however, but entered the house, with the interior arrangements of which Gaston appeared to be perfectly familiar. They passed through a dirty, ill-smelling passage, went across a courtyard, cold and damp as a cell, and ascended a flight of stairs with a grimy balustrade. On the second floor Gaston made a halt before a door upon which several names were painted. They passed through into a large and lofty room. The paper on the walls of this delectable chamber was torn and spotted, and a light railing ran along it, behind which sat two or three clerks, whose chief occupation appeared to be consuming the breakfast which they had brought with them to the office. The heat of the stove, which was burning in one corner of the room, the general mouldiness of the atmosphere, and the smell of the coarse food, were sufficient to turn the stomach of any one coming in from the fresh air.

"Where is M. Verminet?" asked Gaston authoritatively.

"Engaged," replied one of the clerks, without pausing to empty his mouth before he replied.

"Don't you talk to me like that. What do I care whether he is engaged or not? Tell him that Gaston de Gandelu desires to see him at once."

The clerk was evidently impressed by his visitor's

manner, and, taking the card which was handed to him, made his exit through a door at the other end of the room.

Gaston was delighted at this first victory, and glanced at André with a triumphant smile.

The clerk came back almost at once. " M. Verminet," cried he, " has a client with him just now. He begs that you will excuse him for a few minutes, when he will see you"; and evidently anxious to be civil to the gorgeously attired youths before him, he added, " My master is just now engaged with M. de Croisenois."

" Aha," cried Gaston; " I will lay you ten to one that the dear Marquis will be delighted to see me."

André started on hearing this name, and his cheek crimsoned. The man whom he most hated in this world; the wretch who, by his possession of some compromising secret, was forcing Sabine into a detested marriage; the villain whom he, M. de Breulh, and Madame de Bois Arden had sworn to overreach, was within a few paces of him, and that now he should see him face to face. Their eyes would meet, and he would hear the tones of the scoundrel's voice. His rage and agitation were so intense that it was with the utmost difficulty that he concealed it. Luckily for him, Gaston was not paying the slightest attention to his companion; for having, at the clerk's invitation, taken a chair, he assumed an imposing attitude, which struck the shabby young man behind the railing with the deepest admiration.

" I suppose," said he, in a loud voice, " that you know my dear friend, the Marquis?"

André made some reply, which Gaston interpreted as a negative.

"Really," said he, "you know *no* one, as I told you before. Where have you lived? But you must have heard of him? Henri de Croisenois is one of my most intimate friends. He owes me over fifty louis that I won of him one night at baccarat."

André was now certain that he had estimated Verminet's character correctly, and the relations of the Marquis de Croisenois with this very equivocal personage assumed a meaning of great significance to him. He felt now that he had gained a clue, a beacon blazed out before him, and he saw his way more clearly into the difficult windings of this labyrinth of iniquity which he knew that he must penetrate before he gained the secret he longed for.

He felt like a child playing the game called "Magic Music," when, as the seeker nears the hiding place of the article of which he is in search, the strains of the piano swell higher and higher. He now found that the boy whose master he had become, knew, or said he knew, a good deal of this marquis. Why should he not gain some information from him?"

"Are you really intimate with the Marquis de Croisenois?" asked he.

"I should rather think I was," returned Gandelu the younger. "You will see that precious sharp. I know all about him, and who the girl is that he is ruining himself for, but I mustn't talk about that; mum's the word, you know."

At that moment the door opened, and the Marquis appeared, followed by Verminet.

Henri de Croisenois was attired in the most fashionable manner, and formed an utter contrast to the flashy dress of Gaston. He was smoking a cigar, and mechanically tapping his boots with an elegant walking cane. In a moment the features and figure of the Viscount were indelibly photographed upon André's brain. He particularly noticed his eyes, which had in them a half-concealed look of terror, and his face bore the haunted expression of a person who expects some terrible blow to fall upon him at any moment.

At a little distance the Marquis seemed still young, but a closer inspection showed that the man looked even older than he really was, so worn and haggard were his mouth and eyes. Nights at the gaming-table and the anxiety as to where the fresh supplies should come from to furnish the means to prolong his life of debauchery had told heavily upon him. To-day, however, he seemed to be in the best temper imaginable, and in the most cheerful manner he addressed a few words to Verminet, in conclusion of the conversation that had been going on in the inner office.

"It is settled then," remarked he, "that I am to have nothing more to do with a business with which neither of us has any real concern?"

"Just so," answered Verminet.

"Very well, then; but remember that any mistake you may make in the other affair will be attended with the most serious results."

This caution seemed to suggest some new idea to Verminet, for he said something in a low voice to his client at which they both laughed.

Gaston was fidgeting about, very uneasy at the Marquis having paid no attention to him, and he now advanced with a magnificent salutation and a friendly wave of the hand. If the Marquis was charmed at meeting Gandelu, he concealed his delight in a most wonderful manner. He seemed surprised, but not agreeably so; he bent his head, and he extended his gloved hand with a negligent, " Ah, pleased to see you." Then without taking any more notice of Gaston, he turned on his heel and continued his conversation with Verminet.

" The worst part is over," said he, " and therefore no time is to be lost. You must see Mascarin and Martin Rigal, the banker, to-day."

At these words André started. Were these people Croisenois' accomplices? Certainly he had accomplices on the brain just now, and their names remained deeply engraved on the tablets of his memory.

" Tantaine was here this morning," observed Verminet, " and told me that his master wanted to see me at four this afternoon. Van Klopen will be there also. Shall I say a word to him about your fine friend?"

" 'Pon my soul," remarked the Marquis, shrugging his shoulders, " I had nearly forgotten her. There will be a tremendous fuss made, for she will be wanting all sorts of things. Speak to Van Klopen certainly, but do not bind yourself. Remember that I do not care a bit for the fair Sara."

" Quite so; I understand," answered Verminet; " but keep things quiet, and do not have any open disturbances."

" Of course not. Good morning," and with a bow to the managing director and a nod to Gaston, he lunged out of the office, not condescending to take the slightest notice of André. Verminet invited André and Gaston into his sanctum, and, taking a seat, motioned to them to do the same. Verminet was a decided contrast to his office, which was shabby and dirty, for his dress did his tailor credit, and he appeared to be clean. He was neither old nor young, and carried his years well. He was fresh and plump, wore his whiskers and hair cut in the English fashion, while his sunken eyes had no more expression in them than those of a fish.

Gandelu was in a hurry to begin.

"Let us get to business," said he. "Last week you lent me some money."

"Just so. Do you want any more?"

"No; I want to return my bills."

A cloud passed over Verminet's face.

"The first does not fall due until the 15th," remarked he.

"No matter; I have the money with me, and I will pay it on you handing over the bills to me."

"I can't do it."

"And why so, pray?"

"The bills have passed out of my hands."

Gaston could scarcely credit his ears, nor believe in the truth of this last statement, and was certainly upset, not knowing what to do.

"But," stammered he, "you promised, when I signed those bills, that they should never go out of your hands."

"I don't say I did not; but one can't always keep to one's promise. I was forced to part with them. I wanted money, and so had to discount them."

André was not at all surprised, for he had anticipated some such difficulty; and seeing that Gaston had entirely lost his head, he broke in on the conversation.

"Excuse me, sir," remarked he; "but it seems to me that there are certain circumstances in this case which should have made you keep your promise.

Verminet stared at him.

"Who have I the honor of speaking to?" asked he, instead of making a direct reply.

"I am a friend of M. de Gandelu's," returned André, thinking it best not to give any name.

"A confidential friend?"

"Entirely so. He had, I think, ten thousand francs from you."

"Pardon me, five thousand."

André turned toward his companion in some surprise.

Gaston grew crimson.

"What is the meaning of this?" asked the artist.

"Can't you see?" whispered Gaston. "I had ten because I wanted the other five for Zora."

"Oh, indeed," returned André, with a slight uplifting of his eyebrows. "Well, then, M. Verminet, it was five thousand francs that you lent to my young friend here. That was right enough; but what do you say to inducing him to forge a signature?"

"I! I do such a thing?" answered Verminet. "Why, I did not know that the signature was not genuine."

This insolent denial aroused the unhappy Gaston from his state of stupor.

"This is too much, a deuced deal too much," cried he. "Did you not yourself tell me that, for your own security, you must insist upon another name in addition to mine? Did you not give me a letter, and say, 'Write a signature like the one at the bottom of this, it is that of Martin Rigal, the banker in the Rue Montmartre'?"

"An utterly false accusation, without a shadow of

proof; and remember that a libel uttered in the presence of a third party is punishable by law."

"And yet, sir," continued André, "you did not hesitate for a moment in discounting these bills. Have you calculated what terrible results may come of this breach of faith on your part?—what will happen if this forged signature is presented to M. Martin Rigal?"

"Very unlikely. Gandelu is the drawer, Rigal merely the endorser. Bills, when due, are always presented to the drawer," returned Verminet laconically.

Evidently a trap had been laid for Gaston, but the reason was still buried in obscurity.

"Then," remarked André, "we have but one course to pursue: we must trace those notes to the hands in which they now are, and take them up."

"Quite right."

"But to enable us to do so, you must first let us know the name of the party who discounted them."

"I don't know; I have forgotten," answered Verminet, with a careless wave of his hand.

"Then," returned André, in a low, deep voice of concentrated fury, "let me advise you, for your own sake, to make an immediate call upon your powers of memory."

"Do you threaten me?"

"And if you do not succeed in remembering the name or names, the consequences may be more serious than you seem to anticipate."

Verminet saw that the young painter was in dangerous earnest, and rose from his chair, but André was too quick for him.

"No," said he, placing his back against the door;

"you will not leave this room until you have done what I require."

For fully ten minutes the men stood gazing at each other. Verminet was green with terror, while André's face, though pale, was firm and determined.

"If the scoundrel makes any resistance," said he to himself, "I will fling him out of the window."

"The man is a perfect athlete," thought Verminet, "and looks as if he would stick at nothing."

Seeing that he had better give in, the managing director took up a bulky ledger, and began to turn over the leaves with trembling fingers.

André saw that he was holding it upside down.

"There it is," cried Verminet at last.

"Bills for five thousand francs. Gandelu and Rigal, booked for discount to Van Klopen, ladies' tailor."

André was silent.

Why was it that Verminet had suggested Rigal's signature as the one he ought to imitate? and why had he handed the bills over to Van Klopen? Was it mere chance that had arranged it all? He did not believe it, but felt sure that some secret tie united them all together, Verminet, Van Klopen, Rigal, and the Marquis de Croisenois.

"Do you want anything more?" asked the manager of the Mutual Loan Society.

"Are the bills in Van Klopen's hands?"

"I can't say."

"Never mind; he will have to tell me where they are, if he has not got them," returned André.

They left the house, and as soon as they were again in the street André took his companion's arm, and hurried him off in the direction of the Rue de Grammont.

"I don't want to give this thief, Verminet, time to warn Van Klopen of what has taken place; I had rather fall upon him with the suddenness of an earthquake. Come, let us go to his establishment at once."

CHAPTER XXIV.

THE VANISHING BILLS.

HAD André known a little more of the man he had to deal with, he would have learned that no one could fall like an earthquake upon Van Klopen. Shut up in the sanctum where he composed the numberless costumes that were the wonder and delight of Paris, Van Klopen made as careful arrangements to secure himself from interview as the Turk does to guard the approaches to his seraglio; and so André and Gandelu were accosted in the entrance hall by his stately footmen, clad in gorgeous liveries, glittering with gold.

"M. van Klopen is engaged," cried they with one voice.

"Our business is of the utmost importance," asserted André.

"Our master is composing."

Entreaties, threats, and even a bribe of one hundred francs were alike useless; and André, seeing that he was about to be checkmated, was half tempted to take the men by the collar and hurl them on one side, but he calmed himself, and, already repenting of his violence at Verminet's, he determined on a course of submission, and so meekly followed the footmen into the famous waiting-room, styled by Van Klopen his purgatory. The footmen, however, had spoken the truth, for several ladies of the highest rank and standing were awaiting the return of this *arbiter elegantiarum*. All of them turned as the young men entered—all save one, who was gazing out of the window, drawing with her pretty fingers on the window panes. André recognized her in an instant as Madame de Bois Arden.

" Is it possible? " thought he. " Can the Countess have returned here after what has occurred? "

Gaston felt that five charming pairs of eyes were fixed upon him, and studied to assume his most graceful posture.

After a brief time given to arrangement, André grew disgusted.

" I wish that she would look round," said he to himself. " I think she would feel rather ashamed. I will say a word to her."

He rose from his chair, and, without thinking how terribly he might compromise the lady, he took up a position at her side. She was, however, intently watching something that was going on in the street, and did not turn her head.

" Madame," said he.

She started, and, as she turned and recognized André, she uttered a little cry of surprise.

" Great heavens! is that you? "

" Yes, it is I."

" And here? I dare say that my presence in this place surprises you," she went on, " and that I have a short memory, and no feelings of pride."

André made no reply, and his silence was a sufficient rejoinder to the question.

" You do me a great injustice," muttered the Count-

ess. " I am here because De Breulh told me that in
your interests I ought to pardon Van Klopen, and go
to him again as I used to do; so you see, M. André,
that it is never safe to judge by appearance, and a
woman more than anything else."

" Will you forgive me? " asked André earnestly.

The lady interrupted him by a little wave of her
hand, invisible to all save to him, which clearly said,—

" Take care; we are not alone."

She once more turned her eyes towards the street,
and he mechanically did the same. By this means
their faces were hidden from observation.

" De Breulh," went on the lady, " has heard a good
deal about De Croisenois, and, as no doubt you can
guess, but very little to his credit, and quite enough
to justify any father in refusing him his daughter's
hand; but in this case it is evident to me that De
Mussidan is yielding to a secret pressure. We must
ferret out some hidden crime in De Croisenois' past
which will force him to withdraw his proposal."

" I shall find one," muttered André.

" But remember there is no time to be lost. According to our agreement, I treat him in the most
charming manner, and he thinks that I am entirely devoted to his interests, and to-morrow I have arranged
to introduce him to the Count and Countess at the
Hotel de Mussidan, where the Count and Countess
have agreed to receive him."

André started at this news.

" I saw," continued the lady, " that you were quite
right in the opinion you had formed, for in the first
place the common danger has almost reconciled the
Count and Countess affectionately to each other,
though it is notorious that they have always lived in

the most unhappy manner. Their faces are careworn
and full of anxiety, and they watch every movement
of Sabine with eager eyes. I think that they look
upon her as a means of safety, but shudder at the
sacrifice she is making on their account."

"And Sabine?"

"Her conduct is perfectly sublime, and she is ready
to consummate the sacrifice without a murmur. Her
self-sacrificing devotion is perfectly admirable; but
what is more admirable still is the way in which she
conceals the suffering that she endures from her parents. Noble-hearted girl! she is calm and silent, but
she has always been so. She has grown thinner, and
perhaps her cheek is a trifle paler, but her forehead
was burning and seemed to scorch my lips as I kissed
her. With this exception, however, there was nothing
else about her that would betray her tortures. Mo-
deste, her maid, told me, moreover, that when night
came she seemed utterly worn out, and the poor girl,
with tears in her eyes, declared ' that her dear mistress
was killing herself.'"

André's eyes overflowed with tears.

"What have I done to deserve such love?"
asked he.

A door suddenly opened, and André and the
Viscountess turned hastily at the sound. It was Van
Klopen who came in, crying, according to his usual
custom,—

"Well, and whose turn is it next?"

When, however, he saw Gaston, his face grew white,
and it was with a smile that he stepped towards him,
motioning back the lady whose turn it was, and who
protested loudly against this injustice.

"Ah, M. de Gandelu," said he, "you have come, I

suppose, to bespeak some fresh toilettes for that exquisite creature, Zora de Chantemille?"

"Not to-day," returned Gaston. "Zora is a little
indisposed."

André, however, who had arranged the narrative
that he was about to pour into the ears of the famous
Van Klopen, was in too much haste to permit of any
unnecessary delay.

"We have come here," said he hurriedly, "upon
a matter of some moment. My friend, M. Gaston
de Gandelu, is about to leave Paris for some months,
and, before doing so, is anxious to settle all outstand-
ing accounts, and retire all his bills, which may not
yet have fallen due."

"Have I any bills of M. de Gandelu?" said Van
Klopen slowly. "Ah, yes, I remember that I had
some now. Yes, five bills of one thousand francs each,
drawn by Gandelu, and accepted by Martin Rigal. I
received them from the Mutual Loan Society, but they
are no longer in my hands."

"Is that the case?" murmured Gaston, growing
sick with apprehension.

"Yes, I sent them to my cloth merchants at St.
Etienne, Rollon and Company."

Van Klopen was a clever scoundrel, but he sometimes lacked the necessary perception of when he had
said enough; and this was proved to-day, for, agitated
by the steady gaze that André kept upon him, he
added,—

"If you do not believe my word, I can show you
the acknowledgment that I received from that firm."

"It is unnecessary," replied André. "Your statement is quite sufficient."

"I should prefer to let you see the letter."

" No, thank you," replied André, not for a moment
duped by the game that was being played. " Pray take
no more trouble. We shall, I presume, find that the
bills are at St. Etienne. There is no use in taking
any more trouble about them, and we will wait until
they arrive at maturity. I have the honor to wish
you good morning."

And with these words he dragged away Gaston,
who was actually about to consult Van Klopen as to
the most becoming costume for Zora to appear in on
leaving the prison of St. Lazare. When they were a
few doors from the man-milliner's, André stopped and
wrote down the names of Van Klopen's cloth merchants. Gaston was now quite at his ease.

" I think," remarked he, " that Van Klopen is a
sharp fellow; he knows that I am to be relied on."

" Where do you think your bills are? "

" At St. Etienne's, of course."

The perfect innocence of the boy elicited from
André a gesture of impatient commiseration.

" Listen to me," said he, " and see if you can comprehend the awful position in which you have placed
yourself."

" I am listening, my dear fellow; pray go on."

" You drew these bills through Verminet because
Van Klopen would not give you credit."

" Exactly so."

" How, then, do you account for the fact that this
man, who was at first disinclined to trust you, should,
without rhyme or reason, offer to supply you now as
he did to-day? "

" The deuce! that never struck me. It does seem
queer. Does he want to play me a nasty trick? But
which of them is it—Verminet or Van Klopen? "

"It is plain to me that the pair of them have entered into a pleasant little plot to blackmail you."

Young Gandelu did not at all like this turn, and he exclaimed,—

"Blackmail me, indeed! why, I know my way about better than that. They won't get much out of me, I can tell you."

André shrugged his shoulders.

"Then," said he, "just tell me what you intend to say to Verminet when he comes to you upon the day your bills fall due, and says to you, 'Give me one hundred thousand francs for these five little bits of paper, or I go straight to your father with them'?"

"I should say, of course—ah, well, I really do not know what I should say."

"You could say nothing, except that you had been imposed on in the most infamous way. You would plead for time, and Verminet would give it to you if you would execute a deed insuring him one hundred thousand francs on the day you came of age."

"A hundred thousand devils are all the rogue would get from me. That's the way I do things, do you see? If people try and ride roughshod over me, I merely hit out, and then just look out for broken bones. Pay this chap? Not I! I know the governor would make an almighty shine, but I'll choose that sooner than be had like that."

He was quite serious, but could only put his feelings into the language he usually spoke.

"I think," answered André, "that your father would forgive this imprudence, but that it will be even harder for him to do so than it was to send a doctor to number the hours he had to live. He will forgive you because he is your father, and because he loves

you; but Verminet, when he finds that the threat to
go to your father does not appall you, will menace you
with criminal proceedings."

"Hulloo!" said Gandelu, stopping short. "I say,
that is very poor fun," gasped he.

"There is no fun in it, for such fun, when brought
to the notice of a court of justice, goes by the ugly
name of forgery, and forgery means a swinging heavy
sentence."

Gaston turned pale, and trembled from head to foot.

"Tried and sentenced," faltered he. "No, I don't
believe you, but I hold no honors and will turn up
my cards." He quite forgot that he was in the public
street, and was talking at the top of his shrill falsetto
voice, and gesticulating violently.

"The poor old governor, I might have made him
so happy, and, after all, I have only been a torment
to him. Ah, could I but begin once more; but then
the cards are dealt, and I must go on with the game,
and I have made a nice muddle of the whole thing
before I am twenty years of age; but no criminal
courts for me, no, the easiest way out of it is a pistol
shot, for I am an honest man's son, and I will not
bring more disgrace on him than I have already done."

"Do you really mean what you say?" asked André.

"Of course I do. I can be firm enough sometimes."

"Then we will not despair yet," answered the young
painter. "I think that we shall be able to settle this
ugly business, but you cannot be too cautious. Keep
indoors, and remember that I may have urgent need
of you at almost any time of day or night."

"I agree, but remember this, Zora is not to be forgotten."

"Don't fret over that; I will call and see her to-morrow. And now, farewell for to-day, as I have not an instant to lose," and with these words André hurried off.

André's reason for haste was that he had caught a few words addressed by Verminet to Croisenois—" I shall see Mascarin at four o'clock." And he determined to loiter about the Rue St. Anne, and watch the Managing Director when he came out, and so find out who this Mascarin was, who he was certain was mixed up in the plot. He darted down the Rue de Grammont like an arrow from a bow, and as the clock in a neighboring belfry chimed half-past three, he was in the Rue St. Anne. There was a small wine-shop almost opposite to the office of the Mutual Loan Society, and there André ensconced himself and made a frugal meal, while he was waiting for Verminet's appearance, and just as he had finished his light refreshment he saw the man he wanted come out of the office, and crept cautiously after him like a Red Indian on the trail of his enemy.

CHAPTER XXV.

THE SPY.

As Verminet swaggered down the street he had the air of a successful man, of a capitalist, in short, and the Managing Director of a highly lucrative concern. André had no difficulty in following his man, though detective's business was quite new to him, which is no such easy matter, although every one thinks that he can become one. André kept his man in sight, and was astonished at the numerous acquaintances that Verminet seemed to have. Occasionally he said to himself, "Perhaps I am mistaken after all, for fancy is a bad pair of spectacles to see through. This man may be honest, and I have let my imagination lead me astray."

Meanwhile, Verminet who had reached the Boulevard Poissonnière, assumed a totally different air, throwing off his old manner as he cast away his cigar. When he had reached the Rue Montorgueil he turned underneath a large archway. Verminet had gone into the office of M. B. Mascarin, and that person simply kept a Servants' Registry Office for domestics of both sexes. In spite of his surprise, however, he determined to wait for Verminet to come out; and, not to give himself the air of loitering about the place, he crossed the road and appeared to be interested in watching three workmen who were engaged in fixing the revolving shutters to a new shop window. Luckily for the young painter he had not to wait a very long while, for in less than a quarter of an hour Verminet came out, accompanied by two men. The one was tall and thin, and wore a pair of spectacles with colored glasses, while the other was stout and ruddy, with the unmistakable air of a man of the world about him. André would have given the twenty thousand francs which he still had in his pocket if he could have heard a single word of their conversation. He was moving skilfully forward so as to place himself within earshot, when not two feet from him he heard a shrill whistle twice repeated. There was something so strange and curious in the sound of this whistle that André looked round and noticed that the three men whom he was watching had been also attracted by it.

The tall man with the colored glasses glanced suspiciously around him, and then after a nod to his companions turned and re-entered the office, while Verminet and the other walked away arm in arm. André
was undecided; should he try and discover who these
two men were? Near the entrance he saw a lad selling hot chestnuts. "Ah!" said he, "the little chestnut
seller will always be there; but I may lose the others
if I stay here." He followed the two men as quickly
as possible. They did not go very far, and speedily
entered a fine house in the Rue Montmartre. Here
André was for a moment puzzled, as he did not know
to whom they were paying a visit, but noticing an in-
scription on the wall of "Cashier's Office on the first
floor," he exclaimed,—

"Ah! it is to the banker's they have gone!"

He questioned a man coming downstairs and heard
that M. Martin Rigal, the banker, had his offices and
residence there.

"I have struck a vein of good luck to-day," thought
he; "and now if my little friend the chestnut seller
can only tell me the names of these men, I have done
a good day's work. I *do* hope that he has not gone."

The boy was still there, and he had two customers
standing by the chafing-dish which contained the glow-
ing charcoal, and a working lad in cap and blouse was
arguing so hotly with the lad that they did not notice
André's appearance.

"You can stow that chat," said the boy; "I have
told your father the price I would take. You want
my station and stock-in-trade. Hand over two hundred and fifty francs, and they are yours."

"But my dad will only give two hundred," returned
the other.

" Then he don't need give nothing, for he won't get 'em," answered the chestnut vender sharply. " Two hundred francs for a pitch like this! why, I have sometimes taken ten francs and more, and that ain't a lie, on the word of Toto Chupin."

André was tickled with this strange designation, and addressed himself to the lad who bore it.

" My good boy," said he, " I think you were here an hour ago. Did you see anything of three gentlemen who came out of the house and stood talking together for a short time? "

The lad turned sharply round and examined his questioner from tip to toe with an air of the most supreme impertinence; and then, in a tone which matched his look, replied,—

" What does it signify to you who they are? Mind your own business, and be off! "

André had had some little experience of this delightful class of street arab, of which Toto Chupin was so favorable a specimen, and knew their habits, customs, and language.

" Come, my chicken," said he, " spit it out, it won't blister your tongue, to answer a man who asks a civil question."

" Well, then, I saw 'em, sharp enough, and what then? "

" Why, that I should like to have their names if they have such an article belonging to 'em! "

Toto raised his cap and scratched his head, as if to stimulate his brains, and as he brushed up his thick head of dirty yellow hair, he eyed André cunningly.

" And suppose I know the blokes' names and tells 'em out to you, what will you stand? " asked he.

" Ten sous."

The delightful youth puffed out his cheeks, then expelled the pent-up wind by a sudden slap, as a mark of his disgust at the meanness of the offer.

" Pull up your braces, my lord," said he sarcastically, " or you'll be losing the contents of your breeches pockets. Ten sous, indeed! Perhaps you'd like me to lend 'em to yer? "

André smiled pleasantly.

" Did you think, my little man, that I was going to offer you twenty thousand shiners? " asked he.

" Won again! " cried Toto; " I laid myself a new hat that you weren't a fool, and I have collared the stakes."

" Why do you think I am not a fool? "

" Because a fool would have begun by offering me five francs and gone up slick to ten, while you began at a modest figure."

The painter smiled.

" But you were too old a bird to be caught like that," continued the lad; and as he spoke, he stopped, and contracted his brow as if in deep perplexity. Of course he was acquainted with the names, but ought he to give them? Instantly he scented an enemy. Harmless people did not usually ask questions of itinerant chestnut venders, and to open his mouth might be to injure Mascarin, Beaumarchef, or the guileless Tantaine.

This last thought determined the lad.

" Keep your ten sous, my pippin," said the boy; " I'll tell you what you want to know all gratis and for nothing, because I've taken a real fancy to the cut of your mug. The tall chap was Mascarin, the fat un

Doctor Hortebise, and t'other—stop, let me think it out in my knowledge box; ah! I have it, he was Verminet."

André was so delighted that, drawing from his pocket a five-franc piece, he tossed it to the boy.

"Thanks, my noble lord," said Chupin, and was about to add something more in a similar vein, when he glanced down the street. His look changed in an instant, and he fixed his eyes upon the painter's face with a very strange expression.

"What is the matter, my lad?" asked André, surprised at this sudden change.

"Nothing," answered Chupin; "nothing at all; only as you seem a decentish sort of chap, I should recommend you to keep your wits about you, and to look out for squalls."

"Eh, what do you mean?"

"I mean—why—be careful, of course. Hang me if I exactly know what I do mean. It is just an idea that came to me all of a jump. But there, be off; I ain't going to say another word."

With much difficulty André repressed his astonishment. He saw that this young scamp was the possessor of many secrets which might be of inestimable value to him; but he also saw that he was determined to hold his tongue, and that it would at present be a waste of time to try and get anything out of him; and an empty cab passing at this moment, André hailed it, and told the coachman to drive fast to the Champs Elysées. In obedience to the warning that he had just received from Toto, he did not give the name of the *café* where he was to meet De Breulh, for he made up his mind to be careful, yes, extremely careful. He recollected the two odd whistles which had seemed to make Mascarin wince, and which certainly broke off the conference of the three men, and he remembered that it was after a glance down the street that Toto had become less communicative and had given him that curt warning. "By heaven," said he, as the recollection of a story he had read not long ago dawned on him, "I am being followed." He lowered the front glass of the cab, and attracted the coachman's attention by pulling him by the sleeve.

"Listen to me," said he, as the man turned, "and do not slacken your speed. Here, take your five francs in advance."

"But look here——"

"Listen to me. Go as sharp as you can to the Rue de Matignon; turn down it, and, as you do so, go a bit slower; then drive on like lightning, and when you are in the Champs Elysées do what you like, for your cab will be empty."

The driver chuckled.

"Aha," said he; "I see you are being followed, and you want to give 'em leg bail."

"Yes, yes; you are right."

"Then listen to me. Take care when you jump, and don't do it on the pavement, for t'other is the safest."

André succeeded in alighting safely, and turned down a narrow court before his pursuer had entered the street; but it was vain for the young painter to lurk in a doorway, for after five minutes had elapsed there was nothing to be seen, and no spy had made his appearance.

"I have been over-cautious," muttered he.

More than a quarter of an hour had elapsed, and André felt that he might leave his hiding-place, and go in quest of De Breulh; and as he approached the spot chosen for their meeting-place, he saw his friend's carriage, and near it was the owner, smoking a cigar. The two men caught sight of each other almost at the same moment. De Breulh advanced to greet the young man with extended hand.

"I have been waiting for you for the last twenty minutes," said he.

André commenced to apologize, but his friend checked him.

"Never mind," returned he; "I know that you must have had some excellent reasons; but, to tell you the honest truth, I had become rather nervous about you."

"Nervous! and why, pray?"

"Do you not recollect what I said the other evening? De Croisenois is a double-dyed scoundrel."

André remained silent, and his friend, putting his arm affectionately through his, continued,—

"Let us walk," said he; "it is better than sitting down in the *café*. I believe De Croisenois capable of anything. He has the prospect before him of a large fortune,—that of his brother George; but this he has already anticipated. A man in a position like this is not to be trifled with."

"I do not fear him."

"But I do. I am, however, a little relieved by the fact that he has never seen you."

The painter shook his head.

"Not only has he seen me, but I half believe that he suspects my designs."

"Impossible!"

"But I am sure that I have been followed to-day. I have no actual proof, but still I am fully convinced that it was so."

And André recounted all that had occurred during the day.

"You are certainly being watched," answered De Breulh, "and every step that you take will be known to your enemies, and at this very moment perhaps eyes are upon us."

As he spoke he glanced uneasily around; but it was quite dark, and he could see no one.

"We will give the spies a little gentle exercise," said he, "and if we dine together they will find it hard to discover the place."

De Breulh's coachman was dozing on the driving-seat. His master aroused him, and whispered some order in his ear. The two young men then got in, and the carriage started at a quick pace.

"What do you think of this expedient?" asked De Breulh. "We shall go at this pace for the next hour. We will then alight at the corner of the Chaussée d'Autin, and be free for the rest of the night, and those who wish to follow us to-night must have good eyes and legs."

All came to pass as De Breulh had arranged; but as he jumped out he saw a dark form slip from behind the carriage and mingle with the crowd on the Boulevard.

"By heavens," said he; "that was a man. I thought that I was throwing a spy off the track, and I was in reality only treating him to a drive."

To make sure, he took off his glove and felt the springs of the carriage.

"See," said he, "they are still warm from the contact with a human body."

The young painter was silent, but all was now explained: while he jumped from the cab, his tracker had been carried away upon it. This discovery saddened the dinner, and a little after ten André left his friend and returned home.

CHAPTER XXVI.

MASCARIN MOVES.

THE Viscountess de Bois Arden had not been wrong when she told André in Van Klopen's establishment that community of sorrow had brought the Count and Countess of Mussidan nearer together, and that Sabine had made up her mind to sacrifice herself for the honor of the family. Unfortunately, however, this change in the relations of husband and wife had not taken place immediately; for after her interview with Doctor Hortebise, Diana's first impulse had not been to go to her husband, but to write to Norbert, who was as much compromised by the correspondence as she herself. Her first letter did not elicit a reply. She wrote a second, and then a third, in which, though she did not go into details, she let the Duke know that she was the victim of a dark intrigue, and that a deadly peril was hanging over her daughter's head. This last letter was brought back to her by the messenger, without any envelope, and across it Norbert had written,—

"The weapon which you have used against me has now been turned against yourself. Heaven is just."

These words started up in letters of fire before her eyes as the presage of coming misfortune, and telling her that the hour of retribution had now come, and that she must be prepared to suffer, as an atonement for her crimes. Then it was that she felt all was lost, and that she must go to her husband for aid, unless she desired that copies of the stolen letters should be sent to him; and in a little boudoir, adjoining Sabine's own room, she opened her heart and told her husband all. She performed it with all the skill of a woman who, without descending to falsehood, contrives to conceal the truth. But she could not hide the share that she had taken, both in the death of the late Duke of Champdoce and the disappearance of George de Croisenois.

The Count's brain reeled. He called up to his memory what Diana had been when he first saw and loved her at Laurebourg: how pure and modest she looked! what virginal candor sat upon her brow! and yet she was even then doing her best to urge on a son to murder his father.

De Mussidan had had hideous doubts concerning the relations of Norbert and Diana, both before and after marriage; but his wife firmly denied this at the moment when she was revealing the other guilty secrets of her past life. He had believed that Sabine was not his child, and now he had to reproach himself with the indifference he had displayed towards her.

He made no answer to the terrible revelation that was poured into his ears; but when the Countess had concluded, he rose and left the room, stretching out his hands and grasping the walls for support, like a drunken man.

The Count and Countess believed that Sabine had slept through this interview, but they were mistaken, for Sabine had heard all those fatal words—"ruin, dishonor, and despair!" At first she scarcely understood. Were not these words merely the offspring of her delirium? She strove to shake it off, but too soon she knew that the whispered words were sad realities, and she lay on her bed quivering with terror. Much of the conversation escaped her, but she heard enough. Her mother's past sins were to be exposed if the daughter did not marry a man entirely unknown to her—the Marquis de Croisenois. She knew that her torments would not be of very long duration, for to part with her love for André would be to part with life itself. She made up her mind to live until she had saved her parents' honor by the sacrifice of herself, and then she would be free to accept the calm repose of the grave.

But the terrible revelation bore its fruits, for her fever came back, and a relapse was the result. But youth and a sound constitution gained the day, and when she was convalescent her will was as strong as ever.

Her first act was to write the letter to her lover which had driven him to the verge of distraction; and then, fearing lest her father might, in his agony and remorse, be driven to some rash act, she went to him and told him that she knew all.

" I never loved M. de Breulh," said she with a pitiful smile, "and therefore the sacrifice is not so great after all."

The Count was not for a moment the dupe of the generous-souled girl, but he did not dare to brave the scandal of the death of Montlouis, and still less the exposure of his wife's conduct. Time was passing, however, and the miscreants in whose power they were made no signs of life. Hortebise did not appear any more, and there were moments when the miserable Diana actually ventured to hope. " Have they forgotten us?" thought she.

Alas! no; they were people who never forget.

The Champdoce affair had been satisfactorily arranged, and every precaution had been taken to prevent the detection of Paul as an impostor, and engaged as he had been, Mascarin had no time to turn his attention to the marriage of Sabine and De Croisenois. The famous Limited Company, with the Marquis as chairman, had, too, to be started, the shares of which were to be taken up by the unhappy victims of the blackmailers; but first some decided steps must be taken with the Mussidans, and Tantaine was dispatched on this errand.

This amiable individual, though he was going into such very excellent society, did not consider it necessary to make any improvement in his attire. This was the reason why the footman, upon seeing such a shabby visitor and hearing him ask for the Count or Countess, did not hesitate to reply, with a sneer, that his master and mistress had been out some months, and were not likely to return for a week or two. This fact did not disconcert the wily man, for drawing one of Mascarin's cards from his pocket, he begged the kind gentleman to take it upstairs, when he was sure that he would at once be sent for.

De Mussidan, when he read the name on the card, turned ghastly pale.

" Show him into the library," said he curtly.

Florestan left the room, and the Count mutely handed the card to his wife, but she had no need to read it.

" I can tell what it is," gasped she.

" The day for settling accounts has come," said the Count, " and this name is the fatal sign."

The Countess flung herself upon her knees, and taking the hand that hung placidly by his side, pressed her lips tenderly to it.

"Forgive me, Octave!" she murmured. "Will you not forgive me? I am a miserable wretch, and why did not Heaven punish me for the sins that I have committed, and not make others expiate my offences?"

The Count put her gently aside. He suffered intensely, and yet no word of reproach escaped his lips against the woman who had ruined his whole life.

"And Sabine," she went on, "must she, a De Mussidan, marry one of these wretched scoundrels?"

Sabine was the only one in the room who preserved her calmness; she had so schooled herself that her distress of mind was not apparent to the outward eye.

"Do not make yourselves miserable," said she, with a faint smile; "how do we know that M. de Croisenois may not make me an excellent husband after all?"

The Count gazed upon his daughter with a look of the fondest affection and gratitude.

"Dearest Sabine!" murmured he. Her fortitude had restored his self-command. "Let us be outwardly resigned," said he, "whatever our feelings may be. Time may do much for us, and at the very church door we may find means of escape."

CHAPTER XXVII.

A CRUEL SLUR.

FLORESTAN had conducted Tantaine to the sumptuous library, in which the Count had received Mascarin's visit; and, to pass away the time, the old man took a mental inventory of the contents of the room. He tried the texture of the curtains, looked at the handsome bindings of the books, and admired the magnificent bronzes on the mantelpiece.

"Aha," muttered he, as he tried the springs of a luxurious armchair, "everything is of the best, and when matters are settled, I half think that I should like a resting-place just like this——"

He checked himself, for the door opened, and the Count made his appearance, calm and dignified, but very pale. Tantaine made a low bow, pressing his greasy hat against his breast.

"Your humble servant to command," said he.

The Count had come to a sudden halt.

"Excuse me," said he, "but did you send up a card asking for an interview?"

"I am not Mascarin certainly, but I used that highly respectable gentleman's name, because I knew that my own was totally unknown to you. I am Tantaine, Adrien Tantaine."

M. de Mussidan gazed with extreme surprise upon the squalid individual before him. His mild and benevolent face inspired confidence, and yet he doubted him.

"I have come on the same business," pursued the old man. "I have been ordered to tell you that it must be hurried on."

The Count hastily closed the door and locked it; the manner of this man made him feel even too plainly the ignominy of his position.

"I understand," answered he. "But how is it that you have come, and not the other one?"

"He intended to come, but at the last moment he drew back; Mascarin, you see, has a great deal to lose, while I——" He paused, and holding up the tattered tails of his coat, turned round, as though to exhibit his shabby attire. "All my property is on my back," continued he.

"Then I can treat with you?" asked the Count.

Tantaine nodded his head. "Yes, Count, I have the missing leaves from the Baron's journal, and also, well —I suppose you know everything, all of your wife's correspondence."

"Enough," answered the Count, unable to hide his disgust. "Sit down."

"Now, Count, I will go to the point—are you going to put the police on us?"

"I have said that I would do nothing of the kind."

"Then we can get to business."

"Yes, if——"

The old man shrugged his shoulders.

"There is no 'if' in the case," returned he. "We state our conditions, for acceptance or rejection."

These words were uttered in a tone of such extreme insolence that the Count was strongly tempted to hurl the extortionate scoundrel from the window, but he contrived to restrain his passion.

"Let us hear the conditions then," said he impatiently.

Tantaine extracted from some hidden recess of his

coat a much-worn pocketbook, and drew from it a paper.

"Here are our conditions," returned he slowly. "The Count de Mussidan promises to give the hand of his daughter to Henri Marquis de Croisenois. He will give his daughter a wedding portion of six hundred thousand francs, and promises that the marriage shall take place without delay. The Marquis de Croisenois will be formally introduced at your house, and he must be cordially received. Four days afterwards he must be asked to dinner. On the fifteenth day from that M. de Mussidan will give a grand ball in honor of the signing of the marriage contract. The leaves from the diary and the whole of the correspondence will be handed to M. de Mussidan as soon as the civil ceremony is completed."

With firmly compressed lips and clenched hands, the Count sat listening to these conditions.

"And who can tell me," said he, "that you will keep your engagements, and that these papers will be restored to me at all?"

Tantaine looked at him with an air of pity.

"Your own good sense," answered he. "What more could we expect to get out of you than your daughter and your money?"

The Count did not answer, but paced up and down the room, eyeing the ambassador keenly, and endeavoring to detect some weak point in his manner of cynicism and audacity. Then speaking in the calm tone of a man who had made up his mind, he said,—

"You hold me as in a vice, and I admit myself vanquished. Stringent as your conditions are, I accept them."

" That is the right style of way to talk in," remarked
Tantaine cheerfully.

" Then," continued the Count, with a ray of hope
gleaming in his face, " why should I give my daughter to De Croisenois at all?—surely this is utterly unnecessary. What you want is simply six hundred thousand francs; well, you can have them, and leave me
Sabine."

He paused and waited for the reply, believing that
the day was his; but he was wrong.

" That would not be the same thing at all," answered Tantaine. " We should not gain our ends by
such means."

" I can do more," said the Count. " Give me six
months, and I will add a million to the sum I have
already offered."

Tantaine did not appear impressed by the magnitude
of this offer. " I think," remarked he, " that it will
be better to close this interview, which, I confess, is
becoming a little annoying. You agreed to accept the
conditions. Are you still in that mind?"

The Count bowed. He could not trust himself to
speak.

" Then," went on Tantaine, " I will take my leave.
Remember, that as you fulfil your engagement, so we
will keep to ours."

He had laid his hand on the handle of the door,
when the Count said,—

" Another word, if you please. I can answer for myself and Madame de Mussidan, but how about my
daughter?"

Tantaine's face changed. " What do you mean?"
asked he.

"My daughter may refuse to accept M. de Croisenois."

"Why should she? He is good-looking, pleasant,
and agreeable."

"Still she may refuse him."

"If mademoiselle makes any objection," said the old
man in peremptory accents, "you must let me see her
for a few minutes, and after that you will have no
further difficulty with her."

"Why, what could you have to say to my daughter?"

"I should say——"

"Well, what would you say?"

"I should say that if she loves any one, it is not
M. de Breulh." He endeavored to pass through the
half-opened door, but the Count closed it violently.

"You shall not leave this room," cried he, "until
you have explained this insulting remark."

"I had no intention of offending you," answered
Tantaine humbly. "I only——" He paused, and
then, with an air of sarcasm which sat strangely upon
a person of his appearance, went on, "I am aware that
the heiress of a noble family may do many things without having her reputation compromised, when girls in
a lower social grade would be forever lost by the
commission of any one of them; and I am sure if the
family of M. de Breulh knew that the young lady to
whom he was engaged had been in the habit of passing her afternoons alone with a young man in his
studio——"

He paused, and hastily drew a revolver, for it
seemed as if the Count were about to throw himself
upon him. "Softly, softly, if you please," cried he.

" Blows and insults are fatal mistakes. I have better information than yourself, that is all. I have more than ten times seen your daughter enter a house in the Rue Tour d'Auvergne, and, asking for M. André, creep silently up the staircase."

The Count felt that he was choking. He tore off his cravat, and cried wildly, " Proofs! give me proofs!"

During the last five minutes Tantaine had shifted his ground so skilfully that the heavy library table now stood between himself and the Count, and he was comparatively safe behind this extemporized defence.

" Proofs?" answered he. " Do you think that I carry them about with me? In a week I could give you the lovers' correspondence. That, you will say, is too long to wait; but you can set your doubts at rest at once. If you go to the address I will give you before eight to-morrow morning, and enter the room occupied by M. André, you will find the portrait of Mademoiselle Sabine carefully concealed from view behind a green curtain, and a very good portrait it is. I presume you will admit that it could not have been executed without a sitting."

" Leave this," cried the Count, " without a moment's delay."

Tantaine did not wait for a repetition of these words. He passed through the doorway, and as soon as he was outside he called out in cheerful accents, " Do not forget the address, Number 45, Rue Tour d'Auvergne, name of André, and mind and be there before eight a.m."

The Count made a rush at him on hearing this last insult, but he was too late, for Tantaine slammed the door, and was in the hall before the infuriated master of the house could open it. Tantaine had resumed all his airs of humility, and took off his hat to the foot-men as he descended the steps. "Yes," muttered he, as he walked along, "the idea was a happy one. André knows that he is watched, and will be careful; and now that M. de Mussidan is aware that his sweet, pure daughter has had a lover, he will be only too happy to accept the Marquis de Croisenois as his son-in-law." Tantaine believed that Sabine was more culpable than she really had been, for the idea of pure and honorable love had never entered his brain.

CHAPTER XXVIII.

THE TEMPTER.

By this time Tantaine was in the Champs Elysées, and stared anxiously around. "If my Toto makes no mistake," muttered he, "surely my order was plain enough."

The old man got very cross as he at last perceived the missing lad conversing with the proprietor of a pie-stall, having evidently been doing a little jawing with him.

"Toto," he called, "Toto, come here."

Toto Chupin heard him, for he looked round, but he did not move, for he was certainly much interested in the conversation he was carrying on. Tantaine shouted again, and this time more angrily than before, and Toto, reluctantly leaving his companion, came slowly up to his patron.

"You have been a nice time getting here," said the lad sulkily. "I was just going to cut it. Ain't you well that you make such a row? If you ain't, I'd better go for a doctor."

" I am in a tremendous hurry, Toto."

" Yes, and so is the postman when he is behind time. I'm busy too."

" What, with the man you have just left? "

" Yes; he is a sharper chap than I am. How much do you earn every day, Daddy Tantaine? Well, that chap makes his thirty or forty francs every night, and does precious little for it. I should like a business like that, and I think that I shall secure one soon."

" Have patience. I thought that you were going into business with those two young men you were drinking beer with at the Grand Turk? "

Toto uttered a shrill cry of anger at these words. " Business with them? " shrieked he; " they are regular clever night thieves."

" Have they done you any harm, my poor lad? "

" Yes; they have utterly ruined me. Luckily, I saw Mascarin yesterday, and he set me up in the hot-chestnut line. He ain't a bad one, is Mascarin."

Tantaine curled his lips disdainfully. " Not a bad fellow, I dare say, as long as you don't ask him for anything."

Toto was so surprised at hearing Tantaine abuse Mascarin, that he was unable to utter a word.

" Ah, you may look surprised," continued the old man, " but when a man is rolling in riches, and leaves an old friend to starve, then he is not what I call a real good fellow. Now, Toto, you are a bright lad, and so I don't mind letting you know that I am only waiting for a good chance to drop Mascarin, and set up on my own account. Work for yourself, my boy."

"I know that; but it is a good deal easier to say than to do."

"You have tried then?"

"Yes, I have; but I came to grief over it. You know all about it as well as I do, for don't tell me you didn't hear every word I said that night you were hunting up Caroline Schimmel. However, I'll tell you. One day when I saw a lady who looked rather nervous get out of a cab, I followed her. I was decently togged out, so I rang at the door. I was so sure that I was going to make a haul that I would not have taken ninety-nine francs for the hundred that I expected to make. Well, I rang, a girl opened the door, and in I went. What an ass I made of myself! I found a great brute of a man there, who thrashed me within an inch of my life, and then kicked me downstairs. See, he made his mark rather more plainly than I liked." And removing his cap, the boy showed several bruises about his forehead.

During this conversation Tantaine and the lad had been walking slowly up the Champs Elysées, and had by this time arrived just opposite M. Gandelu's house, where André was at work. Tantaine sat down on a bench.

"Let us rest a bit," said he; "I am tired out; and now let me tell you, my lad, that your tale only shows me that it is experience you want. Now, I have any amount of that, and I was really the prime mover in most of Mascarin's schemes. If I were to start on my own account, I should be driving in my carriage in twelve months. The only thing against my success is my age, for I am getting to be an old man. Why, even now I have a matter in my hands which is simply splendid. I have had half the money down, but I want a smart young fellow to pull it through."

"Why couldn't I be the smart young fellow?" asked Toto.

Tantaine shook his head. "You are as much too young as I am too old," answered he. "At your age you are too apt to be frightened, and would shrink back at the critical time. Besides, I have a conscience."

"And so have I," exclaimed Toto; "and it's grown like your own, old man; it can be stretched for miles and folded up into nothing."

"Well, we may be able to do something," returned Tantaine, as, drawing out a ragged check pocket-handkerchief, he wiped his glasses.

"Listen to me, my lad; I'll put what we call a supposititious case to you. You hate those two fellows who have robbed you, for I suppose that is what you meant; well, suppose you knew that they were at work all day on a high scaffold like that one opposite to us, what would you do?"

Toto scratched his head, and remarked after a pause,—

"If that crack-jawed idea you talk of was true," answered he, "those gay lads might as well make their wills, for I'd step up the scaffolding at night and just saw the planks that they are in the habit of clapping their toes on, half through, and when one of the mates stepped on it, why, there would be a bit of a smash, eh, Daddy Tantaine?"

"Not so bad, not so bad for a lad of your years," said the old man with an approving smile.

Toto's bosom swelled with pride.

"Besides," he continued, "I would arrange matters

so well that not a soul would think that I had done the trick."

"The more I hear you speak, Chupin," answered Tantaine, "the more I believe you are the lad I want, and I am sure that we shall make heaps of money together."

"I am cock sure of that too."

"You can use carpenters' tools, I think you once told me?"

"Yes."

"Well," continued Tantaine, "let me tell you then that I know an old man with any amount of money, and there is a fellow whom he hates and detests, a young chap who ran off with the girl he loved."

"The old bloke must have been jolly wild."

"Well, to tell the truth, he wasn't a bit pleased. Now it so happens that this gay young dog spends ten hours a day at least on that very scaffolding opposite to us. The old fellow, who has his head screwed on the right way, had the very same idea as yours, but he is too old and too stout to do the trick for himself; and, to cut the matter short, he would give five thousand francs to the persons who would carry out his idea. Just think, two thousand francs for a few cuts of a saw!"

The boy was violently agitated, but Tantaine pretended not to notice it.

"First, my lad," said he, "I must explain to you in what measure the old gentleman's plans are different from yours. If we did not take care, some other poor devil might break his neck, but I have hit on a dodge to avoid all this."

"I ain't curious, but I should like to hear it."

Tantaine smiled blandly.

"Listen! Do you see high up that little shed built of planks? That is used by the carvers and stone-cutters. Well, this little house, a couple of hundred feet above us, has a kind of a window; well, if this window and the planks below it were cut nearly through, any one leaning against it would be very likely to fall into the street and perhaps to hurt himself."

Chupin nodded.

"Now, suppose," went on Tantaine, "that the enemy of our old gentleman was in that little shed, all at once he hears a woman shriek, 'Help! it is I you love; help me!' what would this young fellow do? Why, he would recognize the voice, rush to the window, lean out, and as the woodwork and supports had been cut away, he would—— Well, do you see now?"

Chupin hesitated for a moment.

"I don't say I won't," muttered he; "but, look here, will the old chap pay down smart?"

"Yes, and besides, did I not tell you that he had given half down?"

The boy's eyes glistened as the old man unpinned the tattered lining of his pocket, and holding the pin between his teeth, pulled out the banknotes, each one for a thousand francs. Chupin's heart rose at the sight of this wealth.

"Is one of those for me?" asked he. Tantaine held the note towards the boy, who shuddered at the touch of the crisp paper and kissed the precious object in a paroxysm of pleasure. He then started from his seat, and regardless of the astonishment of the passers-by, executed a wild dance of triumph.

All was soon settled. Toto was to creep into the unfinished building by night, and not to leave it until he had completed his work. Tantaine, who had a thought for everything, told the boy what sort of a saw to employ, and gave him the address of a man who supplied the best class instruments.

"You must remember, my dear lad," said he, "not to leave behind you any traces of your work which may cause suspicion. One grain of sawdust on the floor might spoil the whole game. Take a dark lantern with you, grease your saw, and rasp out the tooth-nicks of the saw when you have finished your work."

Toto listened to the old man in surprise; he had never thought that he was of so practical a turn. He promised that he would be careful, and imagining that he had received all his directions, rose to leave; but the old man still detained him.

"Here," said he, "suppose you tell me a little about Caroline Schimmel. You told Beaumarchef that she said I had made her scream, and that when she caught me, I should have a bad time of it, eh?"

"You weren't my partner then," returned the lad with an impudent laugh; "and I wanted to give you a bit of a fright. The truth is, that you made the poor old girl so drunk that she has had to go to the hospital."

Tantaine was overjoyed at this news, and, rising from his seat, said, "Where are you living now?"

"Nowhere in particular. Yesterday I slept in a stable, but there isn't room for all my furniture there, so I must shift."

"Would you like to have my room for a day or two?" asked Tantaine, chuckling at the boy's jest. "I have moved from there, but the attic is mine for another fortnight yet."

"I'm gone; where is it?"

"You know well enough, in the Hotel de Perou, Rue

de la Hachette.   Then I will send a line to the land-
lady "; and tearing a leaf from his pocketbook, he
scrawled on it a few words, saying that a young relative of his, M. Chupin, was to have his room.

This letter, together with his banknote, Toto carefully tied up in the corner of his neckerchief, and as
he crossed the street the old man watched him for a
moment, and then stood gazing at the workmen on the
scaffolding.   Just then Gandelu and his son came out,
and the contractor paused to give a few instructions.
For a few seconds Gaston and Chupin stood side by
side, and a strange smile flitted across Tantaine's face
as he noted this.   " Both children of Paris," muttered
he, " and both striking examples of the boasted civiliza-
tion.   The dandy struts along the pavement, while the
street arab plays in the gutter."

But he had no time to spend in philosophical specu-
lations, as the omnibus that he required appeared, and
entering it, in another half-hour he entered Paul Violaine's lodgings in the Rue Montmartre.

The portress, Mother Brigaut, was at her post as
Tantaine entered the courtyard and asked,—

" And how is our young gentleman to-day? "

"Better, sir, ever so much better; I made him a
lovely bowl of soup yesterday, and he drank up every
drop of it.   He looks like a real king this morning,
and the doctor sent in a dozen of wine to-day, which
will, I am sure, effect a perfect cure."

With a smile and a nod Tantaine was making his
way to the stairs, when Mother Brigaut prevented
his progress.

"Some one was here yesterday," remarked she,
" asking about M. Paul."

" What sort of a looking person was it? "

" Oh, a man like any other, nothing particular about
him, but he wasn't a gentleman, for after keeping me
for fully fifteen minutes talking and talking, he only
gave me a five-franc piece."

The description was not one that would lead to a
recognition of the person, and Tantaine asked in tones
of extreme annoyance,—

" Did you not notice anything particular about the
man ? "

" Yes, he had on gold spectacles with the mountings as fine as a hair, and a watch chain as thick
and heavy as I have ever seen."

" And is that all ? "

" Yes," answered she. " Oh ! there was one thing
more—the person knows that you come here."

" Does he ? Why do you think so ? "

" Because all the time he was talking to me he was
in a rare fidget, and always kept his eyes on the
door."

" Thanks, Mother Brigaut; mind and keep a sharp
lookout," returned Tantaine, as he slowly ascended
the stairs.

Every now and then he paused to think. " Who
upon earth can this fellow be ? " asked he of himself.
He reviewed the whole question—chances, probabilities, and risks, not one was neglected, but all in vain.

" A thousand devils ! " growled he; " are the police
at my heels ? "

His nerves were terribly shaken, and he strove in
vain to regain his customary audacity. By this time
he had reached the door of Paul's room, and, on his
ringing, the door was at once opened; but at the sight
of this woman he started back, with a cry of angry
surprise; for it was a female figure that stood before

him, a young girl—Flavia, the daughter of Martin Rigal, the banker.

The keen eyes of Tantaine showed him that Flavia's visit had not been of long duration. She had removed her hat and jacket, and was holding in her hand a piece of fancy work.

"Whom do you wish to see, sir?" asked she.

The old man strove to speak, but his lips would not frame a single sentence. A band of steel seemed to be compressing his throat, and he appeared like a man about to be seized with an apoplectic fit.

Flavia gazed upon the shabby-looking visitor with an expression of intense disgust. It seemed to her that she had seen him somewhere; in fact, there was an inexplicable manner about him which entirely puzzled her.

"I want to speak to M. Paul," said the old man in a low, hoarse whisper; "he is expecting me."

"Then come in; but just now his doctor is with him."

She threw open the door more widely, and stepped back, so that the greasy garments of the visitor might not touch her dress. He passed her with an abject bow, and crossed the little sitting-room with the air of a man who perfectly understands his way. He did not knock at the door of the bedroom, but went straight in; there a singular spectacle at once arrested his attention. Paul, with a very pale face, was seated on the bed, while Hortebise was attentively examining his bare shoulder. The whole of Paul's right arm and shoulder was a large open wound, which seemed to have been caused by a burn or scald, and must have been extremely painful. The doctor was bending over him, applying a cooling lotion to the injured place with a small piece of sponge. He turned sharply round on Daddy Tantaine's entrance; and so accustomed were these men to read each other's faces at a glance that Hortebise saw at once what had happened; for Tantaine's expression plainly said, "Is Flavia mad to be here?" while the eyes of Hortebise answered, "She may be, but I could not help it."

Paul turned, too, and greeted the old man with an exclamation of delight.

"Come here," said he merrily, "and just see to what a wretched state I have been reduced between the doctor and M. Mascarin."

Tantaine examined the wound carefully. "Are you quite sure," asked he, "that not only will it deceive the Duke, who will see but with our eyes, but also those of his wife, and perhaps of his medical man?"

"We will hoodwink the lot of them."

"And how long must we wait," asked the old man, "until the place skins over, and assumes the appearance of having been there from childhood?"

"In a month's time Paul can be introduced to the Duke de Champdoce."

"Are you speaking seriously?"

"Listen to me. The scar will not be quite natural then, but I intend to subject it to various other modes of treatment."

The dressing was now over, and Paul's shirt being readjusted, he was permitted to lie down again.

"I am quite willing to remain here forever," said he, "as long as I am allowed to retain the services of the nurse that I have in the next room, and who, I am sure, is waiting with the greatest eagerness for your departure."

Hortebise fumed, and cast a glance at Paul which

seemed to say, " Be silent "; but the conceited young man paid no heed to it.

" How long has this charming nurse been with you?" asked Tantaine in an unnatural voice.

" Ever since I have been in bed," returned Paul with the air of a gay young fellow. " I wrote a note that I was unable to go over to her, so she came to me. I sent my letter at nine o'clock, and at ten minutes past she was with me."

The diplomatic doctor slipped behind Tantaine, and made violent gestures to endeavor to persuade Paul to keep silence, but all was in vain.

" M. Martin Rigal," continued the vain young fool, " passes the greater part of his life in his private office. As soon as he gets up he goes there, and is not seen for the rest of the day. Flavia can therefore do entirely as she likes. As soon as she knows that her worthy father is deep in his ledgers, she puts on her hat and runs round to me, and no one could have a kinder and a prettier visitor than she is."

The doctor was hard at work at his danger signals, but it was useless. Paul saw them, but did not comprehend their meaning; and Tantaine rubbed his glasses savagely.

" You are perhaps deceiving yourself a little," said he at last.

" And why? You know that Flavia loves me, poor girl. I ought to marry her, and of course I shall; but still, if I do not do so—well, you know, I need say no more."

" You wretched scoundrel!" exclaimed the usually placid Tantaine. His manner was so fierce and threatening that Paul shifted his position to one nearer the wall.

It was impossible for Tantaine to say another word, for Hortebise placed his hand upon his lips, and dragged him from the room.

CHAPTER XXIX.

THE TAFILA COPPER MINES, LIMITED.

PAUL could not for the life of him imagine why Tantaine had left the room in apparently so angry a mood. He had certainly spoken of Flavia in a most improper manner; for the very weakness of which she had been guilty should have caused him to treat her with tender deference and respect. He could understand the anger of Hortebise, who was Rigal's friend; but what on earth had Tantaine in common with the wealthy banker and his daughter? Forgetful of the pain which the smallest movement upon his part produced, Paul sat up in his bed, and listened with intense eagerness, hoping to catch what was going on in the next room; but he could hear nothing through the thick walls and the closed door.

"What can they be doing?" asked he. "What fresh plot are they contriving?"

Daddy Tantaine and Hortebise passed out of the room hastily, but when they reached the staircase they stood still. The doctor wore the same smiling expression of face, and he endeavored to calm his companion, who appeared to be on the verge of desperation.

"Have courage," whispered he; "what is the use of

giving way to passion? You cannot help this; it is too late now. Besides, even if you could, you would not, as you know very well, indeed!"

The old man was moving his spectacles, not to wipe his glasses, but his eyes.

"Ah!" moaned he, "now I can enter into the feelings of M. de Mussidan when I proved to him that his daughter had a lover. I have been hard and pitiless, and I am cruelly punished."

"My old friend, you must not attach too much importance to what you have heard. Paul is a mere boy, and, of course, a boaster."

"Paul is a miserable cowardly dog," answered the old man in a fierce undertone. "Paul does not love the girl as she loves him; but what he says is true, only too true, I can feel. Between her father and her lover she would not hesitate for a moment. Ah! unhappy girl, what a terrible future lies before her."

He stopped himself abruptly.

"I cannot speak to her myself," resumed he; "do you, doctor, strive and make her have reason."

Hortebise shrugged his shoulders. "I will see what my powers of oratory can do," answered he; "but you are not quite yourself to-day. Remember that a chance word will betray the secret of our lives."

"Go at once, and I swear to you that, happen what may, I will be calm."

The doctor went back into Paul's room, while Tantaine sat down on the topmost stair, his face buried in his hands.

Mademoiselle Flavia was just going to Paul, when the doctor again appeared.

"What, back again?" asked she petulantly. "I thought that you had been far away by this time."

"I want to say something to you," answered he, "and something of a rather serious nature. You must not elevate those charming eyebrows. I see you guess what I am going to say, and you are right. I am come to tell you that this is not the proper place for Mademoiselle Rigal."

"I know that."

This unexpected reply, made with the calmest air in the world, utterly disconcerted the smiling doctor.

"It seems to me——" began he.

"That I ought not to be here; but then, you see, I place duty before cold, worldly dictates. Paul is very ill, and has no one to take care of him except his affianced bride; for has not my father given his consent to our union?"

"Flavia, listen to the experience of a man of the world. The nature of men is such that they never forgive a woman for compromising her reputation, even though it be in their own favor. Do you know what people will say twenty-four hours after your marriage? Why, that you had been his mistress for weeks before, and that it was only the knowledge of that fact that inclined your father to consent to the alliance."

Flavia's face grew crimson. "Very well," said she, "I will obey, and never say again that I was obstinate; but let me say one word to Paul, and then I will leave him."

The doctor retired, not guessing that this obedience arose from a sudden suspicion which had arisen in Flavia's mind. "It is done," said he, as he rejoined Tantaine on the stairs; "let us hasten, for she will follow us at once."

By the time that Tantaine got into the street, he

seemed to have recovered a certain amount of his self-command. "We have succeeded," said he, "but we shall have to work hard, and this marriage must be hastened by every means in our power. It can be celebrated now without any risk, for in twelve hours the only obstacle that stands between that youth there and the colossal fortune of the Champdoce will have vanished away."

Though he had expected something of the kind, the face of the doctor grew very pale.

"What, André?" faltered he.

"André is in great danger, doctor, and may not survive to-morrow, and a portion of the work necessary to this end will be done to-night by our young friend Toto Chupin."

"By that young scamp? Why, only the other day you laughed when I suggested employing him."

"I shall this time kill two birds with one stone. Once an investigation is made—let us speak plainly—into André's death, there will be some inquiry made as to a certain window frame that has been sawed through, and suspicion will fall upon Toto Chupin, who will have been seen lurking about the spot. It will be proved that he purchased a saw, and that he changed just before a note for one thousand francs; he will be found in hiding in a garret in the Hotel de Perou."

The doctor looked aghast. "Are you mad?" cried he. "Toto will accuse you."

"Very likely, but by that time poor old Tantaine will be dead and buried. Then Mascarin will disappear, our faithful Beaumarchef will be in the United States, and we can afford to laugh at the police."

"It seems like a success," said the doctor, "but

push on for mercy's sake; all these delays and fluctuations will make me seriously ill."

The two worthy associates held this conversation concealed in a doorway, anxious to be sure that Flavia had kept her promise. In a brief space of time they saw her come out of the house and move in the direction of her father's bank.

"Now," said Tantaine, "I can go in peace, doctor; farewell for the present;" and without waiting for a reply he was walking rapidly away when he was stopped by Beaumarchef, who came up breathless and barred his passage.

"I was looking for you," cried he; "the Marquis de Croisenois is in the office and is swearing at me like anything."

"Go back to the office and tell the Marquis that the master will soon be with him;" and, thus speaking, Tantaine disappeared down a court by the side of Martin Rigal's house.

The Marquis was striding up and down the office, every now and then discharging a rumbling cannonade of oaths. "Fine business people," remarked he, "to make an appointment and then not to keep it!" He checked himself; for the door of the inner office slowly opened, and Mascarin appeared on the threshold. "Punctuality," said he, "does not consist in coming *before*, but *at* the time appointed."

The Marquis was cowed at once, and followed Mascarin into the sanctum and watched him with curious gaze as the redoubtable head of the association seemed to be searching for something among the papers on his desk. When Mascarin had found what he was in search of, he turned and addressed the Marquis.

"I desired to see you," said he, "with reference to the great financial enterprise which you are to launch almost immediately."

"Yes; I understand that we must discuss it, fully understand it, and feel our way."

Mascarin uttered a contemptuous whistle.

"Do you think," asked he, "that I am the kind of person to stand and wait while you feel your way? because if you do, the sooner you undeceive yourself the better. Things that I take in hand are carried out like a flash of lightning. You have been playing while I and Catenac have been working, and nothing remains to be done but to act."

"Act! What do you mean?"

"I mean that offices have been taken in the Rue Vivienne, that the articles of association have been drawn up, the directors chosen, and the Company registered. The printer brought the prospectus here yesterday; you can begin sending them out to-morrow."

"But——"

"Read it for yourself," said Mascarin, handing a printed paper to him. "Read, and then, perhaps, you will be convinced."

Croisenois, in a dazed sort of manner, accepted the paper and read it aloud.

COPPER MINES OF TAFILA, ALGERIA.

Chairman: THE MARQUIS HENRI DE CROISENOIS.

Capital: Four Million Francs.

This Company does not appeal to that rash class of speculators who are willing to incur great risks for the sake of obtaining for a time heavy dividends.

The shareholders in the Tafila Copper Mining Company, Limited, must not look for a dividend of more than six, or at the utmost seven, per cent.

"Well," interrupted Mascarin, "what do you think of this for a beginning?"

"It seems fair enough," answered De Croisenois, "but suppose others than those whose names you have in your black list take shares, what do you say we are to do then?"

"We should simply decline to allot shares to them, that is all. See the Article XX. in the Articles of Association. 'The Board of Directors may decline to allot shares to applicants without giving any reason for so doing.'"

"And suppose," continued the Marquis, "that one of our own people dispose of his share, may we not find our new shareholder a thorn in our side?"

"Article XXI. 'No transfer of stock is valid, unless passed by the Board of Directors, and recorded in the books of the Company,'" read out Mascarin.

"And how will the game be brought to a conclusion?"

"Easily enough. You will advertise one morning that two-thirds of the capital having been unsuccessfully sunk in the enterprise, you are compelled to apply for a winding-up of the Company under Article XVII. Six months afterwards you will announce that the liquidation of the Company has, after all expenses have been paid, left no balance whatsoever. Then you wash your hands of the whole thing, and the matter is at an end."

Croisenois felt that he had no ground to stand upon, but he ventured on one more objection.

"It seems rather a strange thing to launch this enterprise at the present moment. May it not interfere with my marriage prospects? and may not the Count

de Mussidan decline to give me his daughter and risk
her dowry in this manner? One moment, I——"

The agent sneered and cut short the tergiversations
of the Marquis.

" You mean, I suppose," said he, " that when once
you are safely married and have received Mademoiselle Sabine's dowry, you will take leave of us. Not
so, my dear young friend; and if this is your idea,
put it aside, for it is utter nonsense. I should hold
you then as I do now."

The Marquis saw that any further struggle would
be of no avail, and gave in.

*   *   *   *   *

That evening, when M. Martin Rigal emerged from
his private office, his daughter Flavia was more than
usually demonstrative in her tokens of affection.
" How fondly I love you, my dearest father!" said
she, as she rained kisses on his cheeks. " How good
you are to me!" but on this occasion the banker was
too much preoccupied to ask his daughter the reason
for this extreme tenderness on her part.

CHAPTER XXX.

THE VEILED PORTRAIT.

THE danger with which André was menaced was
most terrible, and the importance of the game he was
playing made him feel that he had everything to fear
from the boldness and audacity of his enemies. He
knew this, and he also knew that spies dogged all his
movements. What could be wanted but a favorable

opportunity to assassinate him? But even this knowledge did not make him hesitate for an instant, and all his caution was fully exercised, for he felt that should he perish, Sabine would be inevitably lost. On her account he acted with a prudence which was certainly not one of his general characteristics. He was quite aware that he might put himself under the protection of the police, but this he knew would be to imperil the honor of the Mussidan family. He was sure that with time and patience he should be able to unravel the plots of the villains who were at work. But he had not time to do so by degrees. No, he must make a bold dash at once. The hideous sacrifice of which Sabine was to be the victim was being hurried on, and it seemed to him as if his very existence was being carried away by the hours as they flitted by. He went over recent events carefully one by one, and he strove to piece them together as a child does the portions of a dissected map. He wanted to find out the one common interest that bound all these plotters together—Verminet, Van Klopen, Mascarin, Hortebise, and Martin Rigal. As he submitted all this strange combination of persons to the test, the thought of Gaston de Gandelu came across his mind.

"Is it not curious," thought he, "that this unhappy boy should be the victim of the cruel band of miscreants who are trying to destroy us? It is strange, very strange."

Suddenly he started to his feet, for a fresh idea had flashed across his brain—a thought that was as yet but crude and undefined, but which seemed to bear the promise of hope and deliverance. It seemed to him that the affair of young Gandelu was closely connected with his own, that they were part and parcel of the same dark plot, and that these bills with their forged acceptance had more to do with him than he had ever imagined. How it was that he and Gaston could be connected he could not for a moment guess; yet now he would have cheerfully sworn that such was the case. Who was it that had informed the father of the son's conduct? Why, Catenac. Who had advised that proceedings should be taken against Rose, *alias* Zora? Why, Catenac again; and this same man, in addition to acting for Gandelu, it seems, was also the confidential solicitor of the Marquis de Croisenois and Verminet. Perhaps he had only obeyed their instructions. All this was very vague and unsatisfactory, but it might be something to go upon, and who could say what conclusion careful inquiry might not lead him to? and André determined to carry on his investigations, and endeavor to find the hidden links that connected this chain of rascality together. He had taken up a pencil with the view of making a few notes, when he heard a knock at his door. He glanced at the clock; it was not yet nine.

"Come in," cried he as he rose.

The door was thrown open, and the young artist started as he recognized in his early visitor the father of Sabine. It was after a sleepless night that the Count had decided to take the present step. He was terribly agitated, but had had time to prepare himself for this all-important interview.

"You will, I trust, pardon me, sir," said he, "for making such an early call upon you, but I thought that I should be sure to find you at this hour, and I much wanted to see you."

André bowed.

In the space of one brief instant a thousand suppositions, each one more unlikely than the other, coursed through his brain. Why had the Count called? Who could have given him his address? And was the visit friendly or hostile?

"I am a great admirer of paintings," began the Count, "and one of my friends upon whose taste I can rely has spoken to me in the warmest terms of your talent. This I trust will explain the liberty I have taken. Curiosity drove me to——"

He paused for a moment, and then added,—

"My name is the Marquis de Bevron."

The concealment of the Count's real name showed André that the visit was not entirely a friendly one, and André replied,—

"I am only too pleased to receive your visit. Unfortunately just now I have nothing ready, only a few rough sketches in short. Would you like to see them?"

The Count replied eagerly in the affirmative. He was terribly embarrassed under his fictitious name, and shrank before the honest, open gaze of the young artist, and his mental disturbance was completed by seeing in one corner of the room the picture covered with a green cloth, which Tantaine had alluded to. It was evident that the old villain had told the truth, and that his daughter's portrait was concealed behind this wrapper. She had evidently been here—had spent hours here, and whose fault was it? She had but listened to the voice of her heart, and had sought that affection abroad which she was unable to obtain at home. As the Count gazed upon the young man before him, he was forced to admit that Mademoiselle Sabine had not fixed her affections on an unworthy object, for at the very first glance he had been struck with the manly beauty of the young artist, and the clear intelligence of his face.

"Ah," thought André, "you come to me under a name that is not your own, and I will respect your wish to remain unknown, but I will take advantage of it by letting you know things which I should not dare say to your face."

Great as was André's preoccupation, he could not fail to notice that his visitor's eyes sought the veiled picture with strange persistency. While M. de Mussidan was looking at the various sketches on the walls, André had time to recover all his self-command.

"Let me congratulate you, sir," remarked the Count, as he returned to the spot where the painter was standing. "My friend's admiration was well founded. I am sorry, however, that you have nothing finished to show me. You say that you have nothing, I believe?"

"Nothing, Marquis."

"Not even that picture whose frame I can distinguish through the serge curtain that covers it?"

André blushed, though he had been expecting the question from the commencement.

"Excuse me," answered he; "that picture is certainly finished, but it is not on view."

The Count was now sure that Tantaine's statement was correct.

"I suppose that it is some woman's portrait," remarked the false Marquis.

"You are quite correct."

Both men were much agitated at this moment, and avoided meeting each other's eyes.

The Count, however, had made up his mind that he would go on to the end.

"Ah, you are in love, I see!" remarked he with a forced laugh. "All great artists have depicted the charms of their mistresses on canvas."

"Stop," cried André with an angry glance in his eyes. "The picture you refer to is the portrait of the purest and most innocent girl in the world. I shall love her all my life; but, if possible, my respect for her is greater than my love. I should consider myself a most degraded wretch, had I ever whispered in her ear a word that her mother might not have listened to."

A feeling of the most instantaneous relief thrilled through M. de Mussidan's heart.

"You will pardon me," suggested he blandly, "but when one sees a portrait in a studio, the inference is that a sitting or two has taken place?"

"You are right. She came here secretly, and without the knowledge of her family, at the risk of her honor and reputation, thus affording me the strongest proof of her love. It was cruel of me," continued the young artist, "to accept this proof of her entire devotion, and yet not only did I accept it, but I pleaded for it on my bended knees, for how else was I to hear the music of her voice, or gladden my eyes with her beauty? We love each other, but a gulf wider than the stormy sea divides us. She is an heiress, come of a proud and haughty line of nobles, while I——"

André paused, waiting for some words either of encouragement or censure; but the Count remained silent, and the young man continued,—

"Do you know who I am? A poor foundling, placed in the Hospital of Vendôme, the illicit offspring of some poor betrayed girl. I started in the world with twenty francs in my pocket, and found my way to Paris; since then I have earned my bread by my daily work. You only see here the more brilliant side of my life; for an artist here—I am a common workman elsewhere."

If M. de Mussidan remained silent, it was from extreme admiration of the noble character, which was so unexpectedly revealed to him, and he was endeavoring to conceal it.

"She knows all this," pursued André, "and yet she loves me. It was here, in this very room, that she vowed that she could never be the wife of another. Not a month ago, a gentleman, well born, wealthy, and fascinating, with every characteristic that a woman could love, was a suitor for her hand. She went boldly to him, told him the story of our love, and, like a noble-hearted gentleman, he withdrew at once, and to-day is my best and kindest friend. Now, Marquis, would you like to see this young girl's picture?"

"Yes," answered the Count, "and I shall feel deeply grateful to you for such a mark of confidence."

André went to the picture, but as he touched the curtain he turned quickly towards his visitor.

"No," said he, "I can no longer continue this farce; it is unworthy of me."

M. de Mussidan turned pale.

"I am about to see Sabine de Mussidan's portrait. Draw the curtain."

André obeyed, and for a moment the Count stood entranced before the work of genius that met his eyes.

"It is she!" said the father. "Her very smile; the same soft light in her eyes. It is exquisite!"

Misfortune is a harsh teacher; some weeks ago he would have smiled superciliously at the mere idea of granting his daughter's hand to a struggling artist, for then he thought only of M. de Breulh, but now he would have esteemed it a precious boon had he been allowed to choose André as Sabine's husband. But Henri de Croisenois stood in the way, and as this idea flashed across the Count's mind he gave a perceptible start. He was sure from the excessive calmness of the young man that he must be well acquainted with all recent events. He asked the question, and André, in the most open manner, told him all he knew. The generosity of M. de Breulh, the kindness of Madame Bois Arden, his suspicions, his inquiries, his projects, and his hopes. M. de Mussidan gazed once more upon his daughter's portrait, and then, taking the hand of the young painter, said,—

" M. André, if ever we can free ourselves from those miscreants, whose daggers are pointed at our hearts, Sabine shall be your wife."

CHAPTER XXXI.

GASTON'S DILEMMA.

YES, Sabine might yet be his, but between the lovers stood the forms of Croisenois and his associates. But now he felt strong enough to contend with them all.

" To work! " said he, " to work! "

Just then, however, he heard a sound of ringing laughter outside his door. He could distinguish a woman's voice, and also a man's, speaking in high, shrill tones. All at once his door burst open, and a hurricane of silks, velvets, feathers, and lace whirled

in. With extreme surprise, the young artist recognized the beautiful features of Rose, *alias* Zora de
Chantemille, Gaston de Gandelu followed her, and at
once began,—

"Here we are," said he, "all right again. Did you
expect to see us?"

"Not in the least."

"Ah! well, it is a little surprise of the governor's.
On my word, I really will be a dutiful son for the
future. To-day, the good old boy came into my room,
and said, 'This morning I took the necessary steps to
release the person in whom you are interested. Go
and meet her.' What do you think of that? So off
I ran to find Zora, and here we are."

André did not pay much attention to Gaston, but
was engaged in watching Zora, who was looking
round the studio. She went up to Sabine's portrait,
and was about to draw the curtain, when André exclaimed,—

"Excuse me," said he; "I must put this picture to
dry." And as the portrait stood on a movable easel,
he wheeled it into the adjoining room.

"And now," said Gaston, "I want you to come and
breakfast with us to celebrate Zora's happy release."

"I am much obliged to you, but it is impossible. I
must get on with my work."

"Yes, yes; work is an excellent thing, but just now
you must go and dress."

"I assure you that it is quite out of the question.
I cannot leave the studio yet."

Gaston paused for a moment in deep thought.

"I have it," said he triumphantly. "You will not
come to breakfast; then breakfast shall come to you.
I am off to order it."

André ran after him, but Gaston was too quick, and he returned to the studio in anything but an amiable temper. Zora noticed his evident annoyance.

"He always goes on in this absurd way," said she, with a shrug of her pretty shoulders, "and thinks himself so clever and witty, bah!"

Her tone disclosed such contempt for Gaston that André looked at her in perplexed surprise.

"What do you look so astonished at? It is easy to see you do not know much of him. All his friends are just like him; if you listen to them for half an hour at a stretch, you get regularly sick. When I think of the terrible evenings that I have spent in their company, I feel ready to die with yawning;" and as she spoke, she suited the action to the word. "Ah! if he really loved me!" added she.

"Love you! Why, he adores you."

Zora made a little gesture of contempt which Toto Chupin might have envied.

"Do you think so?" said she. "Do you know what it is he loves in me? When people pass me they cry out, 'Isn't she good style?' and then the idiot is as pleased as Punch; but if I had on a cotton gown, he would think nothing of me."

Rose had evidently learned a good deal, as her beauty had never been so radiant. She was one glow of health and strength.

"Then my name was not good enough for him," she went on. "His aristocratic lips could not bring themselves to utter such a common name as Rose, so he christened me Zora, a regular puppy dog's name. He has plenty of money, but money is not everything after all. Paul had no money, and yet I loved him a thousand times better. On my word, I have almost forgotten how to laugh, and yet I used to be as merry as the day was long."

" Why did you leave Paul then?"

" Well, you see, I wanted to experience what a woman feels when she has a Cashmere shawl on, so one fine morning I took wing. But there, who knows? Paul would very likely have left me one day. There was some one who was doing his best to separate us, an old blackguard called Tantaine, who lived in the same house."

" Ah!" answered he cautiously. " What interest could he have had in separating you?"

" I don't know," answered the girl, assuming a serious air; " but I am sure he was trying it on. A fellow doesn't hand over banknotes for nothing, and I saw him give one for five hundred francs to Paul; and more than that, he promised him that he should make a great fortune through a friend of his called Mascarin."

André started. He remembered the visit that Paul had made him, on the pretext of restoring the twenty francs he had borrowed, and at which he had boasted that he had an income of a thousand francs a month, and might make more, though he had not said how this was to be done. " I think that Paul has forgotten me. I saw him once at Van Klopen's, and he never attempted to say a word to me. He was certainly with that Mascarin at the time."

André could only draw one conclusion from this, either that Paul was protected by the band of conspirators, or else that he formed one of it. In that case he was useful to them; while Rose, who was in their way, was persecuted by them. André's mind came to this conclusion in an instant. It seemed to

him that if Catenac had been desirous of imprison-
ing Rose, it was because she was in the way, and her
presence disturbed certain combinations. Before, however, he could work out his line of deduction, Gaston's
shrill voice was heard upon the stairs, and in another
moment he made his appearance.

"Place for the banquet," said he; "make way for
the lordly feast."

Two waiters followed him, bearing a number of covered dishes on trays. At another time André would
have been very angry at this invasion, and at the
prospect of a breakfast that would last two or three
hours and utterly change everything; but now he was
inclined to bless Gaston for his happy idea, and, with
the assistance of Rose, he speedily cleared a large
table for the reception of the viands.

Gaston did nothing, but talked continually.

"And now I must tell you the joke of the day.
Henri de Croisenois, one of my dearest friends, has
absolutely launched a Company."

André nearly let fall a bottle, which he was about
to place upon the table.

"Who told you this?" asked he quickly.

"Who told me? Why, a great big flaming poster.
Tafila Copper Mines; capital, four millions. And my
esteemed friend, Henri, has not a five-franc piece to
keep the devil out of his pocket."

The face of the young artist expressed such blank
surprise that Gaston burst into a loud laugh.

"You look just as I did when I read it. Henri de
Croisenois, the chairman of a Company! Why, if you
had been elected Pope, I should not have been more
surprised. Tafila Copper Mines! What a joke! The
shares are five hundred francs."

The waiters had now retired, and Gaston urged his friends to take their places at the table, and all seemed merry as a marriage bell; but many a gay commencement has a stormy ending.

Gaston, whose shallow brain could not stand the copious draughts of wine with which he washed down his repast, began all at once to overwhelm Zora with bitter reproaches at her not being able to comprehend how a man like him, who was destined to play a serious part in society, could have been led away, as he had been, by a person like her.

Gaston had a tongue which was never at a loss either to praise or blame, and Zora was equally ready to retort, and defended herself with such acrimony that the lad, knowing himself to be in fault, entirely lost the small remnant of temper which he still possessed, and dashed out of the room, declaring that he never wished to set eyes upon Zora again, and that she might keep all the presents that he had lavished upon her for all he cared.

His departure was hailed with delight by André, who, now that he was left alone with Zora, hoped to derive some further information from her, and especially a distinct description of Paul, whom he felt that he must now reckon among his adversaries. But his hopes were destined to be frustrated, for Zora was so filled with anger and excitement that she refused to listen to another word; and putting on her hat and mantle, with scarcely a glance at the mirror, rushed out of the studio with the utmost speed, declaring that she would seek out Paul, and make him revenge the insults that Gaston had put on her.

All this passed so rapidly that the young painter felt as if a tornado had passed through his humble dwelling; but as peace and calm returned, he began to see that Providence had directly interposed in his favor, and had sent Rose and Gaston to his place to furnish him with fresh and important facts. All that Rose had said, incomplete as her statement was, had thrown a ray of light upon an intrigue which, up till now, had been shaded in the thickest gloom. The relations of Paul with Mascarin explained why Catenac had been so anxious to have Rose imprisoned, and also seemed to hint vaguely at the reason for the extraction of the forged signatures from the simple Gaston. What could be the meaning of the Company started by De Croisenois at the very moment when he was about to celebrate his union with Sabine?

André desired to see the advertisement of the Company for himself; and without stopping to change his blouse, ran downstairs to the corner of the street, where Gaston had told him that the announcement of the Company was placarded up. He found it there, in a most conspicuous position, with all its advantages most temptingly set forth. Nothing was wanting; and there was even a woodcut of Tafila, in Algiers, which represented the copper mines in full working operation; while at the top, the name of the chairman, the Marquis de Croisenois, stood out in letters some six inches in height.

André stood gazing at this wonderful production for fully five minutes, when all at once a gleam of prudence flashed across his mind.

"I am a fool," said he to himself. "How do I know how many watchful eyes are now fixed on me, reading on my countenance my designs regarding this matter and its leading spirit?"

Upon his return to his room, he sat for more than

an hour, turning over the whole affair in his mind, and at length he flattered himself that he had hit upon an expedient. Behind the house in which he lodged was a large garden, belonging to some public institution, the front of which was in the Rue Laval. A wall of about seven feet in height divided these grounds from the premises in the Rue de la Tour d'Auvergne. Why should he not go out by the way of these ornamental grounds and so elude the vigilance of the spies who might be in waiting at the front of the house?

" I can," thought he, " alter my appearance so much that I shall not be recognized. I need not return here to sleep. I can ask a bed from Vignol, who will also help me in every possible way."

This Vignol was the friend to whom, at André's request, M. Gandelu had given the superintendence of the works at his new house in the Champs Elysées.

" I shall," continued he, " by this means escape entirely from De Croisenois and his emissaries, and can watch their game without their having any suspicion of my doing so. For the time being, of course, I must give up seeing those who have been helping me—De Breulh, Gandelu, Madame de Bois Arden, and M. de Mussidan; that, however, cannot be avoided. I can use the post, and by it will inform them all of the step that I have taken."

It was dark before he had finished his letters, and, of course, it was too late to try anything that day; consequently he went out, posted his letters, and dined at the nearest restaurant.

On his return home, he proceeded to arrange his disguise. He had it ready, among his clothes: a blue blouse, a pair of check trousers, well-worn shoes, and a shabby cap, were all that he required, and he then applied himself to the task of altering his face. He first shaved off his beard. Then he twisted down two locks of hair, which he managed to make rest on his forehead. Then he commenced applying some coloring to his face with a paint-brush; but this he found to be an extremely difficult business, and it was not for a long while that he was satisfied with the results that he had produced. He then knotted an old handkerchief round his neck, and clapped his cap on one side, with the peak slanting over one eye. Then he took a last glance in the glass, and felt that he had rendered himself absolutely unrecognizable. He was about to impart a few finishing touches, when a knock came at his door. He was not expecting any one at such an hour, nine o'clock; for the waiters from the restaurant had already removed the remains of the feast.

"Who is there?" cried he.

"It is I," replied a weak voice; "I, Gaston de Gandelu."

André decided that he had no cause to distrust the lad, and so he opened his door.

"Has M. André gone out?" asked the poor boy faintly. "I thought I heard his voice."

Gaston had not penetrated his disguise, and this was André's first triumph; but he saw now that he must alter his voice, as well as his face.

"Don't you know me?" asked he.

It was evident that young Gaston had received some terrible shock; for it could not have been the quarrel in the morning that had reduced him to this abject state of prostration.

"What has gone wrong with you?" asked André kindly.

"I have come to bid you farewell; I am going to shoot myself in half an hour."

"Have you gone mad?"

"Not in the least," answered Gaston, passing his hand across his forehead in a distracted manner; "but those infernal bills have turned up. I was just leaving the dining-room, after having treated the governor to my company, when the butler whispered in my ear that there was a man outside who wanted to see me. I went out and found a dirty-looking old scamp, with his coat collar turned up round the nape of his neck."

"Did he say that his name was Tantaine?" exclaimed André.

"Ah! was that his name? Well, it doesn't matter. He told me in the most friendly manner that the holder of my bills had determined to place them in the hands of the police to-morrow at twelve o'clock, but that there was still a way for me to escape."

"And this was to take Rose out of France with you," said André quickly.

Gaston was overwhelmed with surprise.

"Who the deuce told you that?" asked he.

"No one; I guessed it; for it was only the conclusion of the plan which they had initiated when you were induced to forge Martin Rigal's signature. Well, what did you say?"

"That the idea was a ridiculous one, and that I would not stir a yard. They shall find out that I can be obstinate, too; besides, I can see their little game. As soon as I am out of the way they will go to the governor and bleed him."

But André was not listening to him. What was best to be done? To advise Gaston to go and take

Rose with him was to deprive himself of a great element of success; and to permit him to kill himself was, of course, out of the question.

"Just attend to me," said he at last; "I have an idea which I will tell you as soon as we are out of this house; but for reasons which are too long to go into at present it is necessary for me to get into the street without going through the door. You will, therefore, go away, and as the clock strikes twelve you will ring at the gateway of 29, Rue de Laval. When it is opened, ask some trivial question of the porter; and when you leave, take care that you do not close the gate. I shall be in the garden of the house and will slip out and join you."

The plan succeeded admirably, and in ten minutes Gaston and André were walking along the boulevards.

CHAPTER XXXII.

M. LECOQ.

THE Marquis de Croisenois lived in a fine new house on the Boulevard Malesherbes near the church of St. Augustine, and in a suite of rooms the rental of which was four thousand francs per annum. He had collected together sufficient relics of his former splendor to dazzle the eyes of the superficial observer. The apartment and the furniture stood in the name of his body-servant, while his horse and brougham were by the same fiction supposed to be the property of his coachman, for even in the midst of his ruin the Marquis de Croisenois could not go on foot like common people.

The Marquis had two servants only in his modest establishment—a coachman, who did a certain amount of indoor work, and a valet, who knew enough of cookery to prepare a bachelor breakfast. This valet Mascarin had seen once, and the man had then produced so unpleasant an impression on the astute proprietor of the Servants' Registry Office that he had set every means at work to discover who he was and from whence he came. Croisenois said that he had taken him into his service on the recommendation of an English baronet of his acquaintance, a certain Sir Richard Wakefield. The man was a Frenchman, but he had resided for some time in England, for he spoke that language with tolerable fluency. André knew nothing of these details, but he had heard of the existence of the valet from M. de Breulh, when he had asked where the Marquis lived.

At eight o'clock on the morning after he had surreptitiously left his home in the manner described, André took up his position in a small wine-shop not far from the abode of the Marquis de Croisenois. He had done this designedly, for he knew enough of the manner and customs of Parisian society to know that this was the hour usually selected by domestics in fashionable quarters to come out for a gossip while their masters were still in bed. André had more confidence in himself than heretofore, for he had succeeded in saving Gaston; and these were the means he had employed. After much trouble, and even by the use of threats, he had persuaded the boy to return to his father's house. He had gone with him; and though it was two in the morning, he had not hesitated to arouse M. Gandelu, senior, and tell him how his son had been led on to commit the forgery, and how he threatened to commit suicide.

The poor old man was much moved.

"Tell him to come to me at once," said he, "and let him know that we two will save him."

André had not far to go, for Gaston was waiting in the next room in an agony of suspense.

As soon as he came into the old man's presence he fell upon his knees, with many promises of amendment for the future.

"I do not believe," remarked old Gandelu, "that these miscreants will venture to carry their threats into execution and place the matter in the hands of the police; but for all that, my son must not remain in a state of suspense. I will file a complaint against the Mutual Loan Society before twelve to-day, and we will see how an association will be dealt with that lends money to minors and urges them to forge signatures as security. It will, however, be as well for my son to leave for Belgium by the first train this morning; but, as you will see, he will not remain very many days."

André remained for the rest of the hours of darkness at the kind old man's house, and it was in Gaston's room that he renewed his "make-up" before leaving. The future looked very bright to him as he walked gayly up the Boulevard Malesherbes. The wine-shop in which he had taken up his position was admirably adapted for keeping watch on De Croisenois, for he could not avoid seeing all who came in and went out of the house; and as there was no other wine-shop in the neighborhood, André felt sure that all the servants in the vicinity, and those of the Marquis, of course, among the number, would come there in the course of the morning; so that here he could get into conversation with them, offer them a glass of wine, and, perhaps, get some information from them. The room was large and airy, and was full of customers, most of whom were servants. André was racking his brain for a means of getting into conversation with the proprietor, when two new-comers entered the room. These men were in full livery, while all the other servants had on morning jackets. As soon as they entered, an old man, with a calm expression of face, who was struggling perseveringly with a tough beefsteak at the same table as that by which André was seated, observed,—

"Ah! here comes the De Croisenois' lot."

"If they would only sit here," thought André, "by the side of this fellow, who evidently knows them, I could hear all they said."

By good luck they did so, begging that they might be served at once, as they were in a tremendous hurry.

"What is the haste this morning?" asked the old man who had recognized them.

"I have to drive the master to his office, for he has one now. He is chairman of a Copper Mining Company, and a fine thing it is, too. If you have any money laid by, M. Benoit, this is a grand chance for you."

Benoit shook his head gravely.

"All is not gold that glitters," said he sententiously; "nor, on the other hand, are things as bad as they are painted."

Benoit was evidently a prudent man, and was not likely to commit himself.

" But if your master is going out, you, M. Mouret,
will be free, and we can have a game at cards together."

" No, sir," answered the valet.

" What! are you engaged too? "

" Yes; I have to carry a bouquet of flowers to the
young lady my master is engaged to. I have seen the
young lady; she seems to be rather haughty."

The man, who wore an enormously high and stiff
collar, was absolutely speaking of Sabine, and André
could have twisted his neck with pleasure.

" Let us hope," remarked the coachman, as he hastily swallowed his breakfast, " that the Marquis does
not intend to invest his wife's dowry in this new venture of his."

The men then ceased to speak of their master, and
began to busy themselves with their own affairs, and
went out again without alluding to him any further,
leaving André to reflect what a difficult business the
detective line was.

The customers looked upon him with distrustful
eyes, for it must be confessed that his appearance was
decidedly against him, and he had not yet acquired the
necessary art of seeing and hearing while affecting to
be doing neither; and it was easy for the dullest observer to be certain that it was not for the sake of obtaining a breakfast that he had entered the establishment. André had penetration enough to see the effect
he had produced, and he became more and more embarrassed. He had finished his meal now, and had
lighted a cigar, and had ordered a small glass of
brandy. Nearly all the customers had withdrawn,
leaving only five or six, who were playing cards at a
table near the door. André was anxious to see Croise·

nois enter his carriage, and so he lingered, ordering another glass of brandy as an excuse.

He had just been served, when a man, whose dress very much resembled his own, lounged into the wine-shop. He was a tall, clumsily built fellow, with an insolent expression upon his beardless face. His coat and cap were in an equally dilapidated condition; and in the squeaky voice of the rough, he ordered a plate of beef and half a bottle of wine, and, as he brushed past André, upset his glass of brandy. The artist made no remark, though he felt quite sure that this act was intentional, as the fellow laughed impudently when he saw the damage that he had done. When his breakfast was served, he carelessly spit upon André's boots. The insult was so apparent that André began to reflect.

" Had he not succeeded in eluding his spies, as he thought that he had done? and was it not quite possible that this man had been sent to pick a quarrel with him, and deal him a disabling, or even a fatal blow? "

Prudence counselled him to leave the place at once, but he felt that he could not go until he had found out the real truth. There seemed to be but little doubt on the matter, however; for as the fellow cut up his meat, he jerked every bit of skin and gristle into his neighbor's lap; then, after finishing up his wine, he managed to upset the few drops remaining on to André's arm and shoulder. This was the finishing stroke.

" Please, remember," remarked André calmly, " that there is some one at the table besides yourself."

" Do you think I'm blind, mate?" returned the fellow brutally. " Mind your own business, or——" And to conclude the sentence, he shook his fist threateningly in the young man's face.

André started to his feet, and, with a well-directed blow in the chest, sent the fellow rolling under the table.

At the sound of the scuffle, the card-players turned round, and saw André standing erect, with quivering lips and eyes flashing with rage, while his antagonist was lying on the floor among the overturned chairs.

"Come, come! No squabbling here!" remarked one of the players.

The fellow scrambled to his feet, and made a savage rush at the young man, who, using his right foot skilfully, tripped his antagonist up, and sent him again rolling on the ground. It was most adroitly done, and secured the applause of the lookers-on, who now complained no longer, and were evidently interested in the scene.

Again the rough came up, but André contented himself with standing on the defensive. Some tables, a stool, and a glass were injured, and at last the proprietor came upon the scene of action.

"Get out of this," cried he, "and take care that I don't see your faces here again."

At these words, the rough burst out into a torrent of foul language.

"Don't put up with his cheek," said one of the customers; "give him in charge at once."

Hardly, however, had the manager started to summon the police, than, as if by magic, a body of them appeared; and André found himself walking down the boulevard between a couple, while his late antagonist followed in the safe custody of two more. To have attempted any resistance would have been utter folly, and the young man resigned himself to what he felt he could not help. But as he went on, he reflected on

the strange scene through which he had just passed.
All had gone on so rapidly that he could hardly recall
the events to his memory. He was, however, quite
sure that this unprovoked assault concealed some motive with which at present he was unacquainted.

The police led their prisoners through the doorway
of a dingy-looking old house, and then André saw that
he was not at the regular police-station. The whole
party entered an office, where a superintendent and
two clerks were at work. The ruffian who had assaulted André changed his manner directly he entered
the office; he threw his tattered cap upon a bench,
passed his fingers through his hair, and shook hands
with the superintendent; he then turned to André.

"Permit me, sir," said he, "to compliment you on
being so handy with your fists. You precious nearly
did for me, I can tell you."

At that moment a door opened at the other end of
the room, and a voice was heard to say, "Send them
in."

André and his late antagonist soon found themselves in an office evidently sacred to some one high
up in the police. At a desk near the window was
seated a man, with a rather distinguished air, wearing
a white necktie and a pair of gold glasses.

"Have the goodness to take a seat," said this gentleman, addressing André with the most perfect ur-
banity.

He took a chair, half stupefied by the strangeness of
the whole affair, and waited. Could he be awake, or
was he dreaming? He could hardly tell.

"Before I say anything," remarked the gentleman
in the gold spectacles, "I ought to apologize for a
proceeding which is—well, what shall I call it?—a lit-

tle rough, perhaps; but it was necessary to make use of it to obtain this interview with you. Really, however, I had no choice. You are closely watched, and I did not wish the persons who had set spies on you to have any knowledge of this conference."

"Do you say I am watched?" stammered André.

"Yes, by a certain La Candéle, as sharp a fellow at that kind of work as you could find in Paris. Are you surprised at this?"

"Yes, for I had thought——"

The gentleman's features softened into a benevolent smile.

"You thought," he said, "that you had succeeded in throwing them off the scent. So I had imagined this morning, when I saw you in your present disguise. But permit me, my dear M. André, to assure you that there is great room for improvement in it. I admit that a first attempt is always to be looked on leniently; but it did not deceive La Candéle, and even at this distance I can plainly see your whole make-up; and what I can see, of course, is patent to others."

He rose from his seat, and came closer to André.

"Why on earth," asked he, "should you daub all this color on your face, which makes you look like an Indian warrior in his war-paint? Only two colors are necessary to change the whole face—red and black—at the eyebrows, the nostrils, and the corners of the mouth. Look here"; and taking from his pocket a gold pencil-case, he corrected the faults in the young artist's work.

As soon as he had finished, André went up to the mirror over the chimney-piece, and was surprised at the result.

"Now," said the strange gentleman, "you see the

futility of your attempts. La Candéle knew you at once. I wished to speak to you; so I sent for Palot, one of my men, and instructed him to pick a quarrel with you. The policemen arrested you, and we have met without any one being at all the wiser. Be kind enough to efface my little corrections, as they will be noticed in the street."

André obeyed, and as he rubbed away with the corner of his handkerchief, he vainly sought for some elucidation of this mystery.

The man with the gold spectacles had resumed his seat, and was refreshing himself with a pinch of snuff.

"And now," resumed he, "we will, if you please, have a little talk together. As you see, I know you. Doctor Loulleux tells me that he knows no one so high-minded and amiable as yourself. He declares that your honor is without a stain, and your courage undoubted."

"Ah! my dear sir!" interposed the painter, with a deep blush.

"Pray let me go on. M. Gandelu says that he would trust you with all he possessed, while all your comrades, with Vignol at their head, have the greatest respect and regard for you. So much for the present. As for your future, two of the greatest ornaments of the artistic world say that you will one day occupy a very high place in the profession. You gain now about fifteen francs a day. Am I correct?"

"Certainly," answered André, more bewildered than ever.

The gentleman smiled.

"Unfortunately," he went on, "my information ends here, for the means of inquiry possessed by the police are, of course, very limited. They can only act upon facts, not on intentions, and so long as these are not displayed in open acts, the hands of the police are tied. It is only forty-eight hours since I heard of you for the first time, and I have already your biography in my pocket. I hear that the day before yesterday you were dining with M. de Breulh-Faverlay, and that this morning you were walking with young Gandelu, and that La Candéle was following you like a shadow. These are all facts, but——"

He paused, and cast a keen glance upon André, then, in a slow and measured voice, he continued,—

"But no one has been able to tell me why you dogged Verminet's footsteps, or why you went to Mascarin's house, or why, finally, you disguised yourself to keep a watch on the movements of the most honorable the Marquis de Croisenois. It is the motive that we cannot arrive at, for the facts are perfectly clear."

André fidgeted uneasily in his chair beneath the spell of those magnetic glasses, which seemed to draw the truth from him.

"I cannot tell you, sir," faltered he at last, "for the secret is not mine to divulge."

"You will not trust me? Well, then, I must speak. Remember, all that I have told you was the account of what I knew positively; but, in addition to this, I have drawn my own inferences. You are watching De Croisenois because he is going to marry a wealthy heiress."

André blushed crimson.

"We assume, therefore, that you wish to prevent this marriage; and why, pray? I have heard that Mademoiselle de Mussidan was formerly engaged to M. de Breulh-Faverlay. How comes it that the Count

and Countess de Mussidan prefer a ruined spendthrift
to a wealthy and strictly honorable man? It is for you
to answer this question. It is perfectly plain to me
that they hand over their daughter to De Croisenois
under pressure of some kind, and that means that a
terrible secret exists with which Croisenois threatens
them."

"Your deduction is wrong, sir," exclaimed André
eagerly, "and you are quite wrong."

"Very good," was the calm reply. "Your em-
phatic denial shows that I am in the right. I want
no further proofs. M. de Mussidan paid you a visit
yesterday, and one of my agents reported that his
face was much happier on leaving you than when he
was on his way to your house. I therefore infer that
you promised to release him from Croisenois' per-
secutions, and in return he promised you his daughter's hand in marriage. This, of course, explains your
present disguise, and now tell me again that I am
wrong, if you dare."

André would not lie, and therefore kept silence.

"And now," continued the gentleman, "how about
the secret? Did not the Count tell it you? I do not
know it; and yet I think that if I were to search for
it, I could find it. I can call to my mind certain
crimes which three generations of detectives have
striven to find out. Did you ever hear that De Croisenois had an elder brother named George, who disappeared in a most wonderful manner? What became
of him? This very George, twenty-three years back,
was a friend of Madame de Mussidan's. Might not
his disappearance have something to do with this marriage?"

" Are you the fiend himself?" cried the young man.

" I am M. Lecoq."

André started back in absolute dread at the name of this celebrated detective.

" M. Lecoq!" repeated he.

The vanity of the great detective was much flattered when he saw the impression that his name had produced.

" And now, my dear M. André," said he blandly, "now that you know who I am, may I not hope that you will be more communicative?"

M. de Mussidan had not told his secret to the young artist, but he had said enough for him to feel that the detective was correct in his inference.

" Surely," continued Lecoq, " we ought to be able to come to a more definite understanding, and I think that my openness should elicit some frankness on your side. I saw that you were watched by the very person that I was watching. For three days my men have followed you, and to-day I made up my mind that you could furnish me with the clue I am seeking."

" I, sir?"

" For many years," continued Lecoq, " I have been certain that an organized association of blackmailers exists in Paris; family differences, sin, shame, and sorrow are worked by these wretches like veritable gold mines, and bring them in enormous annual revenues."

" Ah," returned André, " I expected something of this kind."

" Of course, when I was quite sure of these facts," continued Lecoq, " I said to myself, ' I will break up this gang '; but it was easier said than done. There is one very peculiar thing about blackmailing. Those

who carry it on are almost certain of doing so with impunity, for the victims will pay and not complain. Yes,
I tell you that I have often found out these unhappy
pigeons, but never could get one to speak."

The detective was so indignant and acrimonious
withal in his indignation, that André could not repress
a smile.

"Very soon," continued Lecoq, "I recognized the
futility of my attempts, and the impossibility of reaching these scoundrels through their victims, and then I
determined to strike at the plunderers themselves, but
this was a scheme that took patience and time. I have
waited my chance for three years, and for eighteen
months one of my men has been in the service of the
Marquis de Croisenois, and up to now this band of
villains has cost the government over ten thousand
francs. That superlative scoundrel, Mascarin, has put
several white threads in my hair. I believe him to be
Tantaine; yes, and Martin Rigal too. The idea of
there being a means of communication between the
banker's house in the Rue Montmartre and the Servants' Registry Office in the Rue Montorgueil only came
into my head this morning. But this time they have
gone too far, and I have them. The idea of a Limited
Company, the shares of which are to be taken up by
their victims, is not at all a bad one. I know them all,
from the chief, Mascarin-Tantaine-Rigal, down to their
lowest agent, Toto Chupin, and Paul Violaine, the do-
cile puppet of their will. We will get hold of the
whole gang, and neither Van Klopen nor Catenac will
escape. Just now the latter is travelling about with
the Duke de Champdoce and a fellow named Perpignan, and two of my sweet lads are close upon them,
and send in almost hourly reports of what is going

on. My trap has a tempting bait, the spring is strong, and we shall catch every one of them. And now do you still hesitate to confide all you know to me? I swear on my honor that I will respect as sacred what you tell me, no matter what may occur."

André yielded, as did every person who came under the influence of this remarkable man and his strange and inexplicable fascination. If he hid anything from him to-day, would not Lecoq be acquainted with it to-morrow? and so, with the most perfect frankness, he told his story and everything that he knew.

"Now," cried Lecoq, "I see it all clearly. Aha, they want to force young Gandelu to disappear with Rose, do they?"

Beneath his gold-rimmed spectacles his eyes flashed fiercely. He seemed to be occupied in drawing out his plan of campaign.

"From this moment," said he, "be at ease. In another month Mademoiselle de Mussidan shall be your wife; this I promise you, and the promises of Lecoq are never broken."

He paused for an instant, as though to collect his thoughts, and then continued,—

"I can answer for all, except for your life. So many are interested in your disappearance from this world, that every effort will be made to get rid of you. Do not cease your caution for an instant. Never eat twice running at the same restaurant, throw away food that has the slightest strange taste. Avoid crowds in the street; do not get into a cab; never lean from a window before ascertaining that its supports are solid; in a word, fear and suspect everything."

For a moment longer Lecoq detained the young artist.

"Tell me," said he, "have you the mark of a wound on your shoulder or arm?"

"I have, sir; the scar of a very severe scald."

"I thought so; yes, I was almost certain of it," said Lecoq thoughtfully; and as he conducted the young man to the door, he took leave of him with the same words that Mascarin had often used to Paul,—

"Farewell for the present, Duke de Champdoce."

CHAPTER XXXIII.

THROUGH THE AIR.

AT these last words André turned round, but the door closed, and he heard the key grate in the lock. He passed through the outer office, where the superintendent, his two clerks, and his late adversary all seemed to gaze upon him with a glance of admiration and esteem.

He gained the open street.

What did those last words of Lecoq mean? He was a foundling, it is true; but what foundling has not had lofty aspirations, and felt that, for all he knew, he might be the scion of some noble house.

As soon as Lecoq thought that the coast was clear, he opened the door, and called the agent, Palot.

"My lad," said the great man, "you saw that young man who went out just now? He is a noble fellow, full of good feeling and honor. I look upon him as my friend."

Palot made a gesture signifying that henceforth his late antagonist was as something sacred in his eyes.

"You will be his shadow," pursued Lecoq, "and keep near enough to him to rush to his aid at a moment of danger. That gang, of which Mascarin is the head, want his life. You are my right-hand man, and I trust him to you. I have warned him, but youth is rash; and you will scent danger where he would never dream that it lurked. If there is any peril, dash boldly forward, but endeavor to let no one find out who you are. If you must speak to him—but only do so at the last extremity—whisper my name in his ear, and he will know you have come from me. Remember, you are answerable for him; but change your face. La Candéle and the others must not recognize in you the wine-shop bully; that would spoil all. What have you on under that blouse, a *commissionaire's* dress?

"That will do; now change the face."

Palot pulled out a small parcel from his pocket, from which he extracted a red beard and wig, and, going to the mirror, adjusted them with dexterous activity; and, in a few minutes, went up to his master, who was waiting, saying,—

"How will this do?"

"Not bad, not bad," returned Lecoq; "and now to your work."

"Where shall I find him?" asked Palot.

"Somewhere near Mascarin's den, for I advised him not to give up playing the spy too suddenly."

Palot was off like the wind, and when he reached the Rue Montmartre, he caught sight of the person who had been intrusted to his care.

André was walking slowly along, thinking of Lecoq's cautions, when a young man, with his arm in a sling, overtook him, going in the same direction as he was. André was sure that it was Paul, and as he knew that he could not be recognized, he passed him in his turn, and saw that it was indeed the Paul so much regretted by Zora.

"I will find out where he goes to," thought André.

He followed, and saw him enter the house of M. Rigal. Two women were gossiping near the door, and André heard one of them say,—

"That is the young fellow who is going to marry Flavia, the banker's daughter."

Paul, therefore, was to marry the daughter of the chief of the gang. Should he tell Lecoq this? But, of course, the detective knew it.

Time was passing, and André felt that he had but little space to gain the house that Gandelu was building in the Champs Elysées, if he wished to ask hospitality from his friend Vignol.

He found all the workmen there, and not one of them recognized him when he asked for Vignol.

"He is engaged up there," said one. "Take the staircase to the left."

The chief part of the ornamental work was in front, and it was there that the little hut which Tantaine had pointed out to Toto Chupin was erected. Vignol was in it, and was utterly surprised when André made himself known, for he did not recognize him under his strange disguise.

"It is nothing," returned the young man cautiously, as Vignol paused for an explanation; "only a little love affair."

"Do you expect to win a girl's heart by making such a guy of yourself?" asked his friend with a laugh.

"Hush! I will explain matters later on. Can you give me shelter for a night or two?"

He stopped himself, turned terribly pale, and listened intently. He fancied he had heard a woman's scream, and his own name uttered.

"André, it is I—your Sabine; help!"

Quick as lightning André rushed to the window, opened it, and leaned out to discover from whence those sounds came.

The young miscreant, Toto Chupin, had too fatally earned the note with which Tantaine had bribed him. The whole of the front of the window gave way with a loud crash, and André was hurled into space.

The hut was at least sixty feet from the pavement, and the fall was the more appalling because the body of André struck some of the intervening scaffolding first, and thence bounded off, until the unhappy young man fell with a dull thud, bleeding and senseless in the street.

Nearly three hundred persons in the Champs Elysées witnessed this hideous sight; for, at Vignol's cry, every one had stopped, and, frozen with horror, had not missed one detail of the grim tragedy.

In an instant a crowd was collected round the poor, inert mass of humanity which lay motionless in a pool of blood. But two workmen, roused by Vignol's shrieks, were soon on the spot, and pushed their way through the crowd of persons who were gazing with a morbid curiosity on the man who had fallen from a height of sixty feet.

André gave no sign of life. His face was dreadfully bruised, his eyes were closed, and a stream of blood poured from his mouth, as Vignol raised his friend's head upon his knee.

"He is dead!" cried the lookers on. "No one could survive such a fall."

"Let us take him to the Hospital Beaujon!" exclaimed Vignol. "We are close by there."

An ambulance was speedily procured, and the workmen, placing their insensible friend carefully in it, asked permission to carry him to the hospital.

One curious event had excited the attention of some of the lookers on. Just as André fell, a *commissaire* had rushed forward and seized a woman. She was one of the class of unfortunates who frequent the Champs Elysées, and she it was who had uttered the cry that had lured André to destruction. The woman made an effort to escape, but Palot, for it was he, caught her arm.

"Not a word," said he sternly. The wretched creature seemed in abject terror, and obeyed him.

"Why did you cry out?" asked he.

"I do not know."

"It is a lie!"

"No, it is true; a gentleman came up to me, and said, 'Madame, if you will cry out now, André, it is I—your Sabine; help! I will give you two louis.' Of course I agreed. He gave me the fifty francs, and I did as he asked me."

"What was this man like?"

"He was tall, old, and very shabby and dirty, with glasses on. I never set eyes on him before."

"Do you know," returned the *commissaire* sternly, "that the words you have uttered have caused the death of the poor fellow who has just fallen from the house?"

"Why did he not take more care?" asked she indifferently.

Palot, with an angry gesture, handed her over to a police-constable.

" Take her to the station-house," said he, " and do not lose sight of her, for she will be a most important witness at a trial that must soon come on."

" What the woman says is true," muttered Palot. " She did not know what she was doing, and it was Tantaine that gave her the two coins. He shall pay for this; but certainly, if the whole gang are collared, it won't bring the poor young fellow to life."

He had, however, not much time for reflection, for he had to gather up every link of evidence. How was it that this accident had occurred? The frame of the window had fallen out with André, and lay in fragments on the pavement. He picked up one of the pieces, and at once saw what had been done; the wood-work had been sawed almost in two, and the putty with which the marks of the cuts had been concealed still clung to the wood. Palot called one of the workmen, who appeared to be more intelligent than his fellows, pointed out the marks to him, and bade him gather up the fragments and put them in some place of security. This duty being accomplished, Palot joined the crowd; but he was too late, for André had been taken away to the hospital. He looked around to see if there was any one from whom he could gain information, and suddenly perceived on a bench some one whom he had often followed. It was Toto Chupin, no longer clad in the squalid rags of a day or two back. He was dressed in gorgeous array, but his face was livid, his eyes wild, and his lips kept moving convulsively, for he was a victim to a novel sensation—the pangs of remorse— and was meditating whether he should not go to the nearest police-station and give himself up, so that he might revenge himself on Tantaine, who had made him a murderer. For a moment the idea of arresting

Toto passed through Palot's mind, but he, after a moment's thought, muttered,—

" No; that would never do. We should risk losing the whole gang. Besides, he can't get away. I may even have committed an error in arresting that woman. My master will say that I am not to be trusted. He placed one of his friends in my charge, and this is what has happened. I knew that the young man's life was in deadly peril, and yet I let him enter a house in the course of erection; why, I might as well have cut his throat myself."

In a terrible state of anxiety, Palot presented himself at the hospital, and asked for the young man who had just been brought in.

" You mean Number 17? " returned one of the assistant-surgeons. " He is in a most critical state; we fear internal injuries, fracture of the skull, and—in fact, we fear everything."

It was two days before André recovered consciousness. It was midnight when he first woke again to the realities of life. At a glance he guessed where he was. He felt pain when he endeavored to turn over, but he could move his legs and one arm.

" How long have I been here, I wonder? " he thought.

He tried to think, but he was weak, and thoughts would not come at his command, and in a few seconds he dropped off to sleep again; and when he awoke, it was broad day; the ward was full of life and motion, for it was the hour of the house surgeon's visit. He was a young man still, with a cheerful face, followed by the band of students. He went from bed to bed, explaining cases, and cheering up the sufferers. When André's turn came, the surgeon told him that his shoulder was put out, his arm broken in two places, a bad cut on his head, while his body was one mass of bruises; but, for all that, he was in luck to have got off so easily. André listened to him with but a vague understanding of his meaning, for, with the return of reason, the remembrance of Sabine had come, and he asked himself what would become of her while he was confined to his bed in the hospital. As this thought passed through his mind, he uttered a faint groan. One of the students, a stout person, with red whiskers, a white tie, and a rather shabby hat, who looked as if he had just arrived from the country, stepped up to his bed, and leaning over the patient, murmured, " Lecoq." André opened his eyes wide at the name.

" M. Lecoq," gasped he, wondering at the excellence of the disguise.

" Hush, who knows who is watching us? I come to give your mind ease, which will do you more good than all the doctor's stuff. Without in any way committing you, I have seen M. de Mussidan, and have furnished him with a valid excuse for postponing his daughter's marriage for another month. You must remain here; you could not be in a place of greater security; but even here you cannot be too cautious. Eat nothing that is not given you by some one who utters the word ' Lecoq.' M. Gandelu will certainly call to see you. If you want to see or write to me, the patient on your right will manage that; he is one of my men. You shall have news every day; but be patient and prudent."

" I can wait now," answered the young man, " because I have hope."

" Ah," murmured Lecoq, as he moved softly away, " is not hope the true secret of life and happiness? "

CHAPTER XXXIV.

THE DAY OF RECKONING.

M. Lecoq enjoined prudence and caution on André, and the utmost care on the part of his agents, because he was fully aware of the skill and cunning of the adversary with whom he had to cope.

"You should not talk or make a noise," he would say, "when you are fighting."

He could now prove that the head of this association, the man who concealed his identity under a threefold personality, was the instigator of a murder. But he did not intend to make use of this discovery at once, for he had sworn that he would take the whole gang, and his proceedings had been so carefully conducted that his victims did not for a moment suspect the net that was closing around them. The day after the accident to André, Mascarin sent an anonymous communication to the head of the police, giving up Toto as the author of the crime, and saying where he could be found.

"Of course," thought this wily plotter, "Toto will denounce Tantaine, but that worthy man is dead and buried, and I think that even the sharpest agents of the police will be unable to effect his resurrection."

Mascarin had carefully consumed in a large fire every particle of the tattered garments that Tantaine had been in the habit of wearing, and laughed merrily as he watched the columns of sombre smoke roll upwards.

"Look for him as much as you please," laughed he. "Old Daddy Tantaine has flown up the chimney."

The next business was to suppress Mascarin; this was a more difficult operation. Few would care to inquire about Tantaine, but Mascarin was well known as the head of a prosperous business; his disappearance would create a sensation, and the police would take up the matter. His best course would be to conduct matters openly, and sell his business on the plea of family affairs causing him to retire. He easily found a purchaser, and in twenty-four hours the matter had been arranged.

The night before handing over the business to his successor Mascarin had much to do. Assisted by Beaumarchef, he carried into Martin Rigal's private office the papers with which the Registry Office was crammed. This removal was effected by means of a door marked by a panel between Mascarin's office and the banker's private room; and when the last scrap of paper had been removed, Mascarin pointed out a heap of bricks and a supply of mortar to his faithful adherent.

" Wall up this door," said he.

It was a long and wearisome task, but it was at length completed, and by rubbing soot and dust over the new work it lost its appearance of freshness. The evening before Beaumarchef had received twelve thousand francs on the express condition that he would start at once for America, and the leave-taking between him and the master he had so faithfully served was a most affecting one. He knew hardly anything of the diabolical plots going on around him, and was the only innocent person in that house of crime.

Mascarin was in haste to depart; he had annihilated Tantaine in order to free himself from Toto. Mascarin was about to disappear, and he contemplated retaining his third personality, and in it to pass away the remainder of his life honored and respected; but he must first induct his successor into his business; and he went through the books with him, and explained all the practical working of the machinery. This took him nearly all day, and it was getting late when his luggage was put on a cab which he had in waiting. A new plate had already been placed on the door: " J. Robinet, late B. Mascarin."

Knowing that he must carry out the deception completely, Mascarin drove to the western railway station, and took a ticket for Rouen. He felt rather uncomfortable, for he feared that he was being watched, and he made up his mind not to leave a single trace behind him. At Rouen he abandoned his luggage, which he had taken care should afford no clue as to ownership, he also relinquished his beard and spectacles, and returned to Paris as the well-known banker, Martin Rigal, the pretty Flavia's father, having, as he thought, obliterated Mascarin as completely as he had done Tantaine; but he had not noticed in the train with him a very dark young man with piercing eyes, who looked like the traveller of some respectable commercial firm. As soon as he reached his home, and had tenderly embraced his daughter, he went to the private room of Martin Rigal, and opened it with the key that never left his person, and then gazed at a large rough mass of brickwork which disfigured one side of the room, and which was the remains of the wall that erewhile had been so hastily erected in the Office of the Servants' Registry.

" This won't do," muttered he; " it must be plastered, and then repapered."

He picked up the bits of brick and plaster that lay

on the floor, and threw them into the fire, and then pushed a large screen in front of the rough brickwork. He had just finished his work when Hortebise entered the room, with his perpetually smiling face.

"Now, you unbeliever," cried Mascarin gaily, "is not fortune within our grasp? Tantaine and Mascarin are dead, or rather, they never existed. Beaumarchef is on his way to America, La Candéle will be in London in a week, and now we may enjoy our millions."

"Heaven grant it," said the doctor piously.

"Pooh, pooh! we have nothing more to fear, as you would have known had you gone into the case as thoroughly as I have done. Who was the enemy whom we had most need to dread? Why, André. He certainly is not dead, but he is laid up for some weeks, and that is enough. Besides, he has given up the game, for one of my men who managed to get into the hospital says that he has not received a visitor or dispatched a letter for the last fifteen days."

"But he had friends."

"Pshaw! friends always forget you! Why, where was M. de Breulh-Faverlay?"

"It is the racing season, and he is a fixture in his stables."

"Madame de Bois Arden?"

"The new fashions are sufficient for her giddy head."

"M. Gandelu?"

"He has his son's affairs to look after and there is no one else of any consequence."

"And how about young Gandelu?"

"Oh! he has yielded to Tantaine's winning power, and has made it up with Rose, and the turtle doves have taken wing for Florence."

But the doctor was still dissatisfied.

" I am uneasy about the Mussidans," said he.

" And pray why? De Croisenois has been very well received. I don't say that Mademoiselle Sabine has exactly jumped into his arms, but she thanks him every evening for the flowers he sends in the morning, and you can't expect more than that."

" I wish the Count had not put off the marriage. Why did he do so?"

" It annoys me, too; but we can't have everything; set your mind at rest."

By this time the banker had contrived to reassure the doctor.

" Besides," he added, " everything is going on well, even our Tafila mines. I have taxed our people, according to their means, from one to twenty thousand francs, and we are certain of a million."

The doctor rubbed his hands, and a delicious prospect of enjoyments stretched out before him.

" I have seen Catenac," continued Martin Rigal. " He has returned from Vendôme, and the Duke de Champdoce is wild with hope and expectation, and is on the path which he thinks will take him to his son."

" And how about Perpignan?"

Mascarin laughed.

" Perpignan is just as much a dupe as the Duke is; he thinks absolutely that he has discovered all the clues that I myself placed on his road. Before, however, they have quite concluded their investigations, Paul will be my daughter's husband and Flavia the future Duchess of Champdoce, with an income that a monarch might envy."

He paused, for there was a light tap on the door, and Flavia entered. She bowed to the doctor, and, with the graceful movement of a bird, perched herself upon her father's knee, and, throwing her arms round his neck, kissed him again and again.

" This is a very nice little preface," said the banker with a forced smile. " The favor is granted in advance, for, of course, this means that you have come to ask one."

The girl shook her head, and returned in the tone of one addressing a naughty child,—

" Oh, you bad papa! am I in the habit of selling my kisses? I am sure that I have only to ask and to have."

" Of course not, only——"

" I came to tell you that dinner was ready, and that Paul and I are both very hungry; and I only kissed you because I loved you; and if I had to choose a father again, out of the whole it would be you."

He smiled fondly.

" But for the last six weeks," said he, " you have not loved me so well."

" No," returned she with charming simplicity, "not for so long—nearly for fifteen days perhaps."

" And yet it is more than a month since the good doctor brought a certain young man to dinner."

Flavia uttered a frank, girlish laugh.

" I love you dearly," said she, " but especially for one thing."

" And what is that, pray? "

" Ah! that is the secret; but I will tell it you for all that. It is only within the last fortnight that I have found out how really good you have been, and how much trouble you took in bringing Paul to me; but to think that you should have to put on those ugly old clothes, that nasty beard and those spectacles."

At these words the banker started so abruptly to his feet that Flavia nearly fell to the ground.

"What do you mean by this?" said he.

"Do you suppose a daughter does not know her father? You might deceive others, but I——"

"Flavia, I do not comprehend your meaning."

"Do you mean to tell me," asked she, "that you did not come to Paul's rooms the day I was there?"

"Are you crazy? Listen to me."

"No, I will not; you must not tell me fibs. I am not a fool; and when you went out with the doctor, I listened at the door, and I heard a few words you said; and that isn't all, for when I got here, I hid myself and I saw you come into this room."

"But you said nothing to any one, Flavia?"

"No, certainly not."

Rigal breathed a sigh of relief.

"Of course I do not count Paul," continued the girl, "for he is the same as myself."

"Unhappy child!" exclaimed the banker in so furious a voice, and with such a threatening gesture of the hand, that for the first time in her life Flavia was afraid of her father.

"What have I done?" asked she, the tears springing to her eyes. "I only said to Paul that we should be terribly ungrateful if we did not worship him; for you don't know what he does for us. Why, he even dresses up in rags, and goes to see you."

Hortebise, who up to this time had not said a word, now interfered.

"And what did Paul say?" asked he.

"Paul? Oh, nothing for a moment. Then he cried out, 'I see it all now,' and laughed as if he would have gone into a fit."

"Did you not understand, my poor child, what this laugh meant? Paul thinks that you have been my accomplice, and believes that it was in obedience to your orders that I went to look for him."

"Well, and suppose he does?"

"A man like Paul never loves a woman who has run after him; and no matter how great her beauty may be, will always consider that she has thrown herself in his path. He will accept all her devotion, and make no more return than a stone or a wooden idol would do. You cannot see this, and God grant that it may be long before the bandage is removed from your eyes. Can you not read the quality of this foolish boy, who has not a manly instinct in him?"

"Enough!" she cried, "enough! I am not such a coward as to allow you to insult my husband."

He shuddered at the thought that his words might cost him his daughter's love, but Hortebise interposed by putting his arm round Flavia's waist and leading her from the room. When he returned, he observed,—

"I cannot understand your anger. It seems to me that all recrimination is most indiscreet, for you can at any moment break off this marriage."

"Do you think it nothing for me to be at the mercy of that cowardly wretch, Paul?"

"Not more so than you are by the foolish weakness of your daughter. Is not Paul our accomplice? and are we any more compromised because he has discovered the secret of your triple personality?"

"Ah! you have not a father's feelings. Up till now Paul did not know that I was Mascarin, and believed me to be the victim of blackmailers. As a dupe he respected me, as an accomplice he will scorn me. This disastrous marriage must be hastened."

Paul and Flavia's marriage took place at the end of the next week, and Paul left his simple bachelor abode to take possession of the magnificent suite of rooms prepared for him by the banker in his house in the Rue Montmartre. The change was great, but Paul was no longer surprised at anything. He did not feel the faintest tinge of remorse; he only feared one thing, and that was that by some blunder he might compromise his future, when the eventful day arrived which would give him the social position and standing of heir to a dukedom.

When, however, the Duke de Champdoce came, accompanied by Perpignan, the young impostor rose to the level of his masters, and played his part with most consummate skill. The Duke, whose life had been one long scene of misery, and who had so cruelly expiated the sins of his youth, seemed to have become suddenly lenient; and had Paul obeyed him, he would at once have established himself with his young wife at the Hotel de Champdoce, but Martin Rigal put a veto upon this, for he was not quite satisfied that his son-in-law was really the heir to the Champdoce dukedom; and finally it was agreed that the Duke should come to breakfast the next morning and take away Paul. Eleven was the hour fixed, but the Duke appeared at the banker's house at ten, where he, Catenac, Hortebise, and Paul were assembled together in solemn conclave.

"Now, papa," said Flavia, who kept her father on thorns by her gay and frolicsome criticisms, "you will no longer blame me for falling in love with a poor Bohemian, for you see that he is a Champdoce, and that his father possesses millions."

The Duke was now seated on the sofa, holding the hand of the young man whom he believed to be his son tightly in his. The Duchess, to whom he had given a hint of what was going on, had been taken seriously ill from over-excitement, but had recovered herself a little, and the Duke was describing this when he was suddenly interrupted by a series of dull and heavy blows struck upon the other side of the wall of the room. A pickaxe was evidently at work. The whole house was shaken by the violence of the attack, and a screen, which stood near the spot, was thrown down.

The plotters gazed upon each other with pale and terror-stricken faces, for it was evident that the fresh brick wall, the work of Mascarin and Beaumarchef, was being destroyed. The Duke sat in perfect amazement, for the alarm of his host and his friends was plainly evident. He could feel Paul's hand tremble in his, but could not understand why work evidently going on in the next house could cause such feelings of alarm. Flavia was the only one who had no suspicion, and she remarked, "Dear me! I should like to know the meaning of this disturbance."

"I will send and inquire," said her father; but scarcely had he opened the door than he retreated with a wild expression of terror in his face, and his arms stretched out in front of him, as though to bar the approach of some terrible spectre. In the doorway stood an eminently respectable-looking gentleman, wearing a pair of gold-rimmed spectacles, and behind him a commissary of police, girt with his official scarf, while farther back still were half a dozen police officers.

"M. Lecoq," cried the three confederates in one breath, while through their minds flashed the same terrible idea—"We are lost."

The celebrated detective advanced slowly into the room, curiously watching the group collected there. There was an air of entire satisfaction visible on his countenance.

"Aha!" he said, "I was right, it seems. I was sure that I was making no mistake in rapping at the other side of the wall. I knew that it would be heard in here."

By this time, however, the banker had, to all outward appearance, regained his self-command.

"What do you want here?" asked he insolently. "What is the meaning of this intrusion?"

"This gentleman will explain," returned Lecoq, stepping aside to make way for the commissary of police to come forward. "But, to shorten matters, I may tell you that I have obtained a warrant for your arrest, Martin Rigal, *alias* Tantaine, *alias* Mascarin."

"I don't understand you!"

"Indeed. Do you think that Tantaine has cleaned his hands so completely that not a drop of André's blood clings to the fingers of Martin Rigal?"

"On my word, you are speaking in riddles."

A bland smile passed over Lecoq's face as, drawing a folded letter from his pocket, he answered,—

"Perhaps you are acquainted with the handwriting of your daughter. Well, then, listen to what she wrote not so very long ago to the very Paul who is sitting on the sofa there.

"'My Dearest Paul,—

"'We should be guilty of the deepest ingratitude if——'"

" Enough! enough! " cried the banker in a hoarse
voice. " Lost, lost, lost! My own child has been my
ruin! "

The calmest of the conspirators was now the one
who was generally the first to take alarm, and this
was the genial Doctor Hortebise. When he recognized Lecoq, he had gently opened his locket and
taken from it a small pellet of grayish-colored paste,
and, holding it between his fingers, had waited until
his leader should declare that all hope was gone.

In the meantime Lecoq turned towards Catenac.

" And you too are included in this warrant," said he.

Catenac, perhaps owing to his legal training, made
no reply to Lecoq, but addressing the commissary,
observed,—

" I am the victim of a most unpleasant mistake, but
my position——"

" The warrant is quite regular," returned the commissary. " You can see it if you desire."

" No, it is not necessary. I will only ask you to
conduct me to the magistrate who issued it, and in
five minutes all will be explained."

" Do you think so? " asked Lecoq in a quiet tone of
sarcasm. " You have not heard, I can see, of what
took place yesterday. A laborer, in the course of his
work, discovers the remains of a newly-born infant,
wrapped in a silk handkerchief and a shawl. The
police soon set inquiries on foot, and have found the
mother—a girl named Clarisse."

Had not Lecoq suddenly grasped Catenac's arm, the
lawyer would have flown at Martin Rigal's throat.

" Villain, traitor! " panted he, " you have sold me! "

" My papers have been stolen," faltered the banker.

He now saw that the blows struck upon the other

side of the wall were merely a trick, for Lecoq had thought that a little preliminary fright would render them more amenable to reason.

Hortebise still looked on calmly; he knew that the game was lost.

"I belong to a respectable family," thought he, "and I will not bring dishonor upon it. I have no time to lose."

As he spoke he placed the contents of the locket between his lips and swallowed them.

"Ah," murmured he, as he did so, "with my constitution and digestion, it is really hard to end thus."

No one had noticed the doctor's movements, for Lecoq had moved the screen, and was showing the commissary a hole which had been made in the wall large enough for the body of a man to pass through. But a sudden sound cut these investigations short, for Hortebise had fallen to the ground, and was struggling in a series of terrible convulsions.

"How stupid of me not to have foreseen this," exclaimed Lecoq. "He has poisoned himself; let some one run for a doctor. Take him into another room and lay him on a bed."

While these orders were being carried out, Catenac was removed to a cab which was in waiting, and Martin Rigal seemed to have lapsed into a state of moody imbecility. Suddenly he started to his feet, crying,—

"My daughter Flavia! yes, her name is Flavia, what is to become of her? She has no fortune, and she is married to a man who can never provide for her. My child will perhaps starve. Oh, horrible thought!"

The man's strong mind had evidently given way, and his love for his child and the hideous future that lay before her had broken down the barrier that divides reason from insanity. He was secured by the officers, raving and struggling. When Lecoq was left alone with the Duke, Paul and Flavia, he cast a glimpse of pity at the young girl, who had crouched down in a corner, and evidently hardly understood the terrible scene that had just passed.

"Your Grace," said he, turning to the Duke, "you have been the victim of a foul conspiracy; this young man is not your son; he is Paul Violaine, and is the son of a poor woman who kept a petty haberdashery shop in the provinces."

The miserable young fool began to bluster, and attempted to deny this statement; but Lecoq opened the door, and Rose appeared in a most becoming costume. Paul now made no effort to continue his protestations, but throwing himself on his knees, in whining accents confessed the whole fraud and pleaded for mercy, promising to give evidence against his accomplices.

"Do not despair, your Grace," said Lecoq, as he conducted the Duke to his carriage; "this certainly is not your son; but *I* have found him, and to-morrow, if you like, you shall be introduced to him."

CHAPTER XXXV.

"EVERY MAN TO HIS OWN PLACE."

OBEDIENT to the wishes of M. Lecoq, André resigned himself to a lengthy sojourn at the Hospital de Beaujon, and had even the courage to affect that state of profound indifference that had deceived Mascarin. The pretended sick man in the next bed to his told him all that had taken place, but the days seemed to be interminable, and he was beginning to lose patience, when one morning he received a letter which caused a gleam of joy to pass through his heart. " All is right," wrote Lecoq. " Danger is at an end. Ask the house surgeon for leave to quit the hospital. Dress yourself smartly. You will find me waiting at the doors.—L."

André was not quite convalescent, for he might have to wear his arm in a sling for many weeks longer; but these considerations did not deter him. He now dressed himself in a suit which he had sent for to his rooms, and about nine o'clock he left the hospital.

He stood upon the steps inhaling deep draughts of the fresh air, and then began to wonder where the strange personage was to whom he owed his life. While he was deliberating what to do, an open carriage drew up before the door of the hospital.

" You have come at last," exclaimed André, rushing up to the gentleman who alighted from it. " I was getting quite anxious."

" I am about five minutes late," returned Lecoq; "but I was detained," and then, as André began to pour out his thanks, he added, " Get into the carriage; I have a great deal to say to you."

André obeyed, and as he did so, he detected something strange in the expression of his companion's face.

" What ! " remarked Lecoq, " do you see by my face that I have something to tell you? You are getting quite a keen observer. Well, I have, indeed, for I have passed the night going through Mascarin's papers, and I have just gone through a painful scene —I may say, one of the most painful that I have ever witnessed. The intellect of Mascarin," said he, "has given way under the tremendous pressure put upon it. The ruling passion of the villain's life was his love for his daughter. He imagines that Flavia and Paul are without a franc and in want of bread; he thinks that he continually hears his daughter crying to him for help. Then, on his knees, he entreats the warder to let him out, if only for a day, swearing that he will return as soon as he has succored his child. Then, when his prayer is refused, he bursts into a frenzied rage and tears at his door, howling like an infuriated animal; and this state may last to the end of his life, and every minute in it be a space of intolerable torture. Doctor Hortebise is dead; but the poison upon which he relied betrayed him, and he suffered agonies for twenty-four hours. Catenac will fight to the bitter end, but the proofs are clear against him, and he will be convicted of infanticide. In Rigal's papers I have found evidence against Perpignan, Verminet and Van Klopen, who will all certainly hear something about penal servitude. Nothing has been settled yet about Toto Chupin, for it must be remembered that he came and gave himself up."

" And what about Croisenois?"

" His Company will be treated like any other attempt to extort money by swindling, and the Marquis will be sent to prison for two months, and the money paid for shares returned to the dupes, and that, I think, is all that I have to tell you, except that by to-morrow M. Gandelu will receive back the bills to which his son affixed a forged signature. And now," continued Lecoq, after a short pause, " the time has come for me to tell you why, at our first interview, I saluted you as the heir of the Duke de Champdoce. I had guessed your history, but it was only last night I heard all the details."

Then the detective gave a brief but concise account of the manuscript that Paul had read aloud. He did not tell much, however, but passed lightly over the acts of the Duke de Champdoce and Madame de Mussidan, for he did not wish André to cease to respect either his father or the mother of Sabine. The story was just concluded as the carriage drew up at the corner of the Rue de Matignon.

"Get down here," said Lecoq, "and mind and don't hurt your arm."

André obeyed mechanically.

"And now," went on Lecoq, "listen to me. The Count and Countess de Mussidan expect you to breakfast, and here is the note they handed to me for you. Come back to your studio by four o'clock, and I will then introduce you to your father; but till then, remember, absolute silence."

André was completely bewildered with his unexpected happiness. He walked instinctively to the Hotel de Mussidan and rang the bell. The intense civility of the footmen removed any misgivings that he might have felt, and, as he entered the dining-room, he darted back, for face to face with him was the portrait of Sabine which he had himself painted. At that moment the Count came forward to meet him with extended hands.

"Diana," said he to his wife, "this is our daughter's future husband." He then took Sabine's hand, which he laid in André's.

The young artist hardly dared raise his eyes to Sabine's face; when he did so, his heart grew very sad, for the poor girl was but the shadow of her former self.

"You have suffered terribly," said he tenderly.

"Yes," answered she, "and I should have died had it lasted much longer."

André had the greatest difficulty in refraining from telling his secret to his beloved, and it was with even more difficulty that he tore himself away at half-past three.

He had not been five minutes in his studio when there was a knock at the door, and Lecoq entered, followed by an elderly gentleman of aristocratic and haughty appearance. It was the Duke de Champdoce.

"This gentleman," said the Duke, with a gesture of his hand towards Lecoq, "will have told you that certain circumstances rendered it expedient, according to my ideas, that I should not acknowledge you as my heir, but my son. The fault that I then committed has been cruelly expiated. I am not forty-eight; look at me."

The Duke looked at least sixty.

"My sins," continued the Duke, "still pursue me. To-day, in spite of all my desires, I cannot claim you as my legitimate son, for the law only permits me to give you my name and fortune by exercising the right of adoption."

André made no reply, and the Duke went on with evident hesitation,—

"You can certainly institute proceedings against me for the recovery of your rights, but——"

"Ah!" interrupted the young man, "really, what sort of person do you think I am? Do you believe me capable of dishonoring your name before I assumed it?"

The Duke drew a deep breath of relief. André's manner had checked and restrained him, for it was frigid and glacial to a degree. What a difference there was between the haughty mien of André and the gushing effusiveness of Paul!

"Will you permit me," asked André, "to address a few words to you?"

"A few words?"

"Yes. I did not like to use the word 'conditions,' but I think that you will understand what I mean. My daily toil for bread gave me neither the means nor leisure which I required to cultivate my art, for that is a profession that I could never give up."

"You will be certainly your own master."

André paused, as if to reflect.

"This is not all I had to say," he continued at last. "I love and am loved by a pure and beautiful girl; our marriage is arranged, and I think——"

"I think," broke in the Duke, "that you could not love any one who was not a fit bride for a member of our family."

"But I did not belong to this family yesterday. Be at ease, however, for she is worthy of a Champdoce. I am engaged to Sabine de Mussidan."

A deadly paleness overspread the Duke's face as he heard this name.

"Never," said he. "Never; I would rather see you dead at my feet."

"And I would gladly suffer ten thousand deaths sooner than give her up."

"Suppose I refuse my consent? Suppose that I forbid——?"

"You have no claim to exercise paternal authority over me; this can only be purchased by years of tender care. Duke de Champdoce, I owe you nothing. Leave me to myself, as you have hitherto done, and all will be simplified."

The Duke reflected. Must he give up his son, who had been restored to him by such a series of almost miraculous chances, or must he see him married to Diana's daughter? Either alternative appeared to him to be equally disagreeable.

"I will not yield on the point," said he. "Besides, the Countess would never give her consent. She hates me as much as I hate her."

M. Lecoq, who had up to this moment looked on in silence, now thought it time to interpose.

"I think," remarked he blandly, "that I shall have no difficulty in obtaining the consent of Madame de Mussidan."

The Duke, at these words, threw open his arms.

"Come, my son!" said he. "All shall be as you desire."

That night Marie, Duchess de Champdoce, experienced happiness for the first time in the affection and caresses of a son who had been so long lost to her, and seemed to throw off the heavy burden that had so heavily pressed her down beneath its own weight.

When Madame de Mussidan heard that André was Norbert's son, she declared that nothing would induce her to give her consent to his marriage with her daughter; but among Mascarin's papers Lecoq had discovered the packet containing the compromising correspondence between the Duke de Champdoce and herself. The detective handed this over to her, and, in her gratitude, she promised to give up all further opposition to the match.

Lecoq always denied that this act came under the head of blackmailing.

André and Sabine took up their residence after marriage at the Château de Mussidan, which had been magnificently restored and decorated. They seldom leave it, for they love it for its vicinity to the leafy groves, in which they first learned that they had given their hearts to each other. And André frequently points out the unfinished work on the balcony, which was the occasion of his first visit to the Château de Mussidan. He says that he will complete it as soon as he has time, but it is doubtful whether he will ever find leisure to do this for a long time, for before the new year comes there is every chance of there being a baptism at the little chapel at Bevron.